THE AUTHOR

Angela Thirkell was born in London in 1890. She was a member of a distinguished family – her father, J.W. Mackail, was to become Professor of Poetry at Oxford, her grandfather was the artist Edward Burne-Jones, and her cousins included Stanley Baldwin and Rudyard Kipling. J. M. Barrie was her godfather.

In 1911, against the wishes of her parents, she married James Campbell McInnes, a singer. The marriage was to end in divorce in 1917. By then Angela had had two sons, Graham McInnes and Colin MacInnes (both of whose works are published by The Hogarth Press).

Her second marriage, in 1918, was to George Thirkell, an Australian. Early in 1920 they embarked for Australia on a troop ship, an experience which Angela was to describe in her pseudonymous novel *Trooper to the Southern Cross* (1934). They settled in Melbourne, but this marriage too was not a happy one. Angela desperately missed England, to which she returned in 1929 with her third son, Lance.

By this time she had written several magazine articles, and her first book, *Three Houses*, a memoir of her childhood, was published in 1931, with modest success. It was followed in 1933 by two novels, *Ankle Deep* and *High Rising*, and by a further three in 1934. Such a prolific output could scarcely be maintained, but for the rest of her life Angela Thirkell was to produce at least one novel a year, many of them set in Trollope's imaginary county of Barsetshire. They were to win her a devoted worldwide following and a reputation as the supreme exponent of English high comedy, in the tradition of Jane Austen, Mrs Gaskell and, of course, Trollope.

Angela Thirkell died in 1960. She wrote thirty novels in all, a number of which are to be reissued by The Hogarth Press.

THE
BRANDONS

Angela Thirkell

New Introduction by
Libby Purves

THE HOGARTH PRESS
LONDON

Published in 1988 by
The Hogarth Press
30 Bedford Square, London WC1B 3RP

First published in Great Britain by Hamish Hamilton Ltd 1939
Copyright © Angela Thirkell 1939
Introduction copyright © Libby Purves 1988

A CIP catalogue record for this book is available from the British Library.

ISBN 0 7012 0813 9

Printed in Great Britain by
Cox & Wyman Ltd
Reading, Berkshire

INTRODUCTION

Angela Thirkell – ironic, demure, compassionate, satirical – is difficult for a tidy-minded critic to place. She stands, or rather shimmers, somewhere in the middle ground between P.G. Wodehouse and Jane Austen. She could be read as a middle-class Nancy Mitford, a Stella Gibbons without the slapstick, or a Dorothy L. Sayers without the murders. Certainly she stands in the tradition of the beady-eyed female social observer in the corner of the drawing room, letting no nuance escape her and laughing with inward glee as, in her words, 'the conversation runs lightly over hidden depths.' But on the whole, and especially in *The Brandons*, Angela Thirkell is pleasantly unique, in the way that an eccentric aunt is unique, or a legendary godmother. Very observant, very English, and, like Miss Austen, very happy indeed with her little piece of ivory.

For it is a little piece. After all, nothing much happens in *The Brandons* except a picnic, a funeral, and a fête, all of them occurring in one summer in the 1930s, and within a few miles of a dozy Barsetshire village. There is, of course, the ongoing drama of the chicken-pox among the feckless inhabitants of Grumper's End, and the continuing, looming presence of the Gooseberry Fool which is served in every household day after day to save wasting the gooseberry glut; but apart from this, the things that matter happen in the heart. The author does not deal much in scorn, but what there is is reserved for manifestations of the brash and showy outside world and its literature:

'Is that a good book, Sir?' asked Mr Grant.

'Journalism, journalism,' said Mr Miller, looking at *A Wastepaper Basket from Three Embassies* by Jefferson X. Root, who had certainly never set foot in any of them, but was well into his second hundred thousand, 'as practically everything is now.'

But even her dislike of Jefferson X. is tempered by a milder amusement a few lines later, when the learned vicar continues his critique:

'I cannot understand the appeal that this kind of book makes to the public,' said Mr Miller, whose pipe was lying in page two hundred and seventy.

The comedy, and the pathos, rests on the surest of all foundations: the acknowledgement that every human creature has weaknesses, some of which lead to tragedy and some to absurdity. The pipe lying in page two hundred and seventy of the despised book will never date: it is a silent, mocking reproach to everyone who has ever wasted a weekend in the company of Jackie Collins or Harold Robbins. This world of tennis-dresses and marsala, of old Nurses forever altering camisoles and vicar's daughters who scrub out dustbins in gingham pinnies for the Fête, may have vanished forever; but their weaknesses have not. The wonderful pretensions of Mrs Grant, Italianised English bohemian in her 'kind of brigand's cape of coarse blue cloth', have their direct descendants today:

'He is a devoted son, *mio figlio*, but I do not wish him to be tied to my apron strings. There is a charming proverb in Calabria which runs – but you would not understand it in dialect: I will translate roughly, though of course it does not give the *fuoco* of the original – the ass that stays at home will never learn to roam. My husband was always under his mother's domination, *ma! una donna prepotente!* and what was the result? My life made me what I am.'

Mrs Grant is one of the most enjoyable posers in English fiction, on a par with Elfine and Judith Starkadder of *Cold Comfort Farm*, or E.F. Benson's Lucia. Right up to the moment of her final departure for Calabria, she is still burbling of St Francis and her brother the sun:

'No, Hilary, don't come with me. Your gipsy mother needs no speeding on her way.' With great agility she swept herself and her cloak into Wheeler's car, crying '*Avanti*,' which Bert from the garage, who was driving, rightly conjectured to mean Barchester Central Station.

Mrs Grant is an extreme: but nobody, however good or well-meaning, is entirely safe from the author's mocking vision. Delia's ambulance-chasing, Mr Miller's spaniel adoration of Mrs Brandon and incompetence with accounts, Miss Morris's tedious gratitude, Sir Edmund's bluff county competence ('After a weekend of the honest but muddled mental process which Sir Edmund took for thinking...'), Hilary's fearful taste in French poets and Mrs Morland's hairpins are all targets joyfully punctured. Yet at least one pair of these apparently comic characters is involved, at the climax, in one of the most heartstoppingly, restrainedly romantic moments in any novel. It is a rare talent that can create such a balance between satire and real emotion, and the emotion comes all the fresher for the laughing which preceded it: because it has been, and always is in this book, laughter without contempt. One of the curious ways in which Angela Thirkell achieves this detached humour is by following a burst of dialogue with a sudden, deadpan use of reported speech, like the minutes of some haywire Board Meeting:

Mrs Grant said Hilary must get his hair cut and there was a delightful old custom in Calabria by which young men and maidens spent the night under a tree on the night of the full moon and drew lots with the bristles of a hog who had died a natural death, and whoever drew the longest bristle died in childbirth within the year.

Or:

Mr Grant said he didn't go very much [to the movies] but he had seen *Descente de lit* in which Zizi Pavois was superb, and *Menschen ohne Knochen* which, even allowing for propaganda, was an astoundingly moving affair.

Delia said she meant *films*, and there was going to be an awfully good one at Barchester next week called *Going for a Ride* with Garstin Hermon as the villain and she had been told it was absolutely *ghastly*.

Alongside her comic consciousness of weakness in the good, however, the author has a great sympathy for the idea of the Saving Grace. She shows remarkable patience with her heroine, Mrs Brandon, who is, on the face of it, the irritating archetype of the Adored Woman: ineffectual, lazy, dreamy and fey, and utterly preoccupied with clothes. The account of her widowhood is brutally honest:

If there is nothing in one's life that requires pity, one must invent it: for to go through life unpitied would be an unthinkable loss. Mrs Brandon, quite unconsciously, had made of her uninteresting husband a mild bogey, allowing her friends, especially those who had not known him, to imagine a slightly sinister figure that had cast a becoming shadow over his charming widow's life.

Yet Lavinia Brandon has real strengths: her ability to understand, and laugh at, her son's joke about her *couvade*; her firmness and correct, compassionate behaviour at the death of Aunt Sissie; her real kindness, languid and passive as it is. Aunt Sissie herself, dreadful old ogre, 'an elderly Caligula disguised as Elizabeth Fry', seems at first only a comic villainess invented to focus and persecute the charming family Brandon, and a way to introduce the very good joke of a tyrannical rich old aunt whose fortune nobody actually *wants*, who expects visits made out of self-interest but unwittingly receives ones made out of kindness. But even Aunt Sissie, with her humorously salacious preoccupation with Captain Arbuthnot's Indian affairs, and her many anonymous and unnoticed charitable works, gradually takes on that elusive third dimension of human reality. Delia, rowdy and blood-thirsty flapper, emerges towards the end as something of an antidote to her mother: the New Woman, tougher and far less fey than her predecessors, who was about to come into her glory in the War. *The Brandons*, remember, was published in 1939; had it been five years later, Delia would clearly have become a Wren or WRAC, a Nevil Shute heroine. Only Mrs Grant, come to think of it, displays no particular saving grace; but with her brigand's cloak of sublime insensitivity, she probably would not mind the author's disapproval.

Truthfulness without malice, humour without flippancy, are qualities that never date. The joy of coming to a book like this half a century late is that the reader wins twice over: we get our nostalgic escape into a past world of potted-salmon picnics and genteel charity; and we also have the pleasure of seeing a clear and mellow comic light playing, only too revealingly, upon our present lives.

Libby Purves, Saxmundham 1988

1

BREAKFAST AT STORIES

'I WONDER who this is from,' said Mrs Brandon, picking a letter out of the heap that lay by her plate and holding it at arm's length upside down. 'It is quite extraordinary how I can't see without my spectacles. It makes me laugh sometimes because it is so ridiculous.'

In proof of this assertion she laughed very pleasantly. Her son and daughter, who were already eating their breakfast, exchanged pitying glances but said nothing.

'It doesn't look like a handwriting that I know,' said Mrs Brandon, putting her large horn-rimmed spectacles on and turning the letter the right way up. 'More like a handwriting that I *don't* know. The postmark is all smudgy so I can't see where it comes from.'

'You might steam it open and see who it's from,' said her son Francis, 'and then shut it up again and guess.'

'But if I *saw* who it was from I'd *know*,' said Mrs Brandon plaintively. 'In France and places people write their name and address across the back of the envelope so that you know who it is.'

'And then you needn't open it at all if you don't like them,' said Francis, 'though I believe they really only do it to put spies from other places off the scent. I mean if Aunt Sissie wanted to write to you she would put someone else's name and address on the flap, and then you would open it instead of very rightly putting it straight into the waste-paper basket.'

'You don't think it's from Aunt Sissie, do you?' said Mrs Brandon. 'Whenever I get a letter I hope it isn't from her; but mostly' she added, reverting to her original grievance, 'one knows at once by the handwriting who it's from.'

'If it's Aunt Sissie,' said her daughter Delia, 'it will be all about being offended because we haven't been to see her since Easter.'

'Well, we couldn't,' said Mrs Brandon. 'Francis hasn't had a holiday since Easter, and you were abroad and if I go alone she is only annoyed. Besides she is more your aunt than mine. She is no relation of mine at all. That she is a relation of yours you have to thank your father.'

Francis and Delia again exchanged glances. It was a habit of their mother's to make them entirely responsible for any difficulties brought into the family by the late Mr Brandon, saying the words 'your father' in a voice that implied a sinister collaboration between that gentleman and the powers of darkness for which her children were somehow to blame. As for Mr Brandon's merits, which consisted chiefly in having been an uninterested husband and father for some six or seven years and then dying and leaving his widow quite well off, no one thought of them.

'Well, after all, mother, father was as much your father as ours,' said Francis, who while holding no brief for a parent whom he could barely remember, felt that men must stick together, 'at least *you* brought him into the family, and that makes you really responsible for Aunt Sissie. And,' he hurriedly added, seeing in his mother's eye what she was about to say, 'it's no good your saying father wouldn't have liked to hear me speak to you like that, darling, because that's just what we can't tell. Can I have some more coffee?'

Mrs Brandon, who had been collecting her forces to take rather belated offence at her son's remarks, was so delighted to fuss over his coffee that she entirely forgot her husband's possible views on how young men should address their mothers and saw herself very happily as a still not unattractive woman spoiling a handsome and devoted son. That Francis's looks were inherited from his father was a fact she chose to ignore, except if his hair was more than usually untidy, when she was apt to say reproachfully, 'Of course that is your father's hair, Francis,' or even more loftily and annoyingly to no one in particular, 'His father's hair all over again.'

Peace being restored over the coffee, Mrs Brandon ate her own breakfast and read her letters. Francis and Delia were discussing a plan for a picnic with some friends in the neighbourhood, when their mother interrupted them by remarking defiantly that she had said so.

A small confusion took place.

'No, no,' said Mrs Brandon, 'nothing to do with hard-boiled eggs or cucumber sandwiches. It is your Aunt Sissie.'

By the tone of the word 'your' her children realized that they were about to be in disgrace for thinking of picnics at such an hour.

'Then it *was* Aunt Sissie,' said Delia. 'What is the worst, mother? Does she want us to go over?'

'Wait,' said Mrs Brandon. 'It isn't Aunt Sissie. At least not exactly. It is dictated. I will read it to you. And that,' said Mrs Brandon laying the letter aside, 'is why I couldn't tell who it was from. It is written by someone called Ella Morris with Miss in brackets, so as none of the maids are called Morris it must be a new companion.'

'Heaven help her,' said Francis, 'and that isn't swearing, darling, and I am sure father would have said it too. Give me the letter or we shall never know what is in it. Delia, the blow has fallen. Ella Morris, Miss, writes at the wish of Miss Brandon to say that she, Miss Brandon, hereinafter to be known as Aunt Sissie, is at a loss to understand why all her relations have forsaken her and she is an ailing old woman and expects us all to come over on Wednesday to lunch or be cut out of her will. Mother, who gets Aunt Sissie's money if she disinherits us?'

Mrs Brandon said that was not the way to talk.

After half an hour's detailed consideration of the question the Brandon family left the breakfast table, not that the subject was in any way exhausted, but Rose the parlourmaid had begun to hover in an unnerving and tyrannical way. Francis said he must write some letters, Delia went to do the telephoning which she and her friends found a necessary part of daily life, while Mrs Brandon went into the garden to get fresh flowers, choosing with great cunning the moment when the gardener was having a mysterious second breakfast. Certainly anyone who had met her coming furtively and hurriedly but triumphantly in by the drawing-room window, her arms full of the gardener's flowers, would entirely have agreed with her own opinion of herself and found her still not unattractive, or possibly felt that a woman with so enchanting an expression could not have been more charming

9

even in her youth. Mrs Brandon herself, in one of her moods of devastating truthfulness, had explained her own appearance as the result of a long and happy widowhood, and as, after a little sincere grief at the loss of a husband to whom she had become quite accustomed, she had had nothing of consequence to trouble her, it is probable that she was right. Her house and garden were pretty, comfortable, and of a manageable size, her servants stayed with her, Francis had been one of those lucky, even-tempered boys that go through school with the good-will of all, if with no special distinction, and then fallen straight into a good job. As for Delia, she combined unconcealed scorn for her mother with a genuine affection and an honest wish to improve her and bring her up to date. Mrs Brandon thought her daughter a darling, and had gladly given up any attempt at control years ago. The only fault she could find with her children was that they didn't laugh at the same jokes as she did, but finding that all their friends were equally humourless, she accepted it placidly, seeing herself as a spirit of laughter born out of its time.

But human nature cannot be content on a diet of honey and if there is nothing in one's life that requires pity, one must invent it; for to go through life unpitied would be an unthinkable loss. Mrs Brandon, quite unconsciously, had made of her uninteresting husband a mild bogey, allowing her friends, especially those who had not known him, to imagine a slightly sinister figure that had cast a becoming shadow over his charming widow's life. Many of her acquaintances said sympathetically they really could not imagine why she had married such a man. To them Mrs Brandon would reply wistfully that she had not been very happy as a girl and no one else had asked her, thus giving the impression that she had in her innocence seized an opportunity to escape from a loveless home to what proved a loveless marriage. The truth, ever so little twisted in the right direction by her ingenious mind, was that Mr Brandon had proposed to her when she was not quite twenty. Being a kindhearted girl who hated to say no, she had at once fallen in love, because if one's heart is not otherwise engaged there seems to be nothing else to do. Her parents had made no difficulties, Mr Brandon had made a very handsome will and taken his wife to Stories, his charming early Georgian house at Pomfret Madrigal in the Barchester country. Francis was born before she was twenty-one, a deed which filled her with secret pride, though no one else would have guessed it from her usual plaintive and ambiguous statement, 'of course my first baby was born almost at once,' a statement which had made more than one of her hearers silently add the word Brute to Mr Brandon's epitaph.

Delia was born four years later, and Mrs Brandon wrapped up in her nursery, was only beginning to feel ruffled by her husband's dullness when death with kindly care removed him through the agency of pneumonia. As it was a cold spring Mrs Brandon was able to go into black, and the ensuing summer being a particularly hot one gave her an excuse for mourning in white, though she always wore a heavy necklace of old jet to show goodwill.

It was during that summer that Mr Brandon's Aunt Sissie, hitherto an almost mythical figure, had made her first terrifying appearance at Stories. Mrs Brandon was sitting in the ex-library, now called her sitting-room writing to her parents, when the largest Rolls Royce she had ever seen came circling round the gravel sweep. As it drew up she saw that there were two chauffeurs on the front seat. The man who was driving remained at his post to restrain the ardour of his machine, while the second got out and rang the front door bell. The bonnet was facing Mrs Brandon and she could not see who was inside the car without making herself too visible at the window, so she had to wait till Rose, then only a young parlourmaid, but older than her mistress and already a budding tyrant, came in.

'Miss Brandon, madam,' she announced, 'and I've put her in the drawing-room.'

'Miss Brandon?' said her mistress. 'Oh, that must be Mr Brandon's aunt. What shall I do?'

'I've put her in the drawing-room, madam,' Rose repeated, speaking patiently as to a mental defective, 'and she said the chauffeurs was to have some tea, madam, so Cook is looking after them.'

'Then I suppose I must,' said Mrs Brandon, and went into the drawing-room.

It was here that for the first and only time she felt a faint doubt as to the propriety of mourning in white, for her aunt by marriage was wearing such a panoply of black silk dress, black cashmere mantle, black ostrich feather boa and unbelievably a black bonnet trimmed with black velvet and black cherries, that Mrs Brandon wondered giddily whether spinsters could be honorary widows.

'When once I have sat down I don't get up again easily,' said Miss Brandon, holding out a black-gloved, podgy hand.

'Oh, please don't,' said Mrs Brandon vaguely, taking her aunt's lifeless hand. 'How do you do, Miss Brandon. Henry will be so sorry to miss you – I mean he was always talking about you and saying we must take the children to see you.'

'I had practically forbidden him the house for some years,' said Miss Brandon.

To this there appeared to be no answer except Why? – a question Mrs Brandon had not the courage to ask.

'But I would certainly have come to the funeral,' Miss Brandon continued, 'had it not been my Day in Bed. I take one day a week in bed, an excellent plan at my age. Later I shall take two days, and probably spend the last years of my life entirely in bed. My grandfather, my mother and my elder half-sister were all bedridden for the last ten years of their lives and all lived to be over ninety.'

Again it was difficult to find an answer. Miss Brandon murmured something about how splendid and felt it was hardly adequate.

'But I went into mourning for my nephew Henry at once,' said Miss Brandon, ignoring her niece's remark, 'as you see. I have practically not been out of mourning for fifteen years, what with one death and another. A posthumous child?' she added with sudden interest looking piercingly at her niece's white dress.

'Oh, no,' said Mrs Brandon. 'Mamma and papa are still alive.'

'Tut, tut, not you,' said Miss Brandon. 'What is your name?'

Mrs Brandon said apologetically that it was Lavinia.

'A pretty name,' said Miss Brandon. 'When last I saw your husband Henry Brandon, he mentioned you to me as Pet. It was before his marriage and he was spending a week-end with me. I had to say to him, "Henry Brandon, a man who can call his future wife Pet and speak of the Government as you have spoken can hardly make a good husband and is certainly not a good nephew." I suppose he made you suffer a good deal.'

Here if ever was an opportunity for Mrs Brandon to indulge in an orgy of sentiment, but her underlying sense of fairness suddenly choked any complaint she could truthfully have made.

'No, I don't think so,' she said, looking straight at her husband's aunt. 'He was very nice to the children when he noticed them, and he liked me to be nicely dressed, and we were always very comfortable. Would you like to see the children, Miss Brandon?'

She rang the bell and asked Rose to ask Nurse to bring the children down.

'I see you are determined not to give Henry away,' said Miss Brandon, not disapprovingly. 'But when is it? I see no other reason for wearing white so soon.'

Her gaze was again so meaningly fixed upon her niece's white dress that Mrs Brandon began to blush violently.

'I don't think I understand,' she faltered, 'but if that is what you mean of course it isn't. I just thought white was less depressing for the children.'

'I am glad to hear it. That I could *not* have forgiven Henry,' said the disconcerting Miss Brandon, and then the children were brought down, approved, and taken away again.

'Now you can ring for my second chauffeur, Lavinia,' said Miss Brandon. 'He always comes with me to help me in and out of the car. I prefer to have the first chauffeur remain at the wheel, for one never knows.'

She then expounded to Mrs Brandon in the hall, unmoved by the presence of her chauffeur and the parlourmaid, her plans for the disposal of her affairs. As far as Mrs Brandon, shaken by Rose's presence, could understand, Francis and Delia were to be the heirs of their aunt's large fortune, unless she saw fit to leave it to a cousin whom she had never seen. She was then hoisted into her car, the second chauffeur got into his place, the first chauffeur put in the clutch and the equipage moved away. Mrs Brandon, much the worse for her aunt's visit, declined Rose's suggestion of an early cup of tea and went up to the nursery for comfort. Here she found Francis and Delia already having tea. Francis was sitting on a nursery chair with a fat cushion on it. He was wearing a green linen suit with a green linen feeder tied round his neck, and was covered with apricot jam from his large smiling mouth to the roots of his yellow hair. Delia, in a yellow muslin frock with a feeder of yellow towelling, and a yellow ribbon in her brown curls was being fed with strips of bread and butter by Nurse.

'Don't move, Nurse,' said Mrs Brandon, as Nurse sketched the gesture of one who has no intention of getting up. 'Can I have tea with you?'

'If we had known mummie was coming, we'd have had our clean pinny on,' said Nurse severely to Delia.

'Pinny,' said Delia.

'You'd hardly believe the words she picks up, madam,' said Nurse with quite unjustifiable pride considering how many times a day the words clean pinny were said by her. 'We'll get another cup and saucer out of the cupboard, won't we, baby, a nice cup and saucer with a duck on it for mummie. Would you like the duck, madam, or the moo-cow?'

Mrs Brandon expressed a preference for the moo-cow, on hearing which Delia, who was holding a mug of milk to her mouth with both hands, said 'Moo-cow,' into it. The milk spluttered all over her face, Francis began to laugh and choked on a piece of bread and butter and jam, Nurse dashed with first aid from one to another, and Mrs Brandon found herself laughing till suddenly she was crying and couldn't stop. Her children, deeply interested, stopped choking to stare.

'I don't know what's the matter, Nurse,' said Mrs Brandon through her sobs. 'An aunt of Mr Brandon's came to call and it was very upsetting.'

'I don't wonder, madam,' said Nurse, deeply approving her mistress's show of feeling as suitable to a young widow. 'Suppose you go and lie down and I'll bring you the tea in your room. We'll give mummie the nice moo-cow cup of tea, won't we baby? Francis, wipe your mouth on your feeder and say your grace and get down and Nurse will come and wash your hands as soon as she has taken mummie some tea.'

Thanks to the tea and a rest Mrs Brandon quite soon recovered from her mild hysterics, but the affair was not at an end. On Thursdays, which this day happened to be, the nursery maid had her half-day out; by a great oversight the kitchenmaid who took Nurse's supper tray up when the nursery maid was out, had been given special leave to go and see her married sister who had had triplets. On any ordinary occasion Nurse would have gone supperless sooner than condescend to go downstairs, just as the second housemaid would sooner have lost her place than deputize for the kitchenmaid, but the urgent need of communicating gossip drove both sides into some semblance of humanity. As soon as Francis and Delia were asleep Nurse went down to the kitchen and there found the second housemaid talking to Rose.

'Well, Nurse,' said the second housemaid, 'I was just going to take your tray up as Gladys is out.'

'Thanks, Grace,' said Nurse with the courtesy that a superior should always show to an inferior, 'that is very obliging of you, but I hardly feel like touching a thing. Just the bread and butter and that bloater paste and a bit of cheese and a cup of tea.'

She assumed an interesting pallor and smiled faintly.

'Rose feels just like you do, Nurse,' said Grace. 'It's all that upset this afternoon.'

'Madam did mention that she was upset,' said Nurse, exploring the ground, but careful to give nothing away.

'I couldn't hardly touch my own tea,' said Rose. 'That Miss Brandon talking of making her will with Mr Brandon only four months buried and all. No wonder madam didn't fancy her tea after that.'

Cook, who had come in as Rose was speaking, said those chauffeurs were nice young fellers and the young one with the little moustache had worked in the works where her brother was, and there were twenty indoors and out at Miss Brandon's place, and didn't Nurse want a bit of that cold pork.

'Thanks, Cook, ever so,' said Nurse, 'but it would go against my feelings. It gave me quite a turn seeing madam so upset. Seeing Master Francis and baby having their tea seemed to bring it all home as you might say. So I said to madam, If you was to have a nice lay down, madam, you'd feel much better.'

She paused.

'No wonder she was upset,' said Rose. 'I knew she was reel upset because I said if you was to have a cup of tea, madam, now, it would do you good, because it was only half-past four and drawing-room tea isn't till five.'

'My nursery kettle was just on the boil,' said Nurse airily, 'so I took madam a cup of tea and she seemed ever so much better when she'd drunk it.'

This was an appalling piece of provocation on Nurse's part, carefully led up to and deliberately uttered. Between her and Rose there was an unspoken rivalry for the possession of their mistress. Rose had been with Mrs Brandon since her marriage and was therefore the senior, besides holding the important position of un-official lady's maid, but Nurse had through the children an un-assailable hold over the household. Rose might be able to bully her mistress about the hour for tea, or the evening dress she should wear, but it was with Nurse that Mrs Brandon spent an hour or two in the nursery or the garden every day, Nurse that she allowed to help her to get flowers for the church, or to finish the half-dozen hideous and badly cut flannelette nightgowns that were her forced contribution to a thing called Personal Service that levied blackmail on the gentry. Rose knew in her heart that if it came to a showdown Nurse would win, for Mrs Brandon as a mother was as incapable as she was adoring, and this did not improve her feelings. Nurse, equally conscious of this vital fact, was more polite to Rose than anyone could be expected to bear. To-day she had made an incursion into the enemy's territory that would not easily be forgiven. If Mrs Brandon chose to demean herself to have tea in the nursery, Rose could but pity her, while admitting that she had a perfect right to have tea with her own children. But that her mistress should refuse the cup of tea she had so kindly offered and then accept the offering from Nurse, not even in the nursery but in her own room, sacred to Rose's ministrations, that was an insult Rose would not readily forget, and for which she chose to put the entire blame on her rival. So she said, in a general way, that Indian tea wasn't no good for the headache.

Nurse said in an equally general and equally offensive way that so long as tea was made with *boiling* water, it didn't matter if it was Indian or China.

Cook said she found a good dose was the best thing for the headache, but it must be a *good* dose, to which both housemaids added a graphic description of the effect a good dose had on (*a*) a bed-ridden aunt, and (*b*) a cousin who had fits.

Rose said to Cook it was no wonder madam didn't have no appetite for her dinner, poor thing, to which Nurse was just preparing a barbed reply when to everyone's mingled disappointment and relief the kitchenmaid suddenly appeared, and by sitting down and bursting into tears at once became the centre of interest. Cook at once provided a cup of very strong tea and while drinking it the kitchenmaid explained with sobs and gulps that two of the triplets were dead and looked that beautiful that you wouldn't credit it. Everyone applauded her display of feeling and a delightful conversation took place about similar events in everyone's own family circle. Nurse, who only recognized the children of the gentry, circles in which triplets are for some obscure social or economic reason practically unknown, came off poorly in this contest and retired quietly with her tray.

But from that day the silent struggle for the soul of the unconscious Mrs Brandon became the ruling passion in Nurse and Rose. If Nurse brushed and twisted Delia's curls with absent-minded ferocity, or Rose cleaned the silver ornaments in the drawing-room till they were severely dented and had to go to Barchester to be repaired, they were not thinking of their respective charges, but of an enemy above and below stairs. When Francis went to school and Delia had a French governess, Rose's hopes soared high. Mrs Brandon had intended to give Nurse notice, with a huge tip and glowing recommendations, but from day to day she found that she dared not do it, from month to month Nurse's position became stronger, and from year to year Nurse stayed on, partly as maid to Delia, partly as general utility, always in a state of armed neutrality towards Rose.

After this terrifying visit, nearly seventeen years ago, Miss Brandon had never visited Stories again, but from time to time had summoned her niece and her children to Brandon Abbey. These visits seemed to Mrs Brandon to have been the inevitable

occasion for some outburst from her offspring. It was here that
Francis had fallen through a hot-house roof, where he had no
business to be, cutting his leg to the bone and bringing down the
best grape vine in his fall; here that he had laboriously baled all
the water out of the small lily-pond with one of the best copper
preserving pans, abstracted no one ever discovered how from the
kitchen regions, leaving all the high-bred goldfish to die in the
mud. Here it was that Delia, usually so good, had been found in
Miss Brandon's dressing-room, that Holy of Holies, peacocking
before the glass in her great-aunt's mantle and bonnet. Here it
was that Francis, at a later age, had learnt to drive a car with the
connivance of the second chauffeur and run over one of Miss
Brandon's peacocks, while on the same ill-omened visit Delia had
broken the jug and basin in the best spare bedroom where she
had been sent to wash her hands, and flooded the Turkey
carpet.

Miss Brandon had made very little comment on these mis-
fortunes, but her niece noticed that after each of them she had
talked a good deal about the cousin she had never seen, the possible inheritor of her money. Mrs Brandon, who did not care in
the least what her aunt's plans might be, but was genuinely sorry
for the indomitable old lady, yearly becoming more bed-ridden
as she had predicted, was at last goaded into a mild remon-
strance, pointing out to Miss Brandon that if it had not been for
her nephew Henry, the children would never have existed, to
which Miss Brandon had replied cryptically that it took two to
make a quarrel.

Thinking of all this and of her aunt's letter, Mrs Brandon
carried her flowers into the little room known as the flower room,
along one wall of which ran a long marble slab with four basins
in it, relics of a former Brandon with four gardening daughters.
She then fetched yesterday's flowers from the hall and living-
rooms, refilled the vases, and began to arrange her flowers. This
she always called 'my housekeeping', adding that it took more
time than all her other duties put together, but she couldn't bear
anyone else to do it, thus giving the impression of one who was a
martyr to her feeling for beauty. As a matter of fact she spoke no
more than the truth, for Cook arranged the menus, and Nurse

looked after the linen and did all the sewing and darning, so that Mrs Brandon would have been hard put to it to find anything useful to do.

Presently Delia's voice at the telephone in the hall penetrated her consciousness, and she called her daughter's name.

'Oh, bother,' said Delia's voice to her unknown correspondent, 'mummie's yelling for me. Hang on a moment. What is it, mummie?' she inquired, looking into the flower room.

'It's about Aunt Sissie, darling. She said Wednesday, so don't arrange the picnic that day.'

'Oh, mother, any day would do for Aunt Sissie. We must have Wednesday for the picnic or the Morlands can't come.'

'I can't help it,' said Mrs Brandon, massing sweet peas in a bowl. 'We haven't been for ages and she's all alone, poor old thing.'

'Don't be so mercenary, mother,' said Delia. 'Here Francis, come here a moment.'

Francis, who was passing through the hall came to the flower room door and asked what the matter was.

'It's mummie, going all horse-leechy,' said Delia. 'Wednesday's the only possible day for the picnic and now mummie says we must go and be dutiful to Aunt Sissie. I wish Aunt Sissie would give all her money to that cousin of hers straight away and leave us in peace. Oh, mummie, *do* be sensible.'

'I am,' said Mrs Brandon, 'and I don't see why we shouldn't be kind to poor Aunt Sissie even if she *is* rich. If I were very old and alone and spent most of my time in bed, I would be very glad when people visited me.'

At this both her children laughed loudly.

Nurse, on her way upstairs with an armful of sewing, stopped to interfere.

'Oh, Nurse –' said all three at once.

'I want you, Miss Delia, so I can try on your tennis frock,' said she. 'Come up with me now.'

'Oh, Nurse, any time will do. I'm telephoning now. Be an angel and I'll come up presently. Mummie wants us to go over to Aunt Sissie on Wednesday, and that's the only good day for the picnic.'

'Nonsense, Miss Delia,' said Nurse. 'There's plenty of other days in the week. Now come straight up with me and try that dress on.'

Delia followed her old Nurse mutinously upstairs, making faces, till Nurse, who appeared to have, as she had often told the children when they were small thus frightening them horribly, eyes in the back of her head, said sharply that that was enough, and so they vanished.

'Francis, darling,' said Mrs Brandon, who had collected another great bunch of sweet peas and was holding them thoughtfully to her face, 'we *must* go to Aunt Sissie on Wednesday.'

'Yes, I think we must,' said Francis. 'Anyone who didn't know you would think you were mercenary, darling, but I know you haven't the wits to concentrate. You've got a kind heart though, and anyone who looked at you sympathizing with people would think you really cared. Give me a smell of those sweet peas.'

Mrs Brandon held up the flowers and Francis sniffed them violently.

'There are few pleasures like really burrowing one's nose into sweet peas,' he said, much refreshed. 'You're a bit like them, darling, all soft pinky-purply colours and a nice smell. Do you want your tall handsome son to help you to take the flowers to the church? It will look so well if we go together, and everyone will say what a comfort I am to you and what a wonderful mother you have been.'

Mrs Brandon laughed with great good humour and gave Francis a long basket to fill with tall flowers. Then they walked across the garden, up a lane, past the Cow and Sickle, and so into the churchyard by the side gate.

Mrs Brandon could never be thankful enough that her husband had died at Cannes and been decently buried in the English cemetery. If he had been buried in Pomfret Madrigal church she would have had to keep his grave and memory decorated with flowers. If she had undertaken this pious duty herself she would certainly have forgotten it and left the flowers, a wet mush of decay, to scandalize the village. If she had told Turpin the gardener to look after it, not only would the village have been scandalized, but he would have chosen the stiffest asters and

dahlias like rosettes, bedded out begonias, even cultivated im-
mortelles for the purpose, and given the little plot the air of a
County Council Park. The only alternative Mrs Brandon could
imagine was to have what might be called an all-weather grave,
sprinkled with chips from the stone-mason's yard, or battened
down under a granite slab, and to do this to the unconscious Mr
Brandon would have seemed to his widow a little unkind. So Mr
Brandon reposed at Cannes and a sum of money was paid yearly
to keep his memory as green as the climate allowed, while a neat
tablet in Pomfret Madrigal church bore witness in excellent lettering to the dates of his birth and death.

Pomfret Madrigal church was of great antiquity, being the
remains of the former Abbey of that name. Part of it was supposed to date from the reign of King John, but as that particular
part was considered by archaeologists to be buried in the thick
chancel walls, everyone was at liberty to have his own opinion. A
few years previously the Vicar, Mr Miller, a newcomer and an
ardent enthusiast for his new church, had discovered faint traces
of colour in a very dark corner high up on the south wall. Mrs
Brandon, always pleased to give pleasure, had made a handsome
contribution towards a fund for church restoration, a learned
professor famed for extracting mural paintings from apparently
blank walls had visited the church, and the work had been put in
hand. After several months' slow, careful, and to the Vicar
maddeningly exciting work, Professor Lancelot had brought to
light two square feet of what might have been a patterned border,
and a figure, apparently standing on its head, which was vari-
ously identified as Lucifer, Fulke de Pomfret who had impounded
some of the Abbey pigs in revenge for alleged depredations on
his lady's herb garden, and Bishop Wyckens who had made himself extremely unpopular with the Abbey about the matter of
some waste land over at Starveacres. However, all these differences of opinion were drowned and forgotten in Professor Lancelot's supreme discovery that the fragment of border might almost
with certainty be attributed to Nicholas de Hogpen, an extremely
prolific artist practically none of whose work was known. Others
supported the view that the work should stand to the credit of an
unknown monk whose work in Northumberland was described

in an imperfect MS which the owner, Mr Amery P. Otis of Brookline, Mass., would not allow anyone to see. The correspondence on this subject, beginning in the *Journal of the Society of Barsetshire Archaeologists*, had overflowed into the *Sunday Times* and *Observer*, causing several correspondents to write to the Editor about yellow-backed tits who had nested near mural paintings, or the fact that their great-great-grandfather had as a child sat on the knee of a very old man whose grandfather said he remembered someone who said he had heard of the Reformation. The Vicar read every word of correspondence and pasted all the cuttings into an album, as also a photograph from the *Daily Spectrum* with the caption 'Rector of Pomfret Madrigal says Mural Paintings unique,' and an inset called The Rev. Milker.

Since these eventful doings the paintings had gradually receded into the walls and were now invisible except to the eye of faith, which could often be found in the tourist season, guide book in hand, twisting itself almost upside down in its efforts to make out the inverted figure.

The July morning was now very hot. The little churchyard, on a slope facing the south, was shimmering with heat, and the flowers in the jam jars and Canadian salmon tins on the poorer graves were already wilting. In spite of her shady hat and her parasol of a most becoming shade of pink, Mrs Brandon was glad to get into the coolness of the little church. She slipped into a pew, knelt for a moment, and then emerged, apparently spiritually much refreshed.

'What *do* you say, darling, when you do that,' asked Francis. 'I've often wondered.'

Mrs Brandon looked guilty.

'I never quite know,' she said. 'I try to concentrate, but the only way I can concentrate is to hold my breath very hard, and that stops me thinking. And when I shut my eyes I see all sorts of spokes and fireworks. I always mean to ask to be nicer and kinder, but things like Rose wanting to change her afternoon out, or Aunt Sissie's letter, come into my mind at once. But I did have one very good idea, which was that if Rose changes her afternoon we could have the picnic that day and kill two birds with one stone.'

'People have been excommunicated for less than that,' said Francis. 'Pull yourself together, darling; here comes Mr Miller.'

Mr Miller, in the cassock and biretta that were the joy of his life and that no one grudged him, came up.

'Good morning, good morning,' he said, not so much in a spirit of vain repetition as in double greeting.

'I always feel I ought to ask you to bless me,' said Mrs Brandon taking his hand and looking up at him.

'My dear lady!' said Mr Miller, much embarrassed, and only just stopping himself saying 'It is rather you who should bless me.'

'Come off it, mamma,' said Francis kindly but firmly. 'Don't you know my mamma well enough yet, Mr Miller, to realize that she is a prey to saying what she thinks most effective?'

'I don't think you ought to talk like that in church, Francis,' said his mother severely. 'Come along, the altar is waiting for us.'

At this Francis exploded in a reverent guffaw and handed the basket of flowers to the Vicar, saying that he would fill the watering can at the tap in the churchyard and bring it in. So Mr Miller found himself alone with Mrs Brandon and an armful of flowers, and didn't know if he ought to stay with her or visit the poor, who were always kind to him but at the same time gave him the impression that they had just stopped a deeply absorbing conversation, probably about himself, and were only waiting till his back was turned to continue it. Mr Miller was about Mrs Brandon's age and having never met anyone that he felt like marrying had romantic views on celibacy. His richer parishioners liked him and he dined out a good deal, while the poorer part of his flock accepted him with good-humoured tolerance and always put off the christenings till he had come back from his yearly holiday. Funerals unfortunately could not so be postponed, though it was considered distinctly bad taste in Old Turpin, Mrs Brandon's gardener's uncle, to have died four days before the Vicar's return, in particularly hot weather. Weddings were also postponed so that the contracting parties could have the benefit of their own priest, but since the sexton's daughter had produced a fine pair of twins owing to her insistence on waiting to celebrate the nuptials till Mr Miller came back from Switzerland, he had been very firm on the subject.

As was inevitable, he was romantically in love with Mrs Brandon, but luckily for his own peace of mind he did not recognize the symptoms which he mistook for respect and admiration, though why these respectable qualities should make one give at the knees and become damp in the hands, he did not inquire.

Now Francis came back with the watering can and the vestry waste-paper basket for the dead flowers, and Mrs Brandon arranged sheaves of gladioli to her own satisfaction. All three walked down the church together and emerged blinking into the hot noonday glare. Mrs Brandon slowly put up her parasol, looking so angelic that Francis felt obliged to ask his mother what she was thinking about.

'I was wondering,' said she, 'if one *ought* to bring a watering can into the church. Wouldn't it look better to bring the vases outside and fill them at the tap?'

'My mother is the most truthful woman I know,' said Francis to Mr Miller, 'except when she isn't.'

Mr Miller wanted to say that Mrs Brandon's touch would sanctify even a watering can and that Francis ought not to speak lightly of such a thing as Truth, but was overcome by nervousness and said nothing. Francis said, Well, they must be getting along, and Mr Miller was inspired by desperation to ask them into the Vicarage to look at the new wall-paper in his study. Accordingly they walked through the little gate into the Vicarage garden and up by the yew hedge to the sixteenth-century stone Vicarage which was basking in the sun. The new wall-paper, which turned out to be that part of the wall where the damp patch used to be, freshly distempered, was duly admired.

'One does feel,' said Mrs Brandon, sinking elegantly into a very comfortable leather armchair, 'that this house needs a woman.'

Francis, alarmed by his mother's fresh outburst of truthfulness, made gestures behind Mr Miller's back, designed to convey to his mother that the Vicar's cassock and biretta made such a suggestion very unbecoming. Mr Miller felt that if Mrs Brandon were always sitting in that chair on a hot summer morning in the subdued light that filtered through the outside blinds, holding the broken head of a white gladiolus in her gloved hand, the parish would be much easier to manage.

'It really needs a good housekeeper,' said Mrs Brandon, continuing the train of her own thoughts. 'Turpin's Hettie is a nice girl, but she is much too kind to insects. She has never killed a spider in her life. Look!'

And she pointed the gladiolus accusingly at a corner where a fat spider was dealing with a daddy-long-legs.

'Oh dear!' said Mr Miller, in despair.

'I'll hoick her down,' said Francis, looking round for something that would reach the ceiling. 'Can I take one of your oars, Mr Miller?'

Without waiting for permission he took down from the wall the oar with which Mr Miller had stroked Lazarus to victory in Eights Week, and made a pat at the spider. The spider was dislodged, but with great presence of mind clung to the end of the blade with all her arms and legs.

'Get off,' said Francis, waving the oar. 'Help, Mr Miller, she is laying hold with her hands or whatever it says. It's more in your line than mine.'

On hearing this suggestion of clerical interference the spider ran down the oar in a threatening way. Mr Miller flapped feebly at her with his biretta, which caused her, or so Francis subsequently asserted, to bare her fangs and snarl. Mrs Brandon got up and enveloped the spider in her handkerchief, which she then threw out of the window into the heliotrope.

'Thank you, darling,' said Francis, putting the oar back on the wall. 'It takes a woman to fight a woman.'

'I wonder why spiders should be female?' said Mr Miller, so overwrought by his narrow escape that he hardly knew what he was saying.

'I suppose it's because they eat their husbands,' said Mrs Brandon.

'Mamma darling, *don't*,' said Francis, 'not in the Vicarage,' thus completing Mr Miller's confusion.

'Please rescue my handkerchief, Francis,' said Mrs Brandon, 'only see that the spider has really gone.'

25

Francis leant his long form over the window sill, picked up the handkerchief, shook it and returned it to his mother. Mr Miller who had had a wild thought of keeping the handkerchief for himself, realized that his chance was lost.

'It smells so deliciously of heliotrope now,' said Mrs Brandon, holding it to her face. This delightful gesture gave a little comfort to her host, who would be able to reflect that his flowers had furnished the scent that pleased his guest.

Just as the good-byes were getting under way, the study door opened and a dark young man of poetic and pale appearance came in, and seeing company began to back out.

'Wait a moment, Hilary,' said Mr Miller. 'Mrs Brandon, this is Mr Grant who is reading with me. He only arrived last night. And this is Francis Brandon, Hilary Grant.'

Further handshaking took place and it seemed that the visit had really come to an end, when on the doorstep Mrs Brandon suddenly stopped.

'I was thinking,' she said, 'that it would be so nice, Mr Miller, if you would dine with us next Wednesday. It will only be a kind of cold meal, but if you care to come we'd love to have you. And would Mr Grant perhaps come too?'

Mr Miller accepted for himself and his pupil and the Brandons went away.

'Really, mamma,' Francis expostulated, 'I didn't think you had it in you to be so mean!'

'I know quite well what you are hinting,' said his mother, with distant dignity. 'But it isn't my fault if Rose changes her afternoon out, and I have been meaning to ask Mr Miller for some time, and it isn't as if being a clergyman made one not able to eat cold supper. And now I must answer Aunt Sissie's letter. I cannot think how it is that one never has time to do *anything*.'

'Because you never have anything to do, darling,' said Francis. 'You take yourself in, but you can't take in your tall, handsome son. Come along or we shall be late for lunch and Rose will lower.'

26

2

BRANDON ABBEY

In spite of Delia's mild sulks the picnic was put off till Friday and Miss Brandon's invitation, or command, obeyed. The weather remained set fair and as the Brandon family got into the car at twelve o'clock, Francis puffed loudly and said it was worse than a third-class railway carriage that had been standing in a siding. The road to Brandon Abbey was through some of the loveliest scenery in Barsetshire. Leaving Pomfret Madrigal it went through Little Misfit, with a glimpse of the hideous pinnacles of Pomfret Towers in the distance, and then followed for several miles the winding course of the Rising, among water meadows that looked greener than ever in contrast with the sun-parched country. At the Mellings Arms there was a choice of ways. One went through Barchester, the other, marked as a second-class road, went up and over the downs, as straight as the Romans had built it, skirted Rushwater by the beech avenue and so by the Fever Hospital to Brandon Abbey.

As the Mellings Arms came in sight, Mrs Brandon leant forward and tapped on the glass. Francis, who was by the chauffeur, slid the window back and poked his face through.

'Tell Curwen, darling, that we'll go by the downs,' said Mrs Brandon.

Her clear voice carried well and Curwen's back visibly took offence. Francis exchanged a few words with him and turned back to his mother and sister.

'He says there's a bad patch near the top and he doesn't think the springs will stand up to it,' he said.

Mrs Brandon made a face of resignation.

'Don't let that stop us,' said Francis. 'I'm all for the downs myself, aren't you, Delia?'

'Rather,' said Delia. 'We might see the place where the motor char-a-banc was on fire last week.'

Francis shut the window and spoke to Curwen again. That

harbinger of misfortune listened with a stony face and turned the motor's head towards the downs. To Delia's great pleasure the burnt out corpse of the motor char-a-banc was still by the road-side, and Curwen so far unbent as to inform his mistress, via her son, that there was one of the bodies burnt so bad they couldn't identify it, after which he devoted his attention to driving with quite maddening care over the stony patches, wincing at each little jolt as if a pin had been stuck into him.

At twenty minutes past one the gloomy lodge of Brandon Abbey was reached. Miss Brandon always kept her gates shut to mark her disapproval of things in general, and as the lodge-keeper was deaf and usually working in his back garden, Curwen had to get out and go and find him, which he did with the gloomy satisfaction of a prophet whose warnings have been dis-regarded. Another five minutes' driving down the gloomy avenue which wound its way downwards to the hole in which the house was situated, brought them to the front door.

'Welcome to the abode of joy,' said Francis, politely opening the door of the car for his mother and sister. 'I'll ring the front door bell, but I don't suppose anyone will come. No wonder Aunt Sissie spends her time in bed. I would if I lived here.'

Certainly Brandon Abbey was not an encouraging place. The house, a striking example of Scotch baronial, spouting pepper-pot turrets at every angle, had been built in the sixties by Miss Brandon's father, an extremely wealthy jute merchant, on the site of a ruined religious house. The locality, though favour-able for stewponds and contemplation was damp and gloomy in the extreme. Mushrooms sprouted freely in the cellars, damp spread in patches on the bedroom walls, the flooring of the ser-vants' hall was from time to time lifted by unknown fungoid growths. The trees which Mr Brandon had planted far too thickly and far too near the house had thriven unchecked, and screened the house from all but the direct rays of the midday summer sun, which then made the servants' bedrooms under a lead roof in-tolerably hot. On the mossy stones of the terrace the peacocks walked up and down, believing according to the fashion of their kind that everyone was admiring the tail feathers which they had moulted some time ago.

'Nightmare Abbey,' said Francis, after they had waited some time, and rang the bell again. Even as he rang it and said the words, the door was opened by Miss Brandon's permanently disapproving butler, who said Miss Brandon was very sorry she couldn't come down to luncheon, but would like to see Mrs Brandon afterwards. He then showed the family into the drawing-room and left them to meditate till lunch was ready.

'Bother,' said Delia, after hunting in her bag, 'I've left my looking-glass at home.'

She looked round for one, but on the walls, thickly hung with the real masterpieces, the blatant fakes, and, incredibly, the china plates in red velvet frames that Mr Brandon's catholic and personal taste had bought, there was not a mirror to be seen.

'Try the overmantel or what not,' suggested Francis, pointing to the fireplace, above which towered a massive, yet fanciful superstructure of fretwork. Shelves with ball and fringe edgings, turned pillars, Moorish arches, Gothic niches, were among the least of its glories, while here and there were inserted round or diamond-shaped mirrors, hand-painted with sprays of plum blossom, forget-me-not, and other natural products.

By standing on tiptoe on the heavy marble fender Delia could just see her face among some painted bulrushes, and behind it a reflection of the room. In the reflection she saw the door open and a young man come in. Excited by the unexpected apparition she hastily put away her powder puff, turned, knocked down the polished steel fire irons with a frightful crash and stood transfixed with shame. To her great surprise the young man took no notice of the noise, but stood gazing at her mother who was apparently half asleep. Francis was the first to recognize the newcomer as Mr Miller's pupil, and though surprised to see him here, had enough presence of mind to say 'Hello, Grant.'

'Oh, hullo,' said Mr Grant, inquiringly.

'Francis Brandon,' said Francis, 'you remember meeting me at Mr Miller's last week.'

'Of course, I'm so sorry,' said Mr Grant, his eyes still wavering towards Mrs Brandon. 'I mean how do you do.'

'Nicely, thank you,' said Francis. 'This is my sister Delia, and mamma will come to in a minute. Mamma, here is Mr Grant that you met at the Vicarage.'

Mrs Brandon, who had succumbed for a few seconds to the heat and ante-lunch exhaustion, opened her eyes and gave Mr Grant her hand with a smile. Francis was rather afraid that the shock of waking up might prompt her to one of her worse indiscretions, but luckily lunch was announced, and they all went into the dining-room. This impressive apartment was lined with pitch pine and adorned with pictures by deceased R.A.'s, pictures which, as Mr Brandon had informed every visitor, had all been hung on the line. The lofty ceiling was decorated with strips of pitch pine crossing each other diagonally and at each intersection was fixed a naked electric light in a copper lotus. The dado and the panels of the door were of the finest Lincrusta Walton and the bronze clock on the mantelpiece represented a Knight Templar, with the clock face under his horse's stomach.

From the very beginning of lunch it was obvious to Francis and Delia that Mr Grant was in their language a case, and they had the great pleasure of kicking each other under the table whenever he looked at their mother. They were used to her rapid and entirely unconscious conquests, which Francis regarded with malicious enjoyment and Delia with good-humoured contempt. Delia's heart was so far untouched except by the heroes, whether villain or detective, of thrillers and American gangster films, and as Mr Grant, apart from a pair of horn-rimmed spectacles, had nothing in common with these supermen, she mentally labelled him Not Wanted.

Conversation during lunch was of a disjointed nature. Francis and Delia were consumed with curiosity as to why Mr Miller's pupil should be lunching at Brandon Abbey. On ordinary occasions they would have had no inhibitions about asking him what he was doing in their aunt's house, but the presence of the disapproving butler, who never left the room for a moment, not to speak of the two footmen, cramped their style a little. Their mother would have been capable of any indiscretion, but, as her children well saw, she had not yet recovered from her slumber before lunch and although she had grasped the fact that she had met Mr Grant at the Vicarage, she appeared to be under the impression that he was going to be a curate, and was industriously and ignorantly talking on church subjects. Mr Grant was doing his best to second her, but was hampered by an ignorance equal to her own and a tendency to look at her rather than listen to her. Altogether it was a relief to everyone when the butler, as soon as dessert was set on the table, told Mrs Brandon that Miss Brandon would be glad if she would come up and have coffee in her room. Mrs Brandon made a face at her children, sympathetically answered by hideous faces from them, and got up from the table, dropping a pale pink handkerchief as she rose. Mr Grant, who had stood up with her, was about to rescue it when a footman, at a sign from the butler, picked it up and gave it to his superior, who put it on a silver salver and handed it to its owner.

Mrs Brandon looked at the handkerchief, then looked in her bag, and finding that her handkerchief was not there, seemed surprised.

'I must have dropped it,' she said, taking it from the salver. 'Thank you so much.'

She was then wafted away by the butler, and the three young people were left alone with Miss Brandon's glasshouse peaches and grapes, besides the less rare products of the kitchen garden. Francis, approaching his subject cautiously, asked Mr Grant what he was reading with old Miller.

'Classics,' said Mr Grant.

'Is that to go to Oxford, or something?' asked Francis.

'No, I'm afraid I'm through Oxford,' said Mr Grant apologetically. 'Mother thought I'd better read for the bar, and as I did history my classics were a bit sticky, so she sent me here to rub them up. Were you a history man?'

'No, I'm afraid I'm only an Old School Tie,' said Francis in his turn apologetic. 'I wasn't very brainy at school and when a good job turned up in Barchester I jumped at it. I rather wish I'd let mamma send me to a University now, but anyway it's about five years too late.'

'I think you're jolly lucky,' said Mr Grant. 'I wanted to go into a publisher's office when I left school, but I'd got a mouldy kind of scholarship by mistake so they made me take it up, and then mother made me go abroad, and here I am at twenty-three only just beginning.'

'That's exactly as old as Francis,' said Delia. 'When's your birthday?'

Mr Grant said March.

'Well I'm February and Francis is April,' said Delia, 'so that's rather funny. Do you go to the movies much? There's not a bad cinema at Barchester.'

Mr Grant said he didn't go very much, but he had seen *Descente de lit* in which Zizi Pavois was superb, and *Menschen ohne Knochen* which, even allowing for propaganda, was an astounding moving affair.

Delia said she meant *films* and there was going to be an awfully good one at Barchester next week called *Going for a Ride* with Garstin Hermon as the villain and she had been told it was absolutely *ghastly*. As she said these words her pretty brown eyes sparkled, her cheeks flushed in a most becoming way and her hair seemed to curl even more than usual. Mr Grant looked at these phenomena with an historian's appraising eye and thought how much lovelier gentle blue eyes were than bold brown, how preferable was a soft pale skin to the rude glow of health, and how infinitely more touching were loose waves of hair, a little touched with grey, than a mop of corkscrews. Thinking these chivalrous thoughts he said, with the annoyingly tolerant manner that Oxford is apt to stamp upon her sons, that it sounded very exciting.

'Look here, Delia, that's your fourth peach,' said Francis. 'You'll be sick. Let's come out in the garden.'

Accordingly the three young people strolled out into the terrace and sat on the broad balustrade, looking at the foolish peacocks. At the end of the yew avenue the former stewpond, now a formal basin, gleamed among the leaves of the water lilies. The one white peacock, white by courtesy but really looking rather grey, posed self-consciously against the yews. It was all very peaceful and for a time no one had anything to say.

'I'm afraid my aunt's in rather a bad mood to-day,' said Mr Grant at last. 'I do hope she isn't giving Mrs Brandon a bad time.'

'Your aunt?' said Delia.

'Aunt Sissie. She's an aunt of yours too, isn't she?'

'Good Lord,' said Francis, 'you are our long-lost rival. I'm jolly glad to meet you. Aunt Sissie is always ramming you down our throats and I thought you were an old man with a beard. And I jolly well hope you do get this foul Abbey – I mean if you'd like it.'

Mr Grant looked so uncomfortable that even Delia felt that her brother might have been more tactful.

'You see, Aunt Sissie is a bit of a bully,' she said, 'and she thinks she can frighten us by saying she'll leave the money to you, but we really don't care two hoots.'

Mr Grant looked more uncomfortable than ever after this explanation.

'Sorry,' said Francis, vaguely feeling that some reparation was necessary.

'It's all right,' said Mr Grant. 'But it's rather a shock. I knew practically nothing about Aunt Sissie till father died, and then she wrote to mother and said she was a very old woman whose relatives neglected her and would I come and visit her. She didn't say anything about leaving this place or anything. I only came over here yesterday afternoon and I had an awful night in a four-poster stuffed with knobs, and there was a marble bath with a mahogany surround about three hundred yards down the passage, and Aunt Sissie was rather unpleasant, and thank goodness I'm going back to the Vicarage. If I hadn't promised Aunt Sissie I'd stay to tea I'd go at once. I can't stand this.'

He spoke with such vehemence that his hearers were surprised, not understanding that in his mind's eye he saw himself depriving that wonderful Mrs Brandon of her birthright and turning her out into the snow while he lived among peacocks and butlers.

'All right,' said Francis. 'If I get it I'll give it to you and if you get it you give it to me. If I had it I'd sell it for a lunatic asylum. Anyhow it's almost one now.'

'If it were mine I'd burn the damned thing down,' said Mr Grant, toying with the idea of handing over the insurance money to Mrs Brandon anonymously.

Warming to the theme the two heirs, ably supported by Delia, began to alter the house according to their individual tastes, turning the pond into a swimming pool, the enormous servants'

33

hall into a squash court, and the drawing-room into a dance room with bar. By the time they had decided to make their aunt's room into a Chamber of Horrors, charging half a crown for admission, they were all laughing so much that even when Delia suddenly uttered one of her celebrated screams, it was hardly heard above the noise the men were making. Her shriek was merely a prelude to the announcement that if Aunt Sissie was everybody's aunt they must be Hilary's cousins, adding that she hoped he didn't mind her calling him Hilary, but she always did. On inquiry it turned out that Mr Grant's father and the Brandons' father were connected with Miss Brandon's family on quite different sides and no relationship existed, but it was agreed that a state of cousinship should be established.

When Mrs Brandon left the dining-room she found Miss Brandon's maid waiting for her in the hall.

'Good afternoon, Sparks,' said Mrs Brandon. 'How is Miss Brandon to-day?'

'Thank you, madam, a little on the edge,' said Sparks. 'Young Mr Grant's visit seemed to upset her a good deal, being as he reminded her of her brother, Captain Brandon, the one that was killed by a pig in India, madam.'

At any other moment Mrs Brandon might have wondered why Mr Miller's pupil should remind her Aunt Sissie of Captain Frederick Brandon who was killed while pig-sticking in Jubilee year, but her whole attention was concentrated on getting upstairs. The great staircase at Brandon Abbey, square, made of solid oak, had been taken from an Elizabethan house that was being demolished. Mr Brandon, after taking one look at its rich natural colour, had decided that it did not look worth the considerable sum he had given for it, so he dismissed his architect who had advised the purchase and had the whole staircase painted and grained to resemble the oak of which it was made. Having done this he admired the result so much that, with a taste far in advance of his time, he left it bare, instead of covering it as the hall and corridors were covered with a layer of felt, a rich Kidderminster carpet, and a drugget above all. He then gave orders that it was to be waxed and polished twice a week, which had been faithfully carried out ever since, even after Mr Brandon had slipped and broken his ankle and a second footman (who should have been using the back stairs and was at once dismissed) had crashed down the final flight carrying six empty water cans.

Knowing the dangers, Mrs Brandon clung to the banisters and went slowly upstairs. Safely arrived on the landing she followed Sparks along the gloomy corridor to the door that led to Miss Brandon's sitting-room. This door was guarded by two life-size and highly varnished black wooden statues of gorillas, wearing hats and holding out trays for visiting cards, which images had been the terror of Francis and Delia's childhood. Delia always the bolder of the two, had only suspected that they would claw her as she went into her aunt's room, but Francis knew, with the deadly certainty of childhood, that they came over the downs to Stories every Friday night, when Nurse was out, and got under his bed. Perhaps the happiest day of his life was when he was taken to Brandon Abbey in his first prep school holidays, and fresh from a world of men suddenly realized that the gorillas were nothing but very hideous wooden figures, which knowledge he imparted to Delia in a lofty and offhand way, as one who had always known the truth but had not troubled to mention it.

Sparks left Mrs Brandon in the sitting-room while she went to prepare her mistress. Mrs Brandon walked about the room, idly looking at the many faded photographs of old Mr and Mrs Brandon at all stages, of Captain Brandon with military moustache and whiskers, of Miss Brandon from a plump, pretty child with ringlets to a well-corseted young woman in a bustle, after which epoch she had apparently never been photographed again. She wondered idly, not for the first time, what Amelia Brandon's life had been, what secrets her heart might have held, before she became the immense, terrifying old lady whom she had always known. These unprofitable reflections were interrupted by the door into Miss Brandon's room being opened and Mrs Brandon, turning to face Sparks, saw a stranger. It was a woman no longer young, with greying hair and a rather worn face, neatly dressed in dark blue silk.

'Mrs Brandon?' said the stranger. 'I am Ella Morris, Miss Brandon's companion.'

Mrs Brandon found Miss Morris's voice very pleasant.

'Oh, how do you do,' said she, shaking hands. 'Thank you so much for writing for Aunt Sissie and I do hope you aren't having a dreadful time.'

'Nothing to what I have had with my other old ladies,' said Miss Morris composedly. 'I was so sorry not to be down when you came, but Miss Brandon wanted me to read some old letters to her. I hope everything was all right at lunch.'

'Perfect,' said Mrs Brandon. 'And forgive my asking, but knowing Aunt Sissie as I do, have *you* had any lunch.'

'Oh, no,' said Miss Morris as composedly as ever. 'Miss Brandon likes me to read to her while she is lunching. She has a remarkably good appetite. I shall have mine now. Will you come in?'

'How many days a week is she in bed now?' Mrs Brandon asked softly, as they approached the door.

'Six and half, since Whitsun when I came,' said Miss Morris. 'She gets up on Tuesday for the afternoon, and that is why she is always a little fatigued on Wednesday.'

With these ominous words she opened the door, saying, 'Miss Brandon, here is Mrs Brandon.' She then went away and Sparks, who had been keeping guard at the bedside, got up and followed her.

In the huge room, hung with dark tapestries, filled with heavy mahogany furniture, there was very little light. The blinds were drawn against the westering sun and Mrs Brandon, dazzled by the gloom, could only advance slowly towards the fourposter with its embroidered canopy, below which her husband's aunt lay propped upon pillows.

Miss Brandon in a state of nature bore a striking resemblance, with her almost bald head and her massive jowl, to the more decadent of the Roman Emperors. To conceal her baldness she had taken of late years to a rather cheap wig, whose canvas parting was of absorbing interest to the young Brandons as they grew tall enough to look down on it, but when in bed she preferred to discard the wig, and wore white bonnets, exquisitely hand-sewn by Sparks, frilled, plaited and goffered, in which she looked like an elderly Caligula disguised as Elizabeth Fry. Round her shoulders she had a white Cashmere shawl, fine enough to draw through a wedding ring, and about her throat swathes of rich, yellowing lace, pinned with hideous and valuable diamond brooches. Diamonds, rubies, sapphires, emeralds sparkled in the creases of her swollen fingers, and in the watch pocket above her head was the cheap steel-framed watch that her father had bought as a young man with his first earnings.

'Stand still and shut your eyes for a moment,' commanded Miss Brandon's voice from the bed, 'and then you'll be able to see. I can't have the blinds up. My eyes are bad.'

Mrs Brandon obediently halted, shut her eyes, and presently opened them again. The gloom was now less dense to her sight and without difficulty she reached the chair placed by the bedside.

'How are you, Aunt Sissie,' she said, taking her aunt's unresponsive hand, and then sat down.

Miss Brandon said that her legs were more swollen than ever and it was only a question of Time. Her niece, she added, could look at them if she liked.

'Oh, thank you *very* much, Aunt Sissie, but I don't think I could *bear* it,' said Mrs Brandon truthfully.

'You don't have much to bear, Lavinia,' said her aunt grimly, 'and I think you might take a little interest in my sufferings. Even my father's legs weren't as bad as mine. But all you young people are selfish. Hilary wouldn't look at them. What do you think of him?'

'Of whom?' Mrs Brandon asked, a little bewildered.

'Hilary Grant. My nephew. First cousin once removed to be exact, as his father was a son of my youngest aunt. Same relation your children are.'

'Do you mean Mr Grant?' faltered Mrs Brandon. 'I thought he was going to be a clergyman.'

Miss Brandon almost reared in bed.

'I have always been sorry for you, Lavinia, as Henry's wife,' she announced, 'but I am beginning to be sorry for Henry. Have you *no* intelligence?'

'Not much,' said her niece meekly.

'None of you have,' said the invalid. 'Four people having lunch together and can't find out who they are. Why didn't Miss Morris tell you?'

'I didn't see her, Aunt Sissie. She was reading to you, she said, when we got here.'

'Oh, that's what she said, is it,' said Miss Brandon. 'Well, as a matter of fact she is perfectly correct. She was reading some of Fred's letters from India to me. I would like you to read me some, Lavinia. Take a chair nearer the window and pull up the blind a little. Here they are.'

She handed her niece a large sachet, worked in cross-stitch with a regimental crest, containing a bundle of yellowing letters. Mrs Brandon went towards the window and could not resist saying as she went,

'Is it the cousin you sometimes talk about?'

'His son. I didn't like the father and the mother is a fool, but luckily she lives in Italy a good deal. I like young Hilary.'

She said this with such meaning that Mrs Brandon was almost goaded into saying that she wished her aunt would leave everything to Mr Grant at once, and then they needn't ever come to Brandon Abbey again. But when she looked at her aunt's helpless bulk, and thought of her legs, and the years of pain and loneliness she had had and might have to come, she felt so sorry that she said nothing, pulled up the blind a little, sat down and opened the sachet. A marker of perforated cardboard sewn with blue silk on to a faded blue ribbon and stitched with the initials F. B., showed the place where Miss Morris had left off.

'Shall I read straight on?' she asked.

Receiving no reply, she began to read. But Captain Brandon's writing had never been his strong point, the ink was pale with age, the letters were heavily crossed. And they consisted almost entirely of references to fellows in the regiment, or the places where they had been quartered or in camp, she found herself floundering hopelessly.

'You'd better stop, Lavinia,' said her aunt's voice after a time, though not unkindly. 'Miss Morris can do it far better than you can. I think of Fred as if it were only yesterday. He was twelve years older than I was. Sissie was his pet name for me; he didn't like Amelia. When he was a lieutenant he used to let me ride on his knee and pull his moustaches. He was a very fine figure of a man. My father made an eldest son of him, and sent him into the

Army and gave him every advantage. And all the end of it was that Fred was killed. And now I am all that is left. Hilary reminded me of Fred. I should like to think of someone like Fred living here when I am gone.'

Mrs Brandon understood that her aunt was talking to herself and without malice. Neither did she feel any resentment herself at the old lady's outspoken preference for her new nephew. For many years she had felt that the prospect of an inheritance might be bad for Francis. Luckily he had hitherto treated the whole subject as a joke and worked just as hard as if he had no expectations from his aunt and no allowance from his mother. But if by any chance Miss Brandon did bequeath him the Abbey and even a part of her fortune, Mrs Brandon saw no end to the trouble that such a white elephant would bring. What the amount of Miss Brandon's estate might be she had no idea, but she thought the death duties would effectually keep the inheritor from improving or even keeping up the place. Never in fact had the mother of a possible legatee been less grateful. It was almost without knowing that she was speaking that she said, 'I hope that he will then, Aunt Sissie.'

'What?' said Miss Brandon sharply.

Mrs Brandon found what she had just said too difficult to repeat and was silent.

'Read me some of *The Times*,' said Miss Brandon. 'The cricket news. My father was very fond of cricket and I used to know all the names of the county players. It is a poor game now. Go on.'

Mrs Brandon read the descriptions of the chief matches for some time, looking occasionally at the bed to see if her aunt was listening. Gradually she let her voice tail away into a murmur, then gently got up and was tip-toeing towards the door to call Sparks, when a sharp voice from the bed said, 'Lavinia!'

'I'm so sorry,' said Mrs Brandon, returning to the bedside, 'I thought you were asleep.'

'You've never thought in your life,' said Miss Brandon. 'Come here.'

Mrs Brandon approached the bed.

'You are a silly woman, Lavinia,' said her aunt, 'but there's a lot of good in you. I heard what you said quite well. It was no business of yours, but I daresay you are right. I'm going to give you something. It is the diamond Fred brought back from India the last time he came on leave. I always wore it till my hands began to swell, and I wouldn't have it altered because it was set just as Fred gave it to me. If you don't get anything else, you'll get that.'

She took a little case from beside her bed and handed it to her niece, who opened it and saw a diamond ring in an open setting of very thin gold, a store of a thousand lights and twinklings.

'Put it on,' said Miss Brandon. 'That's right. It looks better on you than it ever looked on me. You have a lady's hands. Mine are like my father's, workman's hands. Go away now and send Sparks to me.'

She shut her eyes so determinedly that Mrs Brandon did not dare to thank her, so she kissed the swollen, bejewelled hand very gently and went out of the room. In the sitting-room she found Miss Morris writing letters and told her that Miss Brandon wanted Sparks. Miss Morris rang the bell.

'I hope very much to see you before you go,' she said. 'Miss Brandon has her tea about half-past four and I have ordered tea for you at five if that suits you and then I can come down. Five to seven is my off time. I hope you found Miss Brandon pretty well. She has been looking forward to your visit very much indeed.'

'I never knew anyone who could show their pleasure at seeing one less than Aunt Sissie,' said Mrs Brandon, 'but she was very kind and gave me this ring.'

She held out her left hand on which the diamond was sparkling. Mrs Brandon had exquisite hands and though she was by no means puffed up she might sometimes be found gazing at them with a frank and pensive admiration that amused her best friends. She wore no rings except her wedding ring, having secretly sold her ugly diamond half-hoop engagement ring many years ago. Captain Brandon's Indian diamond now shone in its place.

'It looks perfect on your hand,' said Miss Morris in a matter of fact voice that yet somehow conveyed to Mrs Brandon that her hands were admired and the gift approved. 'I think your son and daughter are in the garden with Mr Grant. Or would you rather rest?'

Again Miss Morris's pleasant voice conveyed an unmistakable meaning, and Mrs Brandon went downstairs feeling rather like a child that has been told it may get down from table. In the hall she picked up her parasol and gloves and went out into the shimmering afternoon. To young Mr Grant, sitting on the edge of the lily-pond, while Francis and Delia tried to tickle for gold-fish, it seemed that never had a goddess been more apparent in her approach. Being in private a poet he tried to think of a suit-able description, rejected the words swimming, floating, gliding, light-footed, winged, and several others, and finally as she came near delivered his soul in the words, 'Oh, Mrs Brandon,' standing up and straightening his tie as he did so.

'Hullo, mamma,' said Francis. 'Don't come any nearer or you will frighten my goldfish. Hilary, take mamma away or she will want to look, and if there's one thing goldfish can't bear it's people looking. There are millions of seats about.'

He waved his hand comprehensively at a stretch of green turf and dark walls of yew and bent himself again to his tickling. Mrs Brandon smiled indulgently and turning to Mr Grant said,

'I think we must be cousins by marriage.'

This statement, which when previously made by Delia had caused Mr Grant no emotion at all, suddenly assumed a totally different aspect. To be Mrs Brandon's cousin was like suddenly becoming a member of the Royal Family, or being asked to tea by the Captain of the Eleven; or like going to Heaven. In a state of unspeakable nervous exaltation he began to explain the rela-tionship, but one half of his mind, and that, if the expression may be permitted, by far the larger half, was trying to visualize the Tables of Affinity in the beginning of the Prayer Book and to remember whether a man might marry his father's aunt's nephew's on another side's wife, or rather widow. So he stam-mered and repeated himself and wished he had shaved more carefully that morning. When he had stammered himself into silence, Mrs Brandon said she thought there was a seat under the tulip tree, so they walked there; and there were two deck chairs, just as if it had been meant.

'Now,' said Mrs Brandon, settling herself comfortably, 'tell me about yourself.'

This kind suggestion naturally threw Mr Grant into a state of even more acute palsy and paralysis, but to please the goddess he explained, in a not very intelligible way, that his father had died some time ago and his mother was rather Italian.

'Have you Italian blood then?' asked Mrs Brandon, interested.

Not like that, Mr Grant explained, but he meant his mother lived mostly in Italy and had got rather Italian, at least, he added in a burst of confidence, the kind of Italian that English people do get.

'I know,' said Mrs Brandon. 'She talks about Marcheses and would like you to kiss people's hands.'

So confounded was Mr Grant by this proof of semi-miraculous understanding, and at the same time so overcome by the idea that he might perhaps be allowed to kiss Mrs Brandon's hand, that he forgot all the hard words he had been about to utter concerning his mother, and wished she had forced him from earliest youth to kiss the hand of every delightful woman he met. Mrs Brandon said she thought the custom of kissing hands was so charming, which inspired Mr Grant's heart with fresh ardour, but that she thought Englishmen could never do it well, at which his heart sank and he thought more unkindly than ever of his mother.

Mrs Brandon pulled off her gloves and looked thoughtfully at her hands.

'Aunt Sissie gave me this ring to-day,' she said. 'Isn't it beautiful?'

She held out her hand. Mr Grant, put his own hand very respectfully beneath it and raised it a little. He looked intently at the diamond and the elegant fingers and imagined himself gently pressing his lips upon them. He then, entirely against his own will, found himself withdrawing his own hand and saying the ring was lovely. This would have been a good moment to add that the hand it adorned was lovelier still, but his voice refused its office and flames consumed his marrow. By the time he came to, Mrs Brandon was telling him about the wall paintings in the church.

'I liked them awfully,' said Mr Grant, 'and all the monuments and things.'

'I suppose you saw my husband's memorial stone,' said Mrs Brandon, assuming quite unconsciously a most intriguing air of melancholy.

'No, I'm awfully sorry I didn't,' said Mr Grant. 'Is it a good one – I mean sculpture or anything?'

'Oh, no; quite simple,' said Mrs Brandon, in a voice that made Mr Grant feel how moving simplicity was, compared with sculpture. 'Just the dates of his birth and death. He died at Cannes, you know, so he couldn't be buried here.'

Mr Grant said again he was awfully sorry.

'That is very sweet of you,' said Mrs Brandon, turning grave blue eyes upon him. 'I don't think much about it. I wasn't very happy. There are things one is glad to forget.'

If Mr Grant's guardian angel had been there he would have been perfectly within his rights to take Mrs Brandon by the shoulders and shake her. Mr Grant, deeply moved by this touching confidence, saw his exquisite new friend in the power of a sadist, a drunkard, a dope fiend, nay Worse, though why it should be worse he didn't quite know, and in his agitation got up and began to walk about.

'Yes, I suppose it is nearly tea-time,' said Mrs Brandon. 'Let's find the children. And you won't mind if I call you Hilary, will you? If we are cousins it seems ridiculous to say Mr Grant.'

'I'd love it,' said Mr Grant.

'And you must call me Lavinia,' said Mrs Brandon, putting her parasol up again as they walked back across the lawn to the pond.

'There is one name I would like to call you,' said Mr Grant, in a low, croaking voice.

Mrs Brandon stopped and looked interested.

'I would like to call you my friend,' said Mr Grant.

'Of course,' said Mrs Brandon, laughing gently, 'that goes without saying. But if you feel I am too old for Christian names, never mind.'

Mr Grant felt that this misunderstanding was so awful that it would be no good trying to explain it. They collected Francis and Delia, who had by now tired of the goldfish, and all four went back to the house for tea. Here Miss Morris was waiting for them at the head of the dining-room table, which was loaded with scones, sandwiches, cakes of all sorts and sizes, sweets and fruit. Mr Grant had not yet arrived at the stage when love makes one resent the sight of food, and all three young people made a very hearty meal. When Miss Morris had finished pouring out the tea she asked Mrs Brandon if it would be inconvenient for her to take Mr Grant back in her car.

'I had ordered Miss Brandon's car to take Mr Grant back,' she said, 'but as he is almost next door to you I thought you wouldn't mind.'

'Of course not,' said Mrs Brandon. 'And now I come to think of it, you are having supper with us to-night, aren't you Hilary, so it all fits in.'

Mr Grant on hearing those lips speak his name lost his senses and said, Oh, of course, he had quite forgotten, and again felt that it was no good trying to explain. Ever since the invitation had been issued on the previous Saturday he had been living for that evening, but in the unexpected joy of seeing Mrs Brandon again at the Abbey, and the whirlpool of emotion into which he had been thrown by finding her even more exquisite than he thought, only the present had existed for him, and so drowned was he in the moment that he had truly and completely forgotten about the evening.

'Well, it's no good forgetting now,' said Francis, 'if you're coming back with us. No need to bother about changing to-night. When Rose is out we relax a little. And anyway there's not much sense in telling old Miller to change because you can hardly tell the difference. He ought to be allowed to dress like a monk or something for dinner; he'd get an awful kick out of it.'

While the younger members were loudly discussing suitable evening dress for Mr Miller, Mrs Brandon turned to Miss Morris and pressed cake upon her. Miss Morris refused it.

'You are too tired to eat,' said Mrs Brandon accusingly. 'You have had nothing for tea, and I'm sure you didn't have enough lunch. Was it a poached egg?'

'Oh, no. Just what you had. Cold salmon, grilled cutlets. I order the meals for Miss Brandon and I make a point of tasting everything. One must keep the servants up to the mark.'

'Yes, tasting,' said Mrs Brandon severely. 'Three grains of rice and a mouthful of cutlet.'

Miss Morris said nothing. Her mouth tightened, but her eyes looked at Mrs Brandon for a moment as if appealing for help.

'I know *exactly* what you feel like,' said Mrs Brandon untruthfully, 'but it's no good going on like that. You need a holiday.'

'I have only been with Miss Brandon since Whitsun, Mrs Brandon.'

'And have you once been outside the grounds? or had a day to yourself? or gone to bed before one o'clock?'

'I really could get out if I wanted to,' said Miss Morris, 'but there's nowhere particular to go, and the motor bus doesn't come any nearer than Pomfret Abbas. And I don't mind going to bed late at all. I used to read to my father a great deal at night.'

'Now what I want you to do,' said Mrs Brandon, 'is to come for a picnic with us on Friday. Francis has a little car and he can come and fetch you and take you back. We are going to the Wishing Well over beyond Southbridge and you will like it very much.'

'How good of you,' said Miss Morris. 'But I can't.'

Her mouth set into a hard line again, but Mrs Brandon saw it tremble, and took a secret resolution.

'Miss Brandon sent her love,' said Miss Morris, deliberately changing the subject and speaking for the whole table to hear, 'and she is very sorry that she doesn't feel up to seeing Mr Brandon, or Miss Brandon – '

'Bountiful Jehovah!' said Francis, piously grateful.

' – or Mr Grant, but she would like you to come up before you go, Mrs Brandon.'

Mrs Brandon said she would come at once then, as they must be getting home, and went upstairs with Miss Morris, saying no more about the picnic.

Miss Brandon was propped up on her pillows, finishing what looked like the remains of a tea that would have fed several people.

'Well,' said she to her niece, 'so you are going. I can't see those

45

young people. They tire me. I suppose they have been getting into mischief as usual.'

'No, Aunt Sissie. Just sitting in the garden.'

'Idling as usual,' said Miss Brandon. 'My father never idled, nor did I.'

Mrs Brandon, suppressing an impulse to say And look at you both now, thanked her aunt for a pleasant visit, at which her aged relative grunted.

'I wanted Miss Morris to come for a picnic with us on Friday,' she said.

'Well, she can't,' said the invalid, who seemed to be imbibing fresh strength as she dipped plum cake into her tea and mumbled it.

'But she said she wouldn't,' Mrs Brandon continued, with great cunning.

'She *wouldn't!*' said Miss Brandon. 'I don't know why girls are so ungrateful now. I never could stand a proud stomach. I suppose you wanted her to help with the sandwiches, Lavinia. Something for nothing.'

Having thus satisfactorily attributed the lowest of motives to her niece and her companion, Miss Brandon drank the rest of her tea and rang the handbell violently. Sparks appeared and was ordered to fetch Miss Morris, while Miss Brandon ate lumps of sugar in a state of mental abstraction which her niece thought it better not to disturb.

'I want you to go with Mrs Brandon on Friday and help with the sandwiches,' said the invalid, as soon as Miss Morris appeared. 'The car will take you, and tell Simmonds to put up some of her potted salmon and crab apple jelly and make some cakes. And you'd better take some of the marsala. You can read to me all Friday evening to make up. Good-bye, Lavinia.'

'Good-bye, Aunt Sissie, and thank you very much for the ring. It is the loveliest diamond I've ever seen,' said Mrs Brandon.

'Fred liked pretty women to have jewellery,' said Miss Brandon with a surprising chuckle. 'It was the diamond bracelet he gave to Mrs Colonel Arbuthnot that made him have to exchange – that was at Poona in seventy-six. I was only a young woman then, but Fred told me everything. Come again, soon, but I don't want to see all those young people. Come alone, and I'll show you my legs.'

Taking this as permission to retire, and seeing no means of reaching her aunt across the tea-things, Mrs Brandon repeated her farewell and went out, followed by Miss Morris.

'Is it all right for Miss Brandon to eat so much?' she inquired as they went downstairs. 'I thought she was on a diet.'

'So she is, but she doesn't take any notice of it. She told Dr Ford last time he came that she was going to die in her own way and he needn't come again if he didn't like it, so he just comes and talks to her occasionally. She likes it. Mrs Brandon, I can't thank you enough, but do you really want me?'

At this slavish question, which no one should ever ask, Mrs Brandon almost felt she didn't. But she looked at Miss Morris's thin shoulders and her worn face and decided that she did.

'I do want you,' she said, 'but I'm not sure if I really want Aunt Sissie's car. Anyway Francis shall drive you back.'

Then they all got into the car. Curwen asked with long-suffering if he should go by the downs, and on receiving the order to go by Barchester managed to express by the set of his shoulders his opinion of employers, their children, and their guest. Francis chose to ride inside, so he and Delia continued their plans for remaking Brandon Abbey, while Mrs Brandon thought of nothing in particular and Mr Grant felt that he now knew what true religion was like. As they approached Pomfret Madrigal, Mrs Brandon told Curwen to drive first to the Vicarage. Francis protested that there was no need to change, and Hilary might as well come straight to Stories and have a singles with him before dinner. But Mr Grant, increasingly conscious of his unsuccessful shave that morning, said he would really like to go to the Vicarage first if nobody minded, and, as an afterthought, that he might as well change. Mrs Brandon smiled approval, Mr Grant was decanted at the Vicarage, the car rolled away and darkness fell on the world.

3

UNDER THE SPANISH CHESTNUT

THE darkness which had covered the universe was not apparent to anyone else. The Vicarage cook was sitting at the kitchen door in the sunshine, knitting a jacket for her married sister's latest; Hettie, the friend of spiders, was in the pantry reading a very nice book in a twopenny edition called *Pure as the Lily*, with the sun glancing on her spectacles, while Mr Miller, reclining in a deck chair under the beech on the lawn, was reading the Bishop of Barchester's pastoral charge, bathed in the late afternoon light. Cook shouted to Hettie that she didn't remember a summer like that, not since her aunt died; Hettie yelled back to Cook that she must hurry up with her vôyle for the Feet, it was that hot, a statement which Cook rightly interpreted as a wise decision of Hettie's to get her new cotton voile dress finished before the annual Church Fête, which took place, with Mr Miller's resigned permission, in the Vicarage grounds; while Mr Miller thought that if there were a hotter place than his garden he wished the Bishop were in it. Seeing his pupil approach he dashed his Bishop's letter to the ground and asked Mr Grant how he had got on at Brandon Abbey.

Quite well, said Mr Grant. His aunt was a peculiar old lady, but quite kind, only he did wish she wouldn't make hints about leaving things to him, because the Abbey was a ghastly place and he would hate to have anything to do with it. Her companion, Miss Morris, was very nice too. And, he added, speaking with some difficulty, Mrs Brandon was there.

'Mrs Brandon. Ah, yes,' said Mr Miller.

There was a silence.

'It's a most extraordinary thing,' said Mr Grant, 'but she is a sort of cousin of mine. I never knew about it till to-day.'

Mr Miller found himself indulging in the sin of envy. To be Mrs Brandon's cousin must be in itself a state of grace to be envied by anyone. Then he rebuked himself, and concentrated on thinking how glad he was that his pupil, whom he already liked, should have this great happiness.

Silence fell again, till Mr Miller, hearing the church clock strike seven, said he supposed they must be thinking of dressing. So they thought about it very comfortably till half-past and then there was rather a scurry. Mr Grant, getting into his white shirt, was for the sixth or seventh time suddenly struck hot with shame and remorse as he remembered the various bricks he had dropped that afternoon. His stud fell from his nerveless hands, rolled across the sloping oak floor and disappeared in the gap under the skirting board. Mr Grant knew he had another stud some-where, but where he couldn't think. After untidying all his draw-ers he went down the passage and knocked at Mr Miller's door.

'I say,' I'm awfully sorry, Mr Miller,' he said, putting his head in, 'but one of my studs has got down a hole in the wall and I can't find my spare one. Could you possibly lend me one?' It's only an ordinary gold one.'

'The worst of my profession is that one doesn't have much to do with studs,' said Mr Miller, who was in his trousers and vest and preparing to put his collar on. 'Wait a minute and I'll see.'

He hunted in a box and found a stud which was just sufficiently unlike Mr Grant's to make that young gentleman conscious of it for the whole evening. He handed it to Mr Grant, and seeing him look with furtive curiosity at his clerical collar, kindly offered to show him how it did up.

'Oh, thanks most awfully,' said Mr Grant. 'I've always wanted to know how that gadget worked. I say, that's awfully interesting. Thanks most awfully.'

He dashed back to his bedroom, hated his own face, hair and tie, wondered if Mrs Brandon would notice a small spot of grease on one of the lapels of his dinner jacket, wished his evening shoes were newer, and hurried downstairs and into Mr Miller's little open car, in which his tutor was already waiting.

'You will enjoy dining at Stories,' said Mr Miller, as they drove along the lane. 'The house is a delightful example of early Georgian; about 1720 I think.'

Mr Grant said that would be awfully jolly and wished his

throat were not so dry, nor his heart banging so absurdly against his ribs.

'And Mrs Brandon is a most charming hostess,' Mr Miller continued.

This understatement could only be met with silence, and nothing more was said till they drew up at the front door.

When Mrs Brandon got home she went upstairs to rest a little before dinner. Not that she was in need of rest, but she vastly enjoyed the ritual of leisurely bath, lying on her sofa in a becoming wrap, and slowly dressing. Francis and Delia went off to play tennis before their skimpier toilets, and their fraternal yells came sweetly to her ears from beyond the walled garden. She took off her hat and rang.

'Did you ring, madam?' said Rose, appearing with great celerity.

'My bath please, Rose, and I'll wear that old pink thing,' said Mrs Brandon, recognizing with some trepidation that Rose had a grievance, and suddenly realizing that she shouldn't have been there at all, as it was her afternoon out.

'I thought you would prefer the black, or the mauve to-night, madam,' said Rose, so meaningly that her mistress had to ask her why.

'You wore the pink if you remember, madam, the last time Sir Edmund dined here.'

'Sir Edmund? But he isn't coming here to-night.'

'I am sorry, I am sure, madam, but understanding from Nurse that Sir Edmund had rung up I thought I had better stay in and take My Afternoon on Friday. If I had taken the message, madam, I should have written it down on the pad, but of course with Nurse taking it I did not wish to interfere, not being any business of mine.'

Without giving her mistress time to answer she disappeared into the bathroom and drowned all attempts at conversation in a roaring of taps, so that she did not hear a knock on the bedroom door.

'Come in,' cried Mrs Brandon, shutting the bathroom door to lessen the noise.

Nurse came in.

'It's about Miss Delia's tennis frock, madam,' she began. 'I'm sure I am ready to work at it all night if need be, but I can't finish it without a fitting, and Miss Delia is playing tennis.'

'Then you'd better tell her to come up to you before she dresses for dinner,' said Mrs Brandon, knowing well that Delia always obeyed Nurse and that this complaint was but a preface to further wrongs.

'Just as you say, madam,' said Nurse, 'and I am sure I am sorry if I have stepped out of my place, but when the telephone rings for quite three minutes, as I said to Cook, being downstairs at the moment, and the other girls upstairs tidying themselves after lunch, and it being Rose's afternoon off and she happened to pass the remark quite distinctly before lunch that she was going to Southbridge on her bike as soon as she had set the dinner table, it is hardly to be surprised at that I went to the phone. Let me take your stockings off, madam, I'm sure you are tired.'

'What *is* all this about the telephone?' asked Mrs Brandon, sinking into a chair.

'Sir Edmund, madam,' replied Nurse, suddenly becoming brisk and business-like. 'He rang up to ask if he could come to dinner and I said you were out all day, madam, so he said he would come at eight and hoped it was all right.'

'Oh well, I suppose he must,' said Mrs Brandon. 'Thanks, Nurse.'

At this minute Rose emerged from the steaming bathroom and saw her rival in the act of putting the bedroom slippers on her mistress's feet. She controlled herself very well, merely saying in an icy voice that she supposed there was nothing more.

'Yes, my old pink dress,' said Mrs Brandon, goaded to defiance. 'Thanks, Nurse. You'd better go and catch Miss Delia before dinner. Now Rose, what is this about Sir Edmund?'

'I understood, madam, from something Nurse let slip,' said Rose coldly, 'that Sir Edmund was coming to dinner, so not being sure what you wished I changed My Afternoon back to Friday.'

In face of this revolting and quite unnecessary self-sacrifice Mrs Brandon could say nothing. She escaped into the bathroom, but not before she had seen Rose pick up the stockings that Nurse had folded and carry them ostentatiously away to be washed. In the bath her spirits revived a good deal. The worst of the interview with Rose and Nurse was over, and she understood her staff well enough to know that they would mobilize and rise to a crisis, and that she could count upon a good dinner. So she finished dressing with a fairly light heart and came downstairs. For a moment she thought of asking Rose if she had remembered the special port for Sir Edmund, but feeling that she could better face her guest's disappointment than her parlourmaid's displeasure she refrained.

Sir Edmund Pridham was an old friend of the Brandons', Mrs Brandon's trustee, and one of those useful middle-aged men who appear to have no particular business but do a hundred unpaid jobs with no thought of the sacrifice of their own time and strength. The Pridhams had lived at Pomfret Madrigal for at least two hundred years, always doing their duty to their tenants, to the church, being Justices of the Peace, sitting on and controlling local committees, once or twice sitting unwillingly but efficiently in Parliament because no one else would contest the seat. The present baronet, a childless widower, had commanded the Barsetshire Yeomanry for two years of the War and when he was invalided with a permanently crippled leg had run the whole county, even bullying the Matron of the Barchester War Hospital and the terrifying head of the Waacs. He knew the country and the people almost as well as old Lord Pomfret, and was entirely unmoved by their affection or dislike. His relations with Mrs Brandon as trustee had always been very pleasant, as he managed her affairs with the same diligence that he applied to everything else and she always signed everything he told her to without asking why. Of late he had insisted that Francis should go thoroughly into his mother's money matters and the two had got on well together.

Of course the county had married him to Mrs Brandon again and again in the last eighteen years or so, but nothing was further from their thoughts. Sir Edmund looked upon Mrs Brandon as what a woman should be, good-looking, docile, not too intelligent, always charming. Her flashes of insight he completely ignored, but he saw through all her self-deceptions with a ruthless though admiring eye, and never missed an opportunity of pointing them out to her. Mrs Brandon liked him very much, accepted his homage and his scorn with equal placidity, consulted him about everything, and except on money matters rarely took his advice.

Presently Rose, her voice divided between the deference due to a baronet and the resentment she was still feeling against Nurse and in a lesser degree against her innocent mistress, announced Sir Edmund. At the sight of his tall figure, which almost filled the drawing-room door, Mrs Brandon felt very comfortable. For years his broad shoulders, straining to the uttermost stitch the well-cut coats that he would not take the trouble to renew, his red neck rigidly confined by a stiff collar and overlapping a little behind, his close-cropped sandy-grizzling hair and moustache, his angry but equitable blue eyes, had represented the safe background of her life. After outraging Rose by asking after her mother's leg, Sir Edmund bore down upon his hostess, who rose to greet him.

'Out to kill, Lavinia,' said Sir Edmund, eyeing her dress with interest. 'Who is it this time?'

'Mr Miller is coming to dinner,' said Mrs Brandon, ignoring her guest's question, 'and Mr Grant who is a cousin of ours, at least he seems to be a cousin of Henry's, and a cousin of Miss Brandon's. We met him there to-day and he is delightful.'

'A cousin of Amelia Brandon's?'said Sir Edmund, who prided himself on knowing the genealogies of the whole county. 'Grant, eh? Now, let's see. Old Mrs Brandon's sister – Mortons they were from Cheshire and a good family, Miss Morton was considered to have thrown herself away on Brandon, till he made all his money – married a man called Grant in the Barsetshire Regiment, met him at the Barsetshire Hunt Ball when she was down here staying with her sister at Brandon Abbey. Their son was born the year Lord Pomfret was made Lord Lieutenant, now what the devil was his name? Edward. That's it. Called after some one – can't think who at the moment. Edward married a damn silly woman and this must be their boy. Hope you've got a good dinner, Lavinia. I'm hungry. Been out all day about those drains.'

53

'Have some sherry then,' said Mrs Brandon, going to the table where Rose had put the decanter. She certainly looked very agreeable in the old pink rag, what she herself called a soft elderly pink, and no wonder that Mr Grant, looking from his considerable height over Mr Miller's shoulder as they came in, was again transfixed by arrows of very respectful desire.

'Well, Miller,' said Sir Edmund, who was Vicar's Churchwarden, read the lessons on Sundays and while supporting all the Vicar's doings in public, bullied him a good deal in private, 'everything all right, eh?'

To this comprehensive question Mr Miller could but answer weakly that it was. Mr Grant bowed rather low over Mrs Brandon's hand, thus affording exquisite pleasure to Francis and Delia who followed hard upon him, and was introduced to Sir Edmund.

'So you are Edward's son,' said Sir Edmund, shaking hands. 'What's your name? Robert?'

Mr Grant, feeling that an apology was necessary said he was sorry but his name was Hilary.

'Hilary, eh? Oh, well, nothing wrong with that. There was a saint called Hilary, a bishop; more in Miller's line than mine. But I should have thought your father would have called you Robert, after your grandfather,' said Sir Edmund, more in sorrow than in anger.

Luckily dinner was coldly announced by Rose and the party drifted into the dining-room. Sir Edmund, lingering behind with his hostess, remarked, in a voice of whose carrying powers he was quite conscious, that he was sorry he had told young Grant that he thought he should have been called Robert, because he remembered now that there had been the deuce of a row between young Grant's father and grandfather on the occasion of young Grant's father's marriage.

'Here, Grant,' he called, 'what's the name of that woman your father married? The dark one?'

Mr Grant looked round, startled.

'My mother, do you mean, sir?' he asked.

'That's right, your mother, you know what I mean. Never mind the name,' said Sir Edmund, who had evidently satisfied himself on the subject.

Conversation at dinner was led by Delia, who had been reading the local weekly and had come across a delightful report of the coroner's inquest on the bodies of the people who were burned in the motor bus.

'It must have been simply *ghastly*, Sir Edmund,' she said with relish. 'The doors and windows got jammed and the ones that got out simply *trampled* on the others and got all cut to bits on the broken glass, and it took two days to sort the others out, and there was one of them that there was so little of him left that they didn't know who he was, and even with the false teeth they couldn't tell because there was another man that died afterwards in the Barchester Infirmary and all he would say was "My teeth, my teeth," only they couldn't understand for ages because he hadn't got any teeth, and you know the way having no teeth makes people so difficult to understand, but anyway one of the nurses who had false teeth herself had a brain wave and said she expected he wanted to know where his false teeth were, because when she was in a car accident once that was the first thing she thought of when she came to, and so they fetched the teeth from the refrigerator or wherever the coroner keeps the bodies, but he was dead then and couldn't identify them. I think they ought to have buried them with him, like Ur and Vikings and all that sort of thing, but they kept them in case anyone could identify them. I'd have put them in the Barchester Museum.'

'In which department?' asked Mr Grant, interested in Delia's maiden fancies.

'Oh, anywhere. Fossils or War Souvenirs or something. I mean then if anyone wanted them they'd always be there.'

'And what happened to the one they couldn't identify?' said Francis.

'Oh, he got buried. It's a pity we couldn't have had him buried here. It would have been *ghastly*. I mean seeing a coffin and knowing there was really nothing to speak of inside. Is it all right to bury people in the churchyard, Mr Miller, when there really isn't any of them to bury except the burnt bits? I mean would the Bishop mind?'

'I have luckily never been faced with such a contingency,' said

Mr Miller, who was very fond of Delia, but had not her strength of mind. 'It is all rather horrible to think of.'

Sir Edmund, who owing to the excellent soup and fish had only been a listener to the foregoing conversation, now spoke as the representative of law and order.

'We all know you'd do your duty, Miller,' he said, wiping his moustache with his table napkin crumpled into a ball. 'But better to marry than to be burnt, eh?'

He then applied himself to the next course. Mr Grant and Francis, catching one another's eye, fell into wild suppressed giggles, and Mrs Brandon applied herself to soothing Mr Miller, which she did so well that the whole dinner was held up while he hung upon her lips and Rose, preferring not to demean herself by making her presence known, stood silently at his elbow with the sweet, till Delia jogged him.

'I say, Mr Miller, it's an ice,' she said earnestly. 'It's an ice, so do hurry up or my bit will go all to squelch. I say, mother, let's have coffee under the chestnut.'

'We might,' said Mrs Brandon doubtfully. 'Rose, do you think we could have the little table out there? Mr Francis would help you with it.'

But Rose had as yet neither forgotten nor forgiven and said, with a manner that froze the blood, that she could manage the table quite well by herself.

'Very well,' said Mrs Brandon, again driven by persecution and injustice to rebel, 'we'll have dessert and coffee and the liqueurs outside, and the port if no one minds.'

Rose, who had a secret passion for anything that savoured of theatre, gave her outwardly grudging consent to this plan, and with the help of one of the housemaids arranged the fruit and wine under the tree and brought her mistress a black lace scarf. Sir Edmund, Mr Miller and Mr Grant took out chairs, while Francis and Delia triumphantly bore silver candlesticks with shaded candles through the dusk. There was not a breath of air and the candles burnt steadily under the great Spanish chestnut. Rose, contemplating the scene from the front door, said to the housemaid that madam really looked quite the thing to-night in her pink, and it was just like the scene in *Moonlight Passion*, the one she saw at the Barchester Odeon last week, where the Italian count gives the feet for Princess Alix. Princess Alix, she added, was taken by Glamora Tudor, the one that they called in Hollywood 'The Woman who Cannot Love,' but madam reely looked every inch as good-looking, and if people who answered the telephone would only write down the messages it would save a lot of trouble to other people she could mention and standing there wouldn't get the dining-room table cleared nor the washing-up done. So she vanished, and the yellow path of light from the front door was suddenly obscured, and in the gathering gloom the radiance of the rising moon could now be seen through the branches.

'The full moon is rising,' Mrs Brandon breathed.

At the sound of her low voice uttering these words Mr Grant nearly fainted.

'Nonsense, Lavinia,' said Sir Edmund, lighting a cigar. 'Full moon doesn't rise till much later. Two or three days off the full. Any child knows that.'

'But I'm not a child,' murmured Mrs Brandon.

At these words Mr Grant's soul took flight and assuming the form of a bird, perched in the chestnut tree, tuning its notes to the music of the spheres which sang 'Mrs Brandon, Mrs Brandon,' leaning its breast against a thorn regardless of botany, embracing in its vision the whole universe, for what worlds could exist outside the pool of candlelight below the leaves? It saw Mrs Brandon, a shadowy goddess, draped in the rose light of evening, veiled in the black lace of tattered clouds, a diamond flashing like a star on her finger. It saw the rest of the party, privileged beyond their knowledge, beyond their worth, laughing and talking in that sacred presence; Sir Edmund pulling at his cigar, Francis and Delia eating more peaches than it would have thought anyone could eat who had already had so many at lunch, Mr Miller – to him alone was vouchsafed a glimpse of the true light, gazing from the shadow at the foundress of the feast. It saw the diamond sparkle and flash again with a thousand fires, growing in size till all earths, all seas, all heavens were included in its bounds, a burning rose at the core. Spreading its wings it flew through an infinity of time and space towards that fiery centre, burning to immolate itself on such a pyre and rise again transfigured to the skies.

'Of course you aren't a child, Lavinia,' said Sir Edmund. 'Can't call a woman of your age a child. What I said was, A child would have more sense.'

Mr Grant's soul returned suddenly to his body, but as no one had noticed its absence in the interval between Mrs Brandon's words and Sir Edmund's reply, its return passed unobserved. Its owner, a little dizzy, helped himself to port. There was a silence in which Mrs Brandon drew her mantilla round her with one hand and gazed meditatively upon the other with its gleaming ring.

'What's that you're wearing, Lavinia?' said Sir Edmund suddenly.

'Only my old pink,' said Mrs Brandon, 'and the Spanish lace shawl that Henry brought from Toledo.'

'No, no, don't be dense. I can see perfectly well what you have on. The ring I mean. Haven't seen that before.'

'It is a diamond. Miss Brandon gave it to me to-day. Isn't it lovely?'

She held out her hand to Sir Edmund.

'A good one,' said he, looking at the ring, but not troubling to raise or support her hand, for which Mr Grant could have killed him. 'Worth a round two hundred, I should say. I'd better have it insured with your other things. Remind me to take it into Barchester next time I go. Queer thing if Amelia Brandon is giving anything away. She must be breaking up. Never knew her give anything to anyone – except charities, of course. Always go to her if we want anything for the hospital. By the way, Lavinia, does she ever mention her will?'

At this appalling frankness everyone was struck dumb.

'I don't think one ought to talk about things like that,' said Mrs Brandon, 'do you, Mr Miller?'

'Now never mind Miller, Lavinia,' said Sir Edmund. 'He knows what's what. Render unto Caesar, eh, Miller?'

'Yes, yes, indeed, Sir Edmund,' said Mr Miller hastily, not wishing to offend his churchwarden, but doubtful as to the applicability or relevance of his statement.

Francis came to the rescue and said Aunt Sissie was always trying to frighten someone by saying she'd leave something to someone else, but no one wanted that awful Abbey and if he or Hilary got it they were going to give it to each other or turn it into a lunatic asylum. Mr Grant corroborated this statement by saying, Rather. On hearing these subversive remarks Sir Edmund nearly burst. To treat the sacred rights of property as a joke was something almost beyond his comprehension, almost worse than robbing the poor box or shooting foxes. If Amelia Brandon left the Abbey, as he had always understood she might, to Lavinia's boy, it would be a big responsibility, but Francis would have to take it on and do the best he could for the place and the tenants, and he would give help and advice if Francis needed it and would take it. If the old lady was going to leave it to this new nephew, who seemed a harmless enough young man for one whose mother was a damn silly woman, that was entirely her affair and no one would grudge it to him. But to talk of a stake in the country, and more especially in Barsetshire, as if it were a shuttlecock to be thrown to and fro or dropped, was worse than Bolshevism, worse than Communism, or Germany, or Italy, or Spain, or Russia, or the United States, or the Labour Party, or any of numerous nations, sects or parties which Sir Edmund found unworthy of his approval.

Filling his glass again, he addressed the two young men on the subject of the rights of property, fixing them with a choleric blue eye that they could not and dared not avoid. Delia melted away and was presently heard playing the gramophone to herself in the drawing-room. A moth fluttered round the candles. Mrs Brandon exclaimed, Mr Miller blew them out, but Sir Edmund's voice rumbled on in the leaf-chequered moonlight. Presently Rose's white apron was seen coming from the house, to the young men a welcome diversion, to Mrs Brandon a vague source of uneasiness. Kindly reluctant to interrupt the gentry in their talk, Rose stood on the outskirts of the group emanating an atmosphere of such condescending tolerance that even Sir Edmund became conscious that something was wrong, and was checked in his flow of speech.

'Yes, Rose?' said Mrs Brandon.

'Curwen would wish to speak to you, madam, if it is convenient,' said Rose.

'It isn't really,' said Mrs Brandon helplessly, 'but I suppose he'll have to. Where is he?'

Rose stepped dramatically aside, revealing the hitherto unsuspected form of Curwen.

'I'm sure I didn't wish to trouble you, madam,' Curwen began, an ill-concealed triumph in his voice.

'Can't hear a word you say. Come up here. Bad enough not seeing anything, without not hearing anything,' barked Sir Edmund in his orderly-room voice. Curwen, an old soldier, automatically moved forward and stood to attention.

'It was going over the downs done it, madam,' he announced with gloomy relish.

'Did what?' asked Sir Edmund. 'Why the devil can't your man speak plainly, Lavinia?'

'Done it in, Sir Edmund,' said Curwen.

Delia, tired of her gramophone, had drifted back again and wanted to know who was done in and if Curwen had seen the body, and if so if she could see it too.

'That's *enough*, Delia,' said Sir Edmund in a state of exasperation. 'Let the man get on with whatever he is trying to say. Carry on, Curwen.'

Curwen, looking straight in front of him, embarked on a long unpunctuated statement from which it appeared that owing to his employer's complete disregard for and want of sympathy with the sensitive works of the car, he had been forced to drive her, by which he meant the car and not his employer, over roads which the County Council had deliberately made to afford employment to garages, the proprietors and employees of which places would, in his opinion, be all the better for six months in the trenches, that he had said at the time what would happen and was therefore guiltless, but that at the same time he would always hold it against himself what had happened. He had taken her, he continued, straight down to Wheeler's the minute he found it and Wheeler, who was an honest sort of chap himself, though that young Bert and Harry couldn't be trusted even to oil her, couldn't possibly get it done before Friday.

'Well, come clean, Curwen; what is it?' said Francis. 'Springs gone? I thought I felt an awful bump when we went over the level crossing.'

'It *might* have been the springs, Mr Francis,' said Curwen regretfully, 'but it happened to be the shock absorber.'

'That's a bit of an anti-climax,' said Francis cheerfully, 'but it dishes the picnic, doesn't it? Can't Wheeler get it done by to-morrow night?'

'Not with the Thursday half-holiday, sir,' said Curwen cheered by the thought. 'That young Bert and Harry are going to Barchester to the cricket.'

'Good thing, cricket,' said Sir Edmund, who was tired of the conversation. 'Not what it was though. Well, Lavinia. I must be getting along. Glad to have met you, Grant. Where are you staying? With Miller? That's right. Mensa, eh? They pronounce it all wrong now. Latin's not what it was in my time.'

With which unfounded aspersion on the classics Sir Edmund heaved himself up to go.

'I suppose you wouldn't care to come to our picnic on Friday?' said Mrs Brandon, taking his hand in farewell.

'No, Lavinia. And what's more you can't have my car. My chauffeur is having his holiday and I'm driving myself over to Rushwater about a bull. You know I never go to picnics. Wasps and jam sandwiches. Good night, Miller.'

He kissed Delia. The whole party moved to the front door. Sir Edmund, assisted by Francis, got into his little car and drove away.

While Francis was dispensing farewell drinks in the drawing-room a complicated discussion took place about the picnic on Friday. Mrs Brandon was in favour of putting it off till her car was back, but her children protested so loudly that she had to give in, though to drive in Francis's little runabout was not any pleasure to her. Mr Miller then offered his car which was gratefully accepted, but as it was very small and uncomfortable and everyone insisted on his coming too, matters were not much more forward till Delia remembered Miss Brandon's offer.

'Look here, mother,' she said. 'Let's telephone to Aunt Sissie and ask if Miss Morris can come and pick you up and you can go comfortably, and then Francis and I can go in the runabout and we'll go round by Starveacres and see where they're dragging for the gypsy that was drowned below the hatches on Monday night, at least Turpin says they think he was, and then Mr Miller and Hilary can come in Mr Miller's car. You're coming, Hilary, aren't you?'

'Of course Hilary is coming,' said Mrs Brandon. So the matter was left, pending a telephone call to Brandon Abbey on the following morning, and good nights were said. Mrs Brandon, not unconscious of the becoming frame that her black mantilla made for her head, came out to see the Vicarage party into their car.

'Come up for tennis some time to-morrow, Hilary,' she said, laying her hands on the door of the car. For all answer Mr Grant, pot-valiant with the moon, the candles, the port, the hot still night, raised it to his lips.

'I was thinking, Mr Miller,' said the goddess, when Mr Grant had finished with her hand, 'that if Hettie would let us have some of her parsnip wine on Friday it would be so nice. Of course we shall bring everything else.'

Mr Miller said Indeed, indeed, yes, and urged his little car homewards. Mrs Brandon went upstairs, thinking not of moonlight, candlelight or the hot scented night air, but of how nice it was to go to bed, however nice a party had been. Rose had left everything exactly as she liked it and just as she was settling to sleep a light tap came at the door. Nurse put her face round it with a caution that would have woken the heaviest sleeper.

'Excuse me, I'm sure, madam,' said Nurse, 'but I saw the light under your door, so I thought it would be all right.'

'Yes?'

'I'd thought you'd just like to know, madam, that Rose and I have had quite an explanation. It is always so unpleasant when there is an unpleasantness of any sort, and much more pleasant when things are explained, as they could easily have been in the first place.'

'Yes, it is,' said Mrs Brandon sleepily. 'That's all right then. Good night, Nurse.'

Outside their bedroom doors Francis and Delia exchanged a few words on life, with special reference to Mr Grant's too visible passion for their mother, which Delia characterized as a bit slooshy if Francis knew what she meant.

'Perhaps it is a bit slooshy,' said Francis, 'but it doesn't look bad, this hand-kissing business. Rather like the Prisoner of Zenda and that sort of thing. I wish mamma had brought up her tall handsome son to kiss her hand. I think I'll take to it.'

His sister murmured the word potty, adding that she dared him to. Francis at once accepted the dare, they rubbed the tips of their noses together, relic of a nursery superstition connected with the binding powers of a dare, and separated for the night.

*

In the Vicarage Mr Miller and his pupil found it difficult to go to bed. There was a very sacred subject on which both would have liked to speak, while both felt a very creditable diffidence in embarking upon it. Although there were more than twenty years between them, they were both at that ingenuous stage of a first love which makes it necessary for the sufferer to celebrate aloud the beauties and virtues of the adored. Later may come doubts, torments, secrecies, jealousies; but in the first golden days the young lover, whether young in years or in experience, far from wishing to conceal the beloved in some unsuspected isle in far-off seas, is more inclined to stand at the cross roads and challenge anyone to mortal combat who denies her charms, or to sing those charms with all comers in the alternate verses beloved of the Muses.

So it was with Mr Miller and Mr Grant, but being English gentlemen they found the approach to these mysteries singularly difficult.

'Well, we really must be turning in,' said Mr Miller, when he and Mr Grant had consumed respectively a glass of orange juice and a lemon squash and said nothing for three quarters of an hour.

'Yes, I suppose we must,' said Mr Grant. 'It was an awfully nice evening.'

'Yes, it was delightful to sit out after dinner. There are so few evenings in an English summer when one can comfortably sit out,' said Mr Miller.

Mr Grant agreed, adding that it was often too cool to sit out comfortably. Also, he said, the light often attracted moths.

Both men thought how a moth had fluttered into the candle under the chestnut, and how Mrs Brandon had exclaimed against it. Both would willingly have celebrated her enchanting childlike terrors, the sweetness of her voice, but neither found himself capable of beginning.

'Well,' said Mr Grant, 'I suppose we ought to be turning in.'

By dint of repeating this comfortable phrase often enough they managed to get themselves upstairs. On the landing they paused.

'Well, we really ought to be in bed,' said Mr Miller. 'Good night, Hilary.'

'Good night,' said Mr Grant. 'And thanks awfully for a splendid evening.'

'Oh, that's all right,' said Mr Miller. 'We really ought to thank Mrs Brandon,' he added in a voice singularly unlike his own.

'Oh yes, Mrs Brandon,' croaked Mr Grant. And having let loose this word of power both were overcome with confusion and separated abruptly. Mr Grant took off his dinner jacket and waistcoat and gazed into the night. Unfortunately his window looked in exactly the opposite direction from Stories, but this presented no obstacle to his mind's eye, which ran lightly up the side of the house like Dracula, scaled the beautiful stone roof, perched on the chimney and thence with extensive view surveyed the landscape. It was during this trance that Mr Grant was suddenly smitten with an idea for a poem, totally new in conception and treatment, containing in itself the finest elements of all previous poetry, yet of an epoch-making originality. Pushing aside the books upon which he had been working earlier in the day, or rather on the preceding day, for it was now well after twelve, he sat down, twisted his legs round the front legs of his chair, titled the chair forwards, and plunged into literary composition.

An hour or so later he heard a light tap at his door. His tutor, also without coat or clerical waistcoat, entered the room. Mr Grant, drunk with his own written words, gazed at him stupidly.

'I couldn't go to sleep,' said Mr Miller, though his dress

afforded no indication of his having tried to do so, 'and I wondered if you had that stud of mine.'

It seemed to Mr Grant in his present demented state of mind eminently reasonable that Mr Miller should want an assurance of the safety of his stud at one in the morning. Wrenching it from his shirt front he handed it to its owner in silence.

'Thanks,' said Mr Miller, apparently much relieved. 'I just wanted to be quite sure, that was all. Are you working?'

'Yes,' said Mr Grant, 'I mean no. At least yes, but not exactly working. Just writing. An idea I had.'

'Oh,' said Mr Miller, interested, but not liking to ask.

'Just an idea,' Mr Grant repeated, longing for a sympathetic audience, but not liking to ask.

'Well,' said Mr Miller, 'I suppose I ought to be turning in. Thanks for the stud. I hope I didn't disturb you.'

'Oh, rather not,' said Mr Grant. 'It was just an idea I had – a sort of idea,' he explained.

Mr Miller, hearing the appeal in Mr Grant's voice, said he didn't suppose he would care to let him look at it. Mr Grant, who wanted nothing more, said he didn't suppose there was anything in it, but if Mr Miller really *cared* – He then pushed a sheet of paper towards his host, saying that it was only an idea.

'Poetry,' said Mr Miller. 'If you don't mind, Hilary, I'll read it aloud to myself. I can't ever quite get the feeling of poetry unless I read it aloud. Let me see,' he added, looking at the various rough drafts and erasures, 'where exactly does it begin? Oh, yes, I see.

> Methinks most like a god is he
> Who in Lavinia's company
> Amazed can sit, and gaze the while
> On the enchantment of her smile.
>
> But when I, wretched, see my saint,
> My tongue is held, my senses faint,
> My eyes are darkened with desire
> And all my veins consumed with fire.

An imitation of Catullus, I see,' said Mr Miller, suddenly becoming professional, 'but free, very free. In a way I think you are right to compress your rendering. It is a more general fault to expand from the original. But you will have to work at it a good deal, Hilary.'

'I never thought of Catullus,' said Mr Grant miserably, his golden vision of a totally original poem dashed to the dust.

'My dear boy, you only have to look at that first line,' said Mr Miller. 'By the way, why Lavinia? Surely Lesbia is good enough?'

Mr Grant said it didn't seem to fit in.

'Lavinia,' said Mr Miller, speaking aloud to himself, 'is Mrs Brandon's name.'

'I know,' said Mr Grant defiantly. 'That's why.'

Mr Miller looked at his pupil, who returned his gaze.

'I think,' said Mr Miller, very kindly, 'that you had better finish undressing and go to bed.'

'I suppose I had. I only once went to bed in my trousers, after a bump supper it was: no, it can't have been that time because they took all my trousers away. Anyway it was jolly uncomfortable,' said Mr Grant yawning. 'Good night, sir, and thanks awfully.'

He tore the paper into fragments, put them in an ash tray, struck a match and watched them burn.

'Good night,' said Mr Miller and went away.

Mr Grant was in bed in two minutes and such is human frailty and such is youth that he was asleep in two minutes more, and slept soundly till long after breakfast time.

- 4 -

A VISIT TO THE WISHING WELL

AFTER a good deal of telephoning, complicated by Miss Brandon's butler's total inability to understand or take any message and Miss Brandon's refusal to let her companion go to the telephone, the use of her car was obtained for the day. It was to come at twelve with Miss Morris, the crab apple jelly, the potted salmon, the cakes and the marsala, and be at Mrs Brandon's disposition as long as she needed it, a concession which would have made Sir Edmund even more unhopeful of Miss Brandon's mental and physical condition.

At half-past eleven on the Friday morning, as Mrs Brandon was thinking of getting ready, Mr Grant came in with a face of such dire portent that even his hostess noticed that something was wrong and asked what it was.

'It's the most ghastly thing,' said Mr Grant. 'My mother is here from Italy. I never knew she was coming. She turned up last night quite late, in a taxi from Barchester, and she has taken a room at the Cow and Sickle.'

'I'm afraid she won't be very comfortable there,' said Mrs Brandon. 'They *will* not have that window in the bedroom made to open and if it did open the pigstye is just outside. But it will be nice for you to have her.'

'It won't,' said Mr Grant, in such anguish that he contradicted his hostess flatly. 'She has come to see how I'm getting on, and it's too awful, because she won't leave me alone and she wants to come to the picnic. It's all my fault. I let out we were going. I did think perhaps Francis would take her, because there's room for three in his car, but I found he'd gone already. Mr Miller will have to take her, that's all, and I'll stay at home and swot, but I thought I must tell you. I simply *loathe* missing the picnic, but there it is. I daresay she won't stay long, because she has a ghastly friend called Lady Norton she is going on to, but I wish to goodness she'd stayed in Italy.'

'She could come with me and Miss Morris in Miss Brandon's car,' said Mrs Brandon kindly. 'Would that help?'

'I say that *is* kind of you,' said Mr Grant. 'Don't you really mind?'

'There's heaps of room,' said Mrs Brandon, 'and it will be perfectly easy. Do tell her that I will call at the Cow soon after twelve. We shall have a delightful day. My friend Mrs Morland who writes books is joining us and her boy who is at South-bridge school, and some young friends of my children, and I hope Dr Ford will look in if he has time. I am so glad you let me know about your mother.'

Thus cheered Mr Grant sped back to the Cow and Sickle, while

Mrs Brandon put on some very special cream and powder to protect her from the sun, a shady hat, the pinky-purply scarf that Francis had approved and long gloves. Being thus prepared for a country expedition she read the newspaper in the drawing-room till Miss Brandon's car arrived and Miss Morris got out of it with a huge bunch of flowers.

'Miss Brandon sent you these,' she said, as her hostess met her in the hall. 'She thought you wouldn't have enough in your garden.'

'They are lovely,' said Mrs Brandon, touching them gently. 'You look tired. Were you up late?'

'Rather late,' said Miss Morris. 'But I'm used to that. What rather alarmed me was the drive here. Miss Brandon ordered the second chauffeur to drive, and as he never gets a real chance he asked me if I would mind if he let her out a bit, to use his own expression. We seem to have taken every corner in Barsetshire at seventy miles an hour on the wrong side of the road.'

Mrs Brandon sympathized warmly.

'Miss Brandon was rather upset this morning,' continued Miss Morris, 'by a letter from Mrs Grant, Mr Grant's mother. It seems that she has come over quite unexpectedly from Italy and is going to stay somewhere in the neighbourhood, but she didn't give any address. Miss Brandon has some kind of prejudice against her and is determined not to see her, so Sparks and the butler have the strictest orders not to open the front door at all to-day. She was so worried that I hardly thought I would get away.'

'I'm so glad you did,' said Mrs Brandon.

'Nothing would have stopped me,' said Miss Morris, 'after you were so kind in asking me.'

'But,' said Mrs Brandon as they got into the car, continuing the train of her own thoughts, 'I must tell you what a dreadful thing has happened. Poor Hilary came up here this morning quite distracted. His mother is here, at the Cow and Sickle, which is a very uncomfortable little inn with roses on the front, and she is coming to the picnic. Now did Rose put the fruit in? Yes, I see it in the corner, so that is all right. I don't know what she is like, but I daresay she is quite nice. You will like our Vicar, Mr Miller, who is coming, and my friend Laura Morland who writes books and several young friends of my children. I never know who they are, but they are all very intelligent and know all about the ballet, and here we are at the Cow.'

Miss Brandon's second chauffeur drew up, a little contemptuously, as near the Cow and Sickle as the immense dray of Messrs Pilward and Sons Entire, which was disgorging casks and bottles at the front door would allow. The two enormous grey cart horses which Messrs Pilward and Sons used with some ostentation for deliveries in the neighbourhood of Barchester, were eating their lunch from modern, labour-saving nosebags hung from the front of the pole; every inch of their glossy coats shone with grooming, every boss of brasswork on their complicated harness glittered, the paintwork of the great dray was spotless in red and black; the draymen, in the scarlet linen coats and black leggings over which the A.U.H.P.B.C., (Amalgamated Union of Horse Propelled Beer Conveyancers) had nearly split, (some saying What about Red Spain, others What about the Blackshirts, both parties agreeing in passing a resolution which called upon the Government to reduce taxation, increase the Air Force, abolish militarism, fight everybody, and establish a thirty hour week with pensions for everyone at fifty) looked like superior if eccentric hunt servants, and Miss Brandon's large, powerful, expensive car was entirely put out of countenance.

Mrs Brandon got out and went to the door.

'Good morning, Spindler,' she said to the proprietor, who was the uncle of the Vicar's cook. 'I've come to fetch a Mrs Grant who is staying here.'

Mr Spindler, a stout gentleman of few words, nodded in the direction of the dray horses. At the head of the nearer horse, so that she had not been visible as the car drove up from behind, was standing what Mrs Brandon at once recognized as an Englishwoman Abroad. Her shoes were sensible, her stockings of lisle thread, her light grey homespun skirt dipped slightly at the back, her jumper was of an orange hue, a green handkerchief was round her neck, a grey felt hat was jammed on to her head, on one arm she carried her homespun jacket. With her free hand in its washleather gauntlet she was offering the horse some sugar on her outspread palm. The horse took its face out of its nosebag, looked at the sugar, blew at it several times, decided in its favour, and in rather a slobbery way mouthed it up, then producing a loud champing, roaring, tearing sound, more appropriate to an engineering works on overtime than to a peaceful Beer Conveyancer eating a blameless lump or two of sugar.

'Excuse me,' said Mrs Brandon advancing, 'but are you Mrs Grant? I am Mrs Brandon.'

Mrs Grant turned. Mrs Brandon saw a handsome face, wavy hair, bobbed and going grey, and a multitude of necklaces of amber, coral and other semi-precious stones, which rattled as their wearer moved.

'That is very kind of you,' said Mrs Grant, holding out her gloved hand which was fresh with a greenish slime from the horse's blowings and mouthings.

Mrs Brandon offered her own white-gloved hand as a sacrifice without flinching, reflecting how glad she was that she had told Rose to put a spare pair in the car.

'I'm so glad you can come to the picnic,' said Mrs Brandon. 'Hilary came up to tell me this morning. Are you ready?'

'I will just get my mackintosh,' said Mrs Grant.

'Oh, I don't think you'll need it,' said Mrs Brandon, thinking that Mrs Grant was already far too warmly and sensibly clad for so hot a day.

'One cannot trust the English climate,' said Mrs Grant, and striding into the hotel she reappeared shortly with a raincoat and a stout walking stick. Miss Morris had already installed herself on one of the folding seats, introductions took place, the usual polite argument about seats was held, Miss Morris was firm, and the car with Mrs Brandon and Mrs Grant on the back seat drove on towards Southbridge.

'What lovely horses those were,' said Miss Morris.

'You are treating animals much better in England,' said Mrs Grant. 'One hardly ever sees an ill-treated or broken-down horse now.'

'I suppose you see lots in Italy,' said Mrs Brandon, rather resenting the aspersion on English humanity.

'Oh no,' said Mrs Grant pityingly. 'Mussolini has stopped all that. Italians *adore* animals now. Wherever I go in Italy I always ask the peasants if they are kind to their animals and their delightful expressive faces simply light up. After St Francis, Mussolini is the greatest animal lover the world has known. I put them together, don't you?'

'I don't quite know. I never actually *met* Mussolini,' said Mrs Brandon cautiously, and somehow implying that she had at some period been introduced to St Francis.

'Of course you wouldn't,' said Mrs Grant. 'No one does. But going everywhere as I do, among very intellectual people in Rome and Florence and among the most illiterate peasants of Calabria, I hear a great deal.'

This statement Mrs Brandon found it impossible to contradict, though it seemed to have no particular relevance to Mrs Grant's argument, and she could not help imagining that both intellectuals and illiterates stood a poor chance of expressing their own views in Mrs Grant's presence. That lady, her necklaces rattling with her enthusiasm, conversed with unceasing fluency on the joys of Italy all through the half-hour's drive to Southbridge, while Mrs Brandon, throwing in a polite interjection from time to time thought of a good way of having her pink evening frock renovated by Nurse's clever fingers and wondered if she would get a black velvet for the autumn.

From every side the picnic party was now converging upon the Wishing Well, a little bubbling spring pleasantly situated in the beech woods above Southbridge. When Mrs Brandon's party arrived, they found Mrs Morland from High Rising already there. Mrs Brandon greeted her affectionately and introduced her guests.

'And where is Tony?' she asked.

Mrs Morland pointed to a pair of grey flannel legs stretched on the ground below a leafy bank.

'You can't see the rest of him,' she said, 'because it is in the Wishing Well. He wanted to see if he could stop the spring by putting his arm into the place where the water bubbles up. Tony! Here is Mrs Brandon.'

The legs made a convulsive movement, clearly signifying 'Bother,' and reared themselves up, together with the body belonging to them. Their owner, his blue short-sleeved shirt soaked with water, his arms muddy to the shoulders, advanced unwillingly upon the group, with an expression of abstracted dislike and resentment.

'This is my youngest boy,' said Mrs Morland to Mrs Grant and Miss Morris. 'He is in his last year at school. I'm afraid he is too dirty to shake hands.'

'I always shake hands,' said Mrs Grant, advancing on Tony with outstretched hand. 'Mother Earth has no terrors for me. The Italian peasants, who never wash, are among the cleanest of God's creatures.'

'It's more Mother Mud,' said Tony, taking Mrs Grant's proffered hand. 'I say, mother, I can't think how the water comes up so clean. That hole is absolutely stinking.'

Miss Morris said How do you do, but made no attempt to shake hands. Tony made a very slight inclination towards her and appeared to be favourably impressed, immediately inviting her to come and see the hole where the stinking mud was. Miss Morris accepted his offer and the two went off to the Wishing Well.

'What a splendid young animal!' said Mrs Grant enthusiastically. 'He reminds me of a young fisherman who used to bring me fresh frutta di mare at a little seaside village in Calabria. Your boy is fairer of course, but he and Tonio might have been twins.'

'Perhaps twins that had a different father,' said Laura Morland, who always tried to sympathize, 'which would account. And my boy is Tony too.'

'And there are people who do not believe in the transmigration of souls!' exclaimed Mrs Grant.

'Is your fisherman dead then?' inquired Mrs Morland 'Because Tony is seventeen, so your man would have had to transmigrate a good while ago, and I don't remember anything particular happening.'

'Non ragioniam di lor,' said Mrs Grant, finding the philosophical level more than she had bargained for.

'No, indeed,' said Mrs Morland. 'And now, Lavinia, where shall we put the food? It is bound to be uncomfortable wherever we sit, but thank heaven it isn't damp.'

Mrs Brandon had brought in the car two folding tables on which she proposed to spread the feast and let everyone help him or herself. These were set up by Miss Brandon's chauffeur, and the three ladies unpacked and arranged the huge store of food provided from High Rising, Brandon Abbey and Stories. While they were thus occupied Mr Miller's little open car came chunking up and its two occupants joined the company, each bearing a large stone jar.

'Good morning, good morning, or rather good afternoon,' said Mr Miller. 'And here is the parsnip wine, Mrs Brandon, to which Hettie insisted on adding some of her dandelion wine. Both are excellent.'

'Thank you so very much,' said Mrs Brandon. 'Have you met Mrs Grant yet?'

Mr Miller expressed his pleasure at meeting his pupil's mother and hoped she would be staying in the neighbourhood for some time, at which Mr Grant groaned almost audibly. Then five or six pleasant young men and women, friends of the young Brandons, arrived; all, as Mrs Brandon had complained, very intelligent, bursting with information about the ballet, and practically indistinguishable, the girls being in trousers and the men a little long in the hair.

'How are you all?' said Mrs Brandon. 'Francis and Delia haven't come yet. They were going to see the place where the gypsy was drowned.'

One of the young men said What energy. One of the young women, apparently called Betty, said they had passed a crowd near the river, ackcherly, as they came along, and they all began to talk cryptically among themselves. Tony, returning from the Wishing Well with Miss Morris, who had miraculously persuaded him to clean the mud off his arms, cast a look of withering contempt on the little group and drifted away towards Miss Brandon's chauffeur, with whom he was soon deep in technical conversation. Mrs Brandon introduced Mr Miller to Miss Morris and had an uneasy feeling that they were not going to take to each other, when much to her relief Francis's car came up, and he and Delia completed the party. Francis, in pursuance of a plan which he and Delia had been perfecting, approached his mother, took her hand, and bowing low over it, kissed it respectfully, saying as he straightened up, 'How charming you look this morning, mamma.'

Mrs Brandon, accepting with tolerance all Francis's whims, said she thought she looked much the same as at breakfast, and had he said how do you do to Mrs Grant. Francis, turning to give the customary careless handshake, was horrified to find a far from clean washleather glove rising towards his face. Rapidly though unwillingly grasping what was expected of him, he bent over it, avoided touching it with his lips, and restored it courteously to its owner.

'Mi piace tanto,' said Mrs Grant in a loud voice to Mrs Brandon, 'to find a young man with manners. All the Italians, high and low, have such exquisite natural manners. I only wish Hilary had profited by his year abroad. Any Italian who came into my house and did not kiss my hand would never be invited again.'

'Serves you right,' said Delia to her brother, making a hideous face, and various of his young friends asked what had bitten him, the girl called Betty adding that it was the first time she had seen anyone kiss anyone's hand, ackcherly, except on the flicks.

'I say,' said Francis who had been examining the feast, 'what about marsala? Is that Aunt Sissie's contribution? When does one drink it, Miss Morris?'

Miss Morris didn't know, so Francis said they would have it as a cocktail and served it round in gaily-coloured tumblers made of some composition.

'Bless Uncle Woolworth for these pretty gauds,' he said, 'even if they are made of high explosives.'

'Ackcherly,' said Betty, 'they're made of milk, because I know a man that told me. They do something to the milk and make things of it.'

'It's a much more elaborate process,' said Tony, who had come back at the sight of food, 'but you wouldn't understand if I told you. Oh, mother, potted salmon! Can I take some to Hooper?'

'Who is Hooper?' inquired Mrs Morland.

'Miss Brandon's chauffeur,' said Miss Morris. 'Yes, please do take him some lunch, Tony.'

Tony made a selection of tempting food and drink and took it to Hooper, but soon returned with his gifts and the depressing intelligence that Hooper was a teetotaller and had brought what he fancied for his own lunch.

'Great bleeding slices of cold beef and a bottle of pickles,' he said with gleaming eyes, 'and a huge chunk of cold plum pudding and some green cheese and some cold tea. Oh mother, can I have lunch with Hooper?'

'No, have lunch here,' said Mrs Morland, 'and you can talk to Hooper afterwards.'

Her son's face, still soft and gently rounded in spite of his years, though faint hollows were just beginning to show below his cheek bones, clouded slightly, but at the sight of sausage rolls and meringues he recovered his spirits and explained at length to the uninterested Betty the methods by which milk was transformed to a bright blue tumbler.

'But how do they get plum pudding in the height of summer?' said Francis to Miss Morris.

'If you lived at Brandon Abbey you wouldn't ask,' said Miss Morris. 'Like Mrs Herbert Pocket's servants, they allow a very liberal table.'

'Oh, heaven bless you, Miss Morris,' said Francis fervently, lifting his marsala towards her. 'And how is Aunt Sissie?'

Miss Morris said pretty well.

'I've been thinking,' said Francis, 'about what Sir Edmund said the other night. You remember, Hilary, about responsibilities and all that.'

'Well?' said Mr Grant.

'Well, I was thinking that perhaps we oughtn't to turn the Abbey into a lunatic asylum. I mean it would be a bit hard on the servants and the gardeners and what not. I thought perhaps you and I could club together and have a sort of what's its name – you know what I mean.'

'You mean a sort of home for old retainers?' asked Mr Grant.

'No, you great ass, they'll all get pensioned off all right. I say, Miss Morris, I'm awfully sorry. I mean I didn't mean anything, I only meant Sparks and that lot,' said Francis crimsoning violently.

'It is quite all right,' said Miss Morris composedly. 'I'd like to hear your ideas for the Abbey.'

'Would you really?' said Francis, much cheered. 'Well, I meant a sort of thing rather like a monastery, only that isn't the word.'

'Ackcherly one can't be a monk in England,' said Betty.

'I never said monk,' said Francis with some heat, 'and anyway one can, because there are a whole lot somewhere in Somerset and they make honey in little cardboard pots.'

'Oh, *those*,' said Betty scornfully.

Her friends then all contributed their views on the subject of monks, appearing to have founded their theories largely on the Ingoldsby Legends. Suddenly Francis's voice dominated the tumult with the word 'Phalanx.'

'That's what I meant, phalanx,' he repeated.

'Phalanstère I expect you mean,' said Tony Morland courteously, managing at the same time to put half a meringue away in one cheek like a monkey in his desire to impart information. 'The theory of the phalanstère was begun and put into practice by Fourier, about 1832, but it was never much of a success. He wanted to organize society into bodies called phalanges, who were to live in phalanstères which were a square league. There is a lot more but you wouldn't understand it. I know about it all because we did it last term.'

'I never heard about him ackcherly,' said Betty.

'It isn't phalan whatever you said,' said one of the young men, who had but imperfectly followed the foregoing conversation. 'Phalangist is what you mean. God! if only the Government had enough planes to bomb them all!'

'Well, they're increasing the Air Force ackcherly,' said Betty.

'The *Spanish* Government,' the young man almost spat at her.

Mr Miller said that Civil Strife was very dreadful.

'Well, anyway you know what I mean,' said Francis. 'And if Hilary and I get the Abbey we'll jolly well not have any politics there. I say, let's go and wish at the Wishing Well.'

This suggestion was received with universal pleasure; by the younger members because it would mean that they needn't help with the clearing up; by the older members because they would be able to clear up in peace without the young; and by Tony Morland because he saw a chance of escaping to his friend Hooper and explaining to him the general outline of European politics in the years after the Congress of Vienna.

It did not take the grown-ups long to tidy away the food and pack up the baskets, and when they had finished Mrs Brandon suggested a visit to the Wishing Well.

'I think we could manage,' she said doubtfully, looking at the fifty yards that separated them from the Well, and putting up her parasol. Escorted by Mr Miller and followed by Mrs Morland, Mrs Grant and Miss Morris, she walked to the green, beech-crowned bank under which the springing water for ever troubled a little pool.

'It is so lovely,' she said. 'If we had a rug we could sit down.'

Mr Miller sprang away, seized a rug from Hooper who was putting it into the car, and was back in an instant. Mrs Grant compared him favourably with several of her Italian acquaintance, who she said, were useless out of doors, though delightful in the drawing-room, and sat down resolutely upon her mackintosh.

'I do hope, Mr Miller,' she said, 'that Hilary is going to do well with you. He is a difficult nature, with a certain morbidezza that English people cannot readily understand.'

'I must say I have found him – ' Mr Miller began, but found he might as well spare his breath, for Mrs Grant, merely lowering her voice to a more powerful diapason continued, 'Like me he adores beauty, but unfortunately he must work. He is a devoted son, mio figlio, but I do not wish him to be tied to my apron strings. There is a charming proverb in Calabria which runs – but you would not understand it in dialect; I will translate roughly, though of course it does not give the fuoco of the original – the ass that stays at home will never learn to roam. My husband was always under his mother's domination, ma! una donna prepotente! and what was the result? My life made me what I am.'

'I do think you are so right,' said Mrs Morland, giving some of her heavy back hair an extra twist and ramming the hairpins into it. 'Boys *always* ought to get away from their mothers. I hardly ever see my three eldest, whom I adore; the eldest is secretary to an American explorer and is always somewhere where he can't send any news, John is doing very well in Burma, and Dick has just rejoined his ship at Malta. Of course Tony is a little different. He is enough to drive anyone mad, because I never know if he is going to be a mentally defective child of five or a man of the world of thirty, but all the same he does need me, and I really don't think he despises me as much as he pretends to,' said Mrs Morland proudly. 'Of course it is a pity that he hasn't a father, but my husband wasn't really very much use, so I dare-say we have got on just as well and I think we shall go on getting on well so long as he doesn't tell me anything. Confidences be-tween people are such a mistake and if he does what he wants to do and doesn't tell me, it's all right, like the time he went through the railway tunnel at Southbridge which is half a mile long and *entirely* forbidden and a train came through when he was there, but most luckily I didn't discover it till a year afterwards.'

'I am really very lucky with Francis,' said Mrs Brandon, taking off one glove and looking at her hand, 'because he tells me nothing at all ever and is never rude. If my husband had lived I am sure he would have wanted to be a father to Francis, and that wouldn't have done at all.'

If the enthralled reader will imagine that these three speeches not only followed rapidly upon one another, but were to a cer-tain extent superimposed, he will have a fair idea of how much the ladies were enjoying themselves and how very much out of it Miss Morris and Mr Miller felt. But they didn't turn to each other for relief and Mrs Brandon still hoped, with all the delicate perception of a nature that feels everything will always be com-fortable, that they weren't going to hate each other at sight.

'I have only just thought of it!' Mrs Morland suddenly ex-claimed in her impressive voice, pushing her hair and her hat wildly back from her forehead with both hands. 'We are all widows!'

'So we are,' said Mrs Brandon, looking round distractedly as if she might see a few more somewhere, 'but not what I would *call* widows.'

'I suppose,' said Mrs Morland, 'the longer one is a widow, the less one *is* a widow. Or is it that one just has it in one or else one hasn't?'

To this entrancing philosophical problem no one was capable of giving an immediate answer, and then Francis and Mr Grant reappeared, saying that the conversation of the others was too intellectual for them.

'Let's all wish,' said Francis. 'You drop a pin or a piece of money into the well and wish and don't tell anybody, and then it comes true. The trouble is one never knows what to wish. Don't let's.'

Mrs Grant said Hilary must get his hair cut and there was a delightful old custom in Calabria by which young men and maidens spent the night under a tree on the night of the full moon and drew lots with the bristles of a hog who had died a natural death, and whoever drew the longest bristle died in childbirth within the year. She then quoted in support of this interesting piece of folk lore several verses of a very old song in an archaic dialect, which she did not, she said, herself fully understand.

'And just as well, probably,' said Francis to Miss Morris in an undertone.

'Io t'amo o pio bove,' said Mrs Brandon suddenly, contemplating her ringed hand.

At this startling statement everyone looked at her.

'My dear mamma, you mustn't say things like that,' said Francis.

'I can't think why it came into my head,' said Mrs Brandon apologetically. 'I suppose it was hearing all that Italian. It's something I had to learn by heart once.'

'A little learning is a dangerous thing,' said Francis sententiously, 'talking of which how glad you ought to be to have a son who gets his quotations right. I say, Mr Miller, did you know that they've got chicken pox down at Grumper's End? The postman told me when he brought up the cat's bit of liver this morning with the letters to save the butcher's boy an extra journey.'

'Indeed? I am sorry to hear it,' said Mr Miller. 'I must go and see them. That means that Jimmy Thatcher won't be able to carry out his duties on Sunday.'

'Jimmy is an enchanting little boy,' Mrs Brandon explained to

79

Miss Morris, 'who helps Mr Miller with the service in a kind of surplice with a frill round his neck. He is very ambitious and wants to be a dentist when he grows up. You would love him, wouldn't she, Mr Miller?'

'I think,' said Miss Morris, her pale cheeks flushing, 'that there is no need for me to tell Mr Miller what I think of such arrangements as he may see fit to make for the celebration of his services.'

There was no mistaking the open hostility in her voice.

'I had hoped, Miss Morris,' Mr Miller began in a low tone, but Miss Morris got up and walked away. Everyone felt uncomfortable and each member of the party tried to cover the awkwardness by dashing into an artificial normality of manner. Mrs Morland and Mrs Grant discovered a very dull common acquaintance who lived on the Riviera and discussed her with zeal. Francis plied Mr Miller with details about the chicken pox at Grumper's End, some gathered from the postman, some invented on the spur of the moment, and Mrs Brandon asked Mr Grant if he would like to have a wish, at the same time stretching out her hand that he might help her to rise.

'How is your work, Hilary?' Mrs Brandon inquired.

'How did you know about it?' Mr Grant asked, going rather pink.

'Well, you are doing classics with Mr Miller, aren't you?' asked Mrs Brandon, puzzled.

'Oh yes, of course. But that's only a sort of lessons. I'm really trying to write a book, at least I don't know if it will ever be a real book, but anyway a sort of article about a French poet called Jehan le Capet, at least his real name was Eugène Duval, but he was a Romantic so he had to have a name that sounded better. No one knows much about him, but I somehow got interested and dug up quite a lot of stuff.'

'Do tell me about him,' said Mrs Brandon, in a voice whose warm interest would not have deceived Sir Edmund or her son Francis for a moment.

'Well, there's not very much,' said Mr Grant, beginning to stammer a little in his excitement at discussing his great work with a goddess. 'He was a Satanist and died very young of absinthe and only published one very small volume called

Belphégor. All his other work was destroyed by his mistress,' said Mr Grant, rapidly slurring over a word which he suddenly felt might sully the goddess's ethereal atmosphere, 'who was really called Angèle Potin, but was known as Nini Le Poumon because she had only one lung because of consumption,' he continued, stammering more than ever as he found his interest in his chosen study involving him in an explanation which must, he felt, be highly offensive to his divinity, 'because she was jealous.'

'Of whom?' asked Mrs Brandon.

'Oh, just jealous,' said Mr Grant vaguely, feeling that a detailed description of Mimi la Salope, Jehanne de Valois, and the other ladies who disputed the unhappy ci-devant Eugène Duval's attentions while alive and his literary remains when dead, were hardly fit offerings to lay on Mrs Brandon's altar.

'It sounds enchanting,' said Mrs Brandon. 'Will you read me some of it one day?'

'Would you really like me to?' asked Mr Grant, incredulous.

'I'd love it,' said Mrs Brandon. 'When are you going to publish it?'

Mr Grant had to confess that he hadn't got as far as a publisher yet. Mrs Brandon said Mrs Morland had a very nice one who she was sure would do and had Hilary a halfpenny to put into the Wishing Well. He had not, but was able to express his devotion by dropping a shining new sixpence to which he was rather attached into the clear moving water. Mrs Brandon, a practical woman, said it would do for them both and now they must wish.

'Only I find it so difficult to wish,' she said plaintively. 'It's like concentrating. I have to hold my breath and shut my eyes tight, and then I go red in the face and can't think of anything at all. Oh, I know what I've wished. I wished –'

'But you mustn't say what you wished,' said Mr Grant. 'You don't get it if you do.'

'Don't you?' said Mrs Brandon. 'What did *you* wish?'

'I can't tell you,' said Mr Grant; and truly; for his incoherent and jumbled wish had been entirely a prayer to be allowed to die some violent and heroic death while saving Mrs Brandon from something or somebody, to have her holding his chill hand, and perhaps letting her cheek rest for a moment against his as his gallant spirit fled, all with a kind of unspoken understanding that he should not be really hurt and should somehow go on living very comfortably in spite of being heroically dead. 'I wouldn't get my wish if I did.'

'Of course, and I do want you to get it,' said Mrs Brandon, melting Mr Grant's marrow with a smile. 'Laura, have you wished?' she asked, as Mrs Morland and Mrs Grant came strolling up to them, followed by Francis and Mr Miller.

'It is a splendid well,' said Mrs Morland. 'Once when Tony was smaller we came here for a picnic, and he was showing off on his bicycle and frightened me dreadfully and I wished the bicycle would somehow get put out of action without hurting him, and it did. I know what I'll wish. I'm frightfully stuck in a serial I've *got* to have ready by September, so I'll wish –'

'You mustn't tell,' broke in Mrs Brandon. 'You won't get it if you do.'

'I think that is what Tony used to call supersistious,' said Mrs Morland severely. 'Don't you, Mr Miller?'

'One might of course condemn the whole ritual as super-stitious and highly pagan,' said Mr Miller, 'but all the same I do not propose to tell my wish.' Upon which he dropped a halfpenny into the well and wished with heathen fervour that Jimmy Thatcher might not get chicken pox.

'Oh, do you write?' Mrs Grant asked Mrs Morland.

'Only to earn my living,' said Mrs Morland apologetically, for although her stories about Madame Koska's dressmaking establishment, where spies, Grand Dukes, drug-smugglers and C.I.D. officers flourished yearly, had a large sale, and she had arrived at the happy point where her public simply asked for 'the new Mrs Morland', instead of mentioning the name of the book, she thought quite poorly of her own hard-working talent and greatly admired people who wrote what she called real books.

'I expect you know my book about Calabria,' said Mrs Grant.

Mrs Morland said the libraries were so stupid and never had the books one wanted.

'I do wish mother wouldn't,' said Mr Grant in a low and un-filial voice to Francis. 'It isn't a book, it's only a sort of little thing in paper covers that she had printed by a very good-looking, bounderish sort of printer somewhere she was staying in Italy, and she behaves as if it were the Encyclopaedia Britannica. What do you think was the matter with Miss Morris?'

Francis said he couldn't think, and he supposed it was something someone had said, but why talking about the chicken pox at Grumper's End should send anyone off their rocker he couldn't imagine. Mr Grant said perhaps someone she was very fond of had died of chicken pox and anyway she was a very good sort, but so was Mr Miller.

Mrs Grant, all her necklaces clashing together, now knelt at the pool and dropping a coin into it moved her lips as if in prayer. Everyone looked on with interest, and her son with weary disgust.

'If only mother wouldn't be so confoundedly in the spirit of the thing,' he complained to Francis. 'I never knew anyone adapt themselves to local customs as she does. She used to make me awfully uncomfortable in Italy, putting little offerings on shrines and things and everyone thought her necklaces were rosaries and it was all frightfully embarrassing, and she would help herself to holy water in the country churches because she didn't like to be out of it.'

'That was a little prayer that the inhabitants of a village on the south coast of Calabria address to the presiding spirit of wells,' she said. 'An invocation from time immemorial. The peasants drink the water and repeat the words that their fathers have taught them.'

So saying she scooped up a handful of water and put it to her lips.

'Don't drink it, Mrs Grant,' cried Mr Miller in great alarm. 'The water is not fit for human consumption. The Medical Officer of Health condemned it as thoroughly infected from the sewage farm at Southbridge.'

Everyone waited anxiously to see Mrs Grant burst, or come out all over spots, but she rose, her homespun skirt rather baggy at the knees, and smiling with tolerance said she believed with St Francis that water was her sister and could do her no harm.

'A lot your mother knows about sisters,' said Francis aside to Mr Grant. 'Wait till she's seen Delia in a temper.'

Mrs Brandon, anxious to change a difficult and controversial subject, said to Mrs Morland that Mr Grant was looking for a publisher and what about her man.

'I think you'd like Adrian Coates very much, Mr Grant,' said Mrs Morland earnestly. 'He is the son-in-law of my old friend George Knox, the one who writes biographies, and his wife is a perfect darling and they have two delightful babies. The elder is called Laura, after me, and the little boy, who will be a year old in March, is called Richard, though after whom I don't know.'

Having given these eminently satisfactory testimonials to her publisher's business capacity, she pushed one or two loose hair-pins into their place and said it must be nearly tea-time. A general move was made to the picnic place, where they found Miss Morris, outwardly as composed as ever, laying out the tea-things with Tony's help. Everyone recognized with annoyance that it would be impossible to find out what was wrong between Mr Miller and Miss Morris until one or other of them could be got at alone, and this in the communal atmosphere of a picnic tea was going to be very difficult.

Mr Grant, though annoyed that his mother should have heard of his publishing plans, about which he knew she would Ask Questions, could not resist talking about himself to a real author, and shaking himself temporarily free from the shackles of Venus transferred his homage to the Muses in the person of Mrs Morland. Her he found kind and communicative but singularly un-helpful, as she did not seem to know anything about the ways of publishers.

'You see,' she said in her impressive voice, 'I have only got one publisher and I was really very lucky because I really met him quite by accident and we have always got on very well. He always gives me a bit more for every book, and if I need anything doing in town, like flowers being ordered for someone's funeral or birthday, or finding out if the name I want to call my new book has been used by someone else, he always gets it done for me at his office. And he plays golf very well, I believe, though I know nothing about the game myself. And Tony likes him,' she added, looking with dislike and adoration at her youngest son, who was helping Betty and Delia to kill wasps by cutting them in two.

'Do you think he would like my book when it is finished?' said Mr Grant.

'What kind of book?'

Mr Grant described to her, with more freedom than he had cared to use when speaking to Mrs Brandon, parts of the career of that unfortunate Satanist, M. Eugéne Duval, which made Mrs Morland laugh so much that she had to get several spare hairpins out of her bag and pin herself together.

'As a matter of fact,' she said, when she had stopped laughing, 'Adrian Coates mostly does either rather bad novels like mine or frightfully dull stuff by journalists about all the European crises and the private lives of dictators, which people somehow like to read I can't think why, but he's always on the look-out for something fresh and I must say your book sounds very funny.'

Mr Grant then had to explain to Mrs Morland that it wasn't really a funny book, and when this was thoroughly grasped Mrs Morland became serious again and asked what *Belphégor* was like.

'Rather wonderful,' said Mr Grant. 'He had a special theory of punctuation. He believed in commas, but not in any other sort of stops. In *Belphégor* you sometimes find a comma after every word. He used to say "La virgule vaut bien la particule".'

'That was just snobbishness, wasn't it, sir?' said Tony Morland, who scenting an intellectual discussion had suddenly deserted the wasp-hunters and come over to his mother. 'He knew he couldn't be an aristocrat, so he pretended to despise them. I know all about him because our French master, Mr Knight, who is a very good man on his job, did the Romantics in the upper Sixth last term. He hasn't got a frightfully good accent, but he knows all about French literature and absolutely hundreds of useful idioms. If I had my notebook here I'd tell you some of them. When I went to France with mother at Easter I used heaps of idioms and surprised people very much. I expect you've heard of Mallarmé, sir,' said Tony kindly, 'well he was just the opposite of your man because he didn't believe in stops at all.'

'What have you read of his?' asked Mr Grant, amused.

'I haven't exactly *read* anything,' said Tony, 'but we did him with Mr Knight, and Mr Knight read us some of the *Aprés-midi d'un faune*.'

'What do you mean *Aprés midi d'un faune*?' asked Betty, who also an intellectual, and subjugated by Tony's free and easy manner of dealing with wasps, had followed him slavishly. 'You can't *read* it. Ackcherly it's a ballet.'

Before Tony could collect his forces for a withering reply, the whole of the younger set, hearing the word ballet, burst into the argument without knowing what it was about, intoxicating themselves by the names of their favourite dancers, Russian and English. Tony quickly recovered himself and plunged headlong into the fray, managing to give the impression of one who had lived in the coulisses from earliest childhood, and ogled the legs of Taglioni. Mrs Morland, who knew that her youngest son had not been more than three or four times to the ballet, marvelled humbly at his grasp of the subject.

'Sadler's Wells!' said Tony scornfully. 'What I call Empire ballet. People don't even dress for it. I'd rather not go to ballet at all if I couldn't go to decent seats at Covent Garden and wear my dinner jacket.'

'Better men than you haven't been ashamed to go in tails,' said the voice of a newcomer whose approach over the grass had not been heard among the warring voices. 'Shut up, Tony and get me some tea,' said Dr Ford, Laura Morland's old friend and physician, the friend of half the county, and at present the medical attendant of Miss Brandon.

Tony collapsed and Dr Ford folded his long legs up and sat down by Mrs Morland, who introduced him to Mrs Grant and her son.

'And I can't think why Tony is so uppish about the ballet,' she said plaintively. 'Adrian Coates has taken him once or twice, and his dinner jacket suit was too small and there was such a gap between his waistcoat and trousers that he had to crouch instead of standing up, to hide it, but I said I simply would not get him a new suit just for one evening, when he couldn't be needing it again till the Christmas holidays and I could get it in the sales.'

'Quite right too,' said Dr Ford. 'Thanks, Tony, that's a nice selection of cakes. And now go away and play with your young friends.'

Tony, who had never yet managed to assert himself against Dr Ford, gave one soft, sullen look at the group of grown-ups and strolled away ostentatiously in the direction of Hooper, hoping that everyone would see him not playing with the young friends.

Mrs Grant began to ask Dr Ford about Miss Brandon's health in a far from tactful way, and his cool parrying of her questions amused all the onlookers so much that Miss Morris, who had been quietly waiting for this chance, was able to speak aside to Mrs Brandon.

'Could we walk to the Wishing Well again, Mrs Brandon?' she asked. 'I forgot to wish.'

Mrs Brandon willingly got up and accompanied her. When they had reached the well Miss Morris opened her bag, took out a penny and dropped it into the water.

'I really ought to wish for a better temper,' she said. 'I can't tell you, Mrs Brandon, how sorry and ashamed I am for the way I behaved just now. If you knew the reasons – but I don't want to justify myself, only to apologize and beg you to forgive me.'

'It was nothing,' Mrs Brandon hastened to reassure her. 'And Mr Miller is a little trying sometimes with his enthusiasm.'

'My father was a clergyman,' said Miss Morris violently.

Mrs Brandon, recognizing from long experience the voice of one who was determined to confess, was torn between a wish not to receive Miss Morris's confidences and the natural lazy kindness that made her so good a listener. Her kindness got the upper hand and she suggested that they should take a little stroll among the beeches. For a few moments they walked in silence, and then Miss Morris said,

'He took pupils. Mr Miller came to him a good many years ago, before he got his theological degree. My father liked him very much and spoke highly of his gifts, but he was horrified to find in him a strong tendency to the doctrines of Rome.'

'Like Cardinal Newman,' said Mrs Brandon sympathetically.

'Thank God he did not go so far. But it caused the deepest grief to my father, and I am afraid high words passed between them. Mr Miller left us very suddenly and my father never

mentioned his name again. I have often thought of him,' said Miss
Morris simply, 'and prayed that he might be forgiven for the
grief he gave my dear father. I didn't know he was Vicar here,
and when I met him and found that he had not changed his ways
of belief I thought of my father and lost my self-control. I am
very, very sorry.'

Mrs Brandon's mind was by now such a jumble of pity, mild
curiosity about the Reverend Mr Morris, and a private feeling
that it was all a fuss about nothing, that she could find nothing
better to say than 'I *am* so sorry,' but Miss Morris seemed comforted by these words, and much to Mrs Brandon's relief did not,
as most women would have done, burst out into a great flood of
confidences. Mrs Brandon asked her a little about her father.
The Reverend Justin Morris, even as described by his daughter,
in whose eyes he was perfect, seemed to have combined in himself
all the less agreeable qualities of the fanatic, the priest, and the
parent. Mrs Brandon gathered from her companion's artless
words that Mr Morris had worked his wife to death and done
his best to kill his daughter. For the last years of his life he had
been almost blind and Miss Morris had acted as working housekeeper, sometimes with a village girl to help her, sometimes alone,
secretary, nurse, and companion, reading aloud to him far into
the night. On his death it was found that he had sunk the whole
of his little fortune in an annuity, and Miss Morris had been
thankful to get, through the interest of various old pupils, for he
had been an excellent theological scholar and coach for those
whose beliefs were like his own, a position as companion to one
elderly lady after another. Her practical sense and her almost
entire self-effacement had made her invaluable to her employers,
and when she had worn herself out in tending one old lady, another was always waiting to snap her up after the funeral. Her
present position with Miss Brandon was, she said, far happier
than any she had yet held, and to read aloud to her employer till
one and two in the morning was no more than she had done for
her father.

'And it is so pleasant to see young people from time to time,'
said Miss Morris. 'I can't tell you how much good your visit
with your children did me, and having Mr Grant for the night.

And then your kindness in getting Miss Brandon to let me come to the picnic to-day. I have so much to be thankful for, and I do hope you will forget my disgraceful show of temper, though I shan't.

Mrs Brandon, saying vague reassuring things in her pleasant voice, led Miss Morris gradually back to the picnic. Dr Ford seemed to have been looking for them, for as soon as he caught sight of them he got up and came in their direction.

'I didn't want to tell you this in public, Miss Morris,' he said, 'but I looked in at the Abbey this afternoon and found Miss Brandon convinced that she was going to die. She has had a good row with Sparks, but it isn't half so much fun bullying a maid as it is bullying a lady. I don't think there is any danger, but she is quite capable of working herself into a fit, which wouldn't do her heart any good, so I said I would bring you home if I could find you. When I left,' said Dr Ford with grim relish, 'Miss Brandon had the head housemaid, who was scared stiff, to sit by her, and Sparks was having hysterics in the housekeeper's room. You are a marvel, Miss Morris, to stand that lunatic asylum.'

'Then I suppose I'd better go back,' said Miss Morris, with no sign of regret for cutting her holiday so short. 'But what about the car? You'll need it to go home, Mrs Brandon.'

'That's all right,' said Dr Ford. 'Sparks told me all about the car, and I told Miss Brandon she couldn't have you and the car as well. Hooper is to take Mrs Brandon home and I'll run you back to the Abbey in my car whenever you like.'

Miss Morris thanked him and said she would go at once if it suited him. She then said good-bye to such guests as were still on the picnic ground and was just going to thank Mrs Brandon for her treat when Mrs Grant came up.

'Do I hear,' said Mrs Grant, 'that Miss Brandon is ill?'

'Not a bit,' said Dr Ford. 'Only temper.'

'I feel it is my duty to see her,' said Mrs Grant, eyeing Dr Ford suspiciously. 'I may not be down here long, and as my husband was one of her nearest relations I certainly ought to pay her a visit. If you are going back, Miss Morris, I will come with you.'

Miss Morris said quietly that she was afraid Miss Brandon could see no one just at present, but if Mrs Grant would write,

Miss Brandon would be glad to hear from her. Mrs Grant, who evidently suspected Miss Morris of spending all her time making her employer alter her will in her favour, uttered a Calabrian exclamation of annoyance, whose tone was singularly like that of a similar English exclamation. Just as Dr Ford was starting up his disgraceful little car, Tony Morland appeared.

'Oh, good-bye, Miss Morris,' he said. 'If I write you a letter will you answer it? Most of my friends are awfully bad at answering letters. I have about seven letters not answered this week. I simply shan't write to them if they don't answer.'

'Of course I will,' said Miss Morris. 'I always answer letters by return of post and I love getting them.'

An expression of mystic satisfaction spread over Tony's face. He made a vague suggestion of a courtly bow somewhere in Miss Morris's direction, returned to Hooper, who said he wouldn't be in Miss Morris's shoes for something, and took up his exposition of European history from 1848, the point at which he had been interrupted by tea, but barely had he outlined to Hooper the downfall of Metternich when a summons came for the car. The younger members had suddenly recollected a cocktail party on the other side of Barchester and were anxious to be off, and the grown-ups were quite ready to go home. After a tremendous amount of arguing and organizing Francis and Delia went off in Francis's car with their friends, taking Mr Grant with them. Mrs Brandon and Mrs Grant were to return in Miss Brandon's car, leaving Mr Miller to drive home by himself.

'Could I come round and see you before dinner?' said Mr Miller urgently to Mrs Brandon as she was getting into the car. 'Oh, dear, oh, dear, the parsnip wine has been in the sun and the cork has blown out. So has the dandelion wine,' he added, gazing helplessly at the wreckage.

Mrs Brandon saw more confidences ahead, but was too kind to say no, though she felt the beginnings of a headache, which Mrs Grant's ceaseless conversation on the way back did not improve. At the Cow and Sickle she deposited Mrs Grant, promising to make an arrangement to meet again soon, and was thankful to find Rose in an excellent temper.

'My bath at once, please Rose,' she said, 'and Mr Miller is

coming to see me before dinner, so you might put the sherry out. Mr Francis and Miss Delia have gone to a cocktail party so they'll probably be late.'

When Mr Miller arrived he found his hostess, robed in filmy black, lying back in the most comfortable armchair, her feet on a low pouf.

'Forgive me if I don't get up,' she said, giving him her hand. 'I'm really rather tired after such a long day and so many people.'

If this was a hint Mr Miller was determined, in spite of his deep admiration, not to take it.

'It is indeed thoughtless of me to intrude my own affairs upon you,' he said, sitting down near her, 'but you are kindness itself and I know you will forgive me.'

Instead of throwing the ink at him and saying she had a headache, as she would dearly like to have done, Mrs Brandon said of course she would, and could she help him at all. It was obvious to the meanest intelligence that Mr Miller was bursting to say something, but hadn't the faintest idea how to begin, and he maundered on about the beauty of the flowers in the drawing-room till Mrs Brandon felt someone more competent must take the matter in hand.

'The flowers came from Brandon Abbey,' she said. 'Miss Morris brought them over this morning. What a very nice person she is. My children like her very much and so does Hilary, and Tony Morland took to her at once.'

Mr Miller said she was a lady for whom he had a very deep respect and then lost his voice and his wits.

'She seems to have had a very difficult father,' said Mrs Brandon, wondering if she would have to ask Mr Miller to stay to dinner.

'I do not wish to speak ill of any minister of the gospel,' said Mr Miller, who evidently did, 'but Mr Morris, in narrowness, bitterness and entire want of charity, was as near a Personal Devil as any man I have known.'

'Miss Morris seems to have been very fond of him,' said Mrs Brandon, her kind heart compelling her to stand up for the absent.

'Miss Morris has a very fine sense of duty,' said Mr Miller, 'but I was for some time an inmate of the family, as a pupil of

Mr Morris, and can speak with authority on what I saw. I doubt whether even the present Bishop of Barchester would have tolerated his views on church discipline. Miss Morris naturally – whether rightly or not it is hardly for me to say – took her father's side, and there was an unhappy but unavoidable breach.'

Mrs Brandon who knew that the Bishop was very Low Church, began dimly to apprehend that what she had romantically hoped to be an old romance between Mr Miller and Miss Morris was only a squabble about doctrine, but wisely kept this regrettable point of view to herself.

'I am very sorry,' she said. 'It is so uncomfortable when one's friends don't like each other.'

'Pray, pray, dear lady, do not mistake me,' cried Mr Miller. 'It is not that I dislike Miss Morris, for whom, as I said, I have a very deep respect, but to judge from what passed at the picnic to-day, she evidently still dislikes and misjudges me. I cannot tell you how sorry I am that so ungracious an incident should have marred our delightful outing. If any of the fault was mine I apologize most sincerely.'

Mrs Brandon assured Mr Miller that no one had blamed him for a moment, told him how handsomely Miss Morris had expressed her regret, and embroidered a little on Miss Morris's mention of her friendly remembrance of Mr Miller before the break. She did not tell him that Miss Morris prayed for him to be forgiven, feeling that this was a liberty which even a clergyman might resent. Mr Miller was so overcome by Mrs Brandon's angelic sweetness that he again lost his voice.

'Do have some sherry,' said Mrs Brandon, waving her hand at the decanter. 'No, not for me thank you, but help yourself.'

Mr Miller filled and sipped and spoke again.

'But that,' he said, 'wasn't really what I wanted to see you about. It was, rather selfishly, about my own affairs.'

This did not at all surprise his hostess, who never expected her friends to come to her about anything else, and she begged him to go on.

'I may have mentioned to you,' said Mr Miller, coughing, 'that I have been working at a little book on Donne – whom I *cannot*,' he added in a burst of confidence, 'bring myself to call Dunne.'

Mrs Brandon said she should think so, she meant she should think not, and wasn't he the one with his head tied up like a turnip in St Paul's. Mr Miller, at once recognizing by her description the well-known statue of the Dean with his grave-clothes done up in a top knot, said indeed, indeed, that was he. His opusculum, he said, was now practically finished, but before sending the typescript to the publishers who had commissioned it, he had a request to make. Might he again trespass on Mrs Brandon's perpetual kindness to allow him to read some of it aloud to her. Nothing was so helpful in forming an estimate of one's own work as to read it aloud to someone whose delicate perception and critical sense would at once detect any flaw.

'How stupid I am,' said Mrs Brandon with great candour. 'I thought it was Miss Morris you wanted to talk about, but it was your book.'

'Miss Morris?' exclaimed Mr Miller. 'Indeed I had hardly thought of her except in so far as the few moments' awkwardness this afternoon might have affected *you*. May I hope you will with your usual kindness forgive my egoism and allow me to bring my little work for your critical approval?'

'Yes, please do,' said Mrs Brandon, casting a sidelong despairing look at the clock which said a quarter to eight. 'I suppose you don't mean now?'

'Well, I have by chance,' said Mr Miller most untruthfully, 'the first chapter of the typescript upon me, if you would care to hear it.'

He produced a folded sheaf of typescript from his coat pocket and lovingly turned its pages.

'I would simply have adored it,' said Mrs Brandon, throwing all the conviction she could into her voice, 'but I have such a stupid head to-night. I think it was the sun, or the long day, or Mrs Grant.'

'How thoughtless, how inconsiderate I am,' said Mr Miller getting up. 'You spend yourself for others, and we selfishly take advantage of you. Forgive me, dear friend, if I may use that word.'

In the middle of the night, thinking sleepily of Hilary Grant's wish to call her friend rather than trespass upon her Christian name, a thought had come to Mrs Brandon, an answer so perfect that she fell into despair at having missed her chance of using it. Now heaven had sent her another chance and she was determined not to let it slip.

'I think I feel about that word rather as Shelley did about the word love,' said Mrs Brandon, her voice sounding to Mr Miller like a distant golden bell,

> ' "One word is too often profaned
> For me to profane it." '

Exhausted (though satisfied) by this sentimental and literary effort she shut her eyes. Mr Miller touched her hand with his finger tips and went quietly away, marvelling at the deep sensitiveness of her nature.

If her son Francis had been there he would certainly have felt justified in his remark that his mother was prey to saying what she thought would be most effective.

– 5 –

READING ALOUD

ACCORDING to telephone advice received from Brandon Abbey Miss Brandon had not died, nor had she worked herself into a fit. Mr Grant worked hard at his classics with Mr Miller, though sorely tried by his mother, who was for ever demanding his company to make a piccolo giro and openly shamed him by alluding to Mr Miller as the parroco. Francis went back to work, but as he didn't have to leave Stories till a quarter to nine and was usually back by soon after six, no one much noticed the difference. Delia had several skirmishes with Nurse in which she came off second best and saw the labourer who had been gored by a bull being carried on a hurdle to the Barchester ambulance. The weather got hotter and hotter and Mrs Grant, tramping the countryside in her homespuns, lamented the cold English climate and pined for the sun of Calabria till everyone wished it had never been invented. The chicken pox at Grumper's

End dragged on from child to child, and though Jimmy Thatcher didn't get it, he was in quarantine from school and from his religious duties and never had such a happy summer in his life.

Mr Miller had not forgotten that Mrs Brandon wished to hear him read his book about Donne, for such he had persuaded himself was her desire, and gradually wore her down to the point of settling a day for the first reading. The hour was to be between tea and dinner and when Mr Miller, all eagerness, arrived with his typescript at half-past five, he found Mrs Brandon seated under the Spanish chestnut.

'I have been looking forward so much to this,' she said. 'I have been reading some of Donne's poetry, which I only knew in anthologies before. I always thought he was the same as George Herbert and mixed them both up with Vaughan and Crashaw, but that,' she said with a proud simplicity, 'was chiefly ignorance. Now that I have read his poems I shall always know exactly who Donne is.'

Mr Miller found this imbecility quite beautiful and could hardly refrain from saying so.

'Shall I begin with the preface, or go straight to the first chapter?' he asked, settling himself near his hostess.

'Oh, the preface; or do you think the first chapter would be nicer?' she asked. 'But here comes Rose to clear away the tea-things. We had better wait till she has finished. I never asked you if you had had any tea. Rose, please bring some fresh tea for Mr Miller.'

In vain did Mr Miller protest not that he had already had tea, for that would have been a lie, but that he didn't really want tea and often went without it altogether.

'Well, this isn't Friday,' said Mrs Brandon, whose ideas on fasting were very sketchy, 'so it will do you good. Yes, Rose, please get fresh tea. It is extraordinary,' she said, as Rose went away, 'how long it always takes to make fresh tea. I believe they fill the largest kettle with cold water and put it on a slow fire. I am always telling Rose that a small kettle boils faster than a big one, but it is hopeless.'

'I might begin the first chapter while the kettle is boiling,' said Mr Miller.

'You look so tired,' said Mrs Brandon. 'Rest a few moments first. It is the heat, and I'm sure you've been down at Grumper's End. Have the Thatchers got it yet?'

Mr Miller said so far they hadn't and that Jimmy would be out of quarantine next week. Mrs Brandon then related several anecdotes of her children's infantile ailments and in time Rose came back with the fresh tea.

'That is perfect,' said Mrs Brandon. 'They have made it with really boiling water, which they so seldom do.'

As Mr Miller preferred his tea without milk or even lemon, its extreme hotness could not be modified. He wished he dared pour it backwards and forwards from cup to saucer and saucer to cup, but this was unthinkable, so he tried to drink it scalding, hurt himself and had to put his cup down. Mrs Brandon, viewing his plight with sympathy, said she believed that putting a silver teaspoon in the cup drew off some of the heat, at least if you put a spoon in a glass when you wanted to pour boiling water into it, it usually didn't crack, though, even so, it often did. Grateful for this kindness Mr Miller put his spoon in his cup, left it there for a moment, and tried to drink. The tea appeared to be as hot as ever, and the spoon, by now at white heat, slid round against his face, causing him considerable anguish.

'I think one ought to take it out first,' said Mrs Brandon, and picking up the spoon with her handkerchief she dropped it into the slop basin.

Mr Miller said he would try a little milk and though he disliked the mixture excessively he was able to swallow enough tea to satisfy his hostess. Refusing a second cup, though she assured him earnestly that it would be cooler this time, he produced his typescript and prepared to begin.

'This is lovely,' sighed Mrs Brandon comfortably. 'Will you just give me that cushion, Mr Miller, and then I shall be able to listen perfectly.'

Mr Miller got up, fetched the cushion, put it reverently at Mrs Brandon's back, sat down again and opened the typescript.

'Drummond of Hawthornden, in his Notes of Ben Jonson's Conversation, on the occasion of Jonson's famous visit to him in 1618,' he began, and then, overcome by the pride of authorship and the excitement of reading aloud to one who, in an earthly way, was perfection itself, choked a little and had to drink the remains of his tepid, milky tea.

'You have clergyman's throat,' said Mrs Brandon in a voice of angelic sympathy. 'Have a little rest before you go on.'

Mr Miller bravely said it was nothing and he was not at all tired.

'I think it is wonderful how you can speak for so long in church,' said Mrs Brandon admiringly. 'If I had to read the service and preach I should be quite voiceless, besides making all sorts of mistakes.'

Mr Miller looked at his saint with an instant's doubt, recovered himself and began again.

'Drummond of Hawthornden, in his Notes of Ben Jonson's Conversation, on the occasion of Jonson's famous visit to him in 1618, reports Jonson – ' he began, when a lawn mower, whose distant whirr had sounded not unpleasantly across the garden, came roaring nearer and nearer and began to move backwards and forwards with hideous recurring crescendo and diminuendo just behind the tree. Mr Miller stopped.

'Do go on,' said Mrs Brandon, but finding her own words almost inaudible, she sat up and looked round.

'That must be Turpin,' she said, while the lawn mower was at the furthest point of its beat. 'I have said again and again that he *must* get the lawns mown before lunch. Do call him, Mr Miller.'

Mr Miller laid down his typescript and went towards the lawn mower, but as the gardener was deaf, and the noise of the machine deafening, and Turpin's eyes were glued to the delicate watered pattern on the grass that he must follow, Mr Miller had to walk the whole length of the lawn beside him before he could get his attention. When Turpin saw who his visitor was he stopped and touched his cap, pleased at the attention, for Hettie gave her employer an excellent character as one who did not too closely inquire into matters of dusting and sweeping, provided his hours of study were not disturbed. Thinking, though erroneously, that his Vicar had come to discuss the weather with him, Turpin gave it as his opinion that this drought wouldn't break for a long time yet, but the gardens were doing wonderful well considering and he had a nice big marrow saving up for the Harvest Festival. He well remembered, he added with a chuckle, the year he had that great whopper of a marrow, and when he came to pick it he found Miss Delia had cut a comic face on the under side with her new pocket knife. At this point Mr Miller, seizing his chance, managed to convey to Turpin by a combination of shouting and pantomime that his mistress wanted to see him.

'Please take the lawn mower right away, Turpin,' said Mrs Brandon, whose gentle voice appeared to be perfectly audible to her gardener. 'You know I will *not* have the lawns done on this side of the house after lunch.'

The substance of Turpin's reply was that Mrs Brandon well knew he always got the lawns done before his dinner now, but if people's cars would splutter the new gravel off the drive on to the grass edge, he couldn't help it if stones got in the machine and Curwen had said he'd run her down in the car to the blacksmith to have the blades re-set, but being as the car was wanted to take Miss Delia over to Rushwater he had to send the garden boy down with her on the barrow, and she was only just back and running so beautiful it seemed a shame not to use her while the weather lasted.

Mrs Brandon replied that the weather would last for a long time and he could do the lawn to-morrow, upon which Turpin touched his cap and departed, the vengeful noise of his machine growing fainter and fainter, till the silence of golden afternoon enfolded the garden.

'How lovely the silence is,' said Mrs Brandon.

'Shall I go on now?' asked Mr Miller.

'Yes *do*,' said Mrs Brandon. 'And begin right at the beginning again, so that I shall miss nothing. Oh, I am so sorry, but could you just pick up that cushion again?'

Mr Miller got up, fetched the cushion, put it with reverence slightly tinged by impatience at Mrs Brandon's back, sat down again and opened the typescript.

'Drummond of Hawthornden,' he began, 'in his Notes of Ben Jonson's Conversation, on the occasion of Jonson's famous visit to him in 1618, reports Jonson as declaring that "He esteemeth John Donne – " '

'Excuse me one moment,' said Mrs Brandon. 'It is Rose. What is it, Rose?'

'Only the tea-things, madam,' said Rose in an aggrieved voice, 'but I can leave them till later if you wish.'

'No, you can take them,' said Mrs Brandon.

'And Nurse wishes to speak to you, madam,' said Rose. 'Seeing Mr Miller was here she didn't like to trouble you, but it's about Miss Delia.'

'Well, tell Nurse to come and tell me what it is,' said Mrs Brandon. 'I'm sure you won't mind,' she added, turning to Mr Miller. 'It won't take a moment and then Rose will have finished clearing away and we can be quite peaceful.'

Mr Miller could but acquiesce.

'I'm sorry to disturb you, madam,' said Nurse, 'but I thought I'd better speak to you. It's about Miss Delia's knickers,' she continued, after a glance at the Vicar and a rapid decision that his cloth protected him. 'She really hasn't a pair fit to wear, not if she goes away to stay anywhere. I really don't know what she does to them. So I thought if you didn't need those three yards of that double width pink crêpe de chine you got in the sales I could start on some at once. I'd just run down to the village on my bike before the shop shuts and see if Miss Thatcher can match me up some pink sewing silk.'

'Yes do, Nurse,' said Mrs Brandon. 'And tell Rose to bring me out my spectacles.'

Nurse went off and was almost immediately seen running to the village on her bicycle.

'Just one moment till I have my spectacles,' said Mrs Brandon to her Vicar. 'I don't really need them, but I like to know where they are. Thank you, Rose. Now, Mr Miller, go on where we stopped. I *am* so sorry for these interruptions, but now we can be perfectly quiet.'

Mr Miller said he thought he had better go back to the beginning again, rather than pick up the thread in the middle of a sentence. He opened his typescript and began:

'Drummond of Hawthornden, in his Notes of Ben Jonson's Conversation, on the occasion of Jonson's famous visit to him in 1618, reports Jonson as declaring that "He esteemeth John

Donne as the first poet in the world for some things". But Jonson also asserted that "Donne ... " '

He read on, sometimes stumbling over a word when he raised his eyes and saw Mrs Brandon's face brooding in quiet beauty on his words. It was difficult to decide, Mrs Brandon reflected, whether she had better get Nurse to alter that apricot slip which she had felt at the time she bought it to be a mistake, or simply cut her losses and give it away. On the whole, give it away, she thought, and having decided this, so exquisite a light of peace and contentment irradiated her face that Mr Miller, turning over the second page, felt that so must angels look.

'That is like Sir Edmund's car,' said Mrs Brandon, a distinct interest in her voice. 'I do hope he won't spoil our reading, Mr Miller. I daresay it is only a message about something and as soon as he has gone we will begin again. I'm glad to see he has his chauffeur back. He drives so badly himself and with his lame leg one never knows what might happen.'

Sir Edmund was seen at the front door holding a short colloquy with Rose, who pointed out to him the party under the chestnut tree, towards whom he then directed his steps.

'Well, Lavinia, out here, eh?' said Sir Edmund. 'Afternoon, Miller. Phew! it's hot.'

'You would like some fresh tea,' said Mrs Brandon.

'No, I wouldn't,' said Sir Edmund. 'Poison to me, Lavinia, as you well know. But if that girl of yours would bring me a brandy and soda, I wouldn't say no.'

'*Would* you mind, Mr Miller,' said Mrs Brandon, 'going to the house and asking Rose to bring out the brandy and a siphon and some glasses, and she might as well bring the sherry too, as Francis will soon be back.'

Mr Miller rose, laid his typescript on his chair, and went to the house. When he got back he found Sir Edmund telling Mrs Brandon about the new drains in a piece of land over near Starveacres.

'Thank you so much, Mr Miller,' said Mrs Brandon. 'Mr Miller was reading aloud to me, Sir Edmund.'

'Bible, eh?' said Sir Edmund.

'No, no. I'm not *ill*,' said his hostess. 'It was a book of his own, all about Donne.'

'Didn't know you were keen on cricket,' said Sir Edmund.

'I was once twelfth man for my college third eleven,' said Mr Miller, 'but I'm afraid I can claim no special knowledge of the subject.'

'What's all this about a book about Bradman then?' asked Sir Edmund.

'I didn't say Bradman, I said Donne,' said Mrs Brandon.

'Well, it's all one,' said Sir Edmund. 'Fine fellows those Australians. I must get that book. What's it called, eh?'

'No, not that kind of Don,' said Mrs Brandon, sticking to her point.

'Don Juan then, eh?' said Sir Edmund with a loud laugh which made Mr Miller want to excommunicate him.

'Don't be dense, Sir Edmund,' said Mrs Brandon severely. 'It is a book about *Donne*, the clergyman that has his head tied up in St Paul's.'

Before Sir Edmund could burst with mystification, Mr Miller, concealing his mortification very well, explained that he was reading to Mrs Brandon the first chapters of a small book on John Donne, Dean of St Paul's from 1621 to 1631, and author of a number of poems, religious and erotic.

'Religious and – well, I suppose you know best, Miller, but it sounds a bit queer to me,' said Sir Edmund, whose chivalry very properly took alarm at the word erotic used in front of a lady. 'Go on, go on, never mind me.'

'I think if you went back to the beginning it would be better,' said Mrs Brandon. 'Then Sir Edmund wouldn't miss anything.'

'That's right. Always do things thoroughly,' said Sir Edmund, composing himself to listen.

Mr Miller turned back to the first page of the typescript and began, a little nervously.

'Drummond of Hawthornden – '

'Just a moment,' said Mrs Brandon. 'Thanks, Rose. Sir Edmund, will you help yourself. Do have a glass of sherry, Mr Miller, or would you rather have brandy and soda?'

Mr Miller politely refused both and waiting till Sir Edmund had filled his glass, prepared to begin again.

'That *stupid* cushion again,' said Mrs Brandon. 'Oh, thank you so much, Mr Miller. Now, we will have a really cosy time.'

It did cross Mr Miller's mind that cosy was not perhaps the *mot juste* for the author of his choice, but he resolutely put the thought from him as savouring of criticism of his hostess, and took up the typescript.

'Drummond of Hawthornden, in his Notes of Ben Jonson's Conversation – '

'Sorry to interrupt you, Miller,' said Sir Edmund, 'but the name Drummond reminds me that old Mrs Perkins down at Grumper's End has sciatica again badly. We'll have to get her into the infirmary, but she's a devilish obstinate old woman. Just thought I'd mention it while it was in my mind. Carry on.'

' – on the occasion of Jonson's famous visit to him in 1618 – ' continued Mr Miller, determined not to go back to the beginning again.

'Sixteen eighteen, eh?' said Sir Edmund. 'That's a deuce of a long time ago, eh? Wonderful old fellows they were.'

At this Mr Miller threw up the sponge, folded his typescript and was wondering whether he could make his excuses without betraying the annoyance in his voice, when Francis's car rushed up the drive, halted, and disgorged Francis and Delia.

'Mother, mother,' shrieked Delia, 'oh, how do you do, Mr Miller, hullo, Sir Edmund, what do you think? Francis came to fetch me from the tennis party and as we were coming down the Southbridge Hill a car came out of Patcher's Lane and a motor bike ran slap into it and the man went right through the windscreen. He wasn't a bit hurt but he was bleeding like anything, so the people in the car took him straight to the Nutfield Cottage Hospital and Dr Ford was there and he put ten stitches in, and the bike is absolutely smashed to bits.'

'If I had my way those hazels at the corner of Patcher's Lane would be cut back,' said Sir Edmund angrily. 'That corner's a perfect death trap. I've told the County Council about it again and again. When someone is killed perhaps they'll take some notice. Well, Lavinia, I must be off. Can I give you a lift, Miller? Early to bed and early to rise, you know.'

Mr Miller, hearing the church clock strike seven, accepted the offer and said good-bye to Mrs Brandon with a shade of stiffness which she noticed but could not account for.

'It was lovely to hear your book,' she said, holding Mr Miller's hand in both her own. 'You must come again and we will have another long reading, that is if you are sure it doesn't tire you,' she added with deep affectionate interest in her voice.

Mr Miller truthfully said that he could have read twice as much to her without being tired and with a look of respectful adoration went away.

'At it again, darling?' said Francis to his mother as the visitors left. 'Seducing the clergy.'

Mrs Brandon said he oughtn't to say things like that and she was going in to have her bath.

*

Dinner passed off peacefully enough except for Delia's lamentations that Dr Ford would not let her see the stitches put in. It was too bad, she said, that she took all the trouble to pass that rotten First Aid exam and now she wasn't allowed to do anything. Even when Sid, the garden boy, had that huge boil on his neck they wouldn't let her see it burst.

'No, I'll say it for you, darling,' said Francis, anticipating his mother. 'Delia, one oughtn't to say things like that. It's enough to take a hard-working young man's appetite away. Oh, I brought out some new dance records. There's an awfully good one called "I'm all of a muddle when I cuddle, cuddle, cuddle." It's played by Cash Campo and his Symposium Boys.'

Accordingly Delia opened the gramophone and Francis turned back a couple of rugs, and he and Delia slid up and down the drawing-room to the glutinous sentiment of 'I'm all of a muddle' and the other records that Francis had brought. Mrs Brandon, at the far end of the room, sat under a shaded light by the window with her embroidery, pleased to see her nice, good-looking offspring enjoying themselves.

Gradually she became conscious of an alien presence, and looking up saw Mr Grant standing outside the open window. She smiled at him.

'Oh,' said Mr Grant, 'I just happened to be passing and I happened to see you. Could I come in?'

The thought did just trouble Mrs Brandon's consciousness that people did not come up the drive, which led nowhere except to her front door, by accident, but as she was quite pleased to see a visitor she invited Mr Grant to join them.

Instead of going round to the front door Mr Grant stood on one leg and then came nearer to the window.

'It was that book of mine you said you'd like me to read to you,' he said, leaning his elbows on the window sill.

'I always hope the sash cord won't break when people do that,' said Mrs Brandon. 'One of them did break once, and the window came down with such a crash that two panes were broken, but most luckily no one was under it at the time.'

'I just happened to have the manuscript with me if you'd care to hear it,' said Mr Grant, standing up.

'I'd love to,' said Mrs Brandon, 'but I don't see how you could possibly read to me here with the gramophone. I'll tell Rose to take you to my sitting-room. Ring the front door bell and I'll catch her in the hall.'

Mr Grant continued his journey, rang the front door bell and was shown by Rose into Mrs Brandon's sitting-room. From the drawing-room beyond came the wail of Cash Campo and his Symposium Boys. The door which led into the drawing-room was opened, the wail rose to a nostalgic shriek, Mrs Brandon carrying, an armful of tapestry work and trailing embroidery wool, came in and shut the door behind her. Mr Grant found himself alone with the most exquisite woman in the world and dropped his manuscript, which fluttered down and lay strewn on the floor.

'Oh, dear,' said Mrs Brandon sympathetically, as she sat down, shedding her scissors, her gold thimble and several skeins of wool.

'I'll pick them up,' said Mr Grant with eager devotion, and leaving his manuscript to its fate he pursued the thimble under a table, retrieved it, collected the scissors and wools, and still on his knees presented them to their owner.

'Hullo, Hilary,' said Francis, looking in. 'What are you doing? Don't propose to mamma, because I've sworn an oath that no home will hold me and a stepfather and I'd hate to turn you out. I say, mamma, do you know where that record of "The Surprise in your Eyes" has got to?'

'I think Nurse borrowed it to play on her little gramophone,' said Mrs Brandon, 'and don't be so silly. And shut the door, darling, because Hilary is going to read to me.'

Francis looked with avuncular tolerance at his young friend and went away. Mr Grant sorted his manuscript and put on his spectacles.

'Are yours for long sight or short sight?' asked Mrs Brandon.

'Astigmatism,' said Mr Grant. 'I squint with one eye and not with the other, or something of the sort. My man says I'll get over it if I wear glasses for a few years.'

'Mine are for short sight,' said Mrs Brandon proudly. 'I can see anything, absolutely anything at a distance, but close to my eyes are quite useless to me.'

Mr Grant found the thought of Mrs Brandon's blue eyes, endowed with the eagle's sight for ranging over the great free distances but betraying their owner for the level of every day's most quiet needs, so moving that he sat silent. Divine poetry alone could, he felt, deal adequately with the theme, but as the only line which immediately presented itself was 'Eyeless in Gaza at the mill with slaves,' which even he recognized to be inappropriate, he gave up the search.

'Now, I am longing to hear about Robert le Diable,' said Mrs Brandon.

'Jehan le Capet,' Mr Grant corrected her.

'Of course, how silly of me. Tell me, was Laura Morland able to help you about a publisher?'

Mr Grant said her publisher, Mr Coates, sounded very nice, but he was afraid no one would really want his book very much. He had, he said, a frightful inferiority complex, which came from the way his mother had brought him up.

'Which reminds me,' said Mrs Brandon, 'that I have never asked your mother to dinner yet. What with one thing coming after another and the days following each other as they do I seem to have got behindhand. I hope she won't think it rude of me.'

'Of course she won't. And anyway she's only been at the Cow

a week and I think she is going on to Lady Norton to-morrow. But she's bound to come back again,' said Mr Grant gloomily, 'and spoil everything as usual. I mean she was never unkind to me or anything, but I have never had a real chance. When I was at school and my father was alive we always went to Frinton for the Easter and summer holidays and stayed at home for Christmas, to please father. Then when he died and I went to Oxford, mother took to going to Italy and made me spend all my holidays there, so you see it really never gave me a chance at all.

Mrs Brandon did not quite follow Mr Grant's argument, but said soothingly that she was sure he would get his book published at once, and that she for one had never noticed his inferiority complex.

Mr Grant said in a hushed voice that was just like her. He felt, he added, quite, quite different when he was with her. He had very few *real* friends, he said, but with the real friends whom he loved he could be himself.

Mrs Brandon, interested in philosophical discussion, said it was extraordinary how one felt quite different with different people and was going on to instance some of the different people that she felt different with, but Mr Grant, though he adored her and was still quite hot and damp from having mentioned that there were a few real friends whom he loved, alternately hoping and fearing that she would have seized his meaning, took the opportunity of a second's pause to enlarge upon the abstract theme of how different one felt with different people, which he did for seven or eight minutes.

'When I met you at Miss Brandon's I was wishing I had never been born,' said Mr Grant byronically, 'but now everything is different.'

There was a short silence.

'Now, do read me your book,' said Mrs Brandon, 'and I will fill in some of my background and then I can listen beautifully.'

'You always listen beautifully,' said Mr Grant in a hoarse voice, but Mrs Brandon was trying to match some wool and either did not hear or took no notice.

'My great difficulty,' said Mr Grant, 'was to know how to

approach my subject. As practically nothing is known about le Capet I thought of treating him fictionally, but I thought that treatment would hardly do.'

He paused, evidently anxious for an opinion. Mrs Brandon said No, of course it wouldn't do.

'On the other hand,' continued Mr Grant, 'one doesn't want to be too prosaic and dry, so I have used a method which I think will combine the best elements of both. If you don't mind, I'll begin at the beginning.'

Without waiting for the goddess's consent to this novel manner of reading a book he plunged recklessly into his first chapter, reading in a quick, unnatural, high-pitched voice and stammering violently, his face very red with mingled emotions. Mrs Brandon, occasionally detaching her thoughts from the apricot slip, a new carpet for the servants' sitting-room, and other weighty affairs, gathered that le Capet's chief claim to immortality was that he had just missed meeting everyone of note in Paris and was in bed with a cold on the first night of *Hernani*. From an altered tone in her young admirer's voice she presently realized that he was reading some of le Capet's verses aloud, tried to anchor her drifting attention and just caught the last line of a poem ending

Sirène, fange, boue, immondices, ordure.

'It's fine,' said Mr Grant, his voice now itself again, 'to be able to say that about the woman you love.'

'I don't think everyone would like it,' said Mrs Brandon with surprising firmness.

Mr Grant came to earth with a bang, and realizing that he had grossly insulted and offended his hostess, got up and said he must go.

'Oh, don't go,' said Mrs Brandon.

Mr Grant sat down again.

'I simply loved it,' said Mrs Brandon. 'I am sure it is going to be an enormous success. Let us go and watch Francis and Delia and you must have a drink. You must be thirsty.'

Mr Grant got up again, moved beyond speech by these exquisite words, and they went into the drawing-room, where Francis dispensed drinks. Mrs Brandon said she was going to

bed and held out her hand to Mr Grant who grasped it with
fervour.

'Tut, tut,' said Francis; and bending low over his mother's
hand he kissed it, while Delia giggled.

'Headache, darling?' he said as he escorted his mother to the
door.

'A little,' said Mrs Brandon. 'I find being read aloud to is very
exhausting. Mr Miller read to me all afternoon and Hilary all
evening and they never seem to get anywhere.'

'You shouldn't let them,' said Francis. 'It's only vanity that
makes you so kind, because you think how nice you look when
you listen. I say, what a ripping title for a fox-trot. Good night,
mamma. Now, Hilary, stop being my stepfather and be a man.
I'll do the gramophone and you dance with Delia.'

Mr Grant did as he was told and enjoyed himself very much,
winding up with a tremendous wrestling match with Francis
and a race down the drive. Not till the following morning did he
remember, with a sense of guilt, that he had not thought of Mrs
Brandon for quite nine hours, for eight and a half of which he
had been asleep.

– 6 –

BRANDON ABBEY AGAIN

ON the following day, much to everyone's relief, Mrs Grant left
the Cow and Sickle to go and stay with her dull friend Lady
Norton, for the last two years a widow whose jointure was the
despair of the nephew who inherited the title. Mrs Brandon went
to say good-bye to her and hoped she had been comfortable.

'Comfort really means nothing to me,' said Mrs Grant. 'In
Calabria I have often slept on a sack stuffed with chestnut husks.'

'The mattresses at the Cow are pretty uncomfortable, but I
don't think there are husks in them,' said Mrs Brandon apologetically. 'Did you manage to get the bedroom window to open?'

'I sleep so well that I hardly notice whether the window is open or shut. In Calabria none of the peasants open their windows. It is an old superstition that evil spirits suck the blood of sleepers if the window is open. Besides, they are out all day. There is a proverb which roughly runs in English, "Do not draw the curtain till the sun's rays are certain." That does not of course give the real meaning at all.'

'Well, I hope you will have a very nice time with Lady Norton,' said Mrs Brandon. 'I believe her garden is beautiful. And we will all take great care of Hilary for you. What a nice boy he is.'

'He is absolutely devoted to me,' said Mrs Grant, toying with her heavy amber necklace. 'Sometimes I almost wish he were less devoted. He never made friends at school and preferred to spend his holidays with me – and his father of course – at Frinton or at home. I always hoped that when he went to Oxford he would make a circle for himself, but he came out to me in Italy every vacation. I loved having him, but he does not understand the Italian mind and cannot get on with my beloved peasants. If only he would marry some nice English girl I should be quite happy, so long as I wasn't expected to take any interest in my grandchildren.'

'I think I should like grandchildren,' said Mrs Brandon. 'They would make me feel important. How are you going to Lady Norton?'

'She is sending the car for me. She is very fond of driving, and while I am with her I shall get her to take me over to Brandon Abbey. My husband was anxious for me to see his Aunt Amelia again, and I feel I ought to go while she is still alive.'

In this sentiment Mrs Brandon fully acquiesced, feeling that a visit after Miss Brandon's death would not be the same thing. She wondered whether she ought to hint at Miss Brandon's disinclination to see her niece by marriage, but came to the conclusion that she had better not interfere. Lady Norton's car then arrived and Mrs Grant's rather shameful luggage, consisting largely of gaily striped bags and baskets, was indignantly put into it by the chauffeur.

'No, no, put my things inside,' said Mrs Grant, coming out to superintend. 'I will go in front with you. They are all human, if we treat them as human beings,' she added in far too audible an aside to Mrs Brandon, who made no comment, knowing well that Lady Norton's chauffeur would die sooner than be human.

Mrs Grant bade embarrassingly affectionate farewells to the staff of the Cow and Sickle, bestowing handsome largess at the same time, and got up beside the unwilling chauffeur, whose face of rigid disapproval boded ill for human relationships. Mrs Brandon walked homewards, considering the matter of the apricot slip. It had come to her in a flash while doing her hair that morning that perhaps Miss Morris would like it and she was determined to leave no stone unturned, although she knew that Nurse, who wanted the slip for Delia, would strongly disapprove. Accordingly she wrote to Miss Morris to ask if the gift would be acceptable. Two or three days passed without an answer, and she was beginning to wonder whether Miss Morris was offended, when after lunch Rose announced a telephone call from Brandon Abbey. It was Miss Morris herself, who told Mrs Brandon that her aunt was not at all well and had expressed a desire to see her.

'She wants to know,' said Miss Morris, 'if you will come over to-morrow afternoon and bring your son and Mr Grant. I understand that her solicitor is also coming, and I can't tell you anything more, because I don't know anything. And I would simply love to have the apricot slip. It is too good of you to think of me.'

'It all sounds extremely uncomfortable,' said Mrs Brandon, 'but of course I'll come if she really wants me, though if it is business I simply cannot understand it ever. I'll bring Hilary and I'll see if Francis can get off work early. How are you?'

Miss Morris said she was quite well, thanked Mrs Brandon again for the slip, and rang off.

As soon as Francis came back his mother told him what Miss Morris had said and they agreed that if the solicitor was coming it must be something to do with legal matters. Francis was at first extremely unwilling to go, feeling that the whole affair savoured of fortune-hunting, and when his mother pressed the point he suggested that they should walk over to the Vicarage and see Mr Grant, who was equally involved.

Mrs Brandon, though she was as disinterested as anyone can

possibly be when a large inheritance is in question, did feel that it would not only be unkind to her old aunt, but a really foolish flying in the face of Providence if this invitation were neglected, and said so with unusual energy. When they got to the Vicarage they found Mr Grant playing tennis with his coach and looked on till the set was finished. Mr Miller, who looked much nicer in flannels than in his clerical garb, or so Mrs Brandon privately thought, came and sat beside her, while Mr Grant and Francis had a little horseplay, but finding it too hot, soon came and sat down on the grass. Mr Grant complained bitterly that Mr Miller always beat him. Mr Miller looked gratified, remembered that pride is sinful, and said he hoped it would be fine for the Harvest Festival. Francis said he was all with them there except that they wanted a little rain at Stories to bring their giant gooseberry on that they were saving up to decorate the font. Mrs Brandon said Francis oughtn't to say things like that, and it was something quite different that she had come to talk about, something that Hilary ought to know. On hearing this Mr Miller offered to go away, but Mrs Brandon begged him not to, saying that his advice would be of the greatest value, and that though luckily Francis and Delia would be quite comfortably off when she was dead, that was no reason for not being polite to people. To this, as a general axiom, Mr Miller gave his approval and asked if she would tell him what the circumstances were that called for his advice; advice, he added, which was ever at her disposal if it could be of any service.

'But I told you,' said Mrs Brandon plaintively, 'About Miss Brandon. After all she *is* a relation.'

'Well, you know darling,' said Francis, 'that listening is your strong suit, not explaining. Leave this to your able and business-like son.'

He then told Mr Grant about Miss Morris's telephone message and said it was all extraordinarily uncomfortable, but he thought they ought to go. It might look like fortune-hunting if they did, but it would be rude and unkind to an old lady if they didn't, and what did Hilary think. Mr Grant said with some vehemence that he loathed the Abbey and never wanted to hear of it again, but if Mrs Brandon thought he ought to go, he would.

'Well, she *is* our relation,' said Mrs Brandon, sticking firmly to her original point. 'What do you think, Mr Miller?'

Mr Miller, who was not quite sure whether he was being appealed to as pastor or neighbour, said visiting the sick was undoubtedly one of the duties laid upon us, a duty from which no material considerations should deter us and he was sure Mrs Brandon would judge for the best.

'Well, I really hardly come into it, because Cousin Amelia never threatened to leave *me* anything,' said Mrs Brandon with great candour, 'but it would be very silly of Hilary and Francis not to go, and very inconsiderate. And the solicitor may be coming about something quite different, like drains, or the kitchen chimney,' said Mrs Brandon, who appeared to confuse solicitors with plumbers and builders. 'You never know.'

'Well, thank you very much for helping, Mr Miller,' said Francis, 'and now that mamma has decided to do what she always meant to do, we can go home again. How's the book, Mr Miller?'

Mr Miller, slightly self-conscious said it had gone to his publishers.

'Oh, shan't I hear any more of it then?' asked Mrs Brandon.

'I was going to ask you a favour, a very great favour,' said Mr Miller in a lower voice, hitching his chair nearer hers. 'Will you think me presumptuous if I ask you to allow me to dedicate my little work to you?'

'To me?' exclaimed Mrs Brandon, in genuine astonishment and delight.

'To whom else?' asked Mr Miller.

'Well, lots of people,' said Mrs Brandon, thinking of the Archbishop of Canterbury and Mr Miller's old stepmother at Harrogate. 'But to me! Oh, Mr Miller, how enchanting of you. I have never had a book dedicated to me before. I couldn't think of anything nicer happening to me. Thank you so very much.'

She looked so pleased and happy, like a child with a new toy as Mr Miller in a flight of fancy afterwards put it to himself, that the author really felt for a moment as if he were doing a kindness rather than receiving one.

'And what exactly will you put in the beginning?' asked Mrs Brandon.

Mr Miller, who had not actually thought of anything except one or two extremely unsuitable lines from Donne's works, hesitated.

'Why not just "To the Listener"?' said Mr Grant.

'You might as well say "To the Daily Telegraph",' said Francis. 'Pull yourself together, my boy. What about a spot of Latin, Mr Miller?'

'I think simply "To L. B. in gratitude",' said Mr Miller.

Mrs Brandon's face assumed such a beatific expression that Mr Miller felt he was already well repaid.

'I was thinking how nice L.B. looked on my dressing case when I was married,' she explained. 'My initials used to be L. O., Lavinia Oliver – Francis's second name is Oliver, you know – and they looked so silly and the girls at school would make jokes about them. L. B. looks much nicer.'

Having stemmed romance by this piece of reminiscence, she said good-bye to Mr Miller.

'Come to lunch to-morrow, Hilary,' she said as she left, 'and we'll go to the Abbey together. Francis is coming separately, from Barchester, and I'm sure it will be most uncomfortable.'

Mr Grant and Mr Miller, finding as usual that speech on the one subject of which their hearts and minds were full was difficult, returned to their tennis, where so fired was Mr Grant by the thought of the morrow that he served eight double faults running and lost two of the new balls among the laurustinus. All evening, when he should have been working at Cicero, he was thinking with envy of Mr Miller, who had really finished a book commissioned by a real publisher, and was going to dedicate it to Mrs Brandon. An idea began to float about in his mind and by the time he came down to breakfast next day it had almost assumed the nature of a resolve. If Mr Miller had not been thinking about the Church Fête and how he could, in a spirit consistent with Christianity, keep his parishioners away from the little rock garden which he sometimes felt to be a stumbling block in the way of complete humility, he would have noticed that his pupil was strangely silent and was jotting down notes on a piece of paper in the manner of one who hopes someone will ask him what he is doing.

The morning passed all too slowly for Mr Grant. At half-past twelve he could contain his impatience no longer and set out for Stories, hoping against hope that by walking slowly he could make the journey last till half-past one, which was Mrs Brandon's lunch-time. By twenty minutes to one he was at the front gate and in despair sat down on the grassy side of the road to die. Before kindly death could ease his pains Delia came up the road on her bicycle. When she saw Mr Grant she stopped and got off.

'Good morning,' said Mr Grant.

'Hullo, Hilary. Feeling sick?' asked Delia.

'Oh, no. I was a bit early for lunch, that's all.'

'I should think you were,' said Delia, 'it's only a quarter to one, but I can easily find some biscuits if you're hungry.'

'It's not that,' said Mr Grant moodily.

'Well, if you are sick, say so,' said Delia, mistaking the moodiness for nausea. 'I'd love to hold your head.'

Mr Grant looked up anxiously. The gleam of the Born Nurse was in Delia's eye and he felt that sooner than forgo her prey she would hypnotize him into feeling ill, so he got up and shook the odds and ends of dry grass and dust off his trousers.

'You'd better come up to the house,' said Delia, accommodating her pace to the invalid's. 'We can eat gooseberries if you're sure you're all right.'

As eating gooseberries appeared to be as good a way as another of passing the time till lunch, Mr Grant accompanied Delia to the kitchen garden where, bent double under the gooseberry nets, torn by the thorny gooseberry bushes, the hot noontide sun beating upon them, they enjoyed a hearty meal of unripe fruit.

'I say,' said Delia, 'are you really writing a book?'

'Damn,' said Mr Grant, as a large and unexpectedly ripe red gooseberry exploded in his hand. 'Sorry, I mean yes.'

'Mother said you read it to her,' said Delia. 'Try this bush, it's a bit riper. All about absinthe and things, isn't it?'

Mr Grant said rather stiffly that it was about a French poet, who had indeed hastened his end by over-indulgence in absinthe, but had produced some very remarkable work.

'There's a man at Nutfield,' said Delia, 'who drinks methylated spirits and power alcohol. Dr Ford says he'll have spontaneous combustion some day. I'd like to be there. It must be marvellous to see anyone spontaneously combusting. You can't do anything to stop them and there's nothing left but a black sticky sort of mess. It must be even more difficult to collect enough to bury than it was with the man who got burned in the motor char-à-banc. Anyway I hope your book will be a best seller. I shall give it to all my friends for Christmas if it isn't more than three and six-pence.'

Touched by this kind interest Mr Grant shyly said he had been thinking of dedicating it to her mother.

'Good idea,' said Delia. 'Mother will love it. What will you put?'

Mr Grant said he didn't know. Something Latin perhaps.

'Oh, I wouldn't do that,' said Delia. 'It puts people off buying if they see Latin. Why don't you say To Cousin Lavinia with Love from Hilary?'

At this brutal suggestion Mr Grant felt a gulf opening be-tween himself and his cousin Delia which only time could bridge. The gong sounded.

'There; now we'll be late,' said Delia. 'If you are too early for a thing you nearly always get too late. Come on. Careful with that net.'

Her words came too late. Mr Grant rather indignantly ex-tricating himself from the gooseberries, found one of his buttons inextricably tangled in the net, wrenched impatiently at it and tore the button together with a strip of grey flannel from his coat. Delia said Now he had done it and they'd better find Nurse. Before he could protest she had hustled him in by the garden door and driven him up two flights of stairs, calling 'Nurse, Nurse' at the top of her voice.

'I'm not deaf, Miss Delia,' said Nurse, appearing at the top of the stairs. 'Why aren't you at lunch?'

'Oh, you know Hilary Grant,' said Delia, leading the way into Nurse's sitting-room, 'the one I told you about that's a sort of cousin. He was eating gooseberries and got his button off. Can you sew it on?'

'And you've got a great ladder in your stocking, Miss Delia,' said Nurse. 'You know what I said about those gooseberry bushes. Why can't you wait till Turpin picks them for the table? Go and change them at once.'

Delia said she hadn't a pair to wear except her good ones. Nurse with conscious magnanimity pointed to a pile of stockings on her table and said they were all mended and quite good enough for the garden. Delia, to Mr Grant's embarrassment, immediately stripped off her stockings and, sitting on the table, put on one of the mended pairs, while, to his even greater embarrassment, Nurse, addressing him as Mr – or possibly, he thought but couldn't be certain of it, Master – Hilary, told him to take his coat off.

'I'll get you one of Mr Francis's to wear,' she said, 'and when you've finished lunch I'll have this nice and ready for you. You can wash in the bathroom here and there's a nail-brush on the shelf.'

With these humiliating words she drove Mr Grant into a bathroom, doled him out a clean towel, and left him in such a state of terror that he spent two long minutes sitting on the side of the bath in case Nurse should think he wasn't having a thorough wash. When at last he ventured out he found Delia waiting for him with one of Francis's coats, and they ran downstairs together.

'Sorry we're late, mother,' said Delia. 'Hilary felt sick, and we ate such a lot of gooseberries his buttons came off, so Nurse is mending them.'

Much to Mr Grant's relief his hostess took no notice of this misleading statement and asked after his mother. As Mr Grant had not heard from her since she went to Lady Norton this subject dropped at once.

'I say, mother,' said Delia, 'you know that book Hilary was reading to you? Who do you think he's going to dedicate it to?'

On hearing this blatant exposition of his heart's secret, Mr Grant went cold with anger and looked at Delia in a way intended to express his disapproval. Delia, a past mistress owing to long practice with her brother Francis in the art of making faces, took his look as a sign of friendliness and made a hideous face back at him.

'I can't think,' said Mrs Brandon.

In despair Mr Grant kicked Delia under the table, forming at the same time the word 'No' with his lips. Delia, realizing at last what he meant, said with great presence of mind that it was a deadly secret.

'Then I won't ask,' said Mrs Brandon, including Mr Grant in a motherly tolerance that made him wince. 'You must read some more to me, Hilary, as soon as we have a free evening.'

After lunch Mrs Brandon went to rest, leaving Mr Grant a prey to Delia, who challenged him to play croquet with some balls she had found in an old set of bowls, and they both laughed so much that Mr Grant quite forgot literature and his consuming passion. Delia, while assuming airs of authority over him in ordinary life, showed a respect for his position as an author which made him feel delightfully grown-up, and he was almost sorry when the car came.

'Aren't you coming?' he asked her.

Delia said she loathed the old Abbey and hoped they'd have a jolly time. Mr Grant was getting into the car where Mrs Brandon was already seated, when Nurse came to the front door.

'Your coat, Mr Hilary,' she said reproachfully.

'You'll hardly want another coat,' said Mrs Brandon. 'It's such a hot day.'

Mr Grant then had to explain that he had torn the button off his coat on the gooseberry bushes, and had furthermore to humiliate himself by getting out of the car, taking off Francis's coat and appearing in his shirt sleeves before his hostess and putting his own coat on again with Nurse's kind help.

'Thanks awfully,' he said, backing away from Nurse, who might, he felt, want to look at his nails, and got back into the car, all his grown-up self-confidence crushed. Mrs Brandon, who was still sleepy after her rest, didn't talk much, and her unhappy young cousin, taking her silence for scorn, wished he were in the Foreign Legion.

When they got to Brandon Abbey they found Miss Morris in the drawing-room giving tea to a stranger whom she introduced as Mr Merton.

'I've heard about you so much from the Keiths,' said Mrs Brandon. 'Isn't Lydia rather a friend of yours? How is she?'

117

'Very well, I believe,' said Mr Merton. 'I was down there for Kate's wedding, and Lydia trod on her own dress in church and ripped a large piece out of it just as the blessing was being given.'

'What happened?' asked Mrs Brandon.

'Kate nearly didn't get married at all,' said Mr Merton, 'because she heard the noise and knew what had happened and wanted to mend it, but luckily she was kneeling down and it all passed over.'

'I wish I had been there,' said Mrs Brandon, 'but I was away. I adore weddings. They always make me cry.'

'Lydia cried like anything,' said Mr Merton proudly. 'In fact she cried so much that I had to take her to see the Barchester Amateur Dramatic Society act *Ghosts*, and that cheered her up.'

While this innocent conversation was going on, Mr Grant was a prey to black fury and despair. Here was a man, not more than a few years older than himself, talking away on terms of friendly intimacy to Mrs Brandon, all because he knew some people called Keith, while he was despised and ignored and treated as a child. Probably this Mr Merton, or whatever his name was, had come down to persuade Miss Brandon to make a new will leaving everything away from her niece, or to embezzle her money, or fraudulently convert, or one of those things that solicitors were always being had up for doing.

'Are you making a new will for Aunt Sissie?' asked Mrs Brandon, with superb disregard of professional feeling. 'You are a lawyer, aren't you?'

'Only a barrister unfortunately,' said Mr Merton, 'and as such not entitled to make people's wills. No, Miss Brandon is an old friend of my father's who is a solicitor, and has an annoying way of summoning me to give her advice that she never takes. What she wants me for this time I don't know. I'm staying with the Dean at Barchester. I hope she won't want to keep me long as I have to get back for tennis at six. How is the old lady?'

Mrs Brandon appealed to Miss Morris, who said Miss Brandon had not been at all well, but seemed better to-day and would like to see Mr Merton as soon as he had had tea.

'It seems very rude to keep you waiting, Mrs Brandon,' she

said, 'but Dr Ford said she must be humoured as much as possible.'

Mrs Brandon said she was in no hurry and as Francis had not yet come she would wait comfortably. So Miss Morris took Mr Merton upstairs and Mrs Brandon, lulled by tea and the hot afternoon, relapsed into a state of semi-consciousness, while the unhappy Mr Grant, torn by hatred of Mr Merton, looked at several large books illustrated by the late Gustave Doré, wishing for the first time in his life that he were an artist, so that he might express his feelings about his rival in an adequate manner. Presently Francis arrived and his mother partially woke up to tell him about Mr Merton. Francis said he remembered him quite well at the Keiths, a very decent sort of fellow.

'And I hope he'll make Aunt Sissie leave everything to the Cats' Home,' he said, 'and serve us all right. What's that you're reading, Hilary? Doré? Those books used to frighten me out of my wits when I was small. There's a lovely one of Arachne turning into a spider with legs simply sprouting out of her. Let's look!'

'Do you remember that spider at Mr Miller's?' said his mother, suddenly regaining complete consciousness.

'A fine British matron she was, too,' said Francis. 'I wonder what happened to her when you threw her out of the window. I expect she walked up the drain pipe and is lurking in your bedroom, Hilary. If she lets herself down from the ceiling on to your face one night, blame mamma.'

'That was the day we first met you, Hilary,' said Mrs Brandon, turning her eyes upon her young relative, who could hardly restrain himself from crying aloud 'God bless you, Mrs Brandon, for remembering that day.' But as Francis was in the room he did restrain himself, though for many days to come the mention of the word spider sent the blood coursing wildly through his veins.

'I can't think what Aunt Sissie wants to talk to Mr Merton about,' said Mrs Brandon.

'You aren't meant to, darling,' said Francis. 'That's why she had Merton to herself instead of having us all in the room at once. You can ask him if you like, but you won't get much change. Hullo, Merton,' he said, as that gentleman came in, 'here

119

you are again. My dear mamma wants to know what devil's work you've been up to with the old lady.'

'Francis, you mustn't say things like that,' said his mother, roused and indignant.

'I am sure that Mrs Brandon hasn't the faintest curiosity about our interview,' said Mr Merton, with a kind of gallantry as from a man of the world to a woman of the world, over the heads of the youngsters, which Mr Grant found inexpressibly galling. 'It was a small matter of business. Mrs Brandon, I am so sorry to have to say good-bye, but I must go back to the Deanery.'

Mrs Brandon shook hands and expressed the hope that Mr Merton would come over and see her one day, an invitation which Mr Grant considered, though showing a divine charity and tolerance, to be entirely misplaced.

'Yes, do,' said Francis. 'We can give you some fairly decent tennis.'

Mr Merton said he would love to and would write to Mrs Brandon, and so took himself off. Mrs Brandon said to Francis what a charming person that Mr Merton was and no wonder all the Keiths liked him so much. Francis quite agreed and Mr Grant gave a hollow mockery of assent. Mrs Brandon then wondered once more why Aunt Sissie wanted them all, yawned and gave it up. By the time that Francis and Mr Grant had exhausted the pleasures of Doré Miss Morris came down again.

'Miss Brandon would be very glad if you could all come up now,' she said, 'and could I speak to you for a moment, Mrs Brandon.'

Mrs Brandon said she would come up with Miss Morris to the sitting-room and asked Francis to show Mr Grant old Mr Brandon's cabinet of dried seaweed and come upstairs in ten minutes.

'No, darling, not the seaweed,' said Francis. 'Hilary doesn't look strong enough. I'll show him the photographs of Venice in the red plush album. They have practically faded altogether so it won't be a tax on the intellect.'

When the ladies reached the sitting-room it was obvious to Mrs Brandon that Miss Morris didn't know how to begin what she wanted to say. It seemed to Mrs Brandon that every friend she had needed winding up before conversation became possible and she kindly applied herself to the task of winding Miss Morris up by asking whether her aunt had been more troublesome than usual. Miss Morris said, No, began to say something else, and stopped.

'Well, what is it?' asked Mrs Brandon in desperation. 'Can I help you at all?'

'It seems a shame to trouble you when you have been so very, very kind to me,' said Miss Morris, 'but I couldn't bear you to misunderstand.'

Visions of Nurse, of Rose, of various holiday governesses, French, German and English, flitted through Mrs Brandon's mind. All had adored her, all had made her life extremely uncomfortable by being jealous of each other and imagining that they had offended her by mistake, or that she was deliberately neglecting them. Nurse and Rose were made of sterner stuff, but all the governesses had cried and had orgies of reconciliation, and Mrs Brandon had once in a fit of exasperation told Sir Edmund that she intended to go into a monastery. Sir Edmund had said he supposed she meant a nunnery and not to talk nonsense, but the idea of a world without women had often charmed her mind, not of course counting sensible women like herself and Mrs Morland and the Dean's wife and a good many more. In Miss Morris she now recognized the stereotyped beginnings of a scene of unnecessary self-abasement which would leave the abased refreshed and strengthened and probably drive herself into a headache as bad as those brought on by being read aloud to.

But she looked at Miss Morris and thought of her dull life, her selfish old father, her poverty, and the really unselfish devotion she had shown to a very tyrannical, self-indulgent, bedridden old lady, and her kind heart melted.

'It wouldn't be a trouble at all,' she said, wondering whether she would be called upon to compose a misunderstanding between Miss Morris and the butler or the housekeeper, or whether Miss Brandon had for once been more outrageously rude than even a paid companion could bear.

'I don't know what you thought when you found Mr Merton here,' said Miss Morris nervously, 'but I can assure you that I didn't know till this morning that he was coming. I usually write

Miss Brandon's letters for her, but she must have written to him herself and given it to Sparks to post.'

'It was very nice to see Mr Merton. I have always heard about him from the Keiths at Southbridge and wanted to meet him.'

'But I mean, I hope you didn't think that I had anything to do with his coming.'

If Mrs Brandon had spoken the truth she would have said that she hadn't thought about it at all, but this would have implied an indifference to her anxious companion which she felt would at once be misinterpreted, so she said she was sure Miss Morris had known nothing about it.

Miss Morris looked grateful, said she couldn't bear to be mis-judged, and stopped short, evidently in need of winding up again. Mrs Brandon looked out of the window. The heat of the long summer afternoon had turned to an oppressive sultriness. The deep unclouded blue of the sky had changed to a fierce copper and though the sun was shining as brightly as ever the sunlight looked baleful. The great trees that surrounded the Abbey and clothed the rising ground before it stood out with unnatural clearness and above them a heavy mass of cloud was slowly rising. A spirt of wind, come and gone in the twinkling of an eye, troubled the tops of the high beeches, and Mrs Brandon wond-ered whether that was a shiver of lightning that ran through the sky, just above the massing clouds. It appeared to her that storm outside and inside the house was to be expected, and with her in-stinct for making things as pleasant as possible she left the ele-ments, which she could not control, to look after themselves, and turned to Miss Morris.

'This is quite an uncomfortable day for everyone,' she said, 'and I expect Aunt Sissie will make it even more uncomfortable, but it is a great comfort to have you here and we are all so grate-ful to you for being so good to Aunt Sissie.'

This, she hoped, would be enough to stem Miss Morris's un-easy desire to grovel, but Miss Morris, with a woman's passion for saying what is far better not put into words, could not be restrained.

'Of course I don't know why Miss Brandon wanted to see Mr Merton,' she said, 'but I do know that his father is her lawyer, and I couldn't bear it if you imagined – people in my position are exposed to all sorts of imaginings – it has happened before when my old ladies have been ill and relations are anxious about things – but I couldn't bear you to think anything like that.'

'But I don't,' said Mrs Brandon, concealing her irritation quite heroically. 'I am perfectly sure that Aunt Sissie will always do exactly what she likes, and in any case what she does is her own affair and none of us will mind in the least what it is. If,' she continued, plunging to the heart of the subject as she heard the voices of the young men in the corridor, 'Aunt Sissie had just made a will and left the Abbey to you, or the Dean of Barchester, or the Salvation Army, we should be perfectly happy.'

'Of course Miss Brandon wouldn't do that,' said Miss Morris, flushing, 'but I did want you to feel that if she did consult Mr Merton about any kind of change in her arrangements I knew nothing about it.'

'No one ever has known anything about Aunt Sissie's wills,' said Mrs Brandon, 'if that is what you mean by arrangements, and I don't suppose they ever will. And now we will forget all about it.'

'I shan't forget your kindness,' said Miss Morris, and was so obviously about to say again that she couldn't bear Mrs Brandon to think what she wasn't thinking, that it was a great relief when Francis and Mr Grant came in. Miss Morris cast one look of slavish devotion towards Mrs Brandon and disappeared into Miss Brandon's room.

'Hilary and I have been admiring the gorillas,' said Francis. 'They wear remarkably well. Do you remember when I put Aunt Sissie's Sunday hat on one of them and how furious she was? She ought to have one of them put up over her tomb; it would look very handsome. And don't tell me not to say that, mamma, because I have said·it.'

'There is going to be a storm,' said Mrs Brandon, looking again at the uneasy sky.

'Not just yet,' said Francis. 'It may even be one of those affairs that go rumble-bumbling all round the hills and then go off and blast an oak at the other end of the county and never come here at all. When does the fun begin?'

'If you mean Aunt Sissie, I don't suppose it will be very

funny,' said Mrs Brandon. 'From the state of poor Miss Morris's nerves I should think Aunt Sissie was in one of her bad moods. I only hope we shall get away before the storm, because I do hate noise.'

Miss Morris now reappeared and said Miss Brandon would like to see them, so they passed into the next room. As usual the blinds were lowered and the curtains half drawn, but Mrs Brandon could see, even in that dim light, that her aunt was greatly changed. The old lady looked as indomitable as ever, but the marks of pain were very evident on her face and she was making an effort to sit up among her pillows. Mrs Brandon took her aunt's hand which lay cold and unresponsive in her own, and said how do you do.

'How do you expect me to do at my age?' said Miss Brandon. 'No, don't go away, Miss Morris. Didn't you hear me say I wanted you. Who is that there? Don't all stand where I can't see you. Oh, Francis. You get more like your father every time I see you, and a poor creature he was. And who is that? Here, young man, which of them are you?'

Mr Grant, struck by the beauty of Mrs Brandon's child-like fear of storms, had been plunged in an exquisite reverie, in the course of which he had been protecting his goddess from the bolts of Jove and she had hidden her lovely face against his shoulder as the thunder crackled and boomed around them. Just as he was saying to her, 'You have nothing to fear, Mrs Brandon, while I am here,' he was rudely awoken by his cousin Francis hitting him in the ribs with his elbow and saying, 'It's Hilary, Aunt Sissie,' and in a lower voice, 'Wake up, you chump.'

'Hilary?' said the old lady. 'Edward Grant's son. Your mother has been writing to me, Hilary. She wants to come and see me. Tell her I won't see her. All I want is to die in peace, and you all come crowding into my bedroom.'

Each of Miss Brandon's visitors felt that this remark was very unfair. They had come at her summons, unwillingly, to satisfy the whim of an ill, lonely aunt, and to be accused of crowding her bedroom was hard to bear.

'I don't very well see how Hilary can tell his mother that,' said Mrs Brandon. 'Let him say that you aren't well.'

'I was never better in my life,' said Miss Brandon angrily. 'I suppose the boy is frightened of his mother. Why don't you all sit down.'

Mrs Brandon took an armchair near her redoubtable aunt's bed and the young men sat a little further away. Francis amused and already a little bored, Mr Grant in a very uncomfortable turmoil of emotions. His aunt's words had gone too near the mark to be pleasant. If he dared to face facts he had to admit this, his mother had more power over him than he liked.

It was not that she made any very unreasonable demands, but her whole attitude to him was that any work he was doing was unimport nt and he never felt safe from her unless she were abroad. His visits to Italy were a sacrifice, for he knew that he would never be allowed to work in peace, but with the good-nature that he inheri.ed from his easy-going father he gave in to his mother's exigencies and managed to get his reading done early in the morning and late at night, and took a very tolerable degree. There had been one moment, at the memory of which he still was shaken with fear, when Mrs Grant, after a quarrel with some Italian authorities had thought of settling in Oxford, imagining that Hilary could live with her and as it were do his homework under her eye. Luckily this scheme had come to nothing and she had remained abroad, but in her short visit to Pomfret Madrigal she had managed to devastate his working hours with her demands that Hilary should walk with her, give her advice that she never took on her Italian affairs, tell her all about what he was reading, and worst of all dine with her at the Cow and Sickle and sit talking or rather being talked to, till the small hours of the morning. He had managed to get through these evenings by withdrawing his mind into itself and indulging in dreams of Mrs Brandon, but he could not master the growing irritation that assailed him whenever he heard the clash of his mother's necklaces, or her voice calling gaily from the garden below his window with some caressing Italian diminutive, which would, he was sure, afford far too much pleasure to Mr Miller's staff.

Again and again he blamed himself for these feelings of irritation, for ingratitude towards a mother who was very fond of him and supported him in comfort; repeatedly did he make good resolutions of patience and forbearance and self-control which broke down as soon as they were made. By the end of the week that his mother spent at the Cow and Sickle he was barely able to control his annoyance and had indeed so far forgotten himself once or twice as to give a snappy or sulky answer, which had caused him subsequent agonies of remorse and even indigestion. To all these emotions his mother was sublimely unconscious, and had now gone off to Lady Norton with the happy assurance that she had cheered up her son in his dull country retreat. As for his Aunt Sissie's remark he could only hope that neither of the Brandons would notice it, and went hot with shame and misery in the darkened room.

'Well,' continued the old lady, 'I suppose you all want to know why I sent for Noel Merton.'

Mr Grant was too far sunk in misery to care. Francis said under his breath that he was damned if he did. Mrs Brandon, with some vague, amorphous idea of saving the situation, was the only one with courage to answer.

'I have never met Mr Merton before, Aunt Sissie,' she said, 'but I had heard about him a great deal from the Keiths at South-bridge. Young Colin Keith is reading law with him, and he was down there for Kate Keith's wedding. He was very amusing about Lydia. He really seems very delightful and I have asked him to come to Stories next time he is at the Deanery.'

During this quite unnecessary speech Miss Brandon had been eyeing her niece by marriage with a stony intensity that penetrated even Mrs Brandon's placid mind. Her voice faltered and trailed away and she sat silent.

'I have said before and shall say it again,' said Miss Brandon, 'that you are one of the silliest women I know, Lavinia, and if Henry were here I should say there were a couple of you. I didn't send for you to hear about the wedding of some young woman in whom I have no interest at all. I have something to tell you and propose to tell it without further interruption.' She picked up some papers from the table by her bed and began sorting them. 'I can't see,' she said angrily. 'Pull the blind up, Miss Morris. How do you expect me to see in the dark?'

Miss Morris began to walk round the great bed to get to the

window, but Francis, who was sitting near it, got up and pulled the blind cord.

'Not too much,' said his aunt warningly.

'Of course not, Aunt Sissie,' he said kindly. 'I think just like this will be enough for you. Hullo, there's a car at the front door.'

'A car?' said the invalid. 'Whose car? No one has any business to bring cars here.'

'I can't see whose, Aunt Sissie,' said Francis, 'except that it's a Rolls, but the county is rather well off in Rollses, so it might be anyone. I think cars ought to have the names of their owners painted very large on the roof so that one could see who is there and not open the front door.'

'Don't talk nonsense,' said the old lady. 'Cars indeed! When I was younger we knew all our friends' carriages by sight, and their horses and their coachmen and footmen. Go and see whose car it is, Miss Morris. I will not have cars in my drive.'

Miss Morris again started on her errand, but again was interrupted. There was a knock at the door and Sparks came in.

'Who is that?' said Miss Brandon. 'Oh, you, Sparks. Well, go and see what all this fuss is about a car at the front door. I will not have strange cars at the front door.'

'It is Lady Norton, miss,' said Sparks, 'and she wants to know how you are, and would like to come up and see you.'

'Tell her I'm quite well and seeing nobody,' said the invalid.

'I did, miss,' said Sparks, 'but there was another lady with her, miss, and she said she must see you because she wasn't in England for long.'

Mr Grant knew that Providence had now reached the end of its tether. Nothing it chose to do to him in the future would have the slightest effect. Let it heap thunders, cataracts, mountains, whirlwinds on his devoted head, he would stand erect, shrug his shoulders and simply say 'Ha-ha.' Meanwhile he greatly wished that he could get under the bed or into a wardrobe, and become practically unconscious. Francis murmured 'Golly' in tones of deep appreciation and prepared himself to enjoy the scene.

'Tell Mrs Grant I can't see anyone. I am very ill,' said Miss Brandon. 'Tell her at once, Sparks, and don't be a fool.'

Sparks looked nervously over her shoulder, opened her mouth, but never got as far as speech, for a noise was heard in the sitting-room, the door was opened, a voice said, 'I have come to see how you are, Amelia,' and in came a tall middle-aged woman in black, with the face of a distinguished horse and the unmistakable air of authority that the best garden in the county gives. Mrs Brandon recognized Lady Norton and felt that events were entirely out of control.

'Well, here I am, a dying old woman, Victoria,' said Miss Brandon, 'and now you can go away again.'

'Nonsense,' said Lady Norton. 'You need cheering up, Amelia. I see you have some visitors. That's very sensible. And I have brought one of my visitors over to see you; Felicia Grant, poor Edward's widow.'

Mrs Grant, who had been almost hidden behind Lady Norton's imposing bulk, came forward with a rattle of coral and amber.

'I have been looking forward to seeing you for a long time, Cousin Sissie,' she said. 'Edward always wanted me to. So when Lady Norton offered to bring me over, I came.'

The noble simplicity of this remark did not appear to affect Miss Brandon, who very disconcertingly shut her eyes and made no reply.

'I was so glad that Hilary had been to see you,' Mrs Grant continued, 'and what luck it is to find him here to-day, and Mrs Brandon and Francis.'

'I said I didn't want to see you,' said Miss Brandon, her eyes still tightly shut, 'and I don't, and what's more I won't.'

'Come, come, Amelia,' said Lady Norton, who had been talking to Mrs Brandon, but the invalid remained silent and blind, merely expressing her dislike of her visitors by playing five finger exercises on her sheet. Mrs Brandon and Lady Norton tried to make a little conversation, but the weight of Miss Brandon's disapproval was too heavy and their voices died away.

'Good-bye,' said Miss Brandon very distinctly.

Lady Norton said she supposed they had better be going. It was useless to try to shake hands with a hostess who was drumming on the bedclothes with her eyes shut, so Lady Norton, not without dignity, made her farewells to Mrs Brandon and Francis, expressed pleasure at having met Hilary, and retreated in good order, carrying Mrs Grant with her.

'See them out, Sparks,' said Miss Brandon, and Sparks followed the visitors, shutting the door behind them.

'And now what have you all to say for yourselves?' said Miss Brandon, opening her eyes and folding her bejewelled hands.

'Well, nothing, Aunt Sissie,' said Mrs Brandon truthfully. 'We came because you asked us to, and here we are. I expect you feel a little tired now, so perhaps we'd better go.'

'Wait a moment,' said Miss Brandon. 'Put my pillows a little higher, Miss Morris.'

Miss Morris came forward, re-arranged the pillows, and helped her employer to raise her unwieldy bulk. The effort obviously cost Miss Brandon a good deal of pain, but for once she made no complaint. Only when the move was accomplished did she utter a kind of grunt and told Miss Morris to get the brandy quickly. Miss Morris measured a tablespoon in a medicine glass and gave it to Miss Brandon.

'And now,' said Miss Brandon, handing the glass back to Miss Morris, 'if you want to know why I asked you to come here it doesn't matter. Noel Merton knows what I had to say, and that's quite enough. I'm an ill old woman and if Victoria Norton sees fit to let fools come into my room and upset me, I can't be blamed for the consequences. Why poor Edward Grant married that woman I never could imagine. A pretentious, selfish woman if ever there was one. I told her I wouldn't see her and I didn't. You can blame your fool of a mother, Hilary Grant, for anything that happens now.'

Mr Grant had been wishing that his mother had never been born, or were a thousand leagues away, but trying as she was, she was still his mother and all the chivalry in him was aroused. It was not easy to defend what he secretly felt to be almost indefensible, or to hold his own against a domineering old lady who was quite capable of deliberately having a fit if crossed, and who had also expressed some liking for him. He longed for Francis's easy assurance, which might have turned the whole thing off as a joke and restored their aunt to some kind of good humour. A thousand years of fright, misery, indecision, seemed to him to have passed before he replied with the slight stammer that nervousness always made him produce.

'I'm sorry, Aunt Sissie, if mother's coming upset you, but I expect she is pretty upset, too, and I'm going to see if she needs me, so good-bye.'

'I said the boy was frightened of his mother,' said Miss Brandon.

If an unseen enemy had suddenly hit Mr Grant in the face he could hardly have suffered more. The knowledge that what his aunt said was partly true, his loyalty to his mother, the extreme distastefulness of the whole scene, the unreality of this half lighted room, the helpless, venomous old lady in the great bed, the consciousness that Mrs Brandon and Francis and Miss Morris were spectators, however unwillingly, of his humiliation, even the increasing sultriness in the atmosphere outside, all were arrayed against him. As he spoke he was facing the window through which Francis had seen Lady Norton's car. The blind was still drawn up. Mrs Brandon saw him turn so pale and then flush so deeply that she was afraid.

'Good-bye, Aunt Sissie,' he said again, and made a step towards the door, but Mrs Brandon said 'Hilary' and slipped her arm through his, so that he had to stand still.

'Really, Aunt Sissie,' she said, 'Mrs Grant may be a little trying, but after all if Lady Norton brought her she couldn't very well help it, and she is just as much a relation of yours as I am. It was nothing to do with Hilary at all. In fact it was really more Lady Norton's fault. So perhaps we had better all go now.'

No one in the room could quite appreciate the heroism underlying this unnecessary, muddle-headed, and on the whole quite unhelpful speech. Francis thought, with amusement, that mother was trying to see everything in as pleasant a light as possible by burying her head in the sand. Mr Grant, wishing that he could have a whole bottle of champagne, or mercifully faint, was only conscious that Mrs Brandon was trying to defend him, and despised himself more than ever. Miss Morris was divided between anxiety for her difficult employer and nervousness at finding herself assisting at a family scene and it is probable that Miss Brandon herself was the only member of the party to appreciate her niece's courage, though she had no intention of admitting it.

'Don't be a fool, Lavinia,' she said sharply. 'Hilary is quite old enough to look after himself. He doesn't need a woman old enough to be his mother hanging round his neck.'

At these words Mr Grant felt the hand that was laid on his arm tremble, though ever so slightly. He took it, pressed it in gratitude, and let Mrs Brandon withdraw it. There was a moment's tense, uncomfortable silence, not improved by a sudden, aimless flash of lightning from the livid sky. Then Francis in a detached voice that barely concealed a white-hot fury said,

'I had better take mother home, Aunt Sissie, and I think it will be better if none of us come here again for the present. Do you agree, Hilary?'

Mr Grant uttered a strangled Yes.

'Good-bye, Aunt Sissie,' said Francis. 'Good-bye, Miss Morris,' and he herded his mother and his cousin out of the room.

'Oh, Miss Morris, I left the apricot slip in a parcel on the hall table,' said Mrs Brandon, turning in the doorway. 'It might just need taking up a little on the shoulders, but I do hope you'll like it.'

Miss Morris made a step towards Mrs Brandon but a call from her employer stopped her, and Francis hustled his mother out and shut the door.

'Help me to lie down again,' said Miss Brandon.

With some difficulty the old lady was rearranged in bed.

'Pull that blind down again,' she said to her companion, 'and read to me for a little.'

Miss Morris took up the book on which they were engaged and began to read. Her employer lay very still and Miss Morris hoped she might be sleeping. When she came to the end of a chapter she paused. Miss Brandon still lay quiet and Miss Morris was assailed by a sudden fear that she might be in a faint, or even dying, after the conditions of the afternoon.

'I suppose you think I am a wicked old woman,' said Miss Brandon, without heat.

'I am afraid Mrs Brandon will be very unhappy,' said Miss Morris.

'Not she,' said Miss Brandon. 'She has a mind like a feather-bed, always had. I wish I could think Edward's wife would be unhappy. What a conceited fool that woman is. I feel really sorry for Hilary.'

'Mr Grant is very nice,' said Miss Morris non-committally, 'and so is Mr Francis Brandon.'

'Oh, you are taking sides too, are you,' said Miss Brandon. 'Well, you can think what you like, but I have spoken my mind to Noel Merton and that's the end. Shut the window and turn the lights on. I can't bear thunder.'

Miss Morris did as she was told and came back to the bed. Her employer, her frilled nightcap a little askew, looked at her with an expression that she could not fathom, a compound of secrecy, amusement, and a tolerance that she was not used to.

'So you stick up for the Brandons, do you?' said the old lady. 'Very well, very well. You're not the first one that has liked Lavinia Brandon, though she is nearly as big a fool as Edward's wife. Fred would have liked Lavinia. That's why I gave her his diamond ring. She is like Mrs Colonel Arbuthnot that Fred got into such hot water over. She was a fool too, but as pretty as they make them. Yes, Fred would have liked her to have the ring and a good deal more besides,' said Miss Brandon with a chuckle of terrifying archness. 'Go on reading. It keeps the thunder out of my head. Fred wouldn't have looked at you.'

'No, I suppose not,' said Miss Morris.

'But someone else might,' said Miss Brandon, 'when I'm dead. Go on with the book. I think I shall fancy my dinner to-night.'

Miss Morris, puzzled, but resigned to the ways of her old ladies, went on reading. Outside the lightning leapt, the thunder crackled and boomed, the rain came down in torrents.

The Brandons and Mr Grant found speech extremely difficult as they went downstairs and into the drawing-room. Mrs Brandon didn't really mind being called a fool, a name which her aunt had freely bestowed upon her on various occasions, and confessed very simply in her own heart that she was one. But to see poor Hilary, who was already so nervous that one often couldn't quite make out what he was saying, and stammered so much over reading his book aloud that one often thought of other things, so baited and badgered, was more than one could bear. Aunt Sissie calling one old enough to be his mother didn't matter, because one was, and the statement was perfectly reasonable, but that he should hear himself accused of sheltering behind her and feeling it with all his sensitiveness made her really angry. In fact when Aunt Sissie let loose those words she had been so shaken by sudden anger that it took Hilary's kind pressure of her hand to make her control herself. Such fresh annoyance surged up in her that she felt she would like to be very cross with someone, a feeling very alien to her gentle nature.

Nor was Mr Grant less furious. His mother had been insulted, not but what she jolly well deserved it for coming meddling with everyone and he wished fervently for the hundredth time that she had stayed in Calabria, but still she was his mother. And far, far worse, Mrs Brandon had been insulted. She had tried to prevent his leaving his aunt in anger, she had taken his arm, she had said 'Hilary', enduing his name with a magic that he had never before known it to possess, she had tried to protect him, she, an exquisite delicate creature, unfitted for harshness and brutal words. When Miss Brandon called her a fool, he had felt her hand tremble. Good God! that such a woman should be tortured on his account. Blast Aunt Sissie! Blast his mother for bringing shame on him and shame on the woman he respectfully adored! Blast everything! He kicked violently at a hassock, which hit a hideous vase that stood against the wall with peacocks' feathers in it and knocked it over.

'Here, look out,' said Francis sharply, for in spite of his assurance he was still fuming with suppressed rage at his aunt's rudeness to his mother and ready to fall foul of anyone. 'Look out. You needn't break Aunt Sissie's things, even if she is an old devil. Yes, mother, I said devil and I meant it, and if you don't like it I can't help it.'

'Oh, all right, all right,' said Mr Grant. 'I haven't broken the beastly thing and I don't want to. I wouldn't touch anything in this house with a barge pole.'

'Well, no one asked you to,' said Francis, and then the heavens suddenly opened and the thunder resounded from the roof-tree, the lightning looked as if it were going to shrivel every tree in the garden, and rain came down hissing and bubbling and steaming.

'Shall we have to drive home through this?' asked Mrs Brandon.

'Well, there isn't any other way,' said Francis, 'and I'm not going to stop in this house if I were paid for it. Isn't Curwen round with the car? I told them to tell him.'

He rang the bell impatiently and repeated his inquiry. It was then revealed by the butler that Curwen had understood Mr Francis to say he was going to drive Mrs Brandon and Mr Grant back in his own car, and so had taken Mrs Brandon's car home.

'All right,' said Francis. 'Of course the roof leaks and I haven't got a spare tyre, but that's all part of the fun. Come along, mother.'

Mr Grant rushed into the hall, wildly hoping to put a coat about Mrs Brandon and shelter her from the storm as she went down the steps, or perish in the attempt, but was immediately frustrated by the butler, who produced an enormous carriage umbrella and held it over her head.

'You'd better get in behind, mother,' said Francis, 'it doesn't leak so much there. You come in front, Hilary, and keep the windscreen wiper going, because it usually sticks.'

Luckily the temperature had not dropped with the rising storm and Mrs Brandon in the back seat of the car, where the leak was barely perceptible, was warm enough, and would have been quite comfortable had not her jangled nerves decided that Francis was driving too fast and taking unnecessary risks. In a crescendo of hysteria she gave instructions to her son which though they drove him nearly mad he bore very well. Even Mr Grant, occupied as he was in pushing the reluctant windscreen wiper to do its duty, in avoiding the steady drip that fell on to the seat between him and Francis, felt a slight irritation mingle with his adoration. By the time they had got through Barchester, skidding on the tram lines, both young men were with difficulty restraining their temper. At Stories Mr Grant got quickly out and ran round to open the car door, but again was thwarted by Rose, who descended, umbrella and raincoat in hand and assisted her mistress into the house.

'I don't suppose you mind if I don't drive you home,' said

Francis. 'I want to put my car away and blow Curwen up. I'm sopped as it is. Why you couldn't catch some of that drip in your hat or something I don't know. And mother cackling like a hen all the time. She's as bad as yours.'

Without a word Mr Grant turned away and walked into the rainy evening, with such thoughts in his mind as he did not care to examine. He found that Mr Miller was dining at the Deanery and Cook, misunderstanding his instructions, had let the kitchen fire out, and Hettie had gone home. Mr Grant said he didn't want any dinner and banged out of the house again. Cook with kindly tolerance put the cold ham and the loaf and butter in the dining-room, and when Mr Grant came in a little later, defeated by the weather and wetter than ever, he was glad to partake of it. When Mr Miller came back at eleven o'clock he found his pupil so hard at work that he very kindly didn't tell him how he had put the Dean down on a quotation from St Augustine, and went rather disappointed to bed, hoping that his unselfishness might be counted to him for righteousness and then reproaching himself for the hope.

Meanwhile Francis, having failed to find Curwen, who was at the Cow and Sickle playing darts with Mr Spindler and Wheeler from the garage, dressed very crossly for dinner, at which meal Delia appeared with red eyes and a swollen face. She had, she explained, been over to Grumper's End to see how the chicken pox was getting on, and on the way back a field mouse had somehow got under her bicycle and been killed. First Aid was of no avail for a squashed mouse, and she said, and indeed looked it, that she had been crying ever since. Mrs Brandon was very sorry about the mouse, but felt compelled to speak to her son Francis again about his driving, thus causing Francis, who hardly ever lost his temper, to have the sulks. Any discussion of the dreadful afternoon they had gone through became impossible and when after dinner Delia, to show her grief, put on all the most depressing crooners' records, it seemed a suitable end to a very unsuccessful day. About half-past nine Sir Edmund looked in and Delia was told to stop playing the gramophone.

'Well Lavinia,' said Sir Edmund, 'had a good day, eh? How's Amelia Brandon?'

To the best of her ability Mrs Brandon described the scene in Miss Brandon's bedroom and expressed the view that if Miss Brandon ever was going to leave anyone anything she now wouldn't, and that she, Mrs Brandon, would be very glad if the Abbey and all the money went to the Salvation Army, so long as she might never hear of it again.

'Mustn't say that, Lavinia. Not the way to talk at all,' said Sir Edmund. 'And what's the matter with Delia, eh? Got a cold? Nasty things colds at this time of year.'

Mrs Brandon was just going to explain what had happened when Nurse appeared at the door. Seeing Sir Edmund she prepared to withdraw with such ostentatious discretion that her mistress was obliged to ask what the matter was.

'It's only Miss Delia's knickers, madam,' said Nurse in a stage whisper. 'I'd be glad if she could come and try them on before she goes to bed so that I can finish them to-night.'

'Go along then, darling,' said Mrs Brandon, 'and perhaps you'd better not come down again if you are too unhappy.'

Delia, sniffing loudly, left the room in Nurse's wake.

'Well, I won't be staying,' said Sir Edmund, not enjoying this depressing domestic atmosphere. 'Good night, Lavinia.'

'Need you go?' said Mrs Brandon, stretching out a hand towards Sir Edmund.

'Now don't try your tricks on me, Lavinia,' said Sir Edmund. 'See you again soon. Good night. Good night, Francis.'

Francis took Sir Edmund to the door. When he got back to the drawing-room he met Rose leaving it with an expression of injured but triumphant virtue.

'Anything up with Rose?' he asked his mother.

'Yes. Nurse's sewing machine has gone wrong, and she asked Rose to lend her the kitchen machine and Rose says she supposes Nurse must have it.'

'That's all right then,' said Francis.

'Yes, but Nurse won't come down and fetch it, and Rose won't carry it up, and the housemaids are out till half-past ten.'

Francis looked at his mother. Then, for the first time since they left Miss Brandon's room, he began to laugh. His mother began to laugh too.

'Well, to hell with old Mother Grant for all the trouble she has brought on us to-day,' said Francis. 'Go along to bed, darling, and I'll put the lights out. What a day! What a day!'

– 7 –

BAD NEWS AT STORIES

By the following morning the storm had rumbled itself away and the weather was as brilliant and hot as ever, though with a pleasant rain-washed freshness. Francis, strolling into the garden before breakfast, was seized by Turpin and taken to admire the giant marrow which had apparently put on several pounds in the night. Turpin expressed the opinion that by the day of the Harvest Festival she would be a whopper.

'When is the Festival?' Francis asked.

Turpin told him the date, a few weeks ahead, and said he also intended to send up some flowers and garden produce for the Feet.

'Good Lord, yes, the Feet,' said Francis. 'That's Saturday week, isn't it? I must lay in some threepences for the coconuts and whatnots.'

Turpin said he didn't hold with them new threepennies, characterizing them as mucky.

'Hardly the *mot juste* for a nice new shining threepence,' said Francis, 'but never mind. Good luck with the marrow.'

He went back to the house. His mother was having breakfast in her room and he was able to tell Delia, now happily recovered from the death of the field mouse, all about the scene at the Abbey. Delia listened with great interest.

'I wish I'd been there,' she said. 'I'd have asked to look at Aunt Sissie's legs. That would have calmed her down all right. You haven't seen them, have you?'

Francis shudderingly said he hadn't, and didn't wish to discuss the matter at breakfast.

'It was the time I went alone with mother, when you were in

France. They were simply *ghastly*,' said Delia with simple enthusiasm, 'and she was ever so bucked at my seeing them. But she had no business to come down on Hilary. If I'd been there I'd have stopped it.'

'Poor old Hilary,' said Francis. 'It was tough luck to be told you are frightened of one woman and sheltering behind another. He looked pretty rotten.'

'Poor Hilary,' Delia echoed, with almost as much compassion as she had shown for the mouse.

'But mother stood up for him like a Trojan,' said Francis. 'I really thought he might be going to faint or something, he looked so queer. He doesn't know Aunt Sissie as well as we do. I must say I got annoyed myself when she started letting off at mother. Next time Aunt Sissie wants to be rude she can just be rude to old Sparks, or Miss Morris. I'm not going there again. Well, I must be off.'

He kissed the top of his sister's head and went off to Barchester. Delia remained at the breakfast table, considering what Francis had said. The thought of Aunt Sissie bullying Hilary made her unaccountably angry. He was so obviously the sort that couldn't look after himself. People who wrote books might be brainy, but they were never quite all there in Delia's opinion, and needed someone with some sense to look after them. It had been just like mother to try to help anyone who was in trouble, but Delia felt that if she had been there she would not only have protected Hilary just as well, but have carried the war into the enemy's country and routed Aunt Sissie thoroughly.

As she was thinking these thoughts she looked up and saw Mr Grant walking about in the drive.

'Hullo, Hilary,' she yelled out of the window. 'Hang on a moment and I'll come out.'

She bolted the rest of her toast and marmalade, took two peaches and went into the garden.

'Have a peach,' she said, handing one to Mr Grant. 'You'd better put your face well forward while you eat it, or it'll all run down your front.'

Mr Grant took her advice and the peaches were eaten.

'Francis was telling me about Aunt Sissie,' said Delia. 'What a beast she must have been. Francis said he thought you were going to pass out.'

'I simply couldn't bear her being so rude to your mother,' said Mr Grant.

'Oh, mother's all right,' said Delia, with the fine confidence of the young that their elders have no feelings at all. 'She never much notices what Aunt Sissie says.'

Mr Grant felt sorry that Mrs Brandon's daughter should be so entirely destitute of sensibility.

'I'll tell you what I wish,' said Delia. 'I wish Aunt Sissie had thrown her stick at you and broken your arm or your leg. Then they'd have had to send for Dr Ford to set it, and I'd have come and helped him. I'm awfully good at that sort of thing. And then I'd have told Aunt Sissie exactly what we all thought of her.'

She gazed at her cousin with an intensity which made him feel that she might rush at him and fracture one of his limbs for the sheer pleasure of helping Dr Ford to set it.

'When Herb Thatcher, that's Jimmy Thatcher's brother down at Grumper's End, broke his arm, I was there and made a splint till the doctor came. It was splendid. But it wasn't Dr Ford, and the other man set it wrong and I got Mrs Thatcher to let Dr Ford see it, and they had to take Herb to the Barchester Hospital and break it again and re-set it, and they wouldn't let me come and see,' said Delia with sad indignation.

'Do you think your mother is in?' said Mr Grant.

'Of course,' said Delia, not at all surprised that her cousin wanted her mother rather than herself. 'I expect she's up now. Come and look.'

She led the way into the hall. Mrs Brandon was just hanging up the telephone receiver. There was on her face a peculiar expression of self-consciousness and amusement and a little pride which Mr Grant couldn't understand, but which if Sir Edmund had been there, he would infallibly have diagnosed as Lavinia up to her tricks again.

'Good morning, Hilary,' she said. 'I do hope you didn't get wet last night.'

'Not a bit,' said Mr Grant untruthfully.

'That was Mr Merton, that we met at the Abbey,' said Mrs

Brandon. 'He rang up to say how sorry he was he couldn't get over to see us, but he wants to come next time he is at the Deanery or the Keiths. You'd like him, Delia.'

'Well, I think I'd better go back and do some work,' said Mr Grant, hating people who rang people up and said they would come and see them.

'Oh, must you?' said Mrs Brandon. 'I thought perhaps you were going to read to me.'

'Well, I had got a few pages on me,' said Mr Grant, going scarlet. 'I was just walking about a bit and saw Delia, so I came in. I hope you don't mind.'

'Always come in,' said Mrs Brandon. 'I've got to see Cook and do a few things, but do read to Delia, and then I'll join you later.'

So saying she drifted away to her sitting-room, still wearing her peculiar happy, mischievous smile. Mr Grant gazed longingly after her.

'Will you really read me some of your book?' asked Delia humbly.

'Would you really like it?' asked Mr Grant, with almost equal diffidence.

'Rather. I've never had a real book read to me,' said Delia, apparently thinking that manuscript made a book more real than print.

'Well, it isn't exactly a *real* book,' said Mr Grant. 'I mean it hasn't been published or anything and I dare say it never will be.'

'Of course it will,' said Delia. 'All books get published. Just look what loads there are of them.'

On hearing these encouraging words Mr Grant's opinion of his cousin rose considerably, and accompanying her to a bench in the garden he began reading. Curiously enough it seemed easier to read to Delia than to her mother. Although he missed Mrs Brandon's inspiration he found that it was pleasant not to be interrupted and pleasant to have an audience that paid attention to what one was reading. He also discovered that Delia, who had spent a year in Paris with a family, had read a great deal of the romantic school of poetry and actually knew one poem of Jehan le Capet's which was in an anthology. All this was balm to an author and disposed him to regard his cousin even more favourably.

Delia, flattered beyond words at Hilary's condescension, drank in every sentence, admired Hilary's French accent, which was indeed very good, and secretly determined to boast to her friend Lydia Keith when next they met of how her cousin who was an author had read aloud a real book to her that no one else had heard.

'Shall I go on?' asked Mr Grant when he had come to the end of the third chapter.

'I'd love it, but I don't think I could *bear* it,' said Delia, who was nearly bursting with admiration of the writing and sentimental pity for le Capet, whose fourth mistress had just abandoned him for an elderly *commis voyageur* taking with her his mother's portrait and ninety francs. And Mr Grant not only understood this peculiar tribute, but was pleased by it.

'It is a bit powerful,' he admitted. 'Perhaps a bit too powerful. I wonder if the public will stand it. But one must tell the truth at all costs.'

Delia said one must, and both young people fell silent, reflecting upon the beauty of this axiom, till Mrs Brandon drifted out to them and asked if the reading had begun. On hearing that it was over she sat down on the bench and said how nice and wouldn't they like to get some gooseberries.

Mr Grant was just elaborating in his mind a plan for picking a dozen of the largest and ripest gooseberries and bringing them to Mrs Brandon on a particularly fine rhubarb leaf, when Rose came out to say that Dr Ford wanted to speak to Mrs Brandon. She was closely followed by Dr Ford himself, whose determination to go and find Mrs Brandon in the rose garden was as great as Rose's determination to keep the flag of convention flying by announcing him properly.

'Come and have some gooseberries, Dr Ford,' said Delia. 'There are some lovely red ones that burst all over you.'

'No thanks,' said Dr Ford. 'I've been at the Abbey this morning and as I had to go over to Southbridge I thought I'd look in and tell you I don't like the look of things.'

141

'Do you mean Aunt Sissie is worse?' asked Mrs Brandon.

Dr Ford said he had sent for a nurse and wouldn't be surprised if she didn't last out the night.

'How dreadful,' said Mrs Brandon. 'You don't think we killed her, do you, Dr Ford?'

'I shouldn't think so,' said Dr Ford. 'Did you try to?'

'No, no,' said Mrs Brandon, 'but we were there yesterday and she was very mysterious, and when Lady Norton and Mrs Grant came it was really quite unpleasant, and Hilary really behaved very well, with the storm working up all the time, and I was afraid she might feel it.'

'I'm glad I'm not having to cross-examine you, Mrs Brandon,' said Dr Ford. 'Grant, you seem to have been there. Can you tell me what really happened?'

Mr Grant explained that Miss Brandon had apparently been going to tell them something about her testamentary dispositions when Lady Norton and his mother, for whom Miss Brandon had a strong dislike, had more or less forced their way in and been summarily ejected.

'And then Aunt Sissie was *beastly* to Hilary,' Delia broke in indignantly. 'Francis told me, and he said Hilary behaved splendidly.'

'You needn't be alarmed,' said Dr Ford. 'The old lady thrives on rows, and one more or less wouldn't hurt her, in fact it probably bucked her up. Judging from what Miss Morris told me about the supper she insisted on eating last night I should say it was the effect of acute indigestion on a weak heart. I'm going to see her again this evening and I'll ring you up.'

He then departed as unceremoniously as he had arrived, followed by Rose's silent scorn.

The immediate and peculiar effect of this news was to make Mrs Brandon suddenly become an invalid and the centre of attraction. Mr Grant and Delia didn't know what to say, both secretly feeling the deep resentment of the young that their elders should do anything disturbing or unusual. This sentiment in Delia's case was complicated by a burning desire to be in at the death, if death there was to be, combined with a certain diffidence in mentioning her wish and the conviction that her mother would not allow it. The tension was broken by the arrival of Nurse, holding something pink.

'I'm sure I didn't know you weren't alone, madam,' she said, looking right through Mr Grant in a disconcerting way, 'or I wouldn't have come out. I saw Dr Ford with you and I said to myself I won't go down just now as Dr Ford is with madam and then I saw him go so I said, Well now madam is alone it will be a good chance to show her Miss Delia's – '

'Dr Ford brought some very upsetting news, Nurse,' said Mrs Brandon, automatically drooping like the flower which the rough ploughshare has touched. 'Miss Brandon is very ill again and he is afraid she won't last out the night.'

'Oh dear, I *am* shocked about that,' said Nurse, in intense enjoyment. 'Shall I get you a cushion, madam?'

'Thank you so much, Nurse,' said Mrs Brandon in a dying voice.

'Couldn't I go and get it?' asked Mr Grant, longing to be of some use and atone for his share in yesterday's crime.

'No, I'll look after madam,' said Nurse in her most nursish voice. 'You and Miss Delia go along now, Mr Hilary. There's some nice gooseberries ripe under the nets.'

Not otherwise had Mr Grant been addressed in his early youth by his own Nannie when she told him not to bother her asking questions but run along and play. Bitterly did he resent the implication that he was worse than useless in a moment of crisis, but realizing that the rites of the Bona Dea were about to be accomplished he felt he would be safer elsewhere and looked at Delia for help.

'You can just stay here a minute while I get a cushion,' said Nurse, and sped away to the house.

'I say, I'm awfully sorry,' said Mr Grant.

Mrs Brandon closed her eyes, looking, as Mr Grant put it to himself, like a martyred saint, and murmured:

'Come and see me this afternoon, Hilary. I shan't be so silly then.'

At these beautiful and unselfish words Mr Grant's heart swelled to such an extent that he was nearly choked, but Nurse's return dispelled romance and he gladly followed Delia to the gooseberry nets.

'It seems so sudden,' said Mrs Brandon. 'Thank you, Nurse, that cushion is just what I wanted.'

As her aunt had been bed-ridden with a weak heart and might have died at any moment for several years, this remark was a tribute rather to her own imagination than to any actual fact, but Nurse thoroughly agreed with her, adding that her own stepsister, who was thirty years older than she was, had been taken just like that.

'I'd like to get some sherry or something, madam,' said Nurse, 'but I don't like to leave you.'

Mrs Brandon with rare heroism said she was all right and only needed to pull herself together and get over it, when by a heaven-sent chance Cook came into the garden to speak to her mistress about making some gooseberry jam.

'Oh, Cook,' said Nurse, who was surveying her cushion-supported mistress with the air of an artist, 'I'm so glad you've come. Dr Ford had some shocking news. It seems poor Miss Brandon is taken worse and they don't expect she'll last the night. I was just going to ask Rose to get a glass of sherry for madam, but I didn't like to leave her.'

'Well, I *am* sorry, mum,' said Cook, who had never seen Miss Brandon and only heard of her as a paragon of bad temper. 'The poor old lady. That's what my tea-leaves meant last night. You remember, Nurse, when you was in the kitchen about Rose's machine, I said there was a funeral in my cup.'

Nurse said she well remembered, and how it had given her quite a funny feeling, for which she could not at the moment account, but which in the light of subsequent events was all too clear, and that they did say the tea-leaves never lied. But there she was standing chattering, she exclaimed, suddenly taking on the bright air of the professional nurse, when what madam needed was a glass of sherry.

'I couldn't touch sherry,' said Mrs Brandon weakly. 'Do you think, Cook, I could have a cup of tea?'

Cook, seeing the chance of a lifetime to get in first with a really exciting piece of news, said she would have the kettle boiling in a moment and tell Rose to get the tray ready. She had left the kettle, she said, nearly on the boil, because she was going to scald the tomatoes for the salad which was much the easiest way to get their skins off, so if she ran back it would be just on the boil, only she must hurry, because when a kettle had come to the boil the water wasn't the same and she wouldn't like to keep madam waiting while she filled the kettle and brought it up to the boil again. Nurse, who had been torn between a wish to be the first to bear the glad tidings to the kitchen and a feeling that she would have scored heavily against Rose by being the first to succour her mistress, decided to keep her position of vantage, and encouraged Cook to go back and get the tea as soon as possible. The kettle must have been exactly on the boil, for in an incredibly short space of time Rose appeared, carrying a tray. Sinking their differences in the face of the common danger, she and Nurse united in tending their mistress, sparing her every effort except that of actually swallowing the tea. Mrs Brandon, who was very much enjoying the fuss and feeling extremely well, then dismissed her attendants and went back to the house. Both the handmaids besought her to have a nice lay down before lunch, but finding her obdurate they retired to the kitchen, loud in praise of her courage. Class distinctions were for once entirely broken down and the whole staff discussed the enthralling news over cups of tea and jam tarts. The general opinion was that Mrs Brandon would immediately inherit a sum varying from two to twenty millions and go to live at the Abbey. If this happened, said Cook, she would give notice, because there were no buses within half a mile and they said the bedrooms were shocking. The kitchenmaid said she had heard that if you hadn't any near relations the Government took it all, but otherwise no untoward incident marred the general excitement and content till a quarter past twelve, when Cook said What about her lunch and what a mercy it was cutlets.

Mrs Brandon and her daughter were alone at lunch. Delia suggested in an off-hand way that it might be a tactful thing to go over and inquire about Aunt Sissie, secretly hoping to see if not a corpse at least a death agony, but receiving no encouragement she dropped the subject, and she and her mother discussed the Fête, for which it was Mrs Brandon's custom to provide a stall with home-made cakes and jam and such garden produce as Turpin saw fit to release.

Meanwhile, through the agency of every tradesman who came to the kitchen door, through Turpin and the garden boy when they went home to dinner, through Nurse having to run down on her bike to match up some more pink sewing silk, through the Vicar's Hettie who had no business to be in Mrs Brandon's kitchen at all, the delightful tidings were spread far and wide. Dr Ford on his way to Southbridge passed Sir Edmund, who was having words with a foreman about the repairs to a cottage, and stopped for a moment to tell him the old lady was sinking, and it was only by the special mercy of Providence that he missed meeting Lady Norton in the chemist's at Southbridge by five minutes.

Owing to a report of midges in the garden Mrs Brandon decided to have tea in the drawing-room. She had hardly begun when Rose brought Mr Miller in, with the air of a junior priest leading the first sacrifice to the altar.

'I cannot tell you,' said Mr Miller, holding her hand a little longer than was strictly necessary, 'how grieved I am by this news.'

'What news?' asked Mrs Brandon, who had really forgotten about her aunt since lunch-time.

'I am not misinformed, I hope,' said Mr Miller anxiously, and feeling even as he spoke that the phrase might have been more happily turned. 'Hilary told me at lunch that your aunt had been taken seriously ill.'

Such is the power of suggestion that Mrs Brandon at once languished, thus causing Mr Miller severely to blame himself for gross want of consideration.

'Poor Aunt Sissie,' she sighed. 'Tell me, Mr Miller, do you think six of Cook's pound cakes and about six dozen of her cream puffs would do for the cake stall? I shall get the rest of the things from Barchester.'

'You always send exactly what is right,' said Mr Miller, admiring the courage that could deal with daily life while an aunt lay dangerously ill. 'Do you think I could be of the slightest use to Miss Brandon? I would not, of course, for the world interfere, but if I could be of any comfort I would willingly go over.'

'How nice of you,' said Mrs Brandon, 'but I really don't think you could do much. Miss Morris is there, and Dr Ford has sent a very good nurse, and he is looking in himself this evening.'

'I was speaking less as a friend than as a priest,' said Mr Miller, and then wondered if he had been harsh.

'Oh, I see what you mean,' said Mrs Brandon. 'That is very nice of you, but I'm afraid Aunt Sissie has a kind of feeling about clergymen. She has quarrelled with every rector and with the Bishop and even with the Dean who is so kind. But you will see us all at Church on Sunday as usual,' she added, by way of appeasing Mr Miller.

Mr Miller gave it up and ate chocolate cake.

'I don't know,' he said when he had finished, 'if it would interest you at all to hear a little more of my Donne. The typescript has gone to the publishers, but I have a carbon copy which is quite legible in parts. We all have our pet economies and I fear that one of mine is carbon paper, which I use far too long.'

'Mine is tissue paper,' said Mrs Brandon, her face and voice assuming an animation hitherto lacking. 'I keep every scrap that comes in parcels, but even so I can hardly keep pace with Rose. She uses such a lot when she packs for me. But I have freed myself from the tyranny of string.'

'The tyranny of string?' the Vicar repeated.

'You know,' said Mrs Brandon earnestly, 'how one keeps all the bits of string off parcels and puts it away in little circles that are always coming undone?'

The Vicar said indeed, indeed he did.

'Well, when I get a parcel now, I simply cut the string and throw the bits into the waste-paper basket,' said Mrs Brandon proudly.

'And what do you do for string then?' asked Mr Miller.

'I buy it,' said Mrs Brandon, with a slight air of bravado. 'You just cut off what you want, and it lasts for quite a long time.'

Mr Miller, much impressed, said he must try that, and was just going to re-introduce the subject of Donne when Delia came in with Mr Grant.

'Oh, mother,' said she, 'oh hullo, Mr Miller, I met Hilary in the drive, so I brought him up to tea. Chocolate cake!'

147

'You said I might come this afternoon,' said Mr Grant, noticing with pleasure that his hostess seemed to have recovered from the shock of Dr Ford's news. But at the same moment she remembered it and assumed a stricken air that wrung Mr Grant's withers.

'I say, mother,' said Delia, who was cutting chocolate cake in a most unfair way, giving herself far more icing than her rightful share, 'Hilary read aloud some of his book to me this morning. It's ripping. I loved that poem, Hilary, about

> Proie sanglante d'une fière et mâle rage,
> Dieu châtré des chrétiens, je crache à ton visage.'

This couplet, delivered in excellent French with a fine melodramatic rendering, was hardly what one would in one's calmer moments choose to recite to one's Vicar, but Delia was assailed by no such scruples. Mr Miller was wondering whether he ought to make a protest, or pretend, thus sacrificing his reputation as a scholar, that he hadn't understood, when Delia, pleased with her own voice, continued,

'When I was young and did that thing of Villon's about the Neiges d'Antan I always thought châtré meant punished. I suppose I was mixing it up with châtié, and no one ever told me. What a lot of words there are in French.'

This last remark gave the opportunity to her paralysed audience, all of whom remembered having made the same mistake and no one ever telling them, to change the subject. Hilary hastily said that Italian had an enormous number of words, and Mr Miller extolled the vocabulary of the ancient Romans.

'I think German is the worst,' said Mrs Brandon, 'not that I know any Latin. It is really nothing but words. If you try to read a German book you spend all your time looking up words, and there doesn't seem to be any special reason for them to mean anything and the minute you have looked them up you forget what they mean. And they all begin with a prefix or a suffix.'

'I hope the news of Aunt Sissie isn't any worse,' said Mr Grant.

Mrs Brandon, who was leaning back in her chair after the arduous duty of pouring out tea, suddenly sat up.

'If anything happened,' she said, impressively, 'I believe I haven't got a single thin black frock.'

'Oh, mother,' said Delia. 'There's that one with the pleated skirt.'

'Delia darling, it is a *rag*. One couldn't wear that frock even in church. You know what I mean, don't you, Mr Miller? And you haven't anything at all, Delia, except that coat and skirt. I must have a talk to Nurse. Oh dear!'

Both gentlemen felt a surge of resentment against Miss Brandon who by her illness was causing anxiety to so exquisite a creature. Conversation rippled spasmodically over hidden depths. What every person in the room wanted to discuss was whether Miss Brandon was going to die this time and what the contents of her will would be, but everyone felt that at such a time it would not be quite nice. Even Mrs Brandon felt a slight constraint and asked Mr Miller if he wouldn't read aloud to them. This chance was not to be neglected and drawing his typescript from his pocket, Mr Miller cleared his throat.

'Will you go on from where we left off?' asked Mrs Brandon.

Mr Miller, who had altered one or two commas since the last reading and wanted to hear how they sounded, said it would perhaps be more interesting for Delia and Hilary if he went back to the beginning. This would have been all very well with the original typescript, but as the first few pages of the carbon copy happened to be particularly blurred, he made but little headway. He apologized for his halting delivery by explaining that he had used the same sheet of carbon which had already served for typing out notices of the Fête and by plunging back into his text just managed to stop Mrs Brandon telling everyone what she did with tissue paper and string.

For at least three minutes the Vicar read happily if haltingly on. Mrs Brandon with a rapt expression let free her inhibitions and thought of how Nurse could alter that pleated black frock. Mr Grant, observing her expression, felt like a clod, while Delia thought how much nicer Hilary's book was than Mr Miller's.

Francis, back from his office, came into the drawing-room unobserved and had a good look at this domestic scene, his mother reclining with the air of langour that always gently amused him in a woman who had no nerves to speak of and an excellent constitution, the rest of the party draped admiringly round her. It surprised him a little to see his cynical sister among the worshippers, but he could not know that she was thinking of Hilary Grant. His mother was the first to see him and welcome him with delight, not only because she was glad to see him, but as a good pretext for interrupting anything that was going on and doing a little fussing.

'Francis, darling,' she said. 'You will excuse us for a moment, won't you, Mr Miller? I'll just order some fresh tea for Francis and then you will go on reading to us. Just ring, Francis.'

As soon as Rose had brought the tea, Mr Miller said to Francis how sorry he was about the news.

'What news?' asked Francis. 'Is the Bishop coming?'

Nothing could be worse than that, said Mr Miller emphatically, and why Barchester always had a Low Church, he would not say Evangelical bishop, and always had since the days of Bishop Proudie, it was not for him to inquire. No: he referred to the news about Miss Brandon.

'She isn't dead, is she?' said Francis.

'Francis, you shouldn't say things like that,' said his mother, 'especially when Mr Miller is here. Dr Ford came to see me this morning and said she is much worse and he has sent a nurse to the Abbey and will ring us up again to-night, so Mr Miller was very kindly reading aloud. Poor Aunt Sissie.'

'Well, that is very sad, but hardly surprising after yesterday,' said Francis. 'And so right of you, dear mamma, to lie there doing a sort of *couvade*, and looking so nice.'

'I don't know what you mean,' said Mrs Brandon, who knew perfectly well but was not going to admit it, and was pleased at being told she looked nice.

'It is a sort of thing the savages do,' said Delia, who liked to air her knowledge. 'If one of them has a baby the husband makes an awful fuss and pretends it's him.'

This lucid explanation of Mrs Brandon's languishing and very becoming airs was too much for Francis and Mr Grant, who burst into ribald laughter. Mr Miller looked at them over his eye-glasses in a quelling manner, but said nothing. Mrs Brandon, suddenly seeing the joke against herself began to laugh too, and Delia was pleased by the success of her remark.

'Poor Aunt Sissie,' said Francis. 'Well, if there's a funeral I'll have to get my hair cut. I ought to have had it done to-day. Give me another bit of cake, Delia.'

Again the conversation ran lightly over secret depths. Francis for all his careless ways and speech, could not bring himself to discuss openly what must be in everyone's mind, and Mr Miller began to rustle his typescript ominously, so that everyone was glad when Sir Edmund walked in.

'Well, Lavinia, anything wrong?' he said. 'Afternoon, Miller. Grass is getting very long outside the north aisle. Pity we can't turn a few sheep in. Afternoon, young people.'

'Not really wrong,' said Mrs Brandon, 'but Dr Ford brought me some rather upsetting news this morning.'

'I met Ford down at the new cottages this morning. A nice mess they are making of them too,' said Sir Edmund. 'Not even a damp-course. I told the foreman I'd see the local health authorities and he wasn't to lay a brick till he'd heard from them. I'll get Pomfret's agent on to it, young Wicklow. He has a head on his shoulders. They aren't on Pomfret's land, but some of his people live there and he won't stand it. Thanks,' he said to Rose who had brought him a brandy and soda. 'Well, Lavinia, I'm sorry about Amelia Brandon, but that's no reason for you to behave like an invalid.'

'I really don't see what else I can do,' said Mrs Brandon. 'She doesn't want to see me and she has Miss Morris and a nurse and all the servants.'

'Well, well, I daresay you're right,' said Sir Edmund. 'Question is: if Amelia Brandon dies, who does the property go to?'

A kind of silent sigh of relief rose from every breast. No one liked to make a suggestion, but there was a general feeling that Sir Edmund would do it for them.

'Must be practical, you know,' said Sir Edmund. 'Well, this is how we stand. Amelia Brandon must have made a will, but no one knows what's in it.'

There was a murmur of assent.

'Well, I look at it this way,' said Sir Edmund, assuming the

151

voice he used on the bench, 'she must have left it to someone. She wouldn't split it up. I remember her telling me that her father had made the place and she meant to pass it on as he had left it. Now we get down to facts. Francis!'

'Yes, sir,' said Francis.

'The way I look at it is this. Either your Aunt Amelia – stupid name Sissie, never liked it – leaves you the property, or she doesn't. If she does, I'm always ready to give you a hand. If she doesn't, she doesn't.'

'Thank you, sir,' said Francis.

'As for Grant,' said Sir Edmund, staring at Mr Grant, 'as I see it the facts are like this. If Amelia Brandon has left the place to him, there it is. If she hasn't, well there we are. Your mother wouldn't want to live there, would she?'

'I don't know,' said Mr Grant. 'I hadn't thought about it. She mostly lives in Italy.'

'Good!' said Sir Edmund. 'Well then, that's that. Of course if she leaves it to someone else, that old uncle of Cedric Brandon's – you'd never have heard of him, he lives at Putney – or the cousin that lives in New Zealand, then of course that alters the state of affairs. That's all, I think.'

'Sir Edmund,' said Delia, 'if Aunt Sissie – well you know what I mean – if she does, what do you suppose will happen to Miss Morris?'

As it happened, no one in the room had thought of Miss Brandon's companion. Mr Miller felt sorry for companions in general and suddenly felt very sorry for Miss Morris in particular.

'Happen, eh?' said Sir Edmund. 'I suppose she'll find another job. Plenty of old ladies about.'

'Yes, but Sir Edmund,' said Delia, 'I mean now, at once, if Aunt Sissie is really as ill as Dr Ford says. I mean it must be pretty ghastly for her to be in that awful Abbey alone.'

Mr Miller made a violent effort.

'Delia is undoubtedly right,' he said. 'Miss Morris should not be left at the Abbey unless she wishes. It might perhaps be possible to find her lodgings in the village for the present. I know they have a furnished bedroom and sitting-room at the shop.

If there were any difficulty of any kind,' he added diffidently, 'and a small contribution would help – '

'Nonsense, Miller,' said Sir Edmund, who knew that the Vicar's income was not large and that much of it went in charity, 'nonsense. There are two rooms at Clematis Cottage and Mrs Bevan is a very nice, clean, respectable woman and I'd see to all that.'

Mrs Brandon had barely heard what her kind-hearted guests were saying. She remembered how worn Miss Morris looked, how patient she had been with the old lady, with what gratitude she had accepted so dull a treat as a picnic. She also remembered with less sympathy how Miss Morris had shown unmistakable signs of devotion to her, but put this away as selfishness. Here was Stories, with two spare bedrooms which were seldom used except at week-ends. The servants would enjoy having a guest in the house so fresh from the excitement of a funeral. Her duty seemed plain.

'I think, Sir Edmund, she had better come here,' she said. 'It is most kind of you and Mr Miller, but I really think she would be better at Stories. She has had a most trying time with Aunt Sissie and looks as if she needed a good rest. I could easily have her for two or three weeks, or more if she doesn't find a new place. I like her and I think we'd get on quite well. Of course I hope this is only a false alarm and that Aunt Sissie will get well again, but if anything does happen I'll go over to the Abbey and fetch her.'

Sir Edmund and Mr Miller expressed their approval of this scheme and Mr Miller went so far as to say that it was just like her.

'Not a bit,' said Mrs Brandon. 'As a matter of fact I hadn't thought about her at all till Delia mentioned her, which was very selfish and forgetful of me. It is really Delia's plan.'

Delia blushed and looked gratified. Sir Edmund and Mr Miller took their leave. Mr Grant lingered to speak to his hostess.

'I do think it is marvellous of you, Mrs Brandon,' he said.

'I suppose you have to go on saying, Mrs Brandon,' said she. 'I wish you would say Cousin Lavinia, or just Lavinia.'

'You know by what name I always think of you,' said Mr Grant in a dark quivering voice.

'No,' said Mrs Brandon, enjoying herself immensely. 'May I hear?'

Mr Grant looked self-conscious, looked down, up, and wildly about him, and said in a hoarse croak:

'I did tell you once. In my mind I call you my friend.'

Having made this avowal he waited for Mrs Brandon to dismiss him for ever from her sight. As she said nothing he dared to raise his eyes and look at her. Her charming face, a little tired, a little dark under the eyes after yesterday's scene, bore an expression as of one whose thoughts are fixed on a distant star.

'I feel,' said Mrs Brandon, in a low, thrilling tone, 'about that word as Shelley felt about the word Love.'

She paused for a moment, to get it right. Mr Grant, on hearing the word Love, a word which he had hardly dared to use even to himself, nearly lost consciousness, but recovered himself in time to hear the goddess's last words.

' "One word",' said Mrs Brandon, ' "is too often profaned for me to profane it".'

Mr Grant, while feeling that it was he rather than Mrs Brandon who intended to profane the word, fully realized the exquisite quality of the rebuke, and mumbling good-bye, hastened after his coach.

Francis, who had frankly been eavesdropping, now approached his mother.

'Really, mamma!' he said.

Mrs Brandon looked at him with the face of a saint and then broke into her mischievous amused smile.

'I couldn't help it,' she said.

'I know you couldn't, darling,' said Francis. 'But what you could have helped was saddling yourself with Miss Morris.'

'I had to,' said his mother. 'She seems to have no friends or relations and she has had a dreadful time with Aunt Sissie. If only she didn't have a slight passion for me, it would be all right. But I do hope Aunt Sissie will get better.'

'So do I,' said Francis, 'if it means you being worn to the bone by Miss Morris's devotion. Perhaps we could interest her in church work.'

'I'm afraid she and Mr Miller don't approve of each other,' said his mother, 'which makes it all more difficult.'

'All true Brandons thrive on difficulties, or else they make them for other people,' said Francis. 'I am an example of the first and Aunt Sissie of the second. To make matters smooth between Miss Morris and Mr Miller shall be my life's work. Come and look at Turpin's marrow, mamma. You will find it has a soothing and inspiriting influence.'

– 8 –

THE LAST OF BRANDON ABBEY

THE more Mrs Brandon thought about her kind offer to take Miss Morris in the event of 'anything happening', as everyone preferred euphemistically to put it, the more she wished she had not felt she must make it. Then she blamed herself and thought again of Miss Morris's position, and how horrid it must be to go from one old lady to another, with no home or background of her own. Dr Ford's report next day was that Miss Brandon was still much the same, and he promised to let Stories know of any change. Mrs Brandon asked if her aunt would like to see her and was greatly relieved to hear that the old lady did not want to see anyone but Sparks and Miss Morris. Her only pleasure, he said, was to hear Miss Morris read Captain Brandon's old letters aloud, when she was not in a semi-conscious condition.

Mrs Brandon told her children the news. Francis went off to work and Delia, oppressed by a shadow that had never before overcast her young spirits, went over to Grumper's End to see how the chicken pox was. Mrs Brandon went up to Nurse's room, where Nurse was pressing one of Delia's evening frocks.

'Dr Ford has just rung up,' said Mrs Brandon. 'He says Miss Brandon is much the same.'

'I'm sure I'm glad to hear that, madam,' said Nurse, who had been hoping for something much more exciting.

'If anything did happen,' said Mrs Brandon, 'I am going to ask her companion, Miss Morris, here for a few weeks. She is a clergyman's daughter and very nice. And I was thinking about that black frock of mine with the pleated skirt. I haven't worn it since the winter, but I think if you took the gold belt off and put on a black one, and just put some of that black lace that is in the cardboard box with the flowers on it, on the top shelf of my big cupboard, round the neck, I could wear it quite nicely.'

As she spoke she looked Nurse firmly in the eye, as if challenging her to prove that the mention of the black frock was anything but a housewife's careful attention to her wardrobe. Nanny, seconding admirably this pretence, said she would just run down and get the dress and see. She was back in a few moments carrying an armful of clothes which she laid on the table.

'I'd better turn the iron off,' said Nurse, 'or we'll be having an accident, like the time that nursery maid left the electric kettle on all afternoon and burnt the hearth rug. I brought up some frocks I thought you might like to go over, madam.'

'I had quite forgotten about that black and white foulard,' said Mrs Brandon. 'It looks well with a black hat. You see what I mean about the pleated frock, Nurse.'

'Yes, madam,' said Nurse. 'It would look quite effective with a black belt and the lace, the way you said. And I brought up this black georgette. You did say it had got a little tight for you, but there didn't seem to be anything to let out, so I wondered if it might do for Miss Delia. I'll try it on her as soon as she gets back. I wish you'd speak to her, madam, about visiting Grumper's End. I know she's had chicken pox twice, but it isn't so much the chicken pox as Other Things she might get there.'

'Yes, Nurse, I'll try to,' said Mrs Brandon, absent-mindedly. 'Why did you bring up the pale green? I thought we were going to give it away.'

'It would dye nicely, madam, and if I sent it to Barchester to-day we'd have it back in two days if it's a special order, and it might come in quite handy.'

'Yes, do,' said Mrs Brandon. 'And there's that lilac georgette.'

'You wouldn't have it *dyed*, madam,' said Nurse, shocked. 'It's all made on the cross and things on the cross do shrink up so when they are dyed. It would come in quite handy for later madam. Really the two black frocks for you, the pleated one and the green one dyed, and your old black frock for Miss Delia would be quite enough. The black and white foulard and the lilac georgette would come in for afterwards, if the weather still keeps hot. I'll finish pressing this frock of Miss Delia's and then I'll send the pale green to be dyed and get on with altering the belt.'

'Well, I think that's all,' said Mrs Brandon and left Nurse to her ironing, both ladies perfectly satisfied by a conversation which had covered Miss Brandon's death, funeral, and the subsequent light mourning, without once mentioning an unpleasant word. On the landing Mrs Brandon found Ethel, the upper housemaid, and paused to tell her that the Green Room might be wanted quite soon, as Miss Morris might be coming from Brandon Abbey if anything happened, and to see that there was clean paper in all the drawers, an order which filled the recipient with ghoulish joy. Thence proceeding to the ground floor she found Rose in the sitting-room, taking away the silver ornaments to clean them.

'Oh, Rose,' she said, 'Dr Ford rang up just now. It seems that Miss Brandon is just the same.'

'Oh, dear, madam,' said Rose.

'Her companion, Miss Morris, has had a very hard time,' said Mrs Brandon, 'and I thought if Miss Morris needed a rest I could have her over here for a fortnight. I told Ethel to see that the Green Room was ready. I was thinking she could use the little dressing-room as a sitting-room if we put a comfortable chair into it.'

Rose, understanding perfectly well the implications of these remarks, said the chair out of the Pink Room would go in nicely, and would Mrs Brandon mention it to Ethel, as really she sometimes hardly liked to say anything to Ethel herself, and was always one for peace and quiet.

This matter adjusted, Mrs Brandon passed on to the kitchen. Cook, who had already heard the news from Nurse and Ethel, said she really was sorry to hear Miss Brandon was no better and she was thinking of making some beef tea and some calves' foot jelly, because it was as well to be prepared and she always liked two clear days for her jellies, and if people had had a shock there was nothing like it.

*

Meanwhile at Brandon Abbey old Miss Brandon's life was slowly ebbing away. It had perhaps not been a very interesting life, or one which contained much affection, but its owner had enjoyed it in her own way. She had admired the father who made a fortune and built the Abbey, and done her best to administer as he would have wished it the vast fortune that he left her. 'Be just before you are generous' was her guiding rule, and made her disliked, for the justice was kept for servants, tenants, tradespeople and such few friends as she had, while the generosity was confined to large subscriptions and donations to various charitable institutions, often appearing as anonymous gifts. The one deep feeling of her life had been her affection, amounting to adoration, for her scapegrace brother, Captain Brandon. To have been in his regiment was a sure passport to her favour, and successive Colonels could have told of help given to any of the regiment whose needs were made known to her. In her younger days more than one officer, who as a subaltern had known Captain Brandon, had come to her when in difficulties with ladies of confirmed or brevet rank, and had been rescued, the only price of his rescue being Miss Brandon's ribald chuckle as she insisted on having the story retailed to her in every detail.

Now she lay half asleep for hours together, watched by Sparks and Miss Morris by day, by the nurse at night, rousing herself from time to time to order Miss Morris to read aloud Captain Brandon's old yellow letters, never tiring of those in which he described the unfortunate entanglement with Mrs Colonel Arbuthnot which had resulted in his having to exchange.

Late in the afternoon a clerk from her solicitors, to whom Miss Morris had written at her request on the previous day, arrived at Brandon Abbey. The old lady summoning her energy insisted on seeing him alone, except for Sparks, and he soon went away again. After this her interest in the world lapsed altogether. At five o'clock next morning the nurse tapped at Miss Morris's door. Miss Morris, who had almost forgotten what a good night's sleep was like, was up and dressed in a very short time and came into Miss Brandon's bedroom. Nurse had drawn up the blind and the early sun was shining into the room, as it had not been allowed to do for many years.

Miss Morris came near the bed. Her employer was lying back on the pillows, her eyes shut, her heavy face in its frilled cap looking very tired and old.

'She will notice you presently,' said the nurse. 'She was asking for you.'

'Never could abide nurses. Meddling fools,' said the old lady in a weak but distinct voice, without opening her eyes.

'It's Miss Morris, Miss Brandon, you asked for her, you know,' said nurse in a voice of patient brightness that fully justified Miss Brandon's dislike.

'Come here,' said the old lady. 'Fred wouldn't have looked at you, but you'll find someone else will, before long. I'm sorry I couldn't fancy my supper last night. It's high time I was dead.'

These may be said to have been Miss Brandon's last sensible words. Miss Morris, who was sitting by her bed did indeed hear her mutter, 'Mrs Colonel Arbuthnot' and give a ghostly chuckle, but otherwise she never spoke again. Presently Miss Morris and the nurse looked at each other. Then Miss Morris went and telephoned to Dr Ford, and because there was nothing else to be done she went back to her room, vaguely wondered in what kind of bedroom she would find herself in her next place, and lay down, dressed as she was, on her bed.

By ten o'clock Mrs Brandon was at the Abbey. When Dr Ford rang her up Francis had offered to come, but as there would have been nothing for him to do she refused his kind offer. Poor Delia, after all her longing to see the last of her aunt, was suddenly overcome by the tender heart that she kept beneath her robust exterior and burst into tears, weeping for her disagreeable aunt as bitterly as if she had been a field mouse. So her mother left her to Nurse and started alone. At the drive gate Curwen suddenly pulled up, as a figure rose from the ditch where it had been sitting.

'Hilary!' exclaimed Mrs Brandon.

'Dr Ford rang Mr Miller up,' said Mr Grant. 'I had an idea

159

you would be going, because of that very kind thing you said about Miss Morris. I didn't like to bother you, but I thought I'd wait here, and if you did come I wanted to ask if I could do anything to help.'

'Get in and come with me,' said Mrs Brandon.

Mr Grant did as he was told. As on a previous journey Mrs Brandon spoke very little, but this time her companion did not take her silence for scorn. To his adoration there began to be added a cooler admiration for someone who was going to do a job that not everyone would have done, and was doing it without any fuss. When they got to the Abbey Mrs Brandon suddenly became an efficient grown-up person and disappeared upstairs with a red-eyed Sparks, leaving Mr Grant a prey to a sense of his own incompetence. The butler offered him sherry in so suitable a voice that Mr Grant, though he disliked sherry early in the morning excessively, was afraid to refuse it, and under the butler's eye not only had to drink it, but also eat two small biscuits with caraway seeds in them, a form of refreshment that he loathed. When he had choked upon the second the butler hastened to refill his glass, and Mr Grant wished Mrs Brandon could see what he was suffering for her sake.

Accompanied by poor Sparks, who was bewailing her mistress as if she had been the kindest of employers, Mrs Brandon visited the dead woman's room, laid on the bed the spray of flowering myrtle that she had brought with her, had a few words with the nurse, and came out again into the little sitting-room with relief that one part of her duty was done. She then set herself to comfort poor Sparks, who found real consolation in telling Mrs Brandon of the various passages she had had with the nurse, even going so far as a dark hint that some nurses got a retaining fee from undertakers, but at this point Mrs Brandon, with as much tact as possible, interrupted and asked where Miss Morris was. Sparks had to confess that she hadn't seen her that morning, but offered to go and look.

Mrs Brandon, left alone, looked for the last time on the serried rows of photographs, wondering by what slow process the plump, pretty child with ringlets had been changed to the shapeless, bed-ridden old woman, feared or disliked by most of those who came in contact with her. Looking absent-mindedly at her own hands according to custom, Mrs Brandon saw the diamond ring and wondered if Miss Brandon was even now meeting Captain Frederick Brandon and if so in what possible kind of heaven. Probably an Indian station, she thought, where Miss Amelia Brandon, keeping house for her gallant brother, would for ever look on his escapades with an indulgent eye and listen to his stories of pretty ladies. But realizing that these were irreligious thoughts, she pulled herself together. Sparks then returned with a face of pleasurable gloom to say that she had knocked at Miss Morris's door, but couldn't get any answer, and she didn't like to think what might have happened.

'She is asleep, I expect,' said Mrs Brandon calmly. 'I had better go and see her. Where is her room?'

From her voice Sparks knew that Mrs Brandon had now stopped being a sympathetic friend and had resumed her position as an employer. With sad resignation she took Mrs Brandon up to Miss Morris's room. Mrs Brandon knocked, received no answer, opened the door and went in. She saw what she expected, Miss Morris lying in an exhausted sleep. She told Sparks, who, having been disappointed of seeing a bleeding corpse with its throat cut was hoping at least for a death by drugs, to go and make some tea and bring it up. To this she added a request for some nice bread and butter, knowing what magic the word nice has in the kitchen. She then sat down and waited.

As she waited she looked at the bedroom. One could not say it was a servant's bedroom, but neither could one call it a guest's room. The furniture obviously consisted of rejects from better bedrooms, the bedstead was of black japanned iron with brass knobs and rails from which all pretence of polish had long since departed, and Mrs Brandon's housekeeping eye could see how the old-fashioned wire mattress sagged and she could imagine how noisy it would be whenever Miss Morris turned. The carpet had been good but was now faded to a nondescript colour, the dressing table had a mirror which had to be wedged with a piece of cardboard to prevent it from turning somersaults, the thin curtains would obviously keep out neither light nor cold.

When Sparks came back Mrs Brandon told her to put the

tray down and then go and get a nice cup of tea for herself, with which crumbs of comfort Sparks departed for the housekeeper's room, there to boast a good deal about what she had seen and heard.

Mrs Brandon poured out a cup of tea, clinking the china as much as possible. Miss Morris stirred a little.

'Do you feel like a cup of tea?' asked Mrs Brandon in her usual placid voice.

Miss Morris sat up, pushed her hair back, and looked wildly at the newcomer for a moment. Then she recovered herself and with almost her usual calm accepted the tea and thanked Mrs Brandon.

'I am afraid I must have been asleep,' she said. 'What time is it?'

'Eleven,' said Mrs Brandon. 'Didn't you have any breakfast?'

'I lay down for a few moments after I left Miss Brandon this morning. Oh, did you know?'

Mrs Brandon said Dr Ford had told her.

'I was rather tired, so I suppose I went to sleep,' said Miss Morris. 'I wonder what I could do now. I suppose I can stay on here for a little and be useful.'

Mrs Brandon looked at Miss Morris, saw the dark circles under her eyes and the shaking of her hands as she held the cup and saucer, and determined to tell the staff what she thought of them for forgetting Miss Morris and never offering her breakfast. Then she determined to tell a lie and said,

'Dr Ford wants you to come back with me to Stories.'

A look of intense relief came into Miss Morris's face and then the mask of the professional companion fell again.

'How very kind of you, Mrs Brandon,' she said, 'but I ought to stay here. I expect I'll be needed.'

'There will be plenty of people to look after everything,' said Mrs Brandon, not caring in the least whether there would be or not, 'and Dr Ford said most particularly that I was to take you with me now. So if you will drink the rest of the tea and eat up that nice bread and butter, I will wait for you downstairs. I will send Sparks up to help you to pack.'

Without waiting for any possible protest she went down to the drawing-room, where Mr Grant was sitting in a horrid atmosphere of sherry, and rang the bell, looking so determined that he dared not address her.

'Please send Sparks to me at once,' she said when the butler appeared.

In a few minutes Sparks came in, still chewing the remains of her nice cup of tea.

'Please go and help Miss Morris to pack,' said Mrs Brandon. 'I'm taking her home with me. And I find that she had no breakfast this morning. How was that?'

Sparks said she supposed the third housemaid, who was supposed to take Miss Morris's breakfast up to her room was upset. They were all upset downstairs, she said, and she could hardly manage more than cocoa and a piece of cake herself.

'Then I'd better see the housekeeper. Please tell her I want to speak to her at once,' said Mrs Brandon with a tone of cold finality that sent Sparks speechless from the room and made Mr Grant cringe inside himself.

She then went to the dining-room, where Mr Grant could hear her telephoning.

The housekeeper came and looked at Mr Grant as if he were a beetle. She then said to no one in particular that she understood Mrs Brandon wished to see her. Mrs Brandon, coming back from the telephone, said she did, and that she wished to know why no one had taken up any breakfast to Miss Morris.

'I am sure I could hardly say, madam,' said the housekeeper.

'Then that is not much use,' said Mrs Brandon with icy politeness. 'Miss Brandon's lawyers are going to send out someone to look after the house till suitable arrangements are made. The person who is sent will give you any orders that are necessary. That is all, thank you.'

If Mr Grant could have got under a sofa, he would gladly have done so. The goddess armed with Jove's thunders was a formidable being whom he had never suspected, and he hardly knew whether to worship or to shut his ears and eyes. He did shut his eyes for a moment. When he opened them the housekeeper had gone, probably shrivelled into nothingness, and the kind goddess was once more apparent.

'I am going to ask you to do something for me, Hilary,' she said. 'I am going to take Miss Morris home with me now. Will you please stay here and see Mr Merton? I managed to get him on the telephone at the Deanery and he is coming out with some-one from the lawyers. Tell him how sorry I am I couldn't stay, and you could bring back any messages from him. I will send Curwen back to fetch you as soon as possible.'

Mr Grant said of course he would.

Miss Morris then came downstairs with Sparks carrying her suitcase. Mr Grant stood up respectfully.

'Give Miss Morris some sherry,' said Mrs Brandon. 'Yes, of course you can drink it; it will do you good.'

Miss Morris obediently drank the sherry and thanked Mr Grant. Mrs Brandon then led her captive to the car and Mr Grant was left alone. His feelings were mixed. The foremost was a kind of anger that Mr Merton, that stranger who spoke with such ease and assurance to Mrs Brandon as if she were an ordinary person, should be coming to the house at all. It was like his impudence to be staying at the Deanery at such a time; even more like it to answer the telephone when Mrs Brandon rang him up; and most like it to be coming out with someone who would give orders. On the other hand Mrs Brandon was not waiting to see him, which made Mr Grant smile a smile of grim satisfaction that afforded him much pleasure till he suddenly saw his face in one of the looking glasses on the overmantel and hastily recomposed it in case any of the servants came in. But though his face now betrayed no emotion, none the less did he inwardly exult. Mr Merton, the man of the world, the gilded popinjay, the roué (for to such heights did Mr Grant's imagination in its flights now ascend), would arrive at the Abbey, all expectation, to find the bird flown and in its place a coldly courteous representative (bearing the form and lineaments of Mr Grant) who would give him any necessary information, hear anything that he might have to say, and then rejoin the goddess, leaving Mr Merton to deal with graves and worms and epitaphs. Turning over in his mind these agreeable thoughts he walked up and down the drawing-room, when suddenly something dreadful occurred to him. It might be that Mrs Brandon was deliberately shunning Mr Merton because she wanted to see him. He had heard, and read in books, that women often fled where they would most fain pursue; that Ravishers (for such Mr Merton was rapidly becoming in his mind) were more inflamed by the fugitive nymph than by bold advances; and, as a happy afterthought, that women were well known to have nothing but contempt for men who were content to worship from afar.

Thus unpleasantly and unfruitfully meditating he did not hear a car drive up. The first thing that attracted his attention was the sound of voices in the hall, and the butler saying to Mr Merton that he thought the young gentleman that come with Mrs Brandon was in the drawing-room. Mr Grant would have ground his teeth if he had known how to do it. 'Young' forsooth, and 'gentleman' indeed! Then Mr Merton came in and said very pleasantly, 'Grant, isn't it? I think we met here before. Mrs Brandon has gone, I expect.'

Mr Grant said she had, and had taken Miss Brandon's companion away with her.

'Splendid,' said Mr Merton. 'I have to get back to town to-day so I haven't much time. I've brought a man from my father's office who is used to this sort of thing and he will take over for the present. Are you staying here?'

'No,' said Mr Grant. 'I'm only waiting for Mrs Brandon to send the car back. She said you might have some messages to send her.'

'I don't think there will be anything special,' said Mr Merton. 'They will let her know about the funeral from the offices of course. Simpson!'

A youngish middle-aged man who looked as if he spent his life carrying out instructions to the letter, came in.

'Mr Simpson from the office, Mr Grant,' said Mr Merton. 'Now, Simpson, you might as well see the servants and I'll go up and see the nurse and then I must go. Well, good-bye, Grant. I hope we'll meet again. Tell·Mrs Brandon not to worry about anything and I hope very much to come over and see her when next I'm down.'

He went upstairs and Simpson went into the dining-room. Mr Grant, consumed with envy of people who knew how things were done and could grapple with nurses, felt the house was no place for him and wandered into the garden, where he had the pleasure of tormenting himself by the remembrance of the afternoon he had spent there with Mrs Brandon, and reflecting how he had then every opportunity of casting himself at her feet and saying 'Oh, Mrs Brandon,' but had not done so. A man like Mr Merton, he felt, would not so basely have wasted his opportunities. In these unprofitable musings he was surprised by Mr Simpson, who came advancing over the grass with the staid yet cheerful step of an undertaker.

'Excuse me, sir,' said Mr Simpson, 'but Mrs Brandon's car is here.'

'Oh, thanks awfully,' said Mr Grant. 'How did you know where I was?'

'Not at all, sir,' said Mr Simpson, apparently in reply to the first of Mr Grant's remarks, and leaving that young gentleman to marvel secretly at the powers of divination that had found him near the lily-pond. Mr Simpson then insisted, much to Mr Grant's discomforture, on seeing him into the car and telling Curwen he would not be wanted again. Mr Grant, who had already seen from Curwen's expression how deeply he resented having to do the journey to Brandon Abbey twice in a morning, feared that this final insult would cause him to overturn the car into a disused quarry, or into the River Rising, out of sheer spite, but Curwen found all the outlet he needed in the back of his neck, which expressive portion of the human body so paralysed Mr Grant that he would have given anything to be allowed to get out and walk. When they got near Pomfret Madrigal Curwen further completed his discomfiture by suddenly opening the glass slide with one hand and asking through the corner of his mouth whether Mr Grant wished to be taken to Stories or to the Vicarage. Thus challenged he dared not say Stories, and said he would get out at the Cow and Sickle and walk, which made Curwen despise him more than ever, as one who was not born to a car.

The Vicarage and its garden looked so peaceful in the sun that Mr Grant found it difficult to believe that anything had really happened. Time seemed to have stopped since he got into Mrs

Brandon's car at her gate and he thought it was probably tea-time, when the church clock striking two made him realize that he was extremely hungry and very late for lunch. He hurried up the flagged path to the house, where he found Mr Miller smoking a pipe over a book and the remains of lunch.

'Hullo,' said Mr Miller. 'I thought you were out.'

'So I was,' said Mr Grant.

'Well, here you are,' said his tutor. 'Had lunch?'

Mr Grant said he hadn't and would awfully like some if it weren't a bother. Mr Miller then rang for Hettie, who conferred with Cook and brought word that there was a nice piece of the beefsteak pie left that could be hotted up in a moment, so Mr Grant sat down to wait and drank a whole glass of beer.

'Thirsty?' said Mr Miller kindly.

'I was,' said Mr Grant. 'I've been at Brandon Abbey. I happened to be passing Stories just as Mrs Brandon was starting, and she asked me to come.'

'I suppose – ' said Mr Miller.

'Oh yes, really dead,' said Mr Grant, fully understanding that Dr Ford's message was not in itself a death certificate.

'And Mrs Brandon?' asked the Vicar.

'She was splendid, sir. She simply took charge of everything. Poor Miss Morris had been up for nights and had not had any breakfast, and Mrs Brandon simply pitched into the servants like anything. I just stayed on a bit to look after things till Mr Merton came. He is some kind of relation of Miss Brandon's lawyers.'

'That must be Noel Merton,' said Mr Miller. 'A very brilliant barrister. I coached him one vacation. I must ask him down here some time. I like to keep up with my old pupils. Is your lunch all right, Hilary?'

'Rather, sir,' said Mr Grant, his mouth full of beefsteak pie with the crust for which the Vicarage cook was doubtfully famous, mashed potatoes, french beans and gravy.

Mr Miller went on with his book and his pipe, while Mr Grant finished his pie and Hettie brought him gooseberry fool and cream with sponge fingers from the baker, and coffee. When Mr Grant had finished, she cleared away, and all the time Mr Grant had a feeling that his host was saving something up to say to him. When Hettie had gone back to the kitchen Mr Miller put his pipe into his book to mark the place and looked confused.

'Is that a good book, sir?' asked Mr Grant.

'Journalism, journalism,' said Mr Miller, looking at *A Waste-paper Basket from Three Embassies* by Jefferson X. Root, who had never certainly set foot in any of them, but was well into his second hundred thousand, 'as practically everything is now.'

He paused again uncomfortably.

'I wonder,' said Mr Grant to ease the tension, 'if the French think it funny that their chief classical authors are called Mr Root and Mr Crow.'

Mr Miller stared for a moment and then laughed and said the Romans had some curious names themselves, and what about Naso and Locusta.

'By the way,' he continued quickly, before his courage could cool. 'I don't want to interfere of course, Hilary, but have you any idea whether your aunt's death will in any way affect you?'

Mr Grant went bright red.

'Of course nothing is further from my mind than any wish to ask indiscreet questions,' Mr Miller pursued, 'but if an older man's advice would at any time be of any use, I thought I would like you to know that it is entirely at your disposal.'

This was an act of truly disinterested kindness on Mr Miller's part, as he had no capacity for or understanding of business at all, and except for the lucky fact that his private income was under a Trust would doubtless have been entirely dependent on his small stipend. As it was he always found himself in or out of pocket over any accounts in connection with church activities, and after the last Fête had been obliged to make up a deficit of seventeen shillings and threepence from his own purse.

Mr Grant, who didn't know this, was much touched, and thanked his coach warmly, after which he too fell into silent confusion.

'I cannot understand the appeal that this kind of book makes to the public,' said Mr Miller, whose pipe was lying in page two hundred and seventy. 'It is like Dr Johnson's mutton, ill-conceived, ill-written, ill-presented.'

Mr Grant laughed a little too loudly.

'By the way,' he said, before his courage could cool, 'you've been so decent to me, sir, that I'd like to say something.'

By way of carrying out this resolution he suddenly stopped speaking and looked with intense interest at the photograph of the Lazarus Eight in 1912 with Mr Miller looking incredibly young and round faced.

'Yes, my boy,' said Mr Miller encouragingly, and then wishing he hadn't used this form of address.

'I only meant,' said Mr Grant, still studying the photograph with an absorbed face, 'that if I did happen to get anything I wouldn't take it.'

Mr Miller vaguely felt that there was some Scriptural precedent for this, but was too much surprised by his pupil's statement to run this fugitive thought to earth, so he made a deprecating kind of noise which might also be taken for agreement, sympathy, or a slight clearing of the throat.

'I think,' said Hilary, 'it would be jolly unfair if I got anything, considering Mrs Brandon is Aunt Sissie's niece, and how jolly good she was to her, going to see her at that awful Abbey. I think I ought to do some work, sir, as I didn't do any this morning.'

He left the room abruptly and could be heard going up to his room. Mr Miller gazed pensively into the garden thinking what fun it must be to be young, to have something to sacrifice for someone worthy of the renunciation. If he had anything he could sacrifice for Mrs Brandon he would willingly have done so, but his oars and his little library, his most cherished possessions, would obviously be of no use to her. With a sigh he picked up his pipe and resumed Mr Root's book at the point where the ingenious author would have seen Lenin, had he not been out of Moscow at the moment. If this sentence is a little ambiguous it must in fairness be said that whether it was Lenin or Mr Root who was out of Moscow, the result would have been much the same and equally dull.

When Delia had finished crying about her Aunt Sissie her spirits began to rise again, and she had a very spirited argument with Nurse about the black georgette frock that was a little too tight for her mother. Nurse, who had an understandable if erroneous belief that Delia, her baby, was still in the nursery, said it made her look much too old and wished to shorten it. Delia, very conscious when it came to a question of good clothes, of her nineteen years, was enchanted by her own imposing appearance and peacocked up and down in front of the glass in her mother's room till Nurse nearly lost her temper, and told Delia to come along like a good girl and take it off.

'Well, if I do take it off,' said Delia, unwillingly beginning to pull the frock off over her head, 'will you swear to shorten it at once, Nurse, so that I can have it on when Miss Morris comes.'

'Certainly not, Miss Delia,' said Nurse, shocked. 'It wouldn't look at all nice to be all in black when poor Miss Morris comes, just as if you'd been Expecting it.'

Delia, now safely extricated from the georgette, said after all one couldn't help expecting it when everyone knew Aunt Sissie was about a hundred and Dr Ford had told them she was very ill, but Nurse, suddenly assuming the position of an authority on etiquette, ignored Delia's protest and carried the dress off to be shortened. Delia got into her ordinary frock again and went into the garden to get flowers for Miss Morris's room.

'Good morning, Turpin,' she said to the gardener, who was tying up dahlias. 'Isn't it awful, Aunt Sissie is dead.'

'That's another of them gone,' said Turpin with gloomy relish. 'How old was she, miss?'

'Oh, I don't know. Eighty-something.'

'My father was ninety-three when Mr Moffat – that was the Vicar before Mr Lane, him as was before Mr Miller – took and buried him,' said Turpin, leaving his hearer to understand that Mr Turpin senior, if not forcibly interred, might have been alive yet. 'And his father, that was my grandfather in a manner of speaking, was nigh on a hundred and hadn't had a tooth in his head for forty years. Ah, they didn't need teeth in those days,' said Turpin, shaking his head over the degeneracy of modern times.

'Well, Aunt Sissie had false teeth and a wig,' said Delia, zealous for the honour of the family.

'What did she want with wigs at her age?' said Turpin. 'The

Lord sends these things to try us and I don't hold with flying in his face with false hair and false teeth like them as are no better than they should be.'

With this cruel aspersion on a profession which, whatever its moral status, certainly does not depend on dentures or postiches for its attractions, Turpin pulled a length of bast from the tress that was tucked into his belt, and resumed his labours. Delia, seeing that further conversation was useless, moved away and began to pick carnations.

'Not them red ones, Miss Delia,' shouted Turpin, who had followed her actions with a suspicious eye. 'I want them for the Feet.'

'All right,' said Delia, now goaded beyond bearing, 'if you think I want red carnations for Miss Morris's room when Aunt Sissie is only just dead, I don't. I'm only getting white flowers.'

So saying she cut two tall white lilies almost viciously, and walked away with them before the outraged Turpin could protest.

'Buds and all!' he muttered, as Delia went off to another flower bed, and then applied himself afresh to his labours, comforting himself with the thought that one death often brought on another.

By this time Delia's blood was up. She stripped the garden of practically every white flower she could find and arranged them all in the Green Room, choosing several rather valuable white Chinese vases that were kept in a cabinet and never used. By the time she had decorated the dressing table, the writing table and the mantelpiece, and massed white phlox in the fender, the room with its pale green curtains and chintzes and its pale green walls, with the light filtering through the half-drawn white blinds, was like a dwelling under a glassy, cool, translucent wave, and Delia was filled with admiration for her own work.

Presently she heard the car come back, so she tidied away all the débris of stalks and leaves, washed her hands, and ran down to the drawing-room where she found her mother and Miss Morris seated in calm and amicable converse. Concealing her disappointment, for she, like Sparks, had hoped at least to see an almost inanimate corpse, she stood on one leg in the doorway.

171

'Come in, darling,' said her mother. 'You remember Delia, don't you, Miss Morris?'

Miss Morris said of course and shook hands. Then Mrs Brandon said it was nearly lunch-time and she expected Miss Morris would like to see her room.

'Will you take Miss Morris up,' she said to Delia, 'while I write a couple of letters.'

Rather nervously Delia led the way, wondering if it was etiquette to talk about people who were dead, or if she ought to let Miss Morris do it first. She opened the door of the Green Room and stood outside for Miss Morris to go in. Her things were already unpacked and laid out, and Ethel was taking her suitcase away, having as a matter of fact delayed to so do till she heard her coming upstairs, so that she might with her own highly favoured eyes gaze upon one who had so lately been near a death-bed and tell the kitchen about it. The account which she gave in the kitchen of Miss Morris looking as pale as chalk and obviously not long for this world was so much the product of her own film-fed mind that we need pay no attention to it, except to remark that it spurred Cook on in her kind preparation of beef tea and calves' foot jelly and so made lunch seven minutes late.

Miss Morris thanked Ethel and stood looking about her. It was perhaps the first time since she had embarked upon her life as a companion that she had been in any bedroom but such as were just too good for the servants. She knew it could not last, that she would probably wake up in a third floor back in Birmingham, or an attic at Droitwich, and hear a bell ringing to summon her to read aloud, or take a little dog for a walk, or pick up stitches in knitting, but until that waking came she was going to be perfectly happy.

'Is it all right?' said Delia anxiously.

'Those flowers!' said Miss Morris, almost with a gasp.

'I did them. Do you like them?' asked Delia, anxious for praise.

'I have never seen anything so lovely in my life,' said Miss Morris, with such sincerity that Delia felt a glow that is not always given to benefactresses. 'They remind me of my father's garden at home.'

172

This was not strictly true, for Mr Morris was interested in nothing but chrysanthemums, but Delia did not know this, and Miss Morris was seeing everything through a haze of grateful sentiment, so both were happy. Miss Morris then opened a very shabby little leather box and took out a photograph which she placed on the table, by her bed. Delia looked at it with interest. It was a middle-aged man in a clerical collar with a thin face, across which his mouth made a tight, hard line, drawn down at the corners.

'Is that your father?' Delia asked.

'Yes,' said Miss Morris. 'It was taken just before he became so ill. He always liked it and it was reproduced in the Parish Magazine after his death.'

If it had been anyone else's father Delia would have thought it looked like a horrid old parson, but being Miss Morris's she looked at it respectfully, while Miss Morris put away her out-door things and washed her hands in the green basin with green soap and dried them on a green towel. Then they went down and had lunch, which was duck and green peas and potato croquettes, followed by gooseberry fool and cream (which every house in Barsetshire was having that week because of not letting the gooseberries be wasted), and home-made sponge fingers. As Miss Morris ate her lunch and drank half a glass of white wine, Rose's opinion of her went down by leaps and bounds. If she confided to Cook, *her* late mistress had been lying stiff, she was sure she would never have been able to touch a thing. But Cook, darkly hinting at delayed shock, though in other words, never ceased in the preparation of calves' foot jelly.

After lunch Miss Morris, on Mrs Brandon's instructions, had a rest in her room on the green chintz sofa, with a Shetland shawl on her feet and a very nice novel of Mrs Morland's to read. She still found it impossible to believe that she was herself. Only a few hours ago she had been the companion, lying exhausted on an iron bedstead with a knobbly mattress, wondering how soon she would be adrift on the world again with a month's not very good wages. Now she was a guest, lying on a sofa in a room full of flowers, among kind, pleasant people whose one wish seemed to be to put her at her ease. She wished she had some pretty frocks to do them honour and some better under-clothes to please the housemaid, but otherwise her cup was full to the brim with happiness. Companions must not cry, so Miss Morris shed no tears, but it was not quite easy to see some of the pages in Mrs Morland's book.

She must have gone to sleep without knowing it for presently the light had crept round and was shining on the white lilies on the mantelpiece and Delia was standing by her side, looking at her with interest.

'I say,' said Delia, her eyes shining with the inspiration of a great plan, 'I thought I'd better tell you it's nearly tea-time.'

Miss Morris thanked her and got up.

'I say,' said Delia again, 'I don't know if you believe in wearing mourning or anything.'

'I suppose I shall have to if I go to the funeral,' said Miss Morris. 'I've got a black coat and skirt and I suppose that would do.'

'You'd be awfully hot in a coat and skirt,' said Delia. 'I've got an awfully good idea. There's a black frock of mother's that's a bit too tight for her and Nurse has been shortening it for me, but if you'd like it I'd awfully like you to have it. I mean you're smaller than I am, so if it's the right length for me it'll be about right for you, I mean the right sort of longness for a person – '

'For someone of my age,' said Miss Morris, kindly finishing the sentence for her. 'Thank you very much, Miss Brandon. I would really be grateful.'

Delia heaved a sigh, partly of relief that her offer had not given offence, partly of regret for what she dearly loved and was only giving up after a severe mental struggle, and produced from behind her back the black frock.

'Could you try it on now!' she said.

Miss Morris was perfectly ready to do so.

'Hang on a minute and I'll get Nurse,' said Delia and rushed upstairs to drag Nurse down and explain the situation to her all in one breath, thus giving her no chance to grumble or expostulate.

'Here's Nurse,' she said, breathless.

'How do you do, Nurse,' said Miss Morris, coming forward and giving her hand with what Nurse considered exactly the right nuance of deference as from an unplaced companion to a pillar of the house, equality as from employee to employee, and proper condescension as from a clergyman's daughter to a children's nurse, which won her complete approval.

'I say, Nurse,' said Delia, 'be an angel and see if that dress fits Miss Morris.'

Nurse helped Miss Morris to take off her well worn blue dress and slip on the georgette, and approved the result. Delia, fired by the pleasure of doing good and now quite reconciled to her sacrifice, insisted on adding a pair of very thin silk stockings to the toilet, and Miss Morris, accepting calmly and gratefully, really looked extremely distinguished, and promised to wear the dress that night. Nurse took it away to press, and on her way upstairs went down to the kitchen, nominally to ask if those pillow slips were back from the wash yet, but really to make easy allusion to what had just passed and to stamp Miss Morris with her official sanction, while Delia took her guest down to tea. Miss Morris, secretly intoxicated by the thought of a dress which she mentally (and correctly) priced at about twenty guineas when new, looked almost sparkling and made her hostess and Delia laugh by describing some of her experiences with old ladies. Mrs Brandon, who had been a little nervous of gratitude, found to her relief that Miss Morris was not showing any symptoms of adoration and everything was going very well when Mr Miller was announced.

Poor Mr Miller had not at all wished to come to Stories that afternoon, but his conscience had told him that if there was anyone in sadness or trouble he ought to see if his help was wanted, so not stopping to consider whether Miss Morris was likely to be sad or troubled about the death of a very irritable old lady, he had put on his Panama and walked over. At his entrance Miss Morris stiffened and became the companion again.

'How are you, Mrs Brandon,' said the caller. 'And Delia. I have just called to express my sincere sympathy, Mrs Brandon. And may I say how glad I am to see you among us, Miss Morris.'

Miss Morris said thank you in a correct, toneless voice. Conversation flagged and became so difficult that Mrs Brandon was reduced to asking Mr Miller when he was going to read some more of his book to her. Mr Miller, in his really single-minded wish to do his duty by the afflicted, had given no thought to himself, and the typescript was in a drawer in his writing table. It had indeed been a source of inward conflict to him, for he had managed quite unnecessarily to persuade himself that to read it aloud to someone as delightful, cultivated and sympathetic as Mrs Brandon, was perhaps in the nature of a sensual gratification and should be discouraged. While putting it away he had come upon a bundle of old papers, and going through them had wondered, as we all do, why on earth he had kept most of them and what practical, emotional, or spiritual value they could ever have had, and had put most of them into the wastepaper basket. Among them were two numbers of the Parish Magazine for 1913 edited by the Rev. Justin Morris, and these Mr Miller had saved, because he thought Miss Morris might care to have them, and these he now took from his pocket.

'I was looking over some papers to-day,' he said to Miss Morris, thinking it better not to say throwing some papers away, 'and found these numbers of your Parish Magazine, which I thought you might care to see. There is a delightful contribution by Mr Morris on some local customs, and a little article by myself which I thought good at the time, but now realize to be a very immature production. But setting that aside, I thought you might possibly care to have the magazines. They remind me of some very happy days in the past.'

It was evident that Mr Miller was getting more and more nervous and talking without knowing really what he was saying. When he had come to an end, Miss Morris replied politely that she had a complete set of the Parish Magazine and would not like to deprive Mr Miller of the numbers in which his own contributions appeared. Mrs Brandon and Delia sat for a moment in horrified silence and then plunged simultaneously into an incoherent conversation about the forthcoming Fête. Mr Miller tried to bear his part in this, but under Miss Morris's silence he became so uneasy that both his hostesses were extremely glad when he said he must go. With great courage he took Miss Morris's ungracious hand, begged her to let him know if he could ever do anything for her and got away.

'I think,' said Miss Morris, as Rose came in to clear away tea, 'I will go upstairs if you don't mind, Mrs Brandon.'

'Yes, do,' said Mrs Brandon, 'and have a good rest. And would you care for dinner in bed? It would be quite easy and perhaps you would be glad to be alone for a bit.'

'I am afraid I am a stupid sort of guest,' said Miss Morris forcing a smile.

'Indeed you aren't,' said Mrs Brandon warmly, hoping to fend off the attack of self-depreciation which she saw in her guest's eye. 'You must do just as you like about dinner. We shall love to see you if you do feel like coming down. If not, you shall have a tray in bed and be as quiet as you like.'

But Miss Morris was not to be baulked.

'I am afraid I behaved unpardonably just now,' she said. 'It was more than kind of Mr Miller to come over, and I am sure his wish to give me those magazines was well meant, but you know what my feeling is about the way he hurt my dear father.'

'What did he do?' asked Delia eagerly, rather hoping for news of some bloody assault with a flat iron or a carving knife.

'Mr Miller and Miss Morris's father did not agree on certain points,' said Mrs Brandon in rather a hurried way. Delia recognized a danger signal, but did not see where the danger was coming from, so she stood by.

'There was no question of agreement. It was a matter of right or wrong,' said Miss Morris, her pale cheeks flushing.

'Well,' said the practical Delia, 'Mr Miller did say that was a jolly good article of your father's and he said those were the good old times or something of the sort. He's awfully nice really, Miss Morris, and we never take any notice of him.'

Miss Morris with an incoherent apology left the room. Rose, who had cleared away as slowly as possible, had the intense pleasure of hearing her give a kind of dry sob as she went upstairs, and so was able to prepare the kitchen agreeably for the worst. Nor was it long before the worst occurred, for Nurse,

177

taking the black dress to Miss Morris's room, knocked, had no answer, went in, and found her trying to take off her blue dress and shaking uncontrollably from head to foot. With the light of battle in her eye Nurse mobilized the household. Mrs Brandon came hurrying upstairs with Delia just in time to receive the full blast of the breakdown which, to do Miss Morris justice, was no more than her due after the last weeks. Beyond kind words Mrs Brandon could not do much, but Delia, well up in first aid, so bullied her patient, standing no nonsense of any sort, that within ten minutes Miss Morris had drunk sal volatile, cried, choked, drunk more sal volatile, somehow got undressed while crying violently all the time, and was in bed with a hot water bottle, in fact with two, as Nurse and Ethel each considered it her own special office. Delia then drove her not unwilling mother away, told Nurse and Ethel she didn't want them, and installed herself firmly by the patient.

When Dr Ford, urgently summoned by Mrs Brandon, arrived, he said there was nothing wrong with Miss Morris at all and a good fit of hysterics would do her good, left a sleeping draught to be taken with a light supper, and promised to look in next day. Just outside the gate of Stories he nearly ran over Mr Grant and pulled up.

'Oh,' said Mr Grant, 'I was just going to ask if Mrs Brandon was all right.'

'I can't think why you want to know,' said Dr Ford unsympathetically. 'Fit as a fiddle. Always is. Miss Morris has just been having hysterics. Do her all the good in the world. Funeral's the day after to-morrow.'

'It's awfully lucky that Miss Morris had Mrs Brandon to look after her,' said Mr Grant reverently.

'Mrs Brandon is one of the most charming women I know,' said Dr Ford, making a horrible noise with his gears, 'but no use in a sick room. Your little friend Delia is the one with a head on her shoulders. She handled that woman as if she had been born a nurse. See you at the funeral, I suppose.'

He clanked away, leaving Mr Grant to consider his words. Deeply did he resent having Delia called his little friend, as if he were in knickerbockers. Deeply did he resent any suggestion that Mrs Brandon was not perfect. The first seed of doubt as to the infallibility of his goddess was sown, and he found the feeling most uncomfortable. Broad-mindedly, he admitted that one might have a worse person than Delia to look after one in a crisis; he could quite see that she might be a tower of strength. But he didn't want towers of strength. For him an exquisite, shrinking, delicate woman, to whom he could say, 'Mrs Brandon, I am here. Have no fear,' and embroidering on this delightful theme he went back to the Vicarage.

Cook felt it would go against her conscience to send up calves' foot jelly till it had stood twenty-four hours, but put her whole soul into the beef tea, and at seven o'clock a tray was ready. Delia annoyed the whole staff, though probably preventing bloodshed, by coming into the kitchen, seizing the tray, and taking it up herself. She then administered the sleeping draught and the beef tea, and when she came down to dinner was able to announce that the patient was dozing. As the drug took possession of her senses, Miss Morris thought of the day that was now ending, from the nurse's call in the early morning to the disgraceful but blessed fit of crying that had left her so relaxed and sleepy. Only one thing troubled her in her half-dreaming state and that was that her father and Mr Miller had been arguing so fiercely about something. She knew her father was right, but Mr Miller had such a pleasant face and such gentle ways that she felt sure he could not be wrong. Surely Mr Miller had said something about those very happy days in the past. Yes, very happy they had been, above all in that summer when Mr Miller was being coached by her father and the weather was so fine. So Miss Morris slid gently back into them, and when Delia came tiptoeing in after dinner, all she had to do was to switch off the reading light, before installing herself in the Green dressing-room where she most unnecessarily proposed to spend that evening and sleep the night.

MISS MORRIS RELENTS

AFTER a good night's rest and a morning in bed, Miss Morris was much better. She thanked Delia warmly for her care, but it was sadly evident that the full force of her gratitude was reserved for Mrs Brandon. When a reserved nature allows itself to show feeling, it does it with a vengeance, and Miss Morris's devotion began to loom alarmingly, taking the form of wanting to help Mrs Brandon with the accounts and the flowers. Mrs Brandon felt that she ought to be touched, but found herself irritated, for her accounts lived in a peculiar muddle which she felt unequal to explaining, and she liked fussing over the flowers herself. However, with real kindness she let Miss Morris help Nurse, who had constituted herself a kind of co-guardian with Delia of their guest's welfare, to go through the linen cupboard and mark some new sheets, which Miss Morris did with exquisitely fine embroidery. Miss Morris also offered to read aloud in the evening, but after one experience gave it up. Francis, alarmed, had made a pretext of work to do and left the room, Delia had slipped away to play the gramophone, and Mrs Brandon had got into such a muddle of trying to get her tapestry right and look as if she were listening, that Miss Morris's sense of humour, almost buried alive by her old ladies, got loose, and she laughed quietly at herself and gave up the attempt. Her own future was going to be a matter of concern, but Mrs Brandon had refused even to hear anything about it till after the funeral, and for a few days Miss Morris resigned herself to drift, enjoying the sunshine and the garden and her comfortable bedroom.

Miss Brandon's funeral took place at the little church of Pomfret Abbas, whose vicar had gone in fear of his patroness for many years, while deeply grateful for her subscriptions to his various charities. It was not expected that many people would be there, for all Miss Brandon's contemporaries were dead and she had few friends.

When the car from Stories arrived with the Brandons and Miss Morris, Sir Edmund was standing at the church porch counting the arrivals.

'Morning, Lavinia,' he said. 'Poor house. Very poor house. Not seen a worse one since old Potter was buried, you know, the man over near Rushwater who used to shoot foxes. Bad time of year for a funeral with nearly everyone away or abroad. Pomfret would have come but he's away on a cruise with the young Fosters. The Dean went to Finland yesterday. Can't think why he went to Finland. Palestine more in his line, I should have thought. Don't stand about in the sun. I've kept places for you inside.'

Francis made Delia giggle by saying *sotto voce* that they wouldn't have been much good outside, and they all followed Sir Edmund up the aisle. Mrs Brandon looked like a ravishing widow in the black pleated frock, Miss Morris looked distinguished in the georgette, and Delia had compromised in her mother's black and white foulard with a black coat over it.

'I put you well up in front,' said Sir Edmund, taking no pains to moderate his voice. 'You are about the nearest relations poor Amelia had. You'll be chief mourner, you know.'

So saying he herded them into the pew usually reserved on happier occasions for the bride's father and mother and went away to look for fresh prey.

Mrs Brandon looked about her and saw a few familiar faces. Roddy Wicklow, Lord Pomfret's agent, evidently representing the family; Mr Leslie from Rushwater House, who had often drawn on Miss Brandon's purse for various county charities; Lord Stoke, who never missed a funeral and had put off going to Aix on purpose to attend; Mr and Mrs Keith from Northbridge Manor. At the back of the church a number of tenants and all the indoor and outdoor servants from the Abbey made a fairly respectable show. Presently Sir Edmund came back with Mr Miller and Mr Grant whom he put into the front pew across the aisle.

'He's a relation too,' said Sir Edmund to Mrs Brandon. 'Nice of Miller to come with him, but a bit awkward for the Vicar here. Must put you off your stroke a bit to see another professional looking at you.'

A rather majestic scuffling was now heard near the door. It was Lady Norton, more imposing than ever in gait and array, wearing a kind of plumed hussar's hat, carrying with her Mrs Grant.

'Good God!' exclaimed Sir Edmund, far more loudly than the atmosphere of a sacred edifice warrants, 'it's Victoria Norton. Who's that with her?'

Mrs Brandon looked round and saw Mrs Grant, wearing her homespun, but paying homage to the conventions by having substituted for her amber and coral beads a heavy jet necklace and jet earrings.

The sexton attempted to usher Lady Norton into an empty pew behind the Brandons, but her ladyship, who was used to sitting on the platform at public meetings, was not so to be put off.

Taking a good look through her lorgnon at the congregation, she spied out Mr Miller and Mr Grant and entered graciously into their pew, driving them up into the far corner.

'You will want to sit by your boy, Felicia,' she said to Mrs Grant. 'Dear me, how he has grown since I saw him at Frinton ten years ago. If you will come on my other side, Mr Miller, then Mrs Grant can sit between me and Hilary.'

After a little confusion Mrs Grant edged past Mr Miller and sat next to her unwilling son. It would not be true to say that he had forgotten about his mother, to whom he dutifully wrote every day at her express desire, but he hoped so much that she would not descend on him again for the present that he had managed to persuade himself that his wish was a fact. Heroically keeping back the scowl which he would willingly have bestowed upon her, he shook hands, not quite sure whether kissing was permissible in church.

'Dear boy,' said Mrs Grant. 'Come stai?'

'Oh, I'm all right,' said Mr Grant, and then mercifully the harmonium pealed and he was safe. That the whole congregation had their eyes riveted on Lady Norton's funereal plumes and his mother's swinging earrings he knew only too well.

The little service was soon over and Miss Brandon's coffin laid in the hideous family grave consisting of a block of red granite weighing about three tons with the words 'I am hiding in thee' picked out in black along the edge, where her parents reposed. Mr Simpson who had been hovering usefully about, then came forward to suggest refreshments, but no one wanted to go to the Abbey and there was no one to be offended if they didn't, so the offer was politely refused and Mr Simpson, entirely unmoved, vanishes from these pages for evermore.

Mrs Brandon and the party exchanged a few civil words with Lady Norton and hoped she was coming to their Church Fête on Saturday. Lady Norton said she would certainly try to, and as Felicia Grant was coming back to Pomfret Madrigal on Saturday, she could drive her over and visit the Fête at the same time.

'I didn't know you were coming back to us so soon,' said Mrs Brandon to Mrs Grant, to break the silence. She then felt she might have put it better.

'Yes, yes, my little giro with Victoria is over,' said Mrs Grant gaily, 'and I am coming back to see something of dear Hilary before I return to Italy. I have got my little room at the Cow and Sickle with our good Mr Spindler.'

Mrs Brandon knew that she ought to ask Mrs Grant to Stories. She had a spare bedroom and a very adequate staff and there was really no excuse at all for not showing hospitality, but she felt that Miss Morris, with her devotion and her willingness to help, was all she could bear, so she delayed for a moment, fighting her lower but really more sensible self.

Mr Miller, with the better excuse of a small and not very competent staff, was going through the same agony. What added to his perplexity was that he knew his pupil would dislike above all things to have his mother on the premises, but his strong sense of duty overpowered all considerations of reason.

'I do hope, Mrs Grant,' he said, 'that you will allow me to offer the hospitality of the Vicarage. The Cow cannot be really comfortable and I have a spare room at your disposal. If you would honour it, we should do our very best to make you comfortable.'

Mr Grant could have martyred his coach with the greatest of pleasure. Yet into his fury crept a certain admiration, for he

knew that in the rather scantily furnished house Mr Miller had
not room in his little bedroom for all his belongings and kept a
good many of them in the cupboard in the spare room, and had
to move them out whenever he had a guest.

'Mr Miller has taken the words out of my mouth,' said Mrs
Brandon untruthfully. 'I don't want to interfere, Mr Miller,
but if Mrs Grant cared to come to Stories I should be delighted
and we are only a step from the Vicarage.'

At this Francis and Delia, who did not know that she was
making amends to her own conscience by trying to give discomfort to every one else, could equally have murdered their
mother.

'How kind you all are,' cried Mrs Grant. 'What can I say?
Even in Calabria I have never received such hospitality. Shall I
do as I used to when all my dear peasants invited me to their
huts, and spend a week in each?'

Francis said 'No' so loudly that it was almost audible, and
Delia made a face at Mr Grant which he answered with another
face before he knew what he was doing. Mr Miller ardently
wished that he had not spoken first and Mrs Brandon as ardently
wished she had let well alone, and all the young people hated
the grown-ups who had landed them in this unconscionable
mess, when Lady Norton, for the first time in her life being of
some real use, told Mrs Grant to take her advice and go back to
the Cow.

'You'll be a fool if you don't, Felicia,' she said. 'Mrs Spindler
was my kitchenmaid for three years and is a very nice woman.
Go to her and you can do what you like, and she can cook
vegetarian things, because Norton had to have them on account
of his gastric trouble. And if you want to go folk-loring in the
evening it won't matter if you are late for meals. Mrs Brandon
and Mr Miller have guests already, so you'll only be a nuisance.'

'Well, I daresay you are right, Victoria,' said Mrs Grant,
enjoying this competition for her favours. 'And I left two trunks
and a lot of Calabrian pottery at the Cow, so I might as well go
back. But we will all meet often and merrily,' she added, jangling
her earrings.

Mrs Brandon and Mr Miller, freed from this pressing terror,

felt they didn't care how often or how merrily they met so long as Mrs Grant was not staying under either of their roofs, and began feverishly to plan dinners and lunches for Mrs Grant.

'Come along, Felicia,' said Lady Norton. 'Lunch will be waiting. Good-bye, Mrs Brandon; good-bye, Mr Miller. I shall certainly come over to the Fête on Saturday.'

After exchanging a few words with friends, largely it is to be feared with the intention of getting them to come to the Fête, Mrs Brandon moved towards the car when a thought struck her. She paused, looked at Miss Morris, went on again and then stopped once more.

'I was thinking,' she said to Miss Morris, 'of asking Mr Miller and Mr Grant to come back to lunch, because I know it is his cook's day off. But if it would be at all uncomfortable for you –'

Miss Morris hastened to say that she would of course like it very much.

'I can't tell you how ashamed I still am of my rudeness the other day,' she said. 'When I think how good you have been to me I feel I can never apologize enough. If only you knew how grateful I am for all your kindness.'

'Then that will be very nice,' said Mrs Brandon, suppressing a desire to say that Miss Morris would give her great pleasure by never being grateful again. Then she issued her invitation to Mr Miller, who said Indeed, indeed they would be delighted to come.

Lunch passed off very pleasantly indeed. Mr Miller was a little nervous at first, but Miss Morris was again the calm, competent woman that Mrs Brandon had first met, and spoke to the Vicar as if he were any ordinary human being. While Rose was about, the conversation was general, though one thought was naturally uppermost in all minds, and when they were at last alone over coffee, Francis was the first to voice it.

'When does one know about people's wills?' he inquired of the company at large. 'Don't tell me not to say things like that, mamma. I thought we all came home to a feast after the funeral and had pork pie and ham and bottled beer and cheese and whisky and then the lawyer read the will aloud and everyone was disappointed.'

Delia, who had talked the matter over thoroughly with Francis and had read one or two Victorian novels, said yes, and another will would be found in a hat box and they would all have a million pounds and she would spend a lot of it at the Fête.

Francis said she was counting her chickens before they were hatched.

'Well, what really *does* happen?' said his mother. 'Mr Miller, you are always having funerals. What do they do?'

Mr Miller had to confess that he had never been present at one of those gatherings dear to the older novelists when the will is read over madeira and seedcake, but he said that judging from his own very small personal experience when his aunt left him two thousand pounds of worthless Brazilian stock, Miss Brandon's lawyers would write to anyone concerned as soon as possible.

'Then if we don't hear from her lawyers we don't get anything,' said Francis cheerfully. 'Come on, Hilary, I'll have a shilling with you on who gets the gorillas.'

Mr Grant being agreeable, each gentleman made a note of the transaction and Francis asked Miss Morris to hold the stakes, which she obligingly consented to do.

Mr Miller then said he must go, as a lot of notices for the Fête still had to be written, about teas and where to park bicycles, and the Assistant-Scoutmaster, Mr Spindler's brother at Little Misfit, who had kindly offered to help him, nearly always got his 'N's' and 'S's' the wrong way round. Everyone felt they ought to help too.

Mr Miller said lingeringly well he must be off. Everyone breathing again at the thought that help with the notices need not now be offered, said what a shame, with an undercurrent of relief which could only have passed unnoticed by one so simple and trusting as the Vicar. As he said good-bye to Miss Morris, she looked uneasy and then said, 'Mr Miller.'

He stopped.

'I don't know if I could be of any help,' said Miss Morris. 'I used to write out all my father's church notices – you probably wouldn't remember – and as I have nothing at all to do here, I thought I could perhaps be of assistance to you.'

'You are kind, very kind,' said Mr Miller, humbly surprised and gratified. 'Indeed, indeed I remember your writing, a real work of art. But ought you to try yourself so much? You have had a severe shock and need rest.'

'Idleness does one no good,' said Miss Morris severely. 'And to make myself useful is my only way of thanking Mrs Brandon for all her wonderful kindness.'

'She is indeed kindness itself,' said Mr Miller, gratified by this praise of his hostess. 'Mrs Brandon, one moment if I may trespass on your time – Miss Morris has kindly offered, most kindly, to help me with the notices for the Fête. While her assistance would be invaluable, for she does beautiful lettering, I feel she should not undertake too much at present.'

'I know,' said Mrs Brandon, voicing her knowledge of her own thoughts rather than of Miss Morris's calligraphy. 'I know. You bring all your notices up here, Mr Miller, and Miss Morris can have a table in the Green dressing-room, where no one will disturb her, and do just as much as she feels like.'

'Excellent, excellent,' cried Mr Miller. 'But Miss Morris must not overtax her strength.'

'I won't let her,' said Mrs Brandon, thus filling both her hearers with a passion of gratitude for her noble unselfishness.

Mr Miller then took his leave, promising to be back within the hour with the necessary materials. Mrs Brandon said not within the hour, because Miss Morris must have a rest, but perhaps at tea-time. Mr Miller was overcome by a sense of guilt at his own selfishness and said doubtless he could do the notices himself, but Mrs Brandon said, 'Tea-time then,' so firmly that he went away without another word.

'You think of nothing but others,' said Miss Morris to Mrs Brandon, fervently. Mrs Brandon smiled, sent her upstairs to rest till tea-time, and went back to the drawing-room where she sank, a little dramatically, on to the sofa.

'When you look at us all with that brave smile, it is obvious what has happened, darling,' said Francis. 'You have as usual been a prey to doing the effective thing and now you are going

187

to pay for it by having Miss Morris be grateful and devoted all over you, and that will make you very tired.'

'I don't see what else I could do,' said Mrs Brandon apologetically. 'If only she wouldn't be grateful she would be no trouble at all.'

'Well, she will be grateful,' said Francis, 'and if you aren't careful she'll stay here for ever and do the flowers. I wonder if we could get Sir Edmund to marry her. Coming to play tennis, Hilary?'

Mr Grant said he was sorry but he must go back to the Vicarage and work.

'All right, I'll take Delia on,' said her brother. 'Come on, Silly-Dilly.'

They went off, leaving Mr Grant with his hostess. Mr Grant said he must be going. Mrs Brandon felt that if anyone said again that he must be going and didn't go at once, she might scream, so she shut her eyes.

'I have tired you,' said Mr Grant, all aglow to abase himself. 'Forgive me for being so selfish. I will go at once, without disturbing you.'

Mrs Brandon felt pleasantly weak with self-pity and said nothing, hoping that her guest would go. Hearing no sound she cautiously opened her eyes again and saw that Mr Grant, far from having gone without disturbing her, was gazing down at her with dark violence.

'You know I would do *anything* for you,' he stammered, and banging into a chair he left the room.

Mrs Brandon shut her eyes again and dropped into a refreshing slumber, from which she was not disturbed till tea was brought in and Miss Morris came down. She was closely followed by Mr Miller with a parcel.

'You see I have taken you at your word, Mrs Brandon,' said Mr Miller, 'and come to tea. And here are the materials, Miss Morris, if you are sure the effort will not tire you. I have cut all the notices to the right size and lightly pencilled upon them the words they should carry. The actual form of the lettering I leave of course entirely to you. I only beg you not to do more than you feel equal to. I fear we need rather a large number, two notices for the Bicycle Park, three of Teas, One Shilling, though of course the words One Shilling will be written in figures, one for the Ice Cream and Soft Drinks tent, and one or two saying This Way to the Fête, Admission Adults Sixpence, Children Twopence. These I shall have put up in the village to catch the unwary tourist. They will also,' said Mr Miller, looking worried, 'require arrows on them, some pointing in one direction, some in another, if I make myself clear.'

'Perfectly,' said Miss Morris. 'You mean an arrow pointing one way on one notice and the other way on another so that people approaching the Vicarage from opposite directions may know which direction to take.'

'I see what you mean,' said Mrs Brandon, who had not been able to concentrate before because of pouring out tea. 'If you are coming *up* the street from the Cow you want an arrow pointing towards the Vicarage; but if you were coming *down* the street from the shop, you'd need an arrow pointing to the Vicarage in the other direction.'

'You are sure it will not be too much for you?' said Mr Miller, looking anxiously at Miss Morris.

'It will remind me of old days,' said Miss Morris. 'I still have the brushes with which I used to do my father's announcements, and with some Indian Ink I believe I could make quite a good effect.'

'Aha!' cried Mr Miller. 'I thought I remembered that you preferred Indian Ink and brought some with me.'

Mrs Brandon said she had a call to make in the village and went away.

'I do feel it indeed a privilege to have Mrs Brandon as a neighbour,' said Mr Miller, gazing at the drawing-room door through which she had just departed.

'I have never met anyone so genuinely kind,' said Miss Morris. 'I would do anything for her to show my gratitude, but unfortunately there is nothing I can do.'

'I am certain,' said Mr Miller earnestly, 'that she feels being allowed to help you in this your hour of need is the greatest privilege she could have. Besides I am sure you are the greatest comfort to her in many ways.'

'I can do the flowers for her,' said Miss Morris, 'and I have offered to help with her accounts. I find that she has considerable difficulty in adding up figures.'

'She has my deepest sympathy,' said Mr Miller. 'I assure you, Miss Morris, that any accounts connected with church or parish work cause me sleepless nights. For my own income that does not matter so much. When I have allotted a tenth part to my poorer brethren all I have to do is not to live outside the rest, and with the help of an occasional guest, such as Hilary Grant, that is quite possible. But on Saturday, for instance, with the Fête, I know, I positively know that I shall be confused. Last year, as I told Mrs Brandon, I found myself seventeen shillings and threepence out of pocket. Not,' he added hastily, 'that I grudged the money, but suppose, which is equally probable, that I had found myself seventeen shillings and threepence to the good. How unjust would have been my stewardship of money that is only in my hands in trust for others.'

He looked so wretched that Miss Morris felt here was someone she could help.

'I suppose you would not care to let me take over the merely technical side of the Fête accounts,' she said, not quite knowing what she meant by the word technical, but feeling that in using it she was being careful to distinguish between helping Mr Miller as a man and as a priest.

'Your kindness – really, Miss Morris,' said the Vicar.

'It would really be a pleasure,' said Miss Morris, the spirit of a thoroughly competent daughter of the clergy beginning to shine in her eye. 'I did all my father's accounts, church and personal, and I have usually done the household accounts for my old ladies.'

'No, I cannot allow myself to trespass upon your kindness, Miss Morris,' said Mr Miller firmly. 'Whatever muddles I have made this year are the outcome of my own stupidity and I must face the consequences. Next year – if it were not too much to ask – '

'I don't know where I shall be next year,' said Miss Morris simply. 'I have to find another situation as soon as possible.'

'Forgive me,' said Mr Miller, much distressed. 'My thoughtlessness is unpardonable. And to think that I should cast my burdens upon you at such a time.'

He made as though he would sweep all the cardboard and Indian Ink into his embrace and carry them off again, but Miss Morris, ignoring this gesture, said she would like to start work at once, so he said good-bye.

'Before you go, Mr Miller, there is one thing I must say,' said Miss Morris. 'If I do not go to church with Mrs Brandon on Sunday, I hope you will not misunderstand me. I know that my presence or absence could make no difference, but I would not like you to think me wanting in courtesy. I cannot so far ignore my dear father's wishes as to attend a form of worship that he disapproved. If there is, within walking distance, a place where worship is conducted as my father would have wished, I shall go to it.'

'I do respect your scruples,' said Mr Miller earnestly. 'There is Tompion over at Little Misfit, two miles by the fields though, too far for you at present; and Carson at Nutfield who would, I am sure, suit you admirably, delightful fellows both, though we do not see eye to eye. But Nutfield is too far. What can be done?'

Miss Morris begged him not to trouble, as she was well used to looking after herself, and thanked Mr Miller for his understanding.

'Your father and I could not, alas, agree to differ,' said Mr Miller, with one of his very rare smiles, 'but I hope that you and I may agree on that, if on nothing else.'

Miss Morris took the cardboard and Indian Ink upstairs to the Green dressing-room and began her work.

*

Francis's idle words about making Sir Edmund marry Miss Morris at once bore fruit in his mother's fertile mind. Happening to meet Sir Edmund in the village she asked him to dine on the following night, and added Mr Grant to the party to make up even numbers. By putting Miss Morris between Francis and Sir Edmund and explaining to Francis exactly the self-effacing role required of him, she hoped to precipitate matters considerably, but being no conspirator by nature she forgot to explain to her son the part he was to play. The result was that Francis and Miss Morris, who had a sort of understanding based on a kindly cynicism about human nature, talked to each other through most of dinner, while Sir Edmund fell a prey to Delia who had, as usual, some interesting local news to impart. A mentally defective labourer on Lord Pomfret's estate had killed the old uncle and aunt with whom he lodged by battering their heads in with a huge billet of wood. He had then knocked up his nearest neighbours, boasted gleefully of what he had done, gone home and thrown himself down the well. With what her family recognized as Delia's luck, she had passed the cottage on her bicycle just as the police were getting the body out. True, they had not allowed her to see it, nor to try artificial respiration, but she had had the intense pleasure of seeing Something with a blanket over it taken away, after which she had had a happy day with the otter hounds.

Sir Edmund said he had heard about it from his bailiff, and the Tiddens were always in trouble of some sort.

'Well, this was Horace Tidden,' said Delia. 'His father was always a bit dotty.'

'That would have been Ned Tidden,' said Sir Edmund, who had the intricate relationships of the countryside at his finger tips. 'He married his cousin, Lily Tidden. She was illegitimate of course. Ford sees her in the County Asylum from time to time. Since she nearly killed one of the nurses she has been quite happy and quiet.'

By these pleasant rural paths the conversation meandered to Grumper's End, where the chicken pox was still about. Delia said she hoped Jimmy Thatcher wasn't sickening, but he had a horrid cough.

Meanwhile Mrs Brandon, thrown back on Mr Grant's society, told him all about the pleated frock and the georgette that was a little too tight and the green frock that was dyed and the black and white foulard and the lilac georgette for afterwards, and Mr Grant felt that he was the kind of man to whom exquisite ladies confided their secrets and could talk about really interesting things; rather like an abbé under the ancien régime.

After dinner Mrs Brandon made another effort to get Sir Edmund into connexion with Miss Morris.

'Do, Sir Edmund,' she said, making room for him on the sofa beside her, 'do have a little talk to Miss Morris. She is such a delightful person and such a help to me with the flowers.'

'Looks a sensible woman,' said Sir Edmund, glancing at Miss Morris, who was examining gramophone records with the three young people. 'Not my style though. A bit too quiet. No life in her. Couldn't get a word out of her at dinner.'

'You didn't try as far as I could see,' said Mrs Brandon.

'You couldn't see at all,' said Sir Edmund. 'Playing your tricks on that young Grant. I've got something I want to say to you, Lavinia.'

'What is it?' asked Mrs Brandon, all flattering attention, hoping to bend Sir Edmund to her desires.

Sir Edmund pulled an envelope out of his pocket.

'You know that row I've been having about those new Council cottages,' he said. 'Well, I've written a pretty strong letter to the *Barchester Chronicle* about them and I'd like you to hear it before it goes. The average reader isn't very intelligent and I'd like to try it on you.'

Mrs Brandon said she would love to hear it, and taking up her tapestry work prepared herself to attend.

'Don't fiddle with that embroidery, Lavinia,' said Sir Edmund. 'You can't do two things at once. No one can. I want you to listen.'

Mrs Brandon, smiling angelically, wrapped her work up again in a silk handkerchief and looked intelligent.

'I'll just tell you exactly how the matter stands about those cottages,' said Sir Edmund, 'then you'll see the point of my letter.'

As his précis of the affair included a description of every battle he had fought with the Barchester County Council during the last forty years, and exactly what he thought of all builders and contractors, Mrs Brandon had plenty of time to construct a charming romance in which Sir Edmund and Miss Morris were married at Barchester Cathedral and she had a new dress for the wedding with one of those little hats with veils that were so becoming. Just as she was thinking how nice it would be if Mr Miller could take part in the marriage ceremony, Sir Edmund said, 'I don't believe you've heard a word I've been saying, Lavinia.'

'Well, quite truthfully I haven't heard much,' said Mrs Brandon. 'You see I was thinking about you so hard that I couldn't listen to you.'

'Don't talk nonsense, Lavinia,' said Sir Edmund, quite unmoved by this subtle flattery. 'I don't suppose you were thinking about me at all. Thinking about a new dress more likely.'

'Well, I was,' said Mrs Brandon meekly. 'At least a dress that I'd had dyed. But what I *really* want to hear is your letter, not about the County Council. I think Miss Morris ought to hear it too. She is so practical. Miss Morris!' she called across the room, 'could you come here for a moment.'

Miss Morris came.

'Sir Edmund has a most interesting letter to read to us,' said Mrs Brandon, 'and we are sure you can help. Do begin again from the beginning, Sir Edmund, and tell Miss Morris all about the cottages.'

Sir Edmund obligingly began all over again, fought all his battles with the County Council and the contractors, and finally read his letter aloud, though with some difficulty, owing to the number of corrections he had made.

'Pretty strong, I think,' he said approvingly when he had finished.

'If you will excuse me, Sir Edmund,' said Miss Morris, who had been listening with impartial intelligence, 'I would suggest – ' and she made one or two very practical suggestions, which would have the double advantage of making the letter intelligible and alleviating the danger of three or four separate libel actions. Sir Edmund, recognizing the value of her remarks, wrote her wording over his own and then looked disconsolately upon the paper which had become a palimpsest several layers deep.

'I could easily type it out for you if you like, Sir Edmund,' said Miss Morris, 'with a copy, and it would reach the *Chronicle* offices in plenty of time. They don't go to press till Tuesday.'

At this point Mrs Brandon, delighted at her success in throwing her two guests together, abstracted herself from their society and went over to the gramophone. Mr Grant was waiting for Francis and Delia who had gone to look for some records that Francis had left in his car, and was enchanted to have his hostess to himself for a moment.

'I have hardly seen you this evening, Hilary,' said Mrs Brandon in a most upsetting way, and apparently forgetting that he had been next to her for all the early part of the evening.

'I was so hoping to have a word with you,' said Mr Grant, who might have been thought by an impartial observer to have had practically nothing else all through dinner. 'I don't know why, but you are the only person I can really talk to about myself.'

Having made this noble avowal Mr Grant went bright red and gazed appealingly at Mrs Brandon, who was enjoying herself immensely. The conversation would doubtless have proceeded along these interesting if well-worn lines had not Rose come into say that Mr Merton wished to speak to Mrs Brandon on the phone. She was absent from the room for nearly ten minutes and when she came back Francis and Delia were with Mr Grant.

'Who were you talking to, darling?' said Francis. 'You have your mysterious mischief face.'

'Mr Merton rang me up,' said Mrs Brandon, ignoring her son's last words. 'He is staying with the Keiths this week-end and is coming over with them to the Fête to-morrow, and said he would like to come and see us. So I said a glass of sherry about six. I couldn't say tea, because we must have Tea, One Shilling to please Mr Miller.'

Francis and Delia expressed loud approval of a visit from Mr Merton. Mr Grant kept his disapproval to himself and christened Mrs Brandon the Belle Dame Sans Merci in his own mind.

'Well, Lavinia, I must be off,' said Sir Edmund, coming up. 'Miss Morris is going to type that letter for me. It will make the Council sit up. Quite a nice woman. She says she wants a job, secretary or something. If I hear of anything I'll let you know.'

195

With this lover-like speech he said good-bye and the party broke up.

'I do hope you had a nice talk with Sir Edmund,' said Mrs Brandon to Miss Morris, when she took her to her room.

'Very nice,' said Miss Morris. 'He has kindly promised to let me know if he hears of any work I could do.'

It was hardly the attitude of one whose heart was involved, and Mrs Brandon could only tell herself that everything must have a beginning. When she had said good night and gone to her room, Miss Morris got out her typewriter and made two fair copies of Sir Edmund's letter. It was now eleven o'clock, but there was still work that her conscience told her must be done. The cards with arrows and directions for reaching the Vicarage had only been sketched in pencil. Miss Morris got out her Indian Ink and her brushes and sat down at the table in the Green dressing-room. As she worked she felt that she was once more at home, doing the notices for her father, and that their pleasant young guest Mr Miller would help to put them up to-morrow morning. It was true that her bedroom at home was an attic, poorly furnished with painted deal furniture and an iron bedstead, and that instead of a shaded reading lamp she would have been working by a little oil lamp while she waited for her father to call out for her to come and read to him. But though so much was changed, one thing was unchanged. Mr Miller, how if he had not behaved so unkindly to her father would have been the most agreeable pupil they had ever had, was in the Vicarage, not far away, and would be putting up to-morrow morning the notices that she was finishing now. There was yet another thing unchanged, but Miss Morris did not notice it, because it was herself, and not being given by temperament or training to introspection, it never occurred to her to consider that Miss Morris, the homeless and penniless companion, was only Ella Morris, the Vicar's daughter, in other circumstances and surroundings. The gulf between her old life and the life of the last twenty-five years was so great that she saw a stranger on the far side of it, having little in common with herself. When she had finished she laid down her brush and pondered on Ella Morris, who had once been so angry with Mr Miller for annoying her father that she could not even pray for him. Then Miss Morris the companion put her work tidily away, but before she lay down she knelt by her bed, as she had been taught to do and had always done, and prayed for Mr Miller as heartily as if he were her enemy.

- 10 -

THE VICARAGE FÊTE - 1

NEXT morning promised well for the Fête. As Mr Grant looked out of his window he saw the valley still shrouded in a light mist which, by a beautiful and poetical flight of fancy, he compared to the filmy veils of sleep from which Mrs Brandon would presently emerge, a goddess made manifest. He then remembered with some annoyance that his mother was coming over that afternoon, but put the disagreeable thought resolutely away and went down to breakfast. Already in the Vicarage paddock stalls were being put up and helpers were getting in the way. A lorry came crashing past the front gate and turned into the field where it unloaded the marquee in which tea was to be served. The roundabout with its steam organ had arrived the night before and was partly erected. Two oily men were carrying boats, ostriches, aeroplane bodies, cocks, horses, swans, and other usual methods of transit, from the van to the platform and fixing them to the brightly polished spiral brass poles which would carry them on their circular path. Mr Miller came in, hot, but not entirely without hope.

'Good morning, sir,' said Mr Grant. 'It looks like a fine day for the Fête.'

'Indeed, indeed it does,' said Mr Miller. 'I have just been putting up some of the Tea, One Shilling notices. I do hope we shall not have so much paper left about as last year. The schoolmaster has spoken about it to the children, and the Women's Institute and the Scouts are collaborating. Mr Spindler has offered us the use of two large dustbins for rubbish of all sorts, and a party of Wolf Cubs are at this moment scrubbing them out. I shall put one near the Confectionery Stall and one near the Ice-Cream Stall. And I must have notices written for them. What would you put, Hilary? ''Rubbish'' or ''Refuse'' or simply ''Waste Paper''?'

Mr Grant thought Rubbish would do.

'I must ask Hettie if we have any old cardboard boxes,' said the Vicar. 'White ones of course, because ink doesn't show on brown, and then I must write the notices.'

'Couldn't I do it, sir?' asked Mr Grant.

'That would indeed be kind,' said the Vicar. 'I will ask about some cardboard at once.'

But before he could ring, Hettie came in with a parcel.

'Please sir, Sid brought this over from Stories,' she said, 'and we was to be sure to be careful with it.'

'Thanks, Hettie,' said the Vicar. 'And do you think we have any pieces of cardboard large enough to write Rubbish on?'

'I'm sure I don't know sir,' said Hettie. 'There's plenty of paper in your study, sir, if you wanted to write rubbish. There was that new lot from the Nutfield Co-op come only a fortnight ago.'

'Mr Miller means he wants to write Rubbish on a large piece of cardboard and put it up,' said Mr Grant.

'Well, I daresay Cook or me could find something if he really wants to write rubbish,' said Hettie, obviously impressed by her master's determination thus to free his soul.

'Look, Hilary,' said Mr Miller excitedly.

He had opened the parcel. In it were three exquisitely written notices of This Way to the Fête, complete with arrows, some pointing one way, some the other.

'Those are ripping, sir,' said Mr Grant. 'And what's under them?'

Mr Miller drew out a rather smaller package. He unwrapped it and took out three placards on which were emblazoned the words NO LITTER. KINDLY PUT ALL RUBBISH IN HERE.

'It is like an answer to prayer,' said Mr Miller.

'And a jolly quick answer too,' said Mr Grant, yielding to

none in his admiration of an omniscient and evidently all-potent Providence. 'I mean you'd only just begun thinking about the rubbish, hadn't you, sir?'

'There are things that we do not understand,' said Mr Miller, truthfully, and at the same time much abashing his pupil. 'But here is a letter which will doubtless explain. You may read it,' he added, pushing it towards Mr Grant.

The letter was neatly typewritten and ran as follows:

Dear Mr Miller,

I am sending you the notices of the Fête. Mrs Brandon is kindly allowing the garden boy to take them over as I am sure you will be early at work. You may remember that my father, who had a great dislike for disorder of any kind, always had receptacles for paper and other rubbish at any church functions. In case this thought has also occurred to you, I am also sending you three notices. If you have no special receptacles for litter, I might suggest that empty dustbins, well scrubbed out with a disinfectant, would answer the purpose. I always cleared the Vicarage dustbin myself for this purpose in old days.

With every good wish for the success of the Fête,

Yours sincerely,
Ella Morris.

'How marvellous of Mrs Brandon to think of sending them over early,' said Mr Grant in a reverent voice.

Mr Miller began to busy himself in tidying the paper and string that were littering the end of the dining-room table. He suddenly remembered a summer morning more than twenty-five years ago and Mr Morris's daughter in a check apron outside the kitchen door, carrying a pail of water and a scrubbing brush. Young Mr Miller had offered to carry the pail, but Miss Morris had said she could quite well manage, but would he be kind enough to get the tin of Jeyes' Fluid off the scullery window sill, as she must clean out the dustbin for the Church Lads' Brigade tea and entertainment. The smell of disinfectant came nostalgically back to him across the years. He stopped smoothing and folding the papers and stood still.

'You look a bit tired, sir,' said Mr Grant, with real concern. 'You haven't had breakfast yet. I'll clear that paper away.'

Mr Miller, remembering that he must be hard at work all day and not fail his parishioners at any point, obediently sat down and made a fairly good breakfast.

'You had better make a good meal now, Hilary,' he said. 'Hettie and Cook always have the day off for the Fête and I'm afraid it will only be the sort of lunch they leave on the table. I sometimes wish that cold tongue and tomatoes had never been invented.'

When Miss Morris, who did not always get up for breakfast, came down about eleven o'clock she found her hostess slightly discomposed.

'I *cannot* make up my mind about this afternoon,' said Mrs Brandon. 'I meant to wear the black and white foulard, the one I lent Delia for the funeral, but Nurse wants me to wear the lilac georgette and make Delia wear the foulard.'

'I think Nurse is right,' said Miss Morris gravely. 'With that pinkish hat and scarf of yours it would look very well.'

'I had thought of that,' said Mrs Brandon. 'But I don't see how one could really count pink as mourning.'

Miss Morris said it was two days after the funeral.

'Yes, I have put it to myself that way,' said Mrs Brandon with an air of broad-mindedness, 'but I somehow feel that one cannot quite go out of mourning on a Saturday. Monday would be all right, but I can't quite *feel* Saturday. But it is all very mixing, because if one goes on wearing mourning for Aunt Sissie it looks as if one were trying to influence her.'

Miss Morris pointed out that as Miss Brandon's will must necessarily have been made before her death, it was highly improbable that it could be in any way influenced by Mrs Brandon's choice of a dress. Mrs Brandon, while admitting the justice of this contention, said that she had a feeling about it. Having thus settled the question she asked Miss Morris what she meant to wear.

'My usual blue dress,' said Miss Morris.

'Wouldn't the black georgette be cooler?' said Mrs Brandon. 'It's going to be frightfully hot. Or if you wouldn't mind the black and white foulard Delia would love not to wear it. She wants to wear a green dress and Nurse is making difficulties.'

'Thank you so much,' said Miss Morris, 'but I think my blue dress would be best. I haven't any reason to wear mourning and a long dress would not be very suitable for me. I thought Mr

Miller might need a little help during the afternoon, and if I take an apron with me I shall be quite prepared.'

'But you mustn't dream of helping,' said Mrs Brandon, genuinely anxious about her protégée's health. 'You aren't up to it. You have no idea how stuffy everything gets, and all the children, and the noise of the roundabout. I am always exhausted after an hour of it.'

'I am quite used to that sort of thing,' said Miss Morris. 'I ran everything for my father when I was a girl and I always got on well with the children. Of course we couldn't afford the round-about – it was a very poor parish – but we had the Temperance Silver Brass Band and the noise they made was quite dreadful.'

Mrs Brandon gave in and with considerable heroism said she would wear the foulard, so that Delia would be free to wear her green frock.

'Lunch has to be at one to-day,' she said. 'I do hope you don't mind, but the maids all take it in turns to go down to the Fête, so it will be a kind of picnic.'

*

The picnic, which included veal cutlets and three vegetables and a chocolate soufflé and gooseberry fool (which was still tyrannizing over the countryside) with little freshly made almond fingers and cream cheese and several sorts of biscuits and coffee and a choice of lemonade, white wine, and cider, was being re-peated with differences all over the neighbourhood. At the Vicarage Mr Miller and Mr Grant were mildly depressed by slices of pressed beef from the Barchester Co-op gently perspiring on a blue dish, three overripe tomatoes, and the remains of yesterday's stewed gooseberries put into a smaller dish. At South-bridge Mr and Mrs Keith, their unmarried daughter Lydia, and their guest Mr Merton had lunch at a quarter past one instead of half-past, so that the parlourmaid and the cook could catch the motor bus. Those excellent fellows Tompion at Little Misfit and Carson at Nutfield, found themselves condemned, by a kind of unwritten law one supposes, to the same pressed beef, tomatoes, and yesterday's stewed gooseberries as were being served at Pomfret Madrigal Vicarage. Mr Tompion, who was famed for his bad luck, had the heel of one piece of pressed beef and the toe or beginning of another, because he had done the shopping himself in Barchester and was too humble to tell the young man at the Co-op to give him a quarter of a pound from a nice piece that was already in cut. Mr Carson, on the other hand, had some nice fresh slices, personally chosen by his housekeeper who liked pressed beef herself, but the gooseberries, which she didn't like, were two days old and tasted of ferment, besides having one or two suspicious patches of fur, so that only fear of the housekeeper made Mr Carson eat them at all. But everyone will be glad to know that both these gentlemen married within the year, Mr Tompion in January a Colonel's daughter from Leamington, and Mr Carson at Easter a very nice widow from the Midlands who stood no nonsense from servants, and both ladies treated their husbands extremely well.

At Norton Park Lady Norton said to Mrs Grant that they would not have a glass of sherry before lunch, so that some of the servants could go in the estate Ford to the Fête, a piece of altruism which made her butler, who was not going, despise her. The only person who really picnicked was Sir Edmund, who disliked lunch and seized the opportunity of having sandwiches, which he ate in front of the Council cottages in a manner highly disconcerting to his enemy the foreman, who felt nervously compelled to work right up to the legal time of knocking off.

Down at Grumper's End Jimmy Thatcher, who had a nasty cough and an obvious temperature, ate far too much pickled pork because his mother said if he didn't finish what was on his plate he could go to bed and stay there, and to hurry up about it.

By half-past two the first piercing blasts of the steam organ announced to the village, most of whom were already on the field, that the Fête had really begun. The gentry did not begin to turn up till later, among the first being the party from Stories. Mrs Brandon had insisted on giving a ten shilling note to each of her party, to be spent at the various stalls. Francis and Delia gladly accepted the gift and Miss Morris's protests were overruled by all three Brandons, who pointed out that she was for the present one of the family. Her protestations were finally cut short by Francis, who with great foresight had laid in two pounds' worth of sixpences, threepenny bits, and coppers at the bank in Barchester that morning, and offered to change everyone's notes for them.

'That is really practical,' said Miss Morris admiringly. 'I can't think why we never thought of that at our Fêtes. I remember what difficulty we always had about change, and as we always had the Fête on a Thursday, which was early closing day, the shop and the bank were shut.'

'Don't be extravagant, Miss Morris,' said Francis. 'And remember I have booked the first ride on the roundabout with you. I bag the cock, but if you don't like the ostrich you and Delia can go in an aeroplane.'

As they walked to the Vicarage Miss Morris's placards drew forth much admiration from the Brandons, who had not yet seen them, and when a carful of obvious strangers was seen to slow down, look at the notice, stop, consult, and turn the car towards the Vicarage gate, Francis, whose relations with Miss Morris were now on much the same gentlemanly and unemotional footing as those of Mr Swiveller and Miss Brass, hit her kindly on the back and said that meant at least ten shillings in teas and side shows. Miss Morris smiled indulgently at Francis and walked quietly on, but her whole being was seething with an excitement she could hardly control. She had been brought up, as the widower parson's daughter, on mothers' meetings, G.F.S. meetings, sewing parties, Sunday School excursions, bazaars, fêtes, rummage sales, and the hundred activities of the Vicarage. She had given ungrudgingly her time, thought and labour, and it was her secret pride that no event for which she had been responsible had ever been a failure. Under her management receipts had always exceeded expenses, even if only by so narrow a margin as three and elevenpence halfpenny, teas had been generous, no children had ever been lost or had accidents, mothers had happily sat wedged in a motor coach for four hours, spent one hour in the pouring rain at Weston-Super-Mare, and happily and damply sung for four hours on the way home. Fractious children had been quelled by her presence, and for all infantile diseases Miss Morris's help and advice were infinitely preferred to those of the district nurse by mothers and patients alike. She knew that there was nothing she could not organize and carry through successfully, which gave her a sense of power, very dear to her heart.

With her father's death all this had come to an end. For twenty years she had hidden herself under the mask of Miss Morris, rather a *reserved* kind of woman, my dear, but quite trustworthy and nursed poor Aunt Emma up to the end, and would do splendidly for your husband's old sister, I am certain. It had been a life of severe self-repression. Not as regarded her old ladies, for to them she felt on the whole a kindly and unsentimental tolerance, but as regarded the arrangements of the houses and hotels where they lived, the organization of service, the discipline of servants, the regulating of expenditure. But in dreams she beheld a parish, every detail of which was under her hand and eye, every relationship known to her, where she would collaborate with all officials and at the same time protect her flock against them, where everything would be a part of one smoothly-running machine of which she was the centre. As for the actual spiritual leader of this parish, she gave him no thought, for her imagination did not work on those lines. If he existed at all it was as a conscientious if shadowy figure who came to her for advice on every point and did not meddle. To-day, for the first time since her servitude had begun, she was to live for a few hours in the familiar life, and though no one heard her, she was saying Ha-ha loudly and exultingly.

Admission Sixpence was paid by Mrs Brandon for the whole party and they entered the field. Mr Grant, who was helping with the coconut shies, had been looking out for them and came forward to meet them.

'I suppose you wouldn't care to try for a coconut, Mrs Brandon,' he said.

Mrs Brandon said she thought not and she would go and buy some things at the Produce Stall and the Fancy Stall and then perhaps sit in the Vicarage garden away from the noise.

'You all go and amuse yourselves,' she said to the three young people, 'and come and fetch me at four o'clock and we'll have tea in the marquee. It is rather horrible but one must. And Francis, ask whoever is in charge of the teas to keep me a table.

I'll get the Keiths to join us and Mrs Morland and your mother, Hilary, and Lady Norton if she stays, so we might be about a dozen. I know they have the two ping-pong tables from the British Legion club room, so do ask them to put them together and that will do nicely.'

'O.K. mamma,' said Francis. 'I go, I go, see how I go. Come with me, Miss Morris. I'm sure you can deal with tea-tents better than I can.'

Miss Morris said she would be very glad if she could be of any help and the two went off.

'And now,' said Mrs Brandon to Delia, 'you won't want to go round the stalls, darling. I know what will happen. I shall have to buy Cook's jam and cake, and Ethel's knitted dish-cloths, and Nurse's baby woollies, and send them all to the hospital. Take Hilary on the roundabout.'

Mr Grant was wounded to the quick by Mrs Brandon's summary relegation of him to the rank of a young person, but Delia gave him no time to feel annoyance. Expressing a fear that someone might have bagged the ostrich, she urged her cousin Hilary rapidly in the direction of the roundabout. The boats and other conveyances were just slowing down and several people were getting off. Calling to Mr Grant to follow her, Delia climbed on to the still moving platform and seized the ostrich on to which she leapt and sat side saddle with an expression of pride and contentment. Under her direction Mr Grant took possession of the cock, whose orbit was within that of the ostrich, and mounted it astride. One of the oily men came round.

'I pay this one,' said Delia, 'and you pay the next, and so on. Two please.' And she held out four pennies.

'Threepence, miss,' said the oily man.

'It was twopence last year,' said Delia.

The oily man was understood to say that it was threepence this year because of the Government, and that even so it was a dead loss to the proprietor, Mr Packer, who ran it on a purely philanthropic basis.

'All right,' said Delia. 'Here's half a crown, and tell Mr Packer I'm going to have my rides at twopence a time. That's seven and a half rides each, and Mr Grant will give you another half-crown and that makes fifteen rides each, or we may use some of them for friends.'

The oily man said he supposed that was all right and went off to collect the other fares.

'Cheek!' said Delia to Mr Grant. 'It's always twopence a ride, and they know it.'

'Are you really going to have fifteen rides?' asked Mr Grant.

'Of course. I adore roundabouts,' said Delia, and the steam organ gave a frightful screech, intended to warn laggards, and burst into 'The Honeysuckle and the Bee', the popular song of the year the organ first appeared in public. The platform began to revolve, Mr Packer's face appeared for a moment above the machinery, even oilier than that of his subordinate, and the whole intoxicating equipage was in motion. To Delia the roundabout had represented since her youthful days the highest point of romance. Seated side saddle, her hair blown by the oil-scented breeze of the ostrich in its career, her elegant legs dangling, Delia felt herself to be d'Artagnan, Sir Lancelot, a Cavalier riding with dispatches to King Charles, a heroine doing something or other for someone she was in love with, Mazeppa, Cortes and several other people. At every flower show she spent most of her money and time, sometimes in a boat or aeroplane body but most often on a bird, and usually descended from her mount in a state of exaltation which lasted until after dinner and sometimes made her rather remote and disagreeable.

Mr Grant, who did not understand his cousin's peculiar devotion to this form of mental stimulus, was ready enough to ride on a cock two or three times, but felt a distinct uneasiness at the thought of half a crown's worth of this exercise. However Delia looked so happy and so pretty, with the flush of excitement on her face, that he determined to endure as long as possible. As the second twopennyworth was coming to an end, he saw a large good-looking girl striding over the grass towards the roundabout, followed by Mr Merton. The last revolution of the platform then carried him away, but as he came round again the girl called out 'Hoy' in piercing tones. Delia looked for the noise, saw it, and shrieked 'Lydia' at the top of her voice. The girl barely waiting for the ostrich to stop, mounted the platform.

'I knew it was you on the ostrich,' she said to Delia. 'I told Noel you'd be here, didn't I, Noel?' she added to Mr Merton who had climbed up after her. 'I say, someone's on my cock.'

'It's only my cousin Hilary,' said Delia. 'He won't mind changing, will you, Hilary. It's Lydia Keith that I was at Barchester High School with. Hullo, Mr Merton.'

Mr Grant, really quite glad of an excuse to dismount, offered his cock to Lydia, who immediately flung a leg over it, explaining that she had put on a frock with pleats on purpose, as she always felt sick if she rode sideways.

'You and Hilary can go in the swan boat behind us,' she shouted to Mr Merton. 'Sorry, I didn't mean to say Hilary, but Delia never said what your name was.'

'Grant,' said the gentleman addressed.

'Well, do you mind if I call you Hilary?' said Lydia. 'Hurry up and get into the swan.'

'We'd better,' said Mr Merton to Mr Grant, 'or Lydia is capable of riding all over the field after us on the cock.'

Accordingly the two gentlemen seated themselves face to face in a kind of canoe with a swan's head and shoulders growing out of its prow.

'It makes me feel a bit like Lohengrin,' said Mr Merton, 'or half of him.'

'Now I know why he always arrives standing, however unbalanced,' said Mr Grant, whose knees were hitting his chin. 'They never thought of people's legs when they made these boats.'

'It was a poor idea to have swans to drag one about anyway,' said Mr Merton. 'I'd always be afraid they might turn round and hiss at me or bite.'

Mr Grant said he didn't suppose Wagner had really worked it out. The steam organ burst into 'Farewell, my Bluebell', a romantic song of adieu familiar to an older generation, and the whole cavalcade was once more set in motion. The oily man came up for Mr Merton's fare, but Mr Grant explained that the two half-crowns were covering expenses for his shipmate and also for the young lady on the cock. The oily man, who by now couldn't hear himself speak, nodded understanding and went away.

As they slowed down again Mr Grant, who found this circular travel very boring, asked Mr Merton, whom much to his annoyance he still couldn't help liking, whether he thought they would have to stay much longer.

'Not if you are feeling as sick as I am,' said Mr Merton, who had been travelling backwards and not liking it. 'Lydia and Miss Brandon will be talking about their old school for ages, and I know that once Lydia is on her cock nothing will get her off. I came here last year with the Keiths and she had thirteen rides.'

'Delia has paid for fifteen,' said Mr Grant, with some pride in his cousin's spirit, 'and I'm supposed to be having fifteen too, but if we got off Miss Keith could use mine.'

'I'd willingly pay half a crown never to have got on the thing at all,' said Mr Merton. 'It's stopping now. Hullo, there's Tony Morland.'

Mr Grant had been aware, during the latter and slower revolutions of this particular twopennyworth, of someone in grey flannels standing near the roundabout and gazing with an expression of detached scorn upon the vagaries of mortals. This person he saw, as the machine came to a standstill, to be the same boy he had met at the picnic.

'I'm frightened of that boy,' he said to Mr Merton as they staggered off the boat. 'He makes me feel I am twenty years his junior and slightly imbecile at that.'

'I know,' said Mr Merton. 'He is a bit like the gentleman in Tennyson, holding no form of creed but contemplating all. But I believe he is human inside. At least his housemaster, who is rather a friend of mine and married Lydia's sister, seems to think so. Hullo, Tony.'

Tony Morland turned his head slightly and saw Mr Merton and Mr Grant.

'How do you do, sir,' he said, with a distant courtesy of manner, as from fallen royalty to one who was respectfully pretending not to see through his incognito. 'How do you do, Mr Grant.'

Both gentlemen felt as if they had been talking in church. Mr Merton was the first to recover himself and asked if Tony was going on the roundabout.

'Perhaps later,' said Tony. 'Did you get to the ballet last week, sir?'

'Not I,' said Mr Merton. 'This is my holiday and I'm not going back to town till I must.'

'It's hardly worth seeing this year,' said Tony negligently. 'There is nothing new except *Les Centaures et les Lapithes* with Bolikoff's *décor*, and I'd hardly advise anyone to go unless they had read Vougeot's *Entrechats Gris*. The whole is a bit determinist, though there's one of the *corps de ballet* that really understands the *pointes*.'

'Do you *have* to talk like that?' asked Mr Merton.

'Yes, sir,' said Tony, the faintest flicker of a smile passing over his face. 'You see I have a friend who talks like that and I have to copy his mannerisms at present. I'll grow out of it. It was much worse last holidays.'

Lydia Keith, swinging past them on the cock, now shouted a greeting at Tony and a command to join the roundabout.

'Aren't you coming, sir?' Tony said to Mr Merton.

'No,' said Mr Merton, casting a nauseated look at the swan boat. 'I'm going to find Mrs Brandon. Do you know where she is?'

'With my mother in the Vicarage garden when I last saw her,' said Tony, and leapt on to the moving platform.

Mr Grant suddenly felt that if Mr Merton was going to make himself pleasant to Mrs Brandon, he, Mr Grant, might as well emigrate, so he boarded the roundabout again as it stopped. Let Mr Merton go and wanton in Mrs Brandon's smiles. For him the free roving life of a Conquistador. He mounted the nearest steed, a dapple grey with a red saddle and bridle painted on it, and found to his surprise that Delia was riding abreast with him on a chestnut with violet trappings.

'I gave the ostrich to Tony,' she said, 'because Lydia wanted to talk to him. I say, Hilary, do you suppose we'll soon know about Aunt Sissie? I know it's rather beastly to say things like that, but I had an idea.'

'About something?' said Mr Grant.

'Yes. Really as a matter of fact about if she did by mistake happen to have – I mean if there was anything even if it was only a very little,' said Delia.

209

As she had stopped speaking Mr Grant came to the conclusion that she had said what she wanted to say. The wording had been obscure in the extreme, but he guessed what she was driving at. He felt that she was in difficulties and decided that as Aunt Sissie's will was not a subject that could be indefinitely avoided, he might as well break the ice and save his cousin any further embarrassment.

'It does seem rather beastly,' he admitted, raising his voice as the steam organ broke again into 'The Honeysuckle and the Bee', 'but after all it's only business. I'll tell you what, Delia, but it's a secret, if I did get anything from Aunt Sissie I'm going to make a will and say if I die first your mother is to have it. I shan't use any of it myself.'

He could not hear through the blaring of the organ his young cousin's hero-worshipping, long-drawn 'Oh, Hilary,' but he read admiration and approval in her eyes and was not displeased.

'And now tell me yours,' he said, as soon as a pause in the sequence of melodies allowed him to make himself heard.

'Well,' said Delia, looking straight in front of her, 'if I did get anything, I don't mean me and Francis but only me, I thought I would give it to Miss Morris. She's had an absolutely rotten time. Do you suppose I could?'

A great many thoughts suddenly dashed into Mr Grant's mind. Among the first was a feeling of shame that Delia and not himself should have been the first to think of this. He realized, with some mental discomfort, that his plan of giving up his potential inheritance to Mrs Brandon, who didn't need it, was a thoroughly selfish piece of self-glorification. If he had been whoever it was who gave his lady his falcon for dinner there might conceivably have been some merit in the sacrifice, though he had always had private doubts as to the amount of eating on a falcon. But to give a quite rich person some money that he didn't need himself, simply to make himself a benefactor in her eyes and be charmingly thanked, was pure egoism. And considering Mrs Brandon, he now saw how probable it was that she, who never thought of or valued money, because she had always had it, would have accepted his tribute with her usual charm, perhaps said 'Dear Hilary, this is too sweet of you,' and laid a hand on his arm, but would have felt no particular obligation, no deep gratitude, and quite likely have refused, lightly, to take it, treating him as a child who did not know what he was doing.

And here was Delia, to whom in his arrogance, absorbed as he was by his romantic devotion to her mother, he had paid little attention, except as a useful person for tennis, who had seen at once where help was needed and was prepared to give it. Perhaps she too was only expressing a devotion, the devotion of a generous nature to anything that had called out its powers of helping, but in the sacrifice she proposed to make there was at least something very practical. He wanted to give what he didn't need to someone who didn't need it, persuading himself that this was a sacrifice to – Well, to what? Thinking of Mrs Brandon as he so often had since he met her, in the night, when he ought to be working, in the melting air of twilight, in the intoxicating warmth of high noon up on the downs, in church (where, he had decided, to think of her was exactly the same as paying attention to the service), in the early morning when the summer mists lay on the world, he had occasionally tried to give his feelings a name. Love, desire; delicious words to intoxicate himself with, but not what he meant. Passion, even with a very small p, would be a desecration of his thought. Adoration, devotion, was perhaps nearer the mark, but did not satisfy him. What human word could ever express one's feeling, at the same time worshipping and protecting, for so exquisite a creature, the child in the woman. As he thought of her in her sunlit, flowery drawing-room, or by candle-light below the chestnut tree, veiled in shadowy lace, her lovely eyes a little tired, her enchanting voice muted, listening to him as he read to her, or telling him about Nurse and Rose, he was suddenly so pierced and torn by whatever it was he felt, that he nearly fell off his dapple grey steed.

'I think your idea is very good too,' said the voice of Delia, who thought his silence might mean that he disapproved her own plan, 'and I expect mother would think it was awfully kind of you. You've got a pretty good crush on her, haven't you? Everyone has,' said Delia proudly.

At these words it would not be quite correct to say that the scales fell from Mr Grant's eyes, for one's eyes are not as a rule opened to one's own peculiarities so quickly and finally. But the word crush, deeply as he disliked and resented it, seemed to fill a gap that no other word had filled. For a fleeting moment he wondered if he had been a little ridiculous. Then he put this doubt at the back of his mind and turned his attention to Delia.

'I think your plan is splendid,' he said, 'and I only wish I'd thought of it myself. It would be simply perfect to give Miss Morris something. I like her awfully, don't you?'

'She's all right,' said Delia tolerantly. 'Of course she will drive mother mad if she stays here long, because she will be humble and grateful. I'm going to see that she has a good rest and get her a bit fatter and then I was thinking Mr Miller's stepmother at Harrogate might have her.'

'Does she want a companion?' asked Mr Grant.

'I don't know,' said Delia, 'but that's no reason why she shouldn't. Mother has an idea of Sir Edmund marrying Miss Morris, but that's all sentiment. Mother is an angel, but she never sees things except the way she wants them, and that's the way things don't go. I say, how many rides have we had?'

Mr Grant said he should think about ten, but would ask. The oily man when appealed to said it was nine for the young lady and four for the other young lady on the cock and three for the gentleman who had got off and seven for this young gentleman and three for the young gentleman on the ostrich.

'All right, that makes twenty-six,' said Delia. 'Four more to go. Oh, Lydia and Tony are getting off. Shall we do the other four, Hilary?'

Mr Grant said he would love to, and offered to stand his cousin as many more as she liked. So they continued their wild career, talking eagerly whenever the music allowed and enjoying their scheme of philanthropy for Miss Morris, till Mr Grant noticed a sudden thinning of the crowd on the field and looking at his watch said it was four o'clock and they must go to the tea-tent.

'Had a nice ride, sir?' asked Mr Packer, raising his dirty face from among the machinery as his customers dismounted.

'Splendid, thanks,' said Mr Grant. 'We might come back after tea. That's an awfully good horse I've been riding.'

'That's Persimmon, sir. All called after Derby winners,' said Mr Packer. 'He's getting on, but there's life in him yet. Needs a new tail, but we all have our troubles.'

Mr Grant asked if a shilling would be of any assistance towards a new tail and on hearing that it would, he handed it over in trust to Mr Packer, who thanked him warmly and said he would drink the young lady's health at the Cow and Sickle when he went to get his bit of supper before the evening rush. Old Persimmon, he added, seeing a slight shade of disappointment on Mr Grant's face at this re-appropriation of the tail-money, wouldn't grudge a man his pint of beer, and to prevent any further argument on the subject disappeared into the machinery again.

'Don't say anything about my plan,' said Delia to her cousin Hilary, as they walked towards the tent. 'I want it all to be a surprise – I mean if anything did happen. And I won't say anything about your plan.'

'My plan is dead,' said Mr Grant with sudden determination. 'If I did have anything, would you mind if I came into your plan? I don't want to shove in if you'd rather not, but I think your plan is so good that I'd like to be in it, if you don't mind.'

'O.K.,' said Delia, 'and it's very nice of you.'

*

Miss Lydia Keith and Mr Anthony Morland, having left the roundabout, as we saw, some time earlier, had done the round of the various side shows pretty thoroughly. At the shooting gallery Tony with his O.T.C. experience was an easy first, hitting a tin rabbit that bobbed up and down at various points on a landscape six times out of six and thus qualifying as the recipient of a small mug left over from the coronation of the summer before, while Lydia, who only fired a gun once a year at the Southbridge Flower Show, missed every time.

'Come on, let's try hitting the weight,' said Lydia, leading the way towards an upright plank with figures on it. As they approached, Mr Spindler from the Cow took up a large blacksmith's hammer, whirled it round his head and brought it down vehemently on a kind of anvil at the base of the plank. A weight rushed about three-quarters of the way up and fell down again.

'Anyone could do that,' said Tony scornfully, and picking up the hammer he aimed a blow at the anvil. The hammer glanced off it and Tony nearly fell over.

'Here, that's not the way,' said Lydia, and wresting the hammer from his grasp she whirled it in the air with all the strength of her hockey-playing muscles. The weight flew up almost to the top and a large rent appeared in the armhole of her dress.

'You've split something,' said Tony with gloomy pleasure.

'Arm, I suppose,' said Lydia, trying to look over her own shoulder. 'Bother! I always split something. Do you remember that awful dress of Geraldine Birkett's that I split for her the summer before last, the one she was sick of? She's gone to college, as if school weren't bad enough. Let's try the coconuts.'

At the coconuts, for which Tony chivalrously though ostentatiously insisted on paying, luck was fairly even, and they were awarded a coconut between them.

'You can have it,' said Tony. 'I've got the mug.'

Lydia held the prize up and looked critically at it.

'It's awfully like someone with a nasty face all close together. I know, it's like the Pettinger,' said Lydia, alluding to the headmistress of the Barchester High School. 'When I had to go into her study before I left and have a holy kind of talk, she looked just like that.'

'What did she say?' asked Tony.

'Oh, I don't know,' said Lydia indifferently. 'Something about an opportunity for something or other. I say, this coconut weighs about a ton.'

'Carry it in your hat,' said Tony.

This seemed to Lydia a good idea. She took off her hat which had a band of ribbon that went round the back of her head to moor it into place, put the coconut in the crown and carried it by the ribbon as if in a basket.

'Come on,' said Tony, 'it's nearly four and your mother said we were to meet her at the tea-tent.'

'What are you going to do with your mug?' asked Lydia, who rather coveted it.

'Give it to someone, I expect,' said Tony. 'As a matter of fact I'm going to give it to Miss Morris. I saw her when I came.'

Lydia asked who Miss Morris was.

'She was at a picnic Mrs Brandon had,' said Tony, 'and she was rather decent. Mother said she was being a companion to Mrs Brandon's aunt and had rather a dull time, so I went to the Wishing Well with her and I told her a lot about the early Christian church, because her father was a clergyman. I did early Christians in history last term, so I know them pretty well.'

'Gosh!' said Lydia. 'Her old lady was that Miss Brandon that father and mother went to the funeral of. I saw Miss Brandon once, like a great black hen with feathers in her hat being rude to people. I expect she Persecuted Miss Morris. I might give Miss Morris the coconut.'

'She'd never be able to open it,' said Tony. 'I'll tell you what. I'll open it at tea-time with the corkscrew in my knife, and we'll drink the juice, and then we'll smash the shell up with something and eat the inside.'

Lydia said she didn't like coconut to eat, because one kept on putting bits into one's mouth and chewing them, but they never seemed to get really chewed and then one had to spit them out. The ribbon of her hat then gave way and the coconut rolled to the ground, so she and Tony dribbled it among the feet of the crowd, right up to the entrance to the tea tent.

Mrs Brandon, after buying conscientiously all the things that were selling least well, and leaving her purchases in a heap at each stall to be fetched by Curwen later, drifted across to the Vicarage garden, where four deck chairs, six rush-bottomed chairs from the dining-room, four cane-bottomed chairs from the bedrooms and three hassocks, were disposed for visitors under the beech tree. Here she disposed herself gracefully in the safest looking of the deck chairs and gave herself up to contemplation. No sound came from the Vicarage, so Mrs Brandon knew that Hettie and Cook were at the Fête. The sound of the steam organ came not unpleasantly from the far side of the field, filling Mrs Brandon with a gentle sentiment for a childhood when those well-worn tunes had been popular favourites. Hot sunshine poured down, and as a faint breeze passed over the garden it brought to Mrs Brandon the scent of Mr Miller's heliotrope in the border beneath the study windows. It reminded her of the spider, which

215

made her think again of Mr Miller and how a woman was needed at the Vicarage. If Mr Miller had a wife, she reflected, he could read his book aloud to her every night instead of having to come over to Stories. Ever since he had so kindly begun to read his Donne to her Mrs Brandon had lived in apprehension of further readings, at some one of which she would, she knew, go to sleep, or hopelessly fail to grapple with some quotation, or otherwise disgrace herself. If only he and Miss Morris did not get on so badly one might have done some match-making in that direction, but though Miss Morris had so nicely come to the rescue and done the notices for the Fête, it was obvious to the meanest intelligence that it was rather a sentiment of duty towards the church that had inspired her than any personal feeling for the Vicar.

Neither had her encounter with Sir Edmund been wholly satisfactory. True she had offered to recast and type his letter to the *Barchester Chronicle*, but Mrs Brandon could not conceal from herself that her secretarial conscience would have made her do the same by anyone who was going to make such a fool of himself as Sir Edmund. It would also, she felt, be unkind to force anyone into marriage with Sir Edmund, if it meant having to listen to his letters to the newspaper more than once a week. If no marriage could be arranged, she must bestir herself about finding a new job for Miss Morris, before her guest had quite overwhelmed and exhausted her with doing the flowers and being grateful. She ran through the other bachelors of her acquaintance mentally, but found none suitable. Francis and Hilary were out of the question. As for Hilary, she thought a wife would not be a bad plan for him either, if only to relieve her from having to listen to any more readings of his French poet, whom she found incomprehensible and faintly distasteful.

Then thoughts of Miss Brandon and that troublesome will, about which they surely must soon know some details, passed through her mind, naturally leading to thoughts of Mr Merton, and at this moment Francis would certainly have observed that his mother had her mysterious mischief face. She had no intention of offering Mr Merton as a husband to Miss Morris, for he seemed to her very amusing and an excellent player at that enchanting game of heartwhole flirtation which she so dearly loved and for which she found so few intelligent players. And as she remembered that Mr Merton was coming over to the Fête with the Keiths and later to Stories for a drink, she did what in the nineties would have been described as dimpling.

'Lavinia,' said an impressive voice.

She looked up and saw Mrs Morland, in a flowered frock and a majestic kind of flowing cape which she wore apologetically.

'Darling Laura, I can't get out of this chair, but I am so glad to see you,' said Mrs Brandon. 'Sit down. Have you been to the Fête?'

'No. Tony has gone off to the roundabout, but I saw that nice Miss Morris near the gate and she told me you might be at the Vicarage, so I came to look for you. Tony has really come to talk to Lydia Keith, who is such a nice girl, with no nonsense about her,' said Mrs Morland, who evidently felt with Mr Edmund Sparkler that this was a high recommendation. 'I didn't mean to come, because I'm all behindhand with a book as usual, but Tony hasn't got his driving licence yet, so I had to bring him.'

'Tell me about the book,' said Mrs Brandon, obeying the law of her nature.

Mrs Morland looked piercingly at her friend, pulled her hat impatiently down on her forehead and shook her head.

'It is very kind of you, Lavinia,' she said, 'and just like you, but certainly not. You know as well as I do that you only asked me to talk about my book because you like to be nice to people and for people to think how nice you are, and so you are, very nice, but you don't really want to hear things, except so that you can think about other things.'

'How clever you are, Laura,' said Mrs Brandon admiringly. 'I suppose it comes of being a novelist. I don't know why it is, but I can't prevent people reading things aloud to me. Mr Miller and Hilary Grant and Sir Edmund all do it, and it is so interesting but I simply *can't* attend, and it makes me so nervous in case I suddenly stop thinking of having my black frock altered or whatever it is and don't say the right thing.'

'I wish I had invented you,' said Mrs Morland, in her turn gazing with admiration at her friend. 'No one would believe in you, but they'd all love you. What is that nice Miss Morris doing now? I did like her so much when you brought her to the picnic.'

Mrs Brandon explained that Miss Morris was staying with her for a rest, before looking for another job, but did not divulge her plans for Miss Morris's future.

'I simply love having her,' she said, 'if only she wouldn't be so grateful. It's bad enough when she will do the flowers for me, but when she thanks me it is very alarming.'

'I know,' said Mrs Morland sagely. 'I know. I wonder if she would like to go to George Knox's old mother. The girl that was with her as companion has married a naval man and Mrs Knox is looking out for someone. Shall I mention it to her?'

'Oh do,' said Mrs Brandon. 'I expect you will see her at tea. What time is it?'

But before Mrs Morland could answer, the imposing form of Lady Norton swept into the garden, accompanied by Sir Edmund.

'Don't move, don't move,' said Lady Norton, who as the widow of an ex-Governor knew exactly how to put people at their ease. 'I have just brought Mrs Grant over and left her at the Cow and Sickle with her luggage; and happening to see Sir Edmund I asked him where you were likely to be.'

'I didn't know where you were, Lavinia,' said Sir Edmund. 'Not my brother's keeper or anything of that sort, but I saw that Miss Morris of yours near the tea-tent and she said you might be up here. She's typed that letter deucedly well for me. I'd like you to see it, Lady Norton. It's about those Council cottages.'

But Lady Norton was so much occupied in renewing her acquaintance with Mrs Morland, for whose works she had a sincere if condescending admiration, that she did not hear.

'I always say to the girl at the library,' said her ladyship, ' "You simply must get me a copy of Mrs Morland's latest book at once." I hope we shall have one for Christmas.'

'Well, not exactly Christmas, but Easter,' said Mrs Morland, with the air of offering a suitable ecclesiastical alternative. 'Easter is early next year.'

'That is all the better for your readers,' said Lady Norton, graciously. 'What were you saying, Sir Edmund?'

'You know those Council houses near the cross roads,' said

Sir Edmund. 'Disgraceful piece of jobbery that whole thing and not even a proper damp course. I've written a pretty stiff letter to the *Chronicle* about it and I'd like to read you what I said.'

Lady Norton, who enjoyed being consulted about things, inclined her head graciously.

'Don't tell me that you wrote that letter, Sir Edmund,' she said when he had finished.

'Not written it?' said Sir Edmund. 'Oh, I see what you mean. Not quite so strong as usual, eh? To tell the truth I had a little help. Miss Morris, a very nice quiet woman too, touched it up a bit and typed it for me. You know her, Lady Norton. Poor Amelia Brandon's companion or secretary or whatever you like to call it.'

'Oh, Miss Morris,' said her ladyship thoughtfully. 'Have you taken her on as secretary then?'

'Good Lord, no,' said Sir Edmund. 'She's staying with Lavinia here. Having a holiday, you know. Anyone would need a holiday after living with Amelia. De mortuis of course, but must face the facts.'

'I was thinking,' said Lady Norton, 'that my eldest niece, the one who lives in Cape Town, is needing a secretary. She does an enormous amount of work among diseased half-castes and writes to me that the life is most interesting. She cannot offer a salary, but the opportunities are unlimited. It might suit Miss Morris. I will write to my niece about it.'

All present felt that this was a plan which had absolutely nothing to recommend it, and comforted themselves by thinking that even with the Air Mail it would take some little time before Lady Norton could get a reply from her niece.

While this conversation was going on the sound of a bell had been heard two or three times. No one had taken any notice of it, but as it at last impinged on Mrs Brandon's consciousness she realized that someone must be trying to get into the Vicarage by the front door.

'I wonder if we had better see what that is,' she said. 'Someone is ringing the front door bell, but I know Hettie and Cook are at the Fête.'

'I'll go and see,' said Sir Edmund. 'Bad plan, leaving a house

empty. Miller ought to have a dog. Often told him so. Quis
custodiet, you know.'

'Perhaps they'll go away if we do nothing,' said Mrs Brandon
hopefully, but at that moment Mrs Grant came round the corner
of the house. She had discarded her jet adornments and was again
wearing her coral and amber and had a wide sash of what are
known as Roman stripes tied round a rather shapeless straw hat.

'Oh, there you are, Victoria,' she said, advancing upon the
party. 'And Mrs Brandon and Mrs Morland and, che piacere!
Sir Edmund, isn't it.'

'Haven't seen you since poor Edward died,' said Sir Edmund
shaking hands.

'I never, never think of him,' said Mrs Grant. 'What is gone
is gone. I am afraid I am rather a pagan, but living so much as I
do among the gracious rural deities of Calabria, the spirit of
Greece beneath the Italian sun, one learns their laughing philos-
ophy. Death comes graciously under that blue sky.'

'Died at Frinton, didn't he?' said Sir Edmund. 'Frinton's all
right if you like it. I don't. Edward never looked well there.'

'I came to find Hilary,' said Mrs Grant, 'but no one answered,
so I gathered that the house was empty. Then I heard voices,
and eccomi!'

Mrs Brandon got up and said it was nearly tea-time and she
expected they would find Hilary and the others down at the tent,
so they all walked across the garden and out through the little
gate into the field.

- 11 -

THE VICARAGE FÊTE - 2

FRANCIS and Miss Morris had gone as Mrs Brandon told them
to the tea-tent. Here they found Mrs Spindler and several helpers
arranging tables, dragging cloths on to the tables, and hurling
crockery and cutlery on to the cloths. On each table Mrs Spindler
put a half-pint mug with too many dahlias crammed into it.

'Good afternoon, Mrs Spindler,' said Francis. 'You seem pretty busy.'

'That's right, Mr Francis,' said Mrs Spindler. 'It never rains but it pours and we're two short. I'm sure I don't know how we'll manage.'

'I say, that's too bad,' said Francis sympathetically. 'I suppose you haven't got the ping-pong tables from the British Legion over here, have you?'

'I'm using them for the urns and cutting the bread-and-butter, Mr Francis,' said Mrs Spindler firmly.

'Mother rather wanted them for her party,' said Francis. 'We shall be about twelve, or fifteen, and she wanted to get everyone together.'

Mrs Spindler said if there hadn't been that unpleasantness with Mrs Wheeler over the matter of that cask, she would have sent some of the scouts down for the trestle table at the garage, but being as it was she didn't see what could be done.

Francis, who was something of a diplomatist, saw that Mrs Spindler was not in a mood for concessions and determined to play his trump card.

'It's a pity about those ping-pong tables,' he said, 'because mother has got rather a special party. This is Miss Morris, old Miss Brandon's companion, who has been very ill. The shock of Miss Brandon's death was too much for her. I hear my aunt never spoke again.'

He paused to study the effect on Mrs Spindler's expression.

'I'm sure Miss Morris would like to meet you,' he added carelessly.

'Well, I'm sure,' Mrs Spindler began, wiping her hands on a cloth. Francis without waiting to hear what she was sure of darted across to Miss Morris, who had stood a little aside and was looking at the tea-urns with a professional eye.

'I say,' he said in a low voice, 'would you mind shaking hands with Mrs Spindler. Her husband keeps the Cow and Sickle, and if she is placated she will let mother have the ping-pong tables for her tea-party. You wouldn't feel equal, would you,' he added as Miss Morris was moving towards Mrs Spindler, 'to saying a few words about Aunt Sissie's death. They would go down awfully well. Mrs Spindler, I want you to meet Miss Morris.'

'Pleased, Miss Morris, I'm sure,' said Mrs Spindler, holding out a damp hand.

'I'm so glad to meet you, Mrs Spindler,' said Miss Morris, shaking hands warmly.

'I'm sure I *am* sorry about poor Miss Brandon,' said Mrs Spindler. 'Mr Spindler read me the piece in the paper about how she was taken, and I passed the remark to him at tea-time that I was sorry for anyone that happened to be there. I lost my own aunt twelve years ago and to this day I don't like to think of it.'

'Thank you so much, Mrs Spindler,' said Miss Morris. 'You must know exactly what I felt like. When the nurse told me all was over I lay down on my bed, just as I was, and never knew anything till Mrs Brandon came in and woke me.'

This strictly truthful account gave Mrs Spindler such pleasure that she relented about the ping-pong tables at once. Two scouts were sent to borrow some wooden cases from the Garden Produce tent. On these Mrs Spindler ordered her helpers to put the urns and the bread-and-butter, while Francis and Mr Miller's Hettie, who had brought down some rock cakes from the Vicarage, put the ping-pong tables together and found a cloth for them.

'Now, I know what you want, Miss Morris,' said Mrs Spindler. 'A nice cup of tea. I've just got the big urn on the boil, but what with being two short and behindhand with the bread-and-butter, I really hardly know where I am.'

'I would love a cup of tea, thank you,' said Miss Morris. 'That is most refreshing. I suppose I couldn't help you with the bread-and-butter?'

'Really, Miss Morris, you mustn't think of such a thing,' said Mrs Spindler, shocked but gratified.

'You'd better let Miss Morris do her worst, Mrs Spindler,' said Francis. 'Her father was a clergyman and what she doesn't know about parish teas isn't worth knowing. Up, Miss Morris, and at them!'

'Well, if Miss Morris doesn't mind,' said Mrs Spindler.

Miss Morris finished her cup of tea and took out of her large sensible bag a neatly folded overall, which she explained she had brought in case. A moment later she was buttering and slicing tin loaves with a calm competence that overpowered Mrs Spindler and the other helpers. Francis was so enchanted by the sight that he borrowed a clean glass-cloth from Mrs Spindler, tied it round him like an apron, and devoted himself to cutting up enormous slabs of cake and making all Mrs Spindler's assistants giggle. Here he was presently found by Noel Merton, who had been distracted from his search for Mrs Brandon by a request from Mr Miller to judge the sack-races. They had discovered, in the intervals of disqualifying boys who deliberately bumped into others, that Mrs Brandon was known to them both.

'What a perfectly delightful woman Mrs Brandon is,' said Mr Merton. 'Isn't Miss Morris, Miss Brandon's companion, staying with her now? I am sure that boy with red hair isn't running under Queensberry rules. He has got one of his feet out of the sack.'

'Dear, dear, no,' said Mr Miller. 'Teddy! Teddy Thatcher! Come here.'

Teddy shuffled up to him.

'Let me look at your sack,' said Mr Miller. 'Now that won't do at all. Your foot is right out of the sack.'

'Please sir, it had a hole in it,' said Teddy.

'Nonsense,' said the Vicar sharply. 'I looked at all the sacks myself. Let me see.'

A closer examination showed that a hole had been cut in the corner and Teddy Thatcher was excommunicated.

'I'm always so glad the Scoutmaster isn't here when that sort of thing happens,' said the Vicar. 'He will talk about honour.'

'How dreadful,' said Mr Merton sympathetically.

'It makes me hot and cold,' said Mr Miller. 'What is it, Teddy? Oh, it was your new pocketknife, was it? Well, don't do it again. Run and get another sack and you can go in for the under fourteen race. Yes, Miss Morris is with Mrs Brandon at present.'

'I thought she seemed a very pleasant, competent person when I once saw her at the Abbey,' said Mr Merton.

'Very pleasant indeed. Her future is a source of considerable anxiety to me,' said Mr Miller, struggling vainly to untie the sack from the neck of one of the young Turpins, who was convinced

223

that he would have to spend the rest of his life in it, armless and legless. 'It's all right, Bobby, don't cry. There you are! Yes; the question of finding another situation arises. Mrs Brandon and I have had a talk about it, but so far there is nothing definite in view.'

'Oh well, I expect it will be all right,' said Mr Merton in what the Vicar felt to be rather a callous way. Then the Vicar blamed himself for imputing evil motives and by that time he was needed to judge the hat-trimming competition, and Mr Merton, gently abstracting himself from these joys, strolled in the direction of the tea-tent where, as we have already said, he found Francis and Miss Morris whom he entertained with small talk, refusing resolutely to cut cake or fill milk jugs.

At four o'clock all Mrs Brandon's guests converged upon the tea-tent, including Lydia's parents, Mr and Mrs Keith, who are quite immaterial to the progress of this book, except in so far as they made the number up to fourteen, thus causing a good deal of distraction. Mrs Brandon, in consultation with Mrs Spindler, counted the party four times, getting a different result each time, partly because they never remembered if Miss Morris and Francis were guests or helpers.

'If we really are fourteen we can't possibly fit into the ping-pong tables,' said Mrs Brandon. 'And I had forgotten Mr Miller. If he joins us we shall be fifteen. Can we put another table up to these, Mrs Spindler?'

'Don't trouble about me. I never take tea,' said Lady Norton, sitting down on one of the school chairs that had been lent for the occasion.

'Then that makes thirteen,' said Mrs Brandon helplessly.

Mrs Grant threw out her hand in what she explained was a Calabrian gesture, useful to ward off the evil eye.

'No, darling, it is fourteen all right,' said Francis. 'Lady Norton will be one of us, even if she doesn't have any refreshment. It's the spirit of the thing that counts. Couldn't we have that little table near the door, Mrs Spindler?'

'Well, Mr Francis, I did put it there because it's a bit uneven in the legs,' said Mrs Spindler. 'Of course you *could* have it.'

'Well, if we could, we can,' said Francis. 'Will you get it, Tony.'

Tony Morland picked the table up, balanced it legs upwards on his head and so carried it across the tent to the loudly expressed terror of all the grown-ups and the even more loudly expressed admiration of Delia and Lydia.

'I often carry desks about the form room like that,' said Tony to the girls as he set the table down.

'What does your master say?' asked Delia, slightly incredulous.

'He doesn't say anything,' said Tony. 'I have them all well under my thumb except Mr Carter. I do history with him and he gives us some jolly useful notes so I let him do what he likes. Come on, I'm going to eat twenty sandwiches.'

'Bravo!' cried Mrs Grant. 'I shall come and sit with you and we will have great fun at our end of the table.'

Anyone else would have been put off by the mask of stolid indifference, thinly masking hatred and contempt, immediately assumed by the three young people, but Mrs Grant was used to breaking down the barriers between herself and the unwilling peasantry of Calabria, and took her seat at the end of the table with Delia, Lydia and Tony.

'Mr Merton, you must sit by me,' said Mrs Brandon, 'and meet Lady Norton.'

Mr Merton said he would love to. Mr Grant, overhearing this, thought some very scornful thoughts about women and took refuge with Mrs Morland who would, he felt, appreciate hearing a little more about Jehan le Capet. Francis and Miss Morris, removing their aprons, joined the party at the children's end as Mrs Grant playfully called it. The conversation at the grown-up end was necessarily a little dull, including as it did Lady Norton and Mr and Mrs Keith, though Mr Merton and Mrs Brandon seemed to find it amusing enough.

'I hope,' said Mr Merton, 'that having tea with you now is without prejudice to my having a glass of sherry with you later. I rather particularly want to see you.'

'Of course not,' said Mrs Brandon. 'Won't Mr and Mrs Keith come too?'

'I think not,' said Mr Merton firmly. 'I have got my own car with me and if you don't mind my bringing Lydia, who clings to me with very flattering affection, we will let the Keiths go home by themselves. In any case they wouldn't stay long, and I know Lydia won't be happy till she has done all the side shows.'

'What a nice girl she is,' said Mrs Brandon. 'She and Delia were at Barchester High School and went to Paris when they left, but not to the same family.'

'She is one of the nicest girls I know,' said Mr Merton, 'and wonderfully toned down since she went to Paris, though she doesn't seem to have learnt any French there.'

A hubbub from the far end of the table now attracted everyone's attention to the finished product of Paris who, together with Delia and Tony Morland, was having a friendly discussion with Mrs Grant about cruelty to animals. The conversation had begun by Mrs Garnt loudly lamenting the cruelty involved in allowing a small pony, property of the grocer, to be let out at threepence a ride for children.

'I know that pony,' said Lydia. 'He used to belong to the butcher at Southbridge. He was called Toby then, but the man who has him now didn't like Toby, so he called him Punch.'

'That is typically English,' said Mrs Grant, 'not to allow an animal any right even in its own name. But if you know that animal's owner, Miss Keith, you should protest. I saw it with my own eyes, with no less that two children on its back at once, being beaten with a stick to make it trot up and down the field.'

'If that is Simpson's pony,' said Delia, joining in the fray, 'you have to beat him. I broke one of mother's parasols over his back two years ago when I had him in the old governess cart for fun.'

'I wish I'd been there,' said Tony, his eyes gleaming. 'I'd have stuck a pin into a stick and jabbed him, all very literary.'

'Have you ever heard of St Francis?' said Mrs Grant meaningly to Tony.

'Yes, I know all about him. We did him in some notes on the monastic orders last term,' said Tony negligently. 'If you want to find out anything about him I can give you the names of one or two really good books. I expect you only know the Brother Elderberry kind. I wrote a pretty good essay on the Influence of the Poverello on Contemporary Society.'

'And do you know what he called animals?' asked Mrs Grant, almost threateningly.

Tony's face assumed a world-weary air which his mother, had she not been so immersed in le Capet, or Dr Ford, had he been present, would at once have recognized as a preparation for showing off. But Lydia, who detested what she called rot, which meant broadly anything she didn't agree with, was ready with an answer before Tony could collect his forces.

'Of course he called them brother and sister and all that,' said she, dominating that end of the table by her powerful voice, 'but that's nothing to go by. I mean in Italian you call people anything. It's a very rich language, though I must say I don't know a frightful lot of it, but what's the use of learning a language if you aren't going there and there's nothing to read except things like Dante. But St Francis lived in the twelfth century – oh, all right, Tony, thirteenth century then, twelve hundreds, it's all the same thing, and you could easily call people brothers and sisters because there weren't so many things to call. I mean it would be absolutely different now with aeroplanes and radio and gas-masks and all that. Anyway it was a pity St Francis went off the deep end about animals like that, because it simply set the Italians against animals for life and they've been doing cruelty to animals ever since. It's in the blood too of course. Look at the ancient Romans. Of course Virgil had some quite modern ideas about kindness to bees in the Georgics, but he tells you to pull their wings off all the same, and I expect he'd have made some jolly good hexameters about beating Simpson's pony if he'd known it. And calling people brothers and sisters doesn't really mean anything.'

> 'If hate killed men, brother Lawrence,
> God's blood, would not mine kill you?'

said Tony approvingly.

'But Browning was speaking of a *Spanish* cloister,' said Mrs Grant, laughingly.

'That's the marvellous part of Browning,' said Lydia. 'I mean he sees human nature everywhere, like Shakespeare, but the Italians haven't got that. Of course St Francis was perfectly

227

marvellous, but he hadn't that deep kind of understanding of people that Browning and Shakespeare have. Of course he was a good bit earlier and I daresay people weren't so developed then.'

She looked round, pleased with herself.

'One only understands St Francis after long study and suffering in the stern school of life,' said Mrs Grant with an annoying and tolerant condescension. 'When you have lived in Italy as much as I have, Miss Keith, you will understand how St Francis's love of animals has become part of daily life now.'

'I read a book about animals in Italy,' said Delia, her eyes gleaming as Tony's had gleamed. 'It was by a clergyman who lived at Genoa or somewhere and it was perfectly *ghastly*. What do you think he saw a man do to a horse in Pisa. He had a great knife, and he –'

'Delia,' said Miss Morris.

There was a tone in her voice, as of a very competent governess, that made Delia much to everyone's relief stop short and say 'Yes, Miss Morris,' exactly as if she had been at school.

'I think I see Mr Miller looking for us,' said Miss Morris, 'and I can't shout up the table at your mother. Could you rescue him?'

Delia, who was seated nearest the door of the tent, got up and rescued Mr Miller who, confused by the dimmer light of the tent after the glare outside and all the noise of talk and crash of crockery, was peering wretchedly about, unable to find his tea-party. Francis admired Miss Morris's well-timed interruption and couldn't make up his mind whether it was deliberate or not. Mr Merton with the utmost good-humour gave up his seat next to Mrs Brandon to the Vicar and came and sat by Lydia on a stool lent by the Badgers' Patrol of the Boy Scouts.

It was very lucky for Mr Grant that he had so kind an audience as Mrs Morland. That worthy creature had a trick of appearing deeply absorbed in what her friends said which was often her undoing, but for the moment she was genuinely amused by what Mr Grant was telling her about his hero and neither of them took any notice of the argument between Lydia and Mrs Grant, which was just as well, or Mr Grant would have been more than usually ashamed of his mother.

'I think le Capet was a genius to have so many mistresses all at once,' said Mrs Morland. 'How on earth did he manage it?'

'He needed them,' said Mr Grant. 'No, I don't mean like that, but he was very poor and very extravagant and they were mostly pretty poor too, so it took several to support him. It was to them that he wrote his poem *Les mains qui donnent*, which some people consider his best.'

It was then that Mrs Morland, putting a stray piece of hair away behind her ear and frowning, made the suggestion that, as Mr Grant subsequently said, changed his whole life.

'Why don't you make a novel of it, Mr Grant,' she said. 'There's a lot of very good material, simply asking to be used. All that Vie de Bohème stuff goes down very well and with a good jacket you ought to get real sales. I'll talk to my publisher, Adrian Coates, about it if you like.'

'I couldn't,' said Mr Grant, shocked, yet agreeably flattered. 'So little is really known about him. In fact I believe I'm about the only person that has done any work on him.'

'Well, there you are,' said Mrs Morland. 'If you are the only one that knows, you can write the book. If you called it something rather vulgar, like "A Poet of the Gutters", or "A Minstrel of Montmartre", it would be a help.'

Mr Grant, throwing himself into the spirit of the thing, then suggested several extremely unsuitable titles which made him and Mrs Morland laugh so much that three of her tortoiseshell hairpins fell under the table, and had to be rescued.

'Thank you so much,' said Mrs Morland as Mr Grant rather red in the face, surged up again bearing the hairpins in triumph.

'Thank *you* as we say,' said Mr Grant. 'You can't think what fun it is to talk to you. You are really the only person I can talk to about myself and my work.'

On hearing this frightful disloyalty to Mrs Brandon the heavens should have sent a thunderbolt straight through the tent on to Mr Grant's head, but they refrained.

'You ought to meet my old friend, George Knox, the biographer,' said Mrs Morland. 'He talks about himself more than anyone I know, but he's very nice. Tony! I think we ought to be going.'

'Oh mother, must we?' said her son. 'I've eaten twenty sandwiches and three slices of cherry cake and I promised Lydia I'd have a sixpenny ice.'

'Very well. After the ice,' said Mrs Morland getting up.

A general move was now being made. Mrs Morland said good-bye to her hostess and seized the opportunity of asking Miss Morris to come to see her at High Rising some day.

'I could easily come over and fetch you and take you back,' she said. 'And I would like you to meet my old friend, George Knox, the biographer, you know. His mother who is French and very nice and has always been very kind to me lives alone, and her companion, Miss Grey, a very nice girl but a little peculiar. has just married a naval man after great exertions, and I know Mrs Knox would be extremely grateful to anyone who would come and live with her. Of course I don't want to bother you, but if you did feel like Mrs Knox and cared to talk to me and George Knox about it, it would be a real kindness.'

'That is very kind indeed of you, Mrs Morland,' said Miss Morris. 'I have no plans at all for the moment, but I can't go on trespassing on Mrs Brandon's kindness and shall be glad to find a place where I can be of use.'

'Then I'll ring you up in about a week, when George Knox is back from visiting his mother,' said Mrs Morland, 'and you shall come to lunch and meet him. Now I have lost Tony. If you see him will you tell him that I have gone to get the car. There is such a jam in the car park.'

She shook Miss Morris warmly by the hand and hurried away. Lady Norton now advanced majestically upon Miss Morris.

'You must get Mrs Brandon to bring you over to see my garden while you are staying with her,' said her ladyship.

Miss Morris, fully realizing that this was not only a royal command but a piece of benevolent condescension, made suitable acknowledgements.

'My eldest niece, who works among diseased half-castes at Cape Town, has written to me that she needs a secretary,' said Lady Norton. 'It is most interesting work, and hearing from Mrs Brandon that you might be available for a new post, I thought it might interest you, especially as I understand that you have been used to parish work. Some of them are discharged lepers,' said Lady Norton by way of making the position sound more attractive.

Miss Morris, who had been offered just as unattractive jobs by people far less well-meaning than Lady Norton, again made suitable acknowledgements and her ladyship passed on. She was closely followed by Mr and Mrs Keith, lamenting the disappearance of their daughter Lydia.

'I think,' said Miss Morris, 'that she may have gone to the ice-cream tent with Mrs Morland's son. They were talking about it.'

Even as she spoke the two reprobates came up.

'Lydia, what *have* you done to your dress?' said Mrs Keith. 'She tears everything, Miss Morris, and now that her sister, my elder girl, is married we never seem to be able to keep her tidy.'

'It was only hitting the weight, mother,' said Lydia, craning her neck as far round as possible and casting an approving eye on the ever-widening rent. 'And it's a foul dress anyway.'

'And where is your hat?' asked her mother helplessly.

'I don't know,' said Lydia indifferently. 'The ribbon got broken when I was carrying the coconut.'

'You were sitting on it at tea-time,' said Tony.

'Bother, so I was,' said Lydia, and went back to the tea table.

'Good-bye, Tony,' said Miss Morris.

Tony took her hand and bowed with an awkward young grace that suddenly touched her.

'If ever you come to Southbridge,' he said, looking up at her from under his dark lashes, 'please come and have tea in my study. I've got matron under my thumb and she'll let us have heaps of scones and things.'

Before Miss Morris could answer he had given her one more of his inscrutable, flickering looks and gone after his mother. Lydia returned from her quest, her hat a good deal the worse for wear in one hand, the coconut in the other.

'I thought you'd like this,' she announced, thrusting it at Miss Morris. 'Some people like the milk. I think it's beastly myself, but it isn't so bad if you smash it to bits and eat the white stuff, only I always spit it out when I've chewed it a bit because you don't seem to get any further.'

231

'Thank you so much,' said Miss Morris gratefully.

Mrs Grant, who had just finished her good-byes to Lady Norton, inquired anxiously if Miss Morris really needed the coconut. If not, she said, she would gladly take it to the Cow and get Mr Spindler to cut it in two and hang the halves up for St Francis's little feathered brothers and sisters. Miss Morris, realizing that Lydia was about to say what she thought of feathered brothers and sisters having the coconut that she had bestowed upon a friend, hastened to assure Mrs Grant that she had a peculiar affection for both the milk and the edible parts of that unwholesome fruit. Mrs Grant smiled pityingly and passed on.

'Anyway St Francis didn't have coconuts,' said Lydia scornfully. 'Good-bye, Miss Morris. Thanks awfully for having the coconut. Tony told me what a rotten time you'd had, and I wanted you to. I hope you'll have awfully good luck now.'

She hurt Miss Morris's hand, and banging into the canvas in a way that nearly shattered it left the marquee in search of her friend Noel Merton.

'I do apologize for Lydia,' said Mrs Keith as she shook hands. 'I thought Paris would improve her.'

'She seems to me a delightful girl,' said Miss Morris warmly.

'Everyone likes her,' said Mrs Keith, 'but I do wish she wouldn't split all her clothes. If you are staying on in this part of the country, I do wish you would come to us for a few days. I feel that Lydia would pay attention to you, and my husband never notices the guests much.'

Miss Morris, who secretly felt that Lydia was quite perfect in her own way, and did not in the least wish that ingenuous young lady to look upon her in the light of a mentor or improver, made some suitably civil remark, said good-bye to Mr Keith, and found herself for a moment alone. She was a little dizzy after the hot tea in the tent and the unusual amount of company she had been seeing, not to speak of the kindness, whether suitable or not, that everyone had shown, and glad to sit on a packing case near the tea-urns and rest. Not one of the offers of posts that had been made to her was in the least what she wanted, yet she felt she ought to examine the possibility of them all. She could not live with Mrs Brandon indefinitely. Every day that she spent in the easy, luxurious atmosphere of Stories seemed to her to be sapping her initiative. It was a fresh daily pleasure to have morning tea and often breakfast in bed, her own bath-room, towels changed nearly every day, leisurely meals, a comfortable bed, lazy quiet afternoons and evenings. Independent as she was, she could not refuse the presents that Mrs Brandon and Delia were always giving her, of stockings, scarves, underthings, a frock, a coat, all offered with such charming good-will that she could not bring herself to deny the affectionate givers the pleasure they took in giving. Every day she stayed was going to make it harder to go. To-day would make it harder than ever. For the first time for many years she had come into her own kingdom again and ruled part of a parish, if only for an afternoon. The blood of generations of vicarage ancestors sang in her veins as she looked upon the tea-urns, the tin loaves, the slabs of cake, the crockery, now all empty, destroyed, dirty but none the less a symbol. She thanked Mr Miller in her heart for having had the Fête on a day when she could be there. Mrs Spindler and her assistants were tidying and packing up. Miss Morris rose and went over to them.

'Thank you so much for letting me help, Mrs Spindler,' she said. 'It has been a most enjoyable experience.'

'Thank *you*, miss, I'm sure,' said Mrs Spindler, forgetting in her enthusiasm to assert her gentility by using Miss Morris's name. 'As I was saying to Mrs Thatcher just now, it's a real pleasure to have a lady that knows how things should be done and what a pity, I said to Mrs Thatcher, there isn't one at the Vicarage. That dirt and waste there you wouldn't believe, miss. Not that the girls mean anything, but it stands to reason you don't get things done the way you do with a good mistress over them. I was passing the remark to Mrs Thatcher that I wouldn't be surprised if Mr Miller hadn't a drop of hot food to-day, with Cook and that Hettie down here since before lunch, wasn't I, Mrs Thatcher?'

Mrs Thatcher, a handsome draggled woman, the mother of Jimmy Thatcher and his four brothers and three sisters, said that was right, and she hoped Jimmy wasn't at the ice-cream stall, as he'd been sick to-day twice.

Miss Morris volunteered to go and look for him, an offer that

Mrs Thatcher accepted with embarrassed relief, begging her to tell Jimmy to come straight along to the tent like a good boy or he'd get the strap when his dad got back. Armed with a description of the afflicted Jimmy, Miss Morris went out of the stuffy marquee into the grounds. There the heat and noise were rather overpowering, but it was good to be in the fresh air again. She went over to the ice-cream stall. Here she found not Jimmy but Mr Miller, giving pennies to small boys to buy a slice of frozen custard-powder and condensed milk between two synthetic wafers apparently made of compressed shavings.

'Excuse me, Mr Miller,' said Miss Morris, 'but have you seen Jimmy Thatcher. His mother wants him.'

'I believe he is at the roundabout,' said Mr Miller, bestowing his last penny. 'May I help you to find him?'

'There is no need,' said Miss Morris, but quite kindly.

'Oh, but do let me,' said Mr Miller. 'No, Herb, you've had one penny and so has Les.'

'Well, thank you very much,' said Miss Morris, remembering that it was the duty of young clergymen – for as such she still considered Mr Miller – to assist vicars' daughters.

But just as Mr Miller had freed himself from the last of the little boys, Mrs Brandon accompanied by Sir Edmund came up.

'Oh, Mr Miller,' she said, 'I did so want a word with you. Could you possibly spare a moment?'

'Would you excuse me, Miss Morris?' said Mr Miller.

'It won't take long,' said Mrs Brandon. 'Sir Edmund, you'll take care of Miss Morris while I talk to Mr Miller, won't you?'

Without waiting for an answer she carried Mr Miller off.

'I only wanted to consult you about church to-morrow,' she said. 'I had got a kind of idea that Miss Morris doesn't like our kind of service and I wondered if you knew what she does like. I suppose I oughtn't to ask you,' said Mrs Brandon, suddenly showing a late-flowering tact, 'when it's your service, but somehow I always look upon you as a friend more than a Vicar.'

With which quite idiotic remark she turned her blue eyes on him with such an air of confidence in his understanding and sympathy that he said, Of course, of course, and he had himself had a little talk with Miss Morris on the matter and had suggested that she should go to Tompion at Little Misfit, or Carson at Nutfield, delightful fellows both, even if a little evangelical in their outlook.

'Then that's all right,' said Mrs Brandon, evidently much relieved.

'I wish I could drive her over myself,' said Mr Miller, quite sincerely, 'but the hours of our services make it impossible.'

Mrs Brandon said he mustn't dream of suggesting such a thing and Curwen, who only went to an evening service at the Methodist chapel, could easily take her over.

'While we are on the subject, I should be glad to know if anything suitable has offered itself in the way of a post. Lady Norton kindly mentioned a niece of hers in Cape Town, but the work, largely among Unfortunates,' said Mr Miller, hoping that Mrs Brandon in her heavenly innocence would not know or ask what he meant, 'seems to me hardly suitable for a lady of Miss Morris's gifts, and in a hot climate.'

'Lady Norton is always busybodying about her nieces,' said Mrs Brandon. 'I certainly shouldn't dream of letting Miss Morris go to South Africa, though I believe it is quite cold in winter, if one can call it winter when it happens in the summer. I hope very much to find something for her nearer home. That's partly why I left her with Sir Edmund. I know he particularly wants to speak to her about something, so I thought we might be tactful and keep away.'

Mrs Brandon smiled mysteriously to herself. Though she had not been feeling very hopeful of Sir Edmund as a wooer for Miss Morris, it seemed to her that a suggestion of his, made to her at tea-time, that he should sound Miss Morris about taking over the secretaryship of the Barsetshire Benevolent Association (founded in 1783), of which he was President, contained the germs of possible romance.

'It would mean,' she continued, following her own train of thought and quite oblivious of that fact that she had not given the Vicar the slightest indication of what she was talking about, 'that she would be living not very far away, and even with her new duties we should be seeing quite a lot of her. Don't you think that would be very nice?'

Mr Miller said indeed, indeed it would be delightful. And looking at it dispassionately what could be more delightful than that a gifted, attractive woman who had been through many years of poverty and self-suppression, should marry a man of quite suitable age, of excellent family and character, comfortably off, and from his house continue her career of beneficence on a larger scale. As a plan Mr Miller could see no fault in it, which made him blame himself all the more for his unwarrantable dislike of the whole idea. Only a thoroughly selfish person could grudge Miss Morris so eminently desirable a marriage, and Mr Miller suddenly knew that sooner or later he must confess to himself that he was that person. Too shy and too oppressed to ask Mrs Brandon any more about the affair, he walked with her up and down the path under the Vicarage garden wall, looking at the Fête with unseeing eyes, hearing the steam organ without knowing what it was, fighting his own feelings, but fatally certain that in the night they would lie in ambush and fall upon him without pity.

Mrs Brandon, walking beside him in the sun, reflected placidly upon life and whether the wedding, if she could bring it about, would take place in the winter or the spring. If in the winter, that blue angora frock with her fur coat and perhaps a new hat would do very well. If it was in the spring she really didn't know. But by that time she would be getting some new clothes. Then she considered what Miss Morris should wear as a bride and decided to take her to town herself and have her suitably dressed. A dark blue tailor-made always looked well, or possibly a wine-coloured dress with a coat to match and a felt hat. Five minutes or so had passed away in these pleasant reflections when Mr Miller, resolutely shaking off the dark cloud that was oppressing him, said he had promised to guide Miss Morris to the roundabout and ought perhaps to be looking for her. Accordingly they went back to the ice-cream stall. Sir Edmund and Miss Morris were nowhere to be seen, but a small boy, who was picking up the uneaten points of larger boys' cones and making a hearty meal off them, said the lady had gone on the horses.

'I can't think that Miss Morris has really gone on the roundabout,' said Mrs Brandon placidly, 'but we'll go and look.'

*

Sir Edmund, left alone with Miss Morris, lost no time in saying what he had to say. In a very few sentences he put the advantages and disadvantages of the Barsetshire Benevolent Association before Miss Morris, named the salary, the hours, the responsibilities, the opportunities for taking on other work of a similar nature and any other points he considered useful. Miss Morris, pleased with his kind businesslike manner, listened attentively and promised to consider the matter and give him an answer as early as possible.

'I would like to mention it to Mrs Brandon if I may,' she said. 'She has been so good to me and I would feel ungrateful if I concealed my plans from her.'

'Tell Lavinia by all means,' said Sir Edmund. 'Woman has less sense for her age than anyone I know, but she doesn't gabble.'

'I don't think you are quite fair to her, Sir Edmund,' said Miss Morris.

'Don't you?' said Sir Edmund. 'Well, look at her now.'

Miss Morris looked and saw nothing worse than Mrs Brandon and Mr Miller pacing up and down under the Vicarage wall.

'Miller's up at Stories pretty often,' said Sir Edmund. 'Nice fellow, but needs a firm hand. Not Lavinia's style at all. I've known her ever since she married. Brandon was a dull dog. Women don't seem to know what's what. What do you say, eh? Clever woman like you ought to notice things.'

Miss Morris, for perhaps the first time in her quiet competent life, was utterly flabbergasted. Any idea of a possible attachment between Mrs Brandon and Mr Miller had never entered her head. She had seen, as who could help seeing, that Mr Miller found Mrs Brandon's charm rather overpowering, but then she felt it herself and could fully sympathize. As for Mrs Brandon, it would never have struck her that, beyond her real kindness to all around her and anyone in trouble, she was capable of any feelings stronger than, or indeed so strong as her complete absorption in her children, her house, and her clothes. The whole idea seemed to her so fantastic that she could not dismiss it as she would have done a more reasonable one, and it made her extremely ill at ease, she could not have said why.

'No, I don't notice anything,' she said pleasantly. 'Shall we go to the roundabout, Sir Edmund? I promised Mrs Thatcher that I would send Jimmy to her. It seems he isn't well and oughtn't to go on the horses.'

Sir Edmund accompanied her to the roundabout, giving her as they went an account of the Thatcher family, their numbers, names, accidents and diseases. Miss Morris listened with professional interest, an interest which she found greatly increased when Sir Edmund mentioned how good Mr Miller had been to them.

'Good Samaritan and all that, you know,' said Sir Edmund. 'Sat up with Thatcher for two nights in the last flu scare, so that Mrs Thatcher and the children could get some sleep. Know for a fact he paid for an extra week's convalescence for Edna Thatcher, that's the one that had the illegitimate baby – no, that was in '36 – it was Doris that had one in '37. Can't think why he wears those clothes though. No need to go about looking like an old woman, Miller, I say to him. There's Jimmy, Miss Morris. Doesn't look too fit, eh?'

To Miss Morris's practised eye Jimmy Thatcher looked indeed far from fit. Mounted on the ostrich he was swept past them at regular intervals, his face green and glistening with perspiration. Miss Morris didn't like the look of it at all, and as the music slowed down she walked quickly round to where Jimmy was convulsively clutching the ostrich's neck.

'Come along, Jimmy,' she said. 'Mother wants you.'

'I can't, miss,' said Jimmy hoarsely.

'Well, try,' said Miss Morris.

'I'll be sick if I do, miss, and it hurts so,' sobbed Jimmy.

Miss Morris put down Lydia's coconut, lifted Jimmy kindly and firmly off his ostrich and sat down on a chair hastily brought by the proprietress of the shooting gallery.

'Boy been eating too many sweets, eh?' said Sir Edmund. 'Better tell his mother. I'll run them home. She's been working in the tent all day.'

'I'm sorry, Sir Edmund,' said Miss Morris, 'but we ought to have a doctor. It's not my business, but it looks very like appendicitis. I've been with several cases. Is there a doctor?'

'Ford isn't here to-day,' said Sir Edmund, who knew every-thing, 'and Macfadden's away on holiday and I'm pretty sure I saw Horton driving over the other side of Barchester as I came. Better get him to the hospital. I've got the car here. Get his mother, one of you boys.'

But Mrs Thatcher, already warned by swift-footed rumour that Jimmy had been taken bad, arrived as he spoke and burst into loud tears. At the same moment Mrs Brandon and Mr Miller came up and learnt what had happened. Mrs Brandon immedi-ately went to find her car where there was a rug, and Miss Morris followed carrying Jimmy. In a few moments they were packed into Sir Edmund's car, Jimmy greener than ever, too much in pain and fright even to cry. Just as they were starting, the proprietress of the shooting gallery came up with Miss Morris's coconut.

'Here's something you left behind, dearie,' she said, thrusting it at its owner.

Jimmy's eyes brightened for a moment.

'Be a good boy, Jimmy, and you can have my coconut,' said Miss Morris.

Jimmy's face assumed the expression of a martyr who sees the gates of heaven beyond the tormentors' swords, as he feebly clutched the prize.

'We'll telephone to you from Barchester, Mrs Brandon,' said Sir Edmund. 'Can you manage, Miss Morris?'

Miss Morris said she thought so, and then caught sight of Delia.

'May Delia come, Mrs Brandon?' she said. 'I'd be rather glad of someone that can keep her head.'

Delia did not wait for her mother's permission. Her face lighted at the idea of going to a hospital with a possible appendix patient, even as Jimmy's had lighted at the coconut. She got into the back seat with Miss Morris and the patient, and the car drove off.

'That was *ripping* of you,' she said to Miss Morris. 'Gosh, doesn't poor Jimmy look *ghastly*.'

There was in her voice and air a mixture of true compassion for the invalid and what almost might be called gloating over the illness, that convinced Miss Morris she couldn't have made a better choice of a companion, who would not only be a support to her, but derive infinite satisfaction from the circumstances of the journey.

'I say, Mrs Thatcher was howling like anything,' said Delia, 'but Mr Miller was awfully nice to her and he was taking her up to the Vicarage to have a good cry and he said he'd keep her there till we telephoned. He's a good old sort for a parson.'

Miss Morris did not even think of chiding Delia for her language. She felt an unreasonable pride that her father's old pupil should have been so kind and thoughtful to the unhappy Mrs Thatcher. Then she remembered what Sir Edmund had said about Mr Miller and Mrs Brandon and told herself that Mr Miller deserved anything good, *anything* that heaven saw fit to send him. The journey to Barchester was soon over.

– 12 –

MR MERTON EXPLAINS

EVERYONE was agreeably excited by Jimmy's sudden appearance as News, some saying that they could see he would die on the way and the Panel ought to do something about it, others maintaining that he would be operated upon at once and die under the operation and the Government ought to do something about it. The crowd had now thinned and gone home to its tea, and the proprietors of the various shows were taking it easy till the evening rush began again about seven o'clock.

Mrs Brandon collected Francis and went home, where she was soon joined by Mr Merton and Lydia. Francis distributed sherry and the peace of Stories fell on the party.

'Excuse me, madam,' said Nurse, appearing in the doorway, 'but is Miss Delia back? I wanted her to try on that slip that I've been altering.'

'She's been taken to the Barchester Hospital,' said Francis.

'Don't be silly, Francis,' said his mother, and explained to Nurse the circumstance under which Delia had gone.

But even this delightful news did not appease Nurse, who said in a chilly way that she couldn't get on with the slip without Miss Delia, and then remained silent in the doorway like a hovering Nemesis.

'I'll tell you what, Nurse,' said Mrs Brandon. 'Could you mend Miss Keith's frock? She tore it at the Fête and her mother was rather upset.'

'Oh, I say, don't bother,' said Lydia, backing. 'It's a foul frock anyway, Mrs Brandon, and I always tear my things.'

'You *have* torn it, miss,' said Nurse, combining approval of the magnificence of the job on hand with deep disapproval of the frock's owner 'If you come upstairs with me, miss, I'll stitch it up. You can't go back like that, and with a gentleman.'

As she spoke she cast a disapproving look at Noel Merton which made him feel that she probably regarded him as a professional seducer, who began his ravishing by tearing the sleeves of his victim's frocks. Lydia, her bold spirit for once outmatched, followed Nurse meekly from the room.

'That is a remarkable woman,' said Mr Merton. 'I have never known anyone who had the faintest effect on Lydia before.'

'It's nothing to the effect she has on us,' said Francis. 'Have some more sherry?'

Mr Merton said he would.

'When I accepted your kind invitation,' he said to Mrs Brandon, 'I did so with the express intention of betraying a confidence, and propose to do so at once, before Lydia comes back and stuns us all. You know my father did Miss Brandon's business. Well, he has told me something about her will and I propose to tell it to you because I know how pleased you will be. His professional letters about it are already in the post and everyone concerned will get them on Monday, so it isn't really a breach of confidence at all.'

'Well, hurry up,' said Francis. 'I'm not a fortune hunter, but I would like to know the worst.'

But before Mr Merton could begin to say whatever it was,

241

Rose announced Mrs Grant and Mr Grant, who had never aroused such annoyance before.

'You will be quite surprised to see us again,' said Mrs Grant, while Francis murmured to Mr Grant that surprised wasn't the word and Mr Grant looked miserable. 'I went up to the Vicarage with my Boy, but there was such confusione, a woman in tears, the parroco consoling her, so different from our dear Calabrian peasants who seek the confessional in the church, never in the presbiterio, that sono rimasta stupefatta. Hilary said you were having a little sherry party and I thought I might be allowed to accompany him as I shall not be here much longer.'

On hearing this delightful news everyone became almost cordial. Mrs Grant refused sherry and asked for lemonade.

'And when do you really have to go?' asked Mrs Brandon.

'Who knows?' replied Mrs Grant. 'There is a proverb in Calabria which runs roughly, "To-morrow has also its own evil – "'

Francis said aloud to himself that to-day had it too and Mr Merton exchanged a glance of sympathy with him.

' – and *che sara sarà*. If I go to-morrow, I go; if not, it is for later,' said Mrs Grant gaily. 'As long as my Boy needs me, I shall be here.'

'Well, I'm afraid I'll have to be getting back to Southbridge,' said Mr Merton to his hostess in amused despair.

'Look here, Mr Merton, it isn't fair to leave us all in this shattering state of suspense,' said Francis. 'After all, Hilary is just as much interested as we are.'

Mr Grant, deeply oppressed by his mother's presence, looked incapable of interest in anything. Mrs Brandon said Francis was perfectly right, though she wasn't sure if one ought to talk about these things.

'Anyway you can't go till Nurse releases Lydia, so you might as well come clean, if you'll excuse the revolting expression,' said Francis to Mr Merton.

'I must explain,' said Mr Merton to the Grants, 'that I was just going to tell Mrs Brandon something about her aunt's will, that I know will interest you all. It will be common property on Monday, but I thought Mrs Brandon would have a particular interest in knowing it now. By a codicil, made just before her death, Miss Brandon has left her companion Miss Morris ten thousand pounds, with some very appreciative remarks about her patience and kindness.'

He finished his sherry, with the consciousness of having made a good point.

'I am *very* glad,' said Mrs Brandon with all the enthusiasm of her kind nature.

'Good old Aunt Sissie,' said Francis. 'Now I can propose to Miss Morris, unless it means cutting you out, Hilary.'

'Good luck,' said Mr Grant, brightening up for the first time since his arrival. 'I'll be best man.'

These expressions of pleasure were genuine and unforced, but Mr Merton, sensitive by nature and training to changes of voice and atmosphere, felt that something was wanting, though he couldn't tell what. Mrs Brandon, Francis and Mr Grant were indeed enchanted to find that Miss Morris had been remembered, but it was impossible for them not to wonder about the rest of the property. There was an uncomfortable pause and silence.

'There was another legacy that my father couldn't quite understand,' said Mr Merton. 'May I help myself to some more sherry?'

'Oh, sorry,' said Francis getting up. 'Hilary?'

'No thanks,' said Mr Grant.

'It was ten thousand pounds to a Captain Arbuthnot,' said Mr Merton. 'He exists all right, but he doesn't seem to be any relation. All we know is that it's an Indian Army family.'

'No, not exactly a relation,' said Mrs Brandon in an abstracted way, 'but there were very old family ties. What sort of age is he?'

'Oh quite young. Under thirty,' said Mr Merton, who was still under forty. 'Do you think Lydia will soon be ready, Mrs Brandon? We really ought to be getting back.'

'But who gets the Abbey?' said Mrs Grant.

The rest of the company, while thinking poorly of such open curiosity, were greatly relieved that anyone had little enough fine feeling to ask what by this time they were all burning to know. Burning is not perhaps quite the right word to express Mrs

Brandon's mild want of interest, or the fact that Francis and Mr Grant (as they found on comparing notes afterwards) both suddenly felt slightly sick; but it will serve.

'Oh, the Abbey and most of the property go as was always arranged,' said Mr Merton. 'Miss Brandon hadn't made a will since the year she inherited her father's estate. She added one or two codicils, but nothing that affects the disposition of the bulk of her property, Hullo Lydia, are you mended now?'

'I say, Mrs Brandon,' said Lydia, knocking a record which was lying on the gramophone lid on to the floor, where it broke in half.

'Do bear your body more seemingly, Lydia,' said Mr Merton, picking up the pieces. 'I apologize for her, Mrs Brandon.'

'Ass!' said Lydia good-humouredly, giving her friend a violent hit which he appeared to expect and indeed enjoy. 'I'm awfully sorry, Mrs Brandon. I say, Noel, what were you talking about codicils?'

'Only Miss Brandon's,' said Mr Merton.

'Oh, the one mother and father went to the funeral of,' said Lydia. 'Who is going to live in the Abbey?'

'It was left in trust with most of the money to be a kind of home for old people, specially anyone connected with certain regiments. I think she had an uncle or a brother she was very fond of in the Army. But what is really interesting, Lydia, is that Miss Morris is to have ten thousand pounds.'

'That's fine!' said Lydia. 'And I gave her the coconut Tony got at the shy. I say, Mrs Brandon, your nurse is a tough guy. I'd like to see her and the Pettinger have a go at each other. I'd back your nurse any day.'

'Miss Pettinger was headmistress of the Barchester High School where Lydia and Delia went,' Mrs Brandon explained to Mrs Grant. 'Well, good-bye, Mr Merton, and thank you so much for telling us about Miss Morris. I shan't say anything till Monday, when your father's letter comes. I can't tell you how pleased we all are. Good-bye Lydia. Never mind about the record. We are always breaking them.'

'Thanks awfully,' said Lydia. 'I do think your house is ripping.'

'So do I,' said Mr Merton. 'Will you let me come and see it and you again while I'm down here?'

'Yes, do,' said Mrs Brandon, adding in a siren's voice, 'Ring me up and come over some day when I am alone.'

Mr Merton shook hands in a deliberately lingering way which made Francis nudge Mr Grant and say 'Mother at it again,' at which Mr Grant was just going to scowl when he realized to his own great surprise that there was nothing to scowl about and smiled at Francis, thinking as he did so that though Mrs Brandon was still one of the nicest people in the world, one looked for something more than charm in a woman; intellect and appreciation of one's work for instance.

'Well,' said Francis, when he returned from seeing the visitors off and had picked up the visiting cards that the whiff and wind of Lydia's progress through the hall had scattered from a table on to the floor. 'Well, there is an end of an old song; for auld sang I cannot nor will not say.'

'I daresay the Abbey will make a very nice home for old people,' said Mrs Brandon, picking up her embroidery, 'that is if they don't mind the damp. After all, Aunt Sissie lived to be very old herself.'

Mrs Grant, who had sat for some time with an expression of deep disapproval, got up and said she and Hilary must be going.

'Do come again soon,' said Mrs Brandon. 'Perhaps you and Hilary would dine with us next week.'

'I always believe in speaking the truth,' said Mrs Grant.

'Yes, truth is so important,' said Mrs Brandon, anxious as usual to agree. 'Would Wednesday suit you perhaps?'

'I feel I owe it to Miss Morris to tell her that I suspected her of trying to get Miss Brandon's property,' said Mrs Grant earnestly.

'Oh I say, mother,' said her son, surprised and horrified.

'I don't think it would really be a good plan,' said Mrs Brandon. 'Mr Merton says Aunt Sissie never altered her will since the one she made when her father died, so Miss Morris really has nothing to do with it at all, and after all ten thousand pounds is really nothing when you think how much money Aunt Sissie had.'

Even Francis had to admit that this was the most muddle-headed piece of special pleading that his dear mamma had ever achieved, but Mrs Grant appeared to find it satisfactory.

'Yes, yes, I see what you mean,' she said with an alarmingly earnest gaze. 'You have intuition about these things.'

'I don't think so,' said Mrs Brandon doubtfully, 'but I do hope you are free on Wednesday.'

This repetition of the invitation seemed to Francis simply asking for trouble, especially when Mrs Grant, having freed her mind of Miss Morris, accepted it.

'Wednesday then will be delightful,' she said. 'We must go now, Hilary. I will go back to the Vicarage with you. It is really a comfort that all this affair of the Abbey is settled. *Finito*.'

She raised her long amber necklace with one hand and let it fall heavily on her coral necklace, her silver chain, and her coloured wooden beads, with a gesture of final doom. She then left, carrying her son, annoyed and speechless with her.

'Well, darling, you said a mouthful asking that Oriental Gipsy Lee with all her clanking necklaces to dinner,' said Francis. 'I expect Hilary will cut his throat if she stays here much longer.'

'Francis, you shouldn't say things like that,' said his mother. 'Darling, you aren't at all sorry, are you?'

'About the Abbey? No, darling. Apart from the glamour of having the most revolting and inconvenient house in Barsetshire bar none, unless it's Pomfret Towers, and the joy of having a large fortune most of which would go in death duties and legacies to other people, I am really honestly quite happy, I may say relieved. And I'm sure Hilary feels exactly the same. By the way who is that Captain Arbuthnot? You seem to know about him.'

Mrs Brandon paused for a moment before answering.

'Aunt Sissie's brother, Captain Brandon, had an entanglement with the wife of a Colonel Arbuthnot in India,' she said. 'He had to exchange his regiment because of it. Aunt Sissie was rather proud of the whole affair. She did say that I was a little like Mrs Arbuthnot,' said Mrs Brandon, looking pleased.

'Mamma, you shock me,' said Francis.

In spite of her son's attempts at dissuasion, Mrs Grant insisted on accompanying him to the Vicarage. He knew that his mother would disgrace him and wished that she would do so at the Cow and Sickle rather than in the presence of Mr Miller, who must be tired by the Fête and looking after Mrs Thatcher. The Vicar was in the garden and Mr Grant couldn't possibly warn him of the fate that was descending on him, so he said rather sulkily to his tutor, 'Here's mother sir,' and escaped into the house. Mrs Grant established herself on the seat by the heliotrope border, and telling Mr Miller that she had come to talk about her boy, proceeded to talk about herself. Mr Miller was very tired. All that week he had been working for the Fête, in addition to his ordinary duties. Since breakfast-time he had been on duty, arranging, planning, judging, composing quarrels, adjusting differences, a buffer for every contending force. Just as he had hoped for a few words with Miss Morris, who had helped so splendidly in the tea-tent, she had been taken away from him by Sir Edmund; but he quickly put that thought away, though he couldn't help stopping to hope that Miss Morris would have everything good that life could give her. Then Jimmy Thatcher had been taken ill, and while he had done nothing, Sir Edmund and Miss Morris had taken the whole affair in hand with a competence which he hopelessly envied. He humbly thought of his own inefficiency. All he could do was to take charge of Mrs Thatcher. After finding Edna, the eldest Miss Thatcher, she who had had an illegitimate baby in '36, and telling her to look after the other children, he had brought Mrs Thatcher to the Vicarage and let her cry and talk in the study. There was no one in the house and Cook and Hettie were lost among the sideshows, so he had been inspired to tell Mrs Thatcher he felt like a cup of tea and introduce her to the kitchen. With loud but less despairing blubberings she had found the tea, milk and sugar, brought the kettle to the boil and produced for him the strongest, sweetest, nastiest cup of tea he had ever tasted. He had persuaded her to sit down with him at the kitchen table and share the odious drink, under whose influence she became as cheerful as circumstances permitted, giving him a graphic account of Thatcher's bad leg. After this he suggested that she should have a rest in Cook's armchair, found for her on the dresser what Cook called a nice book, being a twopenny work of fiction called *Her Dreams Came True*, and left her to herself, promising to tell her as soon as there was any news of Jimmy. He knew he ought to go back to the Fête, but was so tired with the long day and his own anxieties, that he sat for a little in his garden, and so fell a prey to Mrs Grant.

While she talked he tried to listen, tried to focus his attention by looking at her beads and earrings, and then his mind wandered back to its preoccupation with Sir Edmund, till suddenly the name of Miss Morris brought his thoughts back with a jerk to what his guest was saying.

'Excuse me, I didn't quite catch what you said,' he said to Mrs Grant. 'Do you mean that Miss Morris has been left something by Miss Brandon?'

'Not the Abbey, of course,' said Mrs Grant. 'That was always left to some charity, so I understood from Mr Merton, but she is to have ten thousand pounds. If you look on it as capital she will have an income for life if it is properly invested. Not much, but it makes a good background.'

Mr Miller said to himself that even at three per cent one would have thirty pounds a year on a thousand pounds, and three hundred pounds on ten thousand pounds. Then there would be income tax, he supposed, but even so it would make a single woman a good deal better off than he was. So he expressed to Mrs Grant his pleasure at this good news, saying he was sure no one deserved it more.

'By the way,' said Mrs Grant, with a belated attack of conscience, 'Mrs Brandon doesn't mean to tell Miss Morris, because she will hear about it in a lawyer's letter on Monday, but I feel sure she wouldn't mind my telling *you*. So don't give me away.'

Mr Miller assured her that the confidence should be respected, and almost disliked her. So to make amends for this he asked her if she would stay and have a cold meal with him and her son.

'No, thank you,' said Mrs Grant. 'I am going back to the Cow, where I have promised to teach Mrs Spindler to prepare macaroni in the native fashion, that is as far as is possible when the macaroni itself is bought, not made at home. I shan't disturb Hilary, for I know how hard he has to work.'

In proof of this virtuous resolve she called up to her son's window in what Mr Miller could only suppose to be an Italian way, till he put his face unsympathetically out and said good-bye.

When she had gone Mr Miller knew he ought to call his pupil, have the cold tongue and tomatoes, and go back to the Fête, but an overpowering fatigue of mind and body so assailed him that he remained in the garden and was still there when Sir Edmund's car drove up. Mr Miller went to the gate, but Sir Edmund was alone.

'Knew you'd want to know about the boy, Miller,' said Sir Edmund through the car window, 'so I came round this way after I'd dropped Miss Morris and Delia at Stories. It's appendicitis all right. Clever woman Miss Morris. They're going to operate at once. I had a good talk with Miss Morris on the way back, and we understand each other pretty well. Head on her shoulders. Heart too. Not on her shoulders – you know what I mean. I promised Jimmy I'd tell his mother he is all right. Plucky little fellow. Well, I must get along to Grumper's End.'

'Mrs Thatcher is here,' said Mr Miller. 'She was so upset that I thought some tea would do her good.'

Sir Edmund stared at his Vicar with respect and admiration, but made no comment.

'If you would ring me up as soon as there is news of Jimmy,' said the Vicar, 'I'll keep her here, and Cook or Hettie can see her home.'

Sir Edmund nodded and drove off.

Mr Miller and Mr Grant then partook of supper, almost in silence. Mr Grant, bitten by Mrs Morland's idea of a novel, was in a state of literary frenzy. Mr Miller was thinking of a happy future for an admirable intelligent woman, an ideal companion, and at the same time telling himself that such thoughts were better left in an eternal shadow. At nine o'clock Cook and Hettie came back from the Fête and had the rest of the cold tongue and tomatoes with Mrs Thatcher. At nine-fifteen Sir Edmund rang up to say that Jimmy Thatcher had been operated on successfully and was doing well, a piece of news received by Mrs Thatcher with loud and thankful hysterics, by Cook and Hettie with pleasure mingled with a lasting regret that the operation had not delightfully proved fatal. At nine-thirty the Vicar sent Mrs Thatcher home in charge of his servants and by ten o'clock Cook and Hettie were back and had gone to bed, and Mr Grant had retired. Mr Miller sat in his study in the summer darkness, long after the noise and lights of the Fête were over, till he fell asleep with heavy fatigue of mind, and in the unfriendly grey heralding of dawn he woke unrefreshed and went to bed.

*

Dinner at Stories consisted chiefly of a long and happy monologue from Delia, who had not only enjoyed every moment of the drive and insisted on having Jimmy on her lap, but had had the exquisite pleasure of seeing two operation cases being wheeled back from the operating theatre, looking like corpses. Her mother and brother, conspirators, said little and Miss Morris was rather tired. After dinner Delia put on all her crooning records so that talk was unnecessary. Mrs Brandon sat with her embroidery, but her fingers were idle and she looked more often than usual at her graceful hands and Miss Brandon's diamond ring. A gentle melancholy filled her as she thought of Aunt Sissie's legacy to Captain Arbuthnot, probably if one went by dates and ages the grandson of the woman who had for a season enchanted Captain Brandon. As Francis had said, it was the end of an old song. Captain Brandon and his lovely ladies were long forgotten; only in Miss Brandon's memory they had lived. Now she was dead and her memory too would soon be faint. Mrs Brandon suddenly realized how great a compliment Aunt Sissie had paid her when she put Captain Brandon's gift on her finger. What she did not realize was that her indomitable, pagan old aunt had seen and respected in her, for all the silliness that she so trenchantly criticized, an integrity of spirit not so far from her own. The end of an old song.

When good nights had been said Mrs Brandon remembered something she had forgotten, a phenomenon which was frequent in her life. She went to Miss Morris's room and tapped at the door. Miss Morris in her dressing-gown, her hair in two plaits, opened to her.

'I'm so sorry,' said Mrs Brandon, 'I quite forgot to ask you about church to-morrow. Would you like to go to Little Misfit or Nutfield? I just wanted to know so that I could send word to Curwen.'

'I'd like so much to come to church with you if I may,' said Miss Morris.

– 13 –

MISS MORRIS'S LEGACY

SUNDAY passed over quietly. Francis and Delia were spending the day with friends, Mrs Brandon and Miss Morris went to the eleven o'clock service, during which Mrs Brandon did some very useful thinking about clothes for Miss Morris's possible spring wedding, Mr Miller tried hard to keep his mind on his work, and Miss Morris betrayed no thoughts of any kind. The Grants were also there, in the Vicarage pew, and when Mr Grant saw every eye in the church turned upon his mother and her jangling accoutrements, he wished as usual that he were dead, for he was too good a son to wish that fate to his mother. The only thing that sustained him was the thought of the literary composition upon which he had already embarked. As soon as he and Mr Miller had finished their horrid cold supper he had made an excuse of some work to do, and shut himself up with Jehan le Capet. During the evening he mapped out a rough draft of the novel suggested by Mrs Morland and had written a chapter of very realistic description of Jehan le Capet's first mistress, the wife of the proprietor of a rather low eating house in the Quartier Latin called Le Chat Savant. In his enthusiasm he had almost identified himself with his hero and had emerged at about two o'clock in the morning from his work, dazed, exhausted, and with very cold feet, as the poet had often emerged from the side door of the Chat Savant. There was however this difference, that the proprietor's wife always sent her poet away with a little parcel of food in his pocket, whereas Mr Grant having finished on

251

the previous night a tin of biscuits that he kept in his room and being afraid to go downstairs in case Cook or Hettie should hear him, had to go hungry to bed.

Outwardly all the congregation looked much as usual and no one, hearing Sir Edmund read the lessons in his usual orderly-room manner, taking all the difficult names in an unhesitating and often incorrect stride, would have guessed that he was reflecting upon his responsibility for preventing his Vicar and his old friend Mrs Brandon from making fools of themselves.

After the service there was the usual talk outside the church door as the congregation dispersed. When the Vicar came out he approached the little group where Mrs Brandon was standing with Sir Edmund and the Grants. He looked anxious, a fact which did not escape the keen eye of his churchwarden.

'Morning, Miller,' said Sir Edmund. 'That was a queer first lesson. Something to be said for having the Bible in Latin, eh? You look a bit queer too. Had a bad night?'

Mr Miller said he hadn't slept very well.

'It was the Fête,' said Mrs Brandon sympathetically.

'Got the accounts wrong again?' asked Sir Edmund.

Mr Miller said he hadn't been through them yet.

'No, no, of course not. Sunday,' said Sir Edmund. 'Thirteenth after Trinity and all that. Never mind. They'll keep and I daresay you'll get them just as wrong to-morrow. Remember the year you were seventeen and threepence out of pocket. Well, be sure to let me know if there's any deficit. Mustn't muzzle the ox, you know, eh?'

Mr Miller smiled feebly. Not that he in the least resented Sir Edmund's remark about the ox, or the implication that he lined his own pockets out of the takings of the Fête, for he knew his churchwarden's kindness of heart, but there were reasons why he could not bear to think of any deficit being made up by him. One does not like to take too much charity from a man whom one really likes very much and is trying not to dislike.

'Mr Miller,' said Mrs Grant, 'will you mind very much if I take my Boy back to lunch at the Cow? I feel I must see all I can of him before I go.'

Mr Miller, who had counted upon Mr Grant to do justice to the Vicarage roast beef and knew Cook would be annoyed if he said he really couldn't face a heavy lunch, said indeed, indeed she must have Hilary. Mr Grant, who had only come to church out of kindness to his host, and was straining to get back to his novel, looked at his mother in black despair.

'We shall have a little festa,' said Mrs Grant gaily. 'I have told Mrs Spindler exactly how macaroni should be prepared, and we will imagine we are in Calabria.'

Mr Grant looked as if this exercise of the imagination would afford him no pleasure at all, but said nothing.

'Mrs Brandon,' said Mr Miller, 'would I find you in sometime to-morrow afternoon? I very much want to speak to you, alone.'

Although he had said these words in a low voice, they had not escaped Sir Edmund's attention.

'Of course,' said Mrs Brandon. 'Do come to tea and I'll tell Rose I am not at home, only I'm afraid we can't have tea in the garden in that case, because it is really quite impossible to say one is not at home when there one is in full view under the chestnut. I do hope it isn't the accounts, because I can't do them at all.'

Mr Miller assured her that it was not the accounts, but only a small private matter. Sir Edmund, who deliberately overheard this, was more than ever perturbed and resolved to think the matter over seriously.

Mr Miller went back to the Vicarage, told Hettie that Mr Grant would not be in to lunch and sat down alone to a round of beef, which was what Cook and Hettie liked on Sundays. For a moment he thought of putting the helping he had cut for himself under Hettie's eye into an envelope and burying it, but he knew he would not be clever enough to conceal the crime and in any case would be acting a lie. So he chewed his way industriously through red meat, grey potatoes, damp cabbage, and stony apple-pie. With the uninteresting cheese courage was given him to tell Hettie he had had enough and didn't want any coffee as he had to go to Grumper's End. He found a faint satisfaction in sitting in Mrs Thatcher's kitchen, giving her the latest news of Jimmy (who was going on well) and promising to take her to see him at the hospital next week. The cottage appeared to him in an even more deplorable condition than usual. Edna and Doris were washing their hair over the dirty sink, dirty dishes lay about, the youngest Thatchers were playing on the dirty floor with their illegitimate young nephew and niece, a few clothes, washed out in a slovenly way by Edna and Doris, lay about the room because no one could be bothered to hang them out in the sunshine. In the corner Thatcher, unshaven, was enjoying his after-dinner pipe and reading in his Sunday paper about the forthcoming autumn football pools. Everything smelt of frowstiness and stale food. Looking round the young Thatchers, all of whom seemed to thrive upon their parents' slatternly methods, the Vicar blamed himself severely for want of tolerance and wondered how he would manage on thirty-five shillings a week.

Just as he was sitting down to his horrid cold Sunday supper his pupil came in.

'I'm awfully sorry I'm late, sir,' said Mr Grant.

'Come in, come in,' said the Vicar. 'I'm afraid it's only cold beef and pickles. Hettie said they were too busy clearing up after the Fête to do baked potatoes to-night. I am so sorry.'

'That's all right, sir,' said Mr Grant. 'I'm off farinaceous food altogether since lunch. Mother had a most unholy row with Mrs Spindler about macaroni. She wanted to show her how to cook it and Mrs Spindler, who I must say is usually awfully nice, was a bit off colour after the Fête and there were a lot of extra Sunday dinners for motorists and things and she seems to have gone off the deep end altogether. Oh, that's heaps, sir, thanks,' said Mr Grant, hastily withdrawing his plate upon which the Vicar had been heaping slices of beef while Mr Grant talked. 'We did get the macaroni, but it was not a success, and then it was ground rice shape and I felt I must do something not to hurt Mrs Spindler's feelings, so I had two helpings. Oh Lord – Sorry, sir.'

'I am indeed sorry,' said the Vicar. 'I've never known Mrs Spindler be rude to a visitor before.'

'Well, you haven't known my mother before, sir,' said Mr Grant. 'But one good thing is that mother says she must go back to Italy. She has lots of rows with the hotel people there, but somehow rows are different in Italy and people always seem a bit cheered up by them, if you know what I mean. How's Donne, sir?'

'I have been correcting the galley proofs,' said the Vicar, flushing with mild pleasure at his pupil's interest. 'I must say the work has been very well done, and I find very few mistakes. The only thing that worries me now is the question of a dedication.'

'Who were you thinking of dedicating it to?' asked Mr Grant, feeling very respectful towards a person who had real proofs to correct.

'I had thought – ' said the Vicar, and then broke off.

'What about your old college, sir?' asked Mr Grant. 'I should think they'd be jolly pleased.'

'How nice of you,' said the Vicar. 'If it were a work on a classical subject I should not hesitate to make a suggestion. But Donne – . I fear the Master would think such a dedication frivolous. How is your own work?'

'I'm afraid I've been a bit slack lately,' said Mr Grant, guiltily conscious of books unread and essays unfinished. 'I'll put in some solid work to-night and really get down to it next week.'

'I mean your own work,' said the Vicar.

'My own work?' said Mr Grant, going bright pink.

'I suppose it's a novel,' said the Vicar.

'Yes sir. But how on earth did you know?'

'The usual sign,' said the Vicar mildly. 'I've had a good many pupils, you know. When they come down to meals looking drunk and sometimes very cross and nearly always peculiar in manner, it always means a novel. Besides, I wrote one once myself.'

'Did you really, sir?' asked Mr Grant, suddenly seeing his tutor in a new and respectful light. 'Could I read it?'

'I'm afraid not,' said the Vicar, secretly flattered at this interest. 'I tore it up soon after I had finished it. But I remember exactly how I felt when I was writing it and how drunk – if we may use the expression – literary composition made me. I am afraid I wasn't always an easy companion during that period.'

'What was it about, sir?' asked Mr Grant.

'Oh, nothing,' said the Vicar vaguely. 'Quite an ordinary story about two young people who thought they cared for each other and were separated by circumstances. One is told,' he added, more to himself than to his pupil, 'that first novels are nearly always autobiographical.'

He fell into a kind of muse, forgetful of his pupil's presence. Mr Grant felt respectfully uncomfortable and being still young enough to believe that his own affairs must interest all his friends he rather shyly asked the Vicar if he would like to hear about what he was doing.

'What you are doing?' said the Vicar, bringing himself back to life with an effort that his young friend did not notice. 'Indeed, indeed, my dear Hilary, I should be delighted. Don't think I wish to press your confidence in any way, but it would really interest me immensely. Let us go into the garden. It feels so hot and heavy indoors.'

'I was doing a kind of monograph on that French poet, Jehan le Capet that I told you about,' said Mr Grant, as they installed themselves on the seat by the heliotrope border, 'but I was talking about it to Mrs Morland at the picnic and she was awfully helpful about publishers and things and then I met her again at the Fête and she said why not make a novel out of it?'

'Why not?' said Mr Miller.

'So,' continued Mr Grant, enchanted by this encouragement, 'I thought I'd have a stab at it. Mrs Morland's awfully nice and she's a real author. I mean people ask for her books in libraries. And she's the sort of person you can really talk to about anything. I mean things you couldn't talk to other people about.'

'Yes, I should think Mrs Morland is extraordinarily broad-minded about things she really knows nothing about,' said the Vicar, a remark whose unexpected profundity rather staggered Mr Grant. 'And now tell me how you propose to treat your novel.'

Encouraged by the growing darkness which enabled one to say words like 'mistress' in front of one's tutor without feeling uncomfortable, Mr Grant embarked upon his subject, and having once begun saw no reason to stop. The Vicar found his pleasant eager young voice no hindrance to his own thoughts and they sat, each full of his own dreams, till the late full moon had risen above the trees.

*

On Monday morning Francis, coming down just before half-past eight to have his breakfast and go off to his work, was very much surprised to find his dear mother already downstairs and walking about the room. To see her so early and to see her restless were phenomena which, taken together, could not fail to strike an intelligent observer.

'Good Lord!' said Francis, 'it's Monday.'

'The post is usually a bit late on Mondays,' said Mrs Brandon, looking out of the window.

'I say,' said Delia, as she came in, 'has the post come?'

'Not yet,' said her mother. 'He never does on Monday because of helping his cousin at the dairy.'

'I do hope Miss Morris will get down before he comes,' said Delia. 'I want to see if she'll throw a fit or something when the news comes. Do you suppose it will come this morning, mother.'

'Mr Merton said so,' said Mrs Brandon, 'and he ought to know because he's a lawyer.'

'People do sometimes die of shock when they get very good news,' said Delia hopefully, but at the moment Miss Morris came in, looking as neat and collected as ever, and this interesting conversation had to stop.

Miss Morris ate her breakfast with good appetite, wondering a little why Francis and Delia were talking in such a disjointed way.

'You don't often come down to breakfast, do you, Mrs Brandon?' she asked.

'Sometimes, but not very often, at least I hardly ever do, but just now and then, or really hardly ever, unless you count the days one has to get up early, like going abroad,' said Mrs Brandon with the air of one giving a thoroughly lucid explanation.

Francis and Delia began to laugh. Francis choked and Delia hit him on the back and they would probably both have had hysterics had not Rose come in with the letters. One might have heard a pin drop, as Francis dramatically said to Mr Grant later in the day, while Miss Morris looked over her little pile of letters.

'They all look like business,' she said. 'I shan't spoil my breakfast with them.'

If maddened frustration could kill, Francis and Delia would

certainly have killed her on the spot. Even Mrs Brandon thought vaguely that Miss Morris was perhaps a little inconsiderate but a fat envelope bulging with patterns of material for new curtains held her attention for the moment. Francis got up and went to the sideboard to find a little something to round off his breakfast. After cutting himself two slices of ham he returned to his place, and said to Miss Morris, as carelessly as possible, 'Why not look at them now, Miss Morris? It's unlucky to leave letters unopened at breakfast.'

He looked across at his sister to demand her sympathetic applause for this brilliant piece of diplomacy, but Delia did not respond. To her brother's alarm she was sitting with a flushed face and her mouth open, and staring fixedly at nothing.

'Hi, Delia, what's up?' Francis asked. 'Has something stuck in your gullet? Wait a minute and I'll come and hit your back.'

To this kind suggestion Delia's only answer was the words, 'Two hundred pounds!'

'Pounds of what?' said Francis. 'Pull yourself together, my girl.'

'Aunt Sissie! Two hundred pounds!' Delia gasped. 'It says so in a letter. Mother, is it real, do you think?'

She pushed a letter across the table to her mother who read it with provoking coolness and said she thought it was quite real.

'Well!' said Francis, who had got up again and was reading the letter over his mother's shoulder, 'who would have thought Aunt Sissie had it in her. Now we can get those records, Delia.'

'I'll tell you what,' said Delia, 'I'll give you half.'

'No, you jolly well won't,' said Francis. 'Oh Good Lord! hang on a moment. I've got a hunch.'

He dashed back to his place, tore open his letters, held up one of them and said triumphantly.

'There! Two hundred pounds for me too. Well, well, well. Good old Aunt Sissie. Let's go to Monte Carlo and stake it all and double it and take away the number we first thought of. I'll give you half, Delia, to make up for the half you're giving me. I say, mother, what about you?'

'Aunt Sissie gave me my ring,' said Mrs Brandon, looking with complacency at her graceful hand which bore only her wedding ring and Captain Brandon's diamond. 'I am so glad she remembered you both, and two hundred pounds is such a nice sum, because you feel it isn't worth investing.'

Miss Morris then said, with every evidence of sincerity, how glad she was of this good fortune and quite agreed – she who had counted less than half that sum as riches for a year – that the great thing about two hundred pounds was that one could spend it; that it became indeed a kind of solemn duty to spend it. By the time she had finished saying this her young friends could have shaken her till every tooth in her head rattled, but the conventions forbid one to press one's guests, who may have very good reasons for their conduct, to open their letters in one's presence.

'Well, I must be off,' said Francis. 'If I get the sack for being late, two hundred pounds won't support me till I get the Old Age Pension. How soon do we get the money, mother?'

'I haven't the faintest idea, darling,' said Mrs Brandon. 'Ask Mr Merton.'

'When is he coming?' asked Francis.

Mrs Brandon said she didn't know, but Mr Merton had said he would telephone. Her son Francis looked at her and grinned at his sister.

'What you mean, darling, is that you asked him to ring you up,' said Francis. 'Well, I must be off.'

He made a last face at Delia, indicative of hatred for people who would not read their letters, and went away to his car. Delia, after gazing with silent animosity upon the unconscious Miss Morris, went into the garden. Mrs Brandon, giving the whole matter up as a bad job, went off to see Cook in her sitting room, leaving Miss Morris looking at the advertisement pages of *The Times*. Cook was in a good mood and Mrs Brandon was soon able to apply herself to her correspondence. She was in the middle of writing an account of the Fête to her old governess, who lived in Cheltenham, when Miss Morris came in and asked if she could spare a moment.

'Of course,' said Mrs Brandon, laying down her pen with a gentle feeling of excitement. 'Can I do anything?'

'I don't quite understand this letter,' said Miss Morris, apparently as composed as ever.

Mrs Brandon asked if she might see it. Miss Morris handed a letter to her and Mrs Brandon noticed that her hand was shaking.

'Sit down and let me look at it,' said Mrs Brandon, who knew perfectly well what the contents were, but wanted to give Miss Morris time. 'It seems quite clear to me. Aunt Sissie has left you ten thousand pounds, and I must say it does her the greatest credit, or did, or is it does?'

'But it's not fair,' said Miss Morris with unusual vehemence. 'Francis and Delia have two hundred pounds each and you have nothing, and I have all this money.'

'No, please don't look at it like that,' said Mrs Brandon. 'As a matter of fact it is a very good thing for the children not to have any more, because they will both be really very comfortably off, and as for me I shouldn't know what to do with it, and besides, I have my diamond. Please, please do believe me that it is the nicest and best thing Aunt Sissie could have done, and let me say for us all how very pleased we are.'

With which words Mrs Brandon got up and kissed Miss Morris warmly.

'I can't believe it. You are too generous,' said Miss Morris, in a voice which threatened tears.

'Drink this at once,' said Mrs Brandon, unscrewing the top of the little flask of brandy that she kept in the top drawer of her bureau in case, and thrusting it into Miss Morris's hand. Miss Morris, hypnotized by her hostess's firm attitude, tilted the flask, drank more of the contents than she expected and coughed so violently that emotion was for the time being dispelled.

'I'm not really a bit generous,' said Mrs Brandon, voicing as usual the first muddled thoughts that came into her head, 'because I didn't make the will, but I'm sure if Aunt Sissie had asked me I'd have said twenty thousand.'

'I can't take it,' said Miss Morris.

'You could subscribe to ever so many charities,' said Mrs Brandon, 'and do good secretly, but I *do* hope you'll spend some on clothes and let me help you, because I know that's what Aunt Sissie would have liked.'

'Miss Brandon would have liked you to have pretty clothes.

She wouldn't have approved of them for me,' said Miss Morris with ruthless realism. 'But if I could help anyone who is in need –'

She paused and looked with a rapt expression into the distance.

'Of course you could,' said Mrs Brandon, seizing her opportunity. 'Pomfret Madrigal is simply full of people in need and then there is our division of Barsetshire, and the whole county, and Zenana missions, whatever they are, and heaps of charities. Mr Miller is coming to see me after tea and I could ask him about deserving cases in the village to start with if you like.'

'That would be true kindness,' said Miss Morris, 'and so like you. I think, if you don't mind, I had better go upstairs to my room and be quiet for a little. If only my dear father could see –'

She broke off, too moved for further speech.

'He can see *everything*,' said Mrs Brandon firmly, for though she had no particular conviction that the Rev. and late Justin Morris, who seemed to have been as selfish as they make them, was looking down from his particular brand of heaven upon his daughter with a benevolent and approving eye, yet she felt that any idea to that effect in Miss Morris's mind was eminently suitable for a clergyman's daughter and should be encouraged.

Miss Morris threw a grateful glance towards her hostess and escaped, to thank Heaven with grateful tears in her bedroom for making it possible for her to help the poor, and more especially the poor who were in Mr Miller's flock.

Mrs. Brandon, left alone, amused herself by trying to calculate upon the blotting paper how much a year Miss Morris would have, but as she didn't know how much per cent one was likely to get and had a vague though mistaken idea that Compound Interest, which she could never do at school, somehow came into it with some letters of the alphabet, not to speak of blotting paper being a very unfavourable medium for arithmetical computation, she had not got very far when Delia came into the room, carrying a vase of flowers.

'I say, mother,' she said, 'does Miss Morris know yet? I saw her going upstairs when I was bringing the flowers in, but I didn't like to ask, so I did the dining-room vases and this one for her room, but I didn't like to take it upstairs till I knew everything was all right.'

'Yes, she opened her letters just after you had gone out,' said Mrs Brandon, 'but I wouldn't go up just yet. She is probably crying. Poor thing, how glad I am for her.'

'So'm I,' said Delia. 'I say, mother, what about Hilary? Do you suppose he comes in on this? If not Francis and I must do something about it. He was just as much Aunt Sissie's cousin or whatever it is as we are.'

*

The object of Delia's interest had meant to get up at cockcrow to strike while the iron was hot, or in other words to continue his novel while the inspiration was upon him, but so soundly did he sleep that it was not till Hettie had knocked twice that he realized the precious early morning hours had flown. Having realized it he at once went to sleep again and did not wake till half-past nine. Full of shame he rushed through his bath and dressing and came downstairs three steps at a time only to find the dining-room empty. Hettie, coming in to ask rather grudgingly if he would like some fresh tea, said Mr Miller had been sent for to Starveacres Hatches and didn't know when he would be back. Mr Grant looked miserably at the tepid, black infusion in the tea-pot and said it would do nicely, and Hettie retired. He poured himself out a cup, drank shudderingly of it, looked with distaste at a cold poached egg, and decided on milk and bread and butter. Over this blameless meal he began to read his letters, and by this time it will surprise no one to learn that the second letter he opened was from Miss Brandon's solicitors, announcing a bequest of two hundred pounds.

His first thought was of pure joy at having two hundred pounds of his own, for though his father had arranged an income for him, it was not to be his own till he was twenty-five, until which time he had to live on the allowance his mother gave him, an allowance which, though not ungenerous, did not allow for much saving. Two hundred pounds would be a godsend. One could buy books, go to Iceland, have really good seats at the Opera and in short indulge one's fancy. His second thought was one of apprehension. Had his mother also received a legacy, and if not would she resent his having one. Her annoyance, if she had to be annoyed, would not last, but while it did she was capable of flying into one of the scenes which, while part of calm everyday life to her beloved Calabrians, had the effect of volcanoes and geysers on the colder-blooded English and would put him to shame for ever in Pomfret Madrigal. With some annoyance he decided he had better neglect his classics and his novel and go down to the Cow before his mother went out. But on the way he passed the lane leading to Stories and could not resist the temptation of going up the drive to see if anyone was about. Catching sight of Delia through the morning room window, he came in and found her with her mother.

'Good morning, Hilary,' said Mrs Brandon. 'Have you come to congratulate Miss Morris?'

'Because you can't just now,' Delia remarked antiphonally, 'because she's having a good howl in her room. Good old Miss Morris.'

'I'd rather forgotten about that,' said Mr Grant, feeling brutal, 'but I'm awfully glad. She deserves it if anyone does. I really came to tell you something.'

'But what is *marvellous*,' said Delia, taking no notice of him, 'is that Aunt Sissie has left me two hundred pounds for myself. Good old Aunt Sissie. I say, Hilary, have you got anything? If not I'll give you half of mine.'

Mr Grant suddenly felt so selfish that he could have sunk through the floor. All he had thought of was how to spend his own money, and now Delia, who must have as many secret wishes as he had, was offering him half her inheritance from sheer kindness. He tried to say something but stammered so badly that he had to stop. Mrs Brandon, feeling that the young people must really deal with their affairs themselves, resumed her letter writing with some ostentation.

'All right, Hilary, no need to gobble,' said Delia kindly. 'Just as you like, only I'd awfully like to give you something. It might help your book along a bit.'

'You do have the most marvellous ideas,' said Mr Grant, at last recovering partial control of his speech.

Delia looked pleased.

'You will have it, won't you?' she asked anxiously.

'It's absolutely *decent* of you,' said Mr Grant vehemently, 'but as a matter of fact Aunt Sissie left me two hundred pounds too. I do hope you won't mind.'

'Delia darling,' said Mrs Brandon, 'do take Hilary into the garden. I must finish writing to poor old Miss Heaton about the Fête and I have just written hundred pounds instead of roundabout.'

Accordingly the young people went into the garden, where Mr Grant, now himself again, told Delia all about Mrs Morland's suggestion. Delia showed as much interest and excitement about the proposed novel as any author could wish, and it was she who made the brilliant suggestion that in the extremely remote case of the publishing trade being blind and misguided enough not to accept the novel, Hilary should use some of his legacy in paying for a part of the expenses of publication, thus conferring a lasting benefit on the reading public. So pleasantly did the morning pass that it was too late for Hilary to go to the Cow, and he had to hurry back to the Vicarage where lunch was at one.

'I really can't say thank you enough,' he said to Delia as he left. 'You simply are the only person I can really talk to about my book. You really understand.'

Pleased with her cousin's praise, Delia went back to the house and let Nurse try on a camisole without a single murmur, which made Nurse look at her a little suspiciously.

– 14 –

MRS BRANDON AT HOME

MR MILLER arrived punctually for his assignation with Mrs Brandon, who had given orders that she would see no one till the Vicar had gone.

'Now, tell me all about everything,' said Mrs Brandon, in her most comfortable voice.

'I really hardly know how to begin what I want to say to you,

Mrs Brandon, without a breach of confidence,' said Mr
Miller.

'Tell me exactly what it is then,' said Mrs Brandon.

'You see, it concerns not only myself, but Mrs Grant,' said the
Vicar.

'Mrs Grant?' said Mrs Brandon, taken quite aback, and
wondering whether Mrs Grant had come to tell Mr Miller that
the Mafia were on her track, or alternatively whether he was
going to propose to his pupil's mother. Neither alternative
seemed probable.

'You see she came to the Vicarage on Saturday evening, after
she had been at Stories, and told me something which perhaps I
oughtn't to know, but which has caused me very grave concern.'

Mrs Brandon simply couldn't think of anything at Stories
which, repeated by Mrs Grant, could cause Mr Miller any concern, and looked at him in perplexity.

'My only excuse,' said Mr Miller, 'is that I didn't realize what
she was talking about till it was too late.'

'And I shan't either,' said Mrs Brandon, stung by his floundering to what was for her an unusually sharp retort. 'What on earth
did she say?'

'She said, but doubtless I understood her wrongly, that Miss
Brandon had left Miss Morris a sum of money in her will,' said
Mr Miller, looking appealingly at Mrs Brandon as if she might
be able to reassure him.

'That is quite true,' said Mrs Brandon. 'Ten thousand pounds.
I don't know how much a year that comes out to, because Delia
interrupted me when I was doing the sum, but it was very nice of
Aunt Sissie.'

Mr Miller said nothing. Mrs Brandon, realizing that as usual
she would have to help him to express himself, took up her
embroidery in a soothing way and asked if he wanted to see Miss
Morris who was upstairs.

'No,' said Mr Miller, jibbing violently. 'At least nothing would
give me more pleasure, but I feel it would be better not to. I had
hoped so much – she was so kind about the notices for the Fête –
she helped in the tea-tent – you saw how she dealt with Jimmy
Thatcher. And then she came to church with you yesterday.

265

Perhaps I oughtn't to have noticed that, but I couldn't help seeing her in your pew. But of course this inheritance, about which no one can be more unfeignedly glad and thankful than I, puts her in a position where it is impossible for me to speak to her on a matter that is very near to my heart.'

Mrs Brandon looked with great compassion on Mr Miller, whose halting words were obviously being forced from him with considerable anguish, while he industriously picked to pieces a rose, fallen from a vase.

'Miss Morris is very anxious to use some of this legacy in helping the poor,' said Mrs Brandon. 'She asked me particularly about the poor in your parish, and I promised her I would find out. Perhaps if you made a list of people who needed help you could talk it over with her, though really we aren't a needy parish at all and no one is in the least grateful.'

'I could do that,' said Mr Miller, carefully picking up the rose petals and putting them on an ash tray. 'It is just like her to think of such a use for the money. As a matter of fact a little judicious help would be welcome at Grumper's End. Poor Mrs Thatcher does nothing but cry about Jimmy, who is in no danger at all, and Doris and Edna only think of clothes and lipstick, and the kitchen is worse than I've ever seen it, with the sink full of dirty dishes and all the children on the floor.'

'That sounds just the thing for Miss Morris,' said Mrs Brandon. 'I'm sure she'll adore it.'

Mr Miller tried to explain that while on the one hand he did not for a moment mean that Miss Morris herself should go to Grumper's End, yet on the other hand the presence of anyone so helpful and kind would be of the utmost benefit to the Thatcher family, but he entangled himself so hopelessly in what he was saying that Mrs Brandon cut him short by saying that she would tell Miss Morris about the Thatchers at once.

'I know she isn't doing anything to-morrow,' she said, 'so I'll tell her she might as well go down there about half-past eleven. No; Mrs Thatcher will be getting the children's dinner then. Say about half-past three, and then she can be back here for tea. It was so nice of you to come.'

This was so unmistakably a *congé*, though said in the kindest way, that Mr Miller rose. Mrs Brandon laid down her embroidery and accompanied him to the front door, where he turned and took both her hands in his. He was standing on a lower step and their eyes were on a level.

'Thank you and God bless you,' he said. 'I can't see my path clearly, but you have been kind beyond measure to me and I shall never forget it.'

'How very nice of you,' said Mrs Brandon, leaving her hands in his and vaguely noticing that someone was at the bottom of the steps. 'And don't forget; to-morrow at half-past three.'

'Bless you again, with all my thanks and devotion,' said Mr Miller. He did not kiss her hands, for this might have savoured of idolatry, but he pressed them respectfully and went down the steps, nearly cannoning into Sir Edmund, who acknowledged his greeting with a kind of grunt.

'Came to see you about an investment, Lavinia,' said Sir Edmund, 'but now I'm here there's another matter I might as well speak about. Where's Delia? Don't want her and Francis coming in all the time.'

'Delia is out somewhere and Francis won't be back till dinnertime,' said Mrs Brandon, 'so we are quite safe. Do come in.'

She led the way to the drawing-room and re-established herself with her embroidery. Sir Edmund let himself down into the armchair in which his vicar had been sitting and lit a cigarette. His feelings were at the moment in such a seething condition that he could hardly trust himself to speak. For some time he had had his suspicions of Mr Miller, and the scene he had just witnessed had fully confirmed them. With his own eyes he had seen Mrs Brandon and Mr Miller standing on the front door steps holding hands like lovers; with his own ears he had heard Mr Miller express undying devotion and Mrs Brandon making an assignation. Neither of the guilty couple had even had the grace to look ashamed. If one looked at the matter calmly, as he erroneously imagined himself to have done since Saturday, there was no reason why a wealthy, charming widow, with a grown-up son and daughter, should not marry to please herself; and though Miller was poor, his character was excellent, his learning uncontested, and his family quite as good as Mrs Brandon's. But it didn't seem right to Sir Edmund, and the more he thought of it the less he liked it. After a week-end of the honest but muddled mental process which Sir Edmund took for thinking, he had brought himself to the conclusion that Lavinia was on the verge of making a fool of herself and it must be stopped. After what he had just seen the folly was but too evident, and as for the manner of stopping it, Sir Edmund saw but one course open to him.

'Bit lonely here sometimes, eh, Lavinia?' he said, breaking the peaceful silence.

Mrs Brandon said she never felt lonely. Francis was always back to dinner, and Delia was usually at home, and what with people coming to the house and one thing and another, she never seemed to have enough time.

'Can't keep Francis and Delia for ever,' said Sir Edmund. 'Leave the nest and all that sort of thing, you know.'

'Yes, I hope so,' said Mrs Brandon. 'I think it is dreadful when children stay at home for ever. I have sometimes thought that Francis was attracted by the Archdeacon's daughter at Plumstead, such a nice girl, and the Dean's daughters are delightful too. Delia is a bit young, but I'm sure she'll be delighted to get married presently, and I shall let her have my second-best pearls and my grandmother's lace veil. And then I shall have the grandchildren here and Nurse will be quite happy for once.'

'That's not the point, Lavinia,' said Sir Edmund, who had waited with ill-concealed irritation for the end of her remarks. 'Point is, you're getting on. We're all getting on. Need to settle down a bit for our old age, eh?'

Mrs Brandon said yes, she supposed so, and had Sir Edmund heard that Miss Brandon had left the children two hundred pounds each.

'Good God! what's happened to the property then?' asked Sir Edmund.

'Mr Merton did explain, but I wasn't listening very much,' said Mrs Brandon, matching a wool with her head on one side. 'It is all to be a home for somebody, a kind of charity. It seems a very good idea, because what with the damp and the distance from the main road, no one could live there.'

'Suppose Amelia knew her own mind,' said Sir Edmund

doubtfully. 'More than most women do. Well, I'm glad you won't be at the Abbey. Can keep my eye on you better on this side of the county. Wish I could keep it on you a bit more. See what I mean, eh?'

'I'm afraid my business is rather a trouble for you sometimes,' said Mrs Brandon plaintively, 'but I couldn't possibly do it myself.'

'Of course you can't. That's why I want to be in a position where I can look after you. If I were here, or you were over at my place, I could keep an eye on things properly. What about it, Lavinia. You know me pretty well and I know you pretty well. You've not much sense, but you're a good woman. Your Miss Morris could come as secretary to us both. Clever woman that.'

Mrs Brandon, who was used to being scolded by Sir Edmund, and had not been listening much to what he was saying, came to life at the last words.

'Oh, but Miss Morris won't need to be a secretary now,' she said. 'Didn't you know? Aunt Sissie left her ten thousand pounds. How much would that be a year?'

'Don't be a fool, Lavinia,' said Sir Edmund, exasperated. 'How can I tell how she's going to invest it? If she's the woman I think, she'll leave it where Amelia had it. Good business woman, Amelia.'

'And what is annoying,' continued Mrs Brandon, wrinkling her forehead over her wools, 'is that Mr Miller is really very devoted to her, but he has that noble kind of feeling that I really call rather silly that he oughtn't to say so now.'

Sir Edmund stared at his hostess, his face and neck going such a deep purple that she was almost perturbed. Luckily Rose came in with brandy and soda, and as Sir Edmund gulped down a very stiff drink, his face assumed its ordinary brick-red appearance again.

'He came to me about it this afternoon,' Mrs Brandon went on. 'Miss Morris wants to do something for the poor here, so I said to Mr Miller, Why not give Miss Morris a list of people that really need help, and he said the Thatchers at once, so I said I'd tell Miss Morris to go down and have a look at them to-morrow at half-past three.'

Her mysterious mischief face was bent over her work and Sir Edmund was able to look at her at his ease. Seldom had he more admired his trying and charming friend. She might have no sense, but she had lightened his heart of an immense load. If marrying her had been the only way of saving her from marrying the Vicar, he had been prepared to do his duty, but not only had she apparently no thoughts of marrying Mr Miller, but was actively engaged in scheming for him to marry Miss Morris. Sir Edmund heaved such a sigh of relief that Mrs Brandon looked up in alarm.

'Most sensible thing you could do, Lavinia,' he said approvingly. 'More sense than I gave you credit for. Must be getting along now. I'll come in again about that investment some other time.'

Such was his pleasure at his escape that as he said good-bye to Mrs Brandon he put an arm round her and kissed the side of her head. She accepted the attention in the spirit in which it was offered, laughed, and promised to let him know how things went.

When Francis came back a little later, he found his mother snipping off dead roses in a very elegant way in front of the house.

'Hullo, darling,' he said. 'I saw Merton in Barchester to-day, and he wants to know if you would give him a glass of sherry to-morrow.'

'Of course I will,' said Mrs Brandon. 'Shall I ring him up?'

'No need,' said Francis sternly. 'I have saved your fair name by telling him to come unless he hears to the contrary. Anything happened to-day? I see in your face that it did.'

'Miss Morris was terribly pleased about the money and is going to do good to the poor,' said Mrs Brandon. 'And Mr Miller came to see me and then Sir Edmund came. And it has only just occurred to me, Francis, that he was trying to propose to me for a moment, but he got over it, I am glad to say, almost before he had spoken.'

'Really, mother, you shouldn't say things like that,' said Francis. 'Come in. It's time to dress.'

*

On the following afternoon Miss Morris set out for Grumper's End on foot, refusing Mrs Brandon's offer of the car. In her hand she carried her large, sensible bag containing her overall. Mr Thatcher was out at work, but as school had not yet begun all the young Thatchers were making holiday in the narrow lane, or on the kitchen floor. Edna and Doris were absent-mindedly poking bits of tinned salmon into their unhallowed offsprings' mouths, and three hens and a very large half-caste dog were walking aimlessly in and out of the kitchen. As Miss Morris came down the lane, a couple of young Thatchers rushed into the cottage to tell their mother that Jimmy's Lady was coming, a piece of news that caused Mrs Thatcher to dust a chair with an old stocking and begin to cry again.

Miss Morris appeared at the door and asked if she might come in. As Mrs Thatcher could only sniff and gulp, and Edna and Doris burst into loud, primitive giggles, Miss Morris accepted this welcome, and sitting down on the chair that Mrs Thatcher pushed at her, said it was a nice day and how was Jimmy. Mrs Thatcher appeared to be incapable of speech. Doris nudged her sister Edna and smacked her child, and said Mr Miller was coming to take mother to the hospital in his car.

'Well, if Mr Miller is coming, we ought to get the kitchen a little tidier,' said Miss Morris.

Fascinated by this eccentric statement, Mrs Thatcher stopped crying. Edna and Doris stopped giggling, and the children all crowded round to look at Jimmy's Lady. Miss Morris opened her bag, took out her overall, put it on, and assumed command. In answer to her questions Doris said there was a bit of soap somewhere, and Edna volunteered that the scrubbing brush was somewhere in the yard and she dessaid the towel was somewhere. Miss Morris looked round, and recognizing Teddy, who had been in the sack race, gave him some money and told him to run up to the shop as fast as he could and bring back yellow soap, washing soda, a dish mop, a wire saucepan cleaner, a small bottle of Jeyes' Fluid, and three cloths for drying up. She then filled both the kettles. Doris, entering into the spirit of these preparations carried them to the kitchen range, while Edna drove Ernie Thatcher out to bring in some more sticks, and chased all the

271

other children into the garden, where they clustered round the door in horrified interest, gazing at Jimmy's Lady and their illegitimate young nephew and niece, who were tied to their chairs.

Just as the kettles were coming to the boil, Teddy came back with his shoppings and the change.

'Now, Edna and Doris, if you'll give me a hand we'll get the sink tidied up,' said Miss Morris, 'and then we can clean the children.'

Recognizing an irresistible natural force, Edna and Doris, again giggling irrepressibly, so exerted themselves that the unpleasant pile of dishes, plates, cutlery and saucepans was soon washed and neatly stacked, and the sink scoured with soda and disinfectant and clean enough to wash in. In a fury of zeal Doris dragged all her young brothers and sisters into the kitchen and washed their hands and faces, while Edna, disinterring from a loathsome heap of rubbish in a cupboard a broom with half a handle, swept everything that was on the kitchen floor out into the yard.

'That's very nice,' said Miss Morris approvingly. 'Now we'll just wash out these cloths and Teddy can hang them on the fence to dry. Suppose you and Doris tidy yourselves a little, Edna. Have you a comb?'

Doris said she hadn't seen it not since Friday, when Edna was combing Micky. On inquiring which of the children Micky was, Miss Morris was informed that it was the large half-caste dog. Without showing any signs of emotion, that admirable woman took a small comb out of her bag and gave it to the girls, saying that they could keep it and she would send them some shampoo powder. While they wrestled with their tangled golden curls in front of a small chipped mirror, Miss Morris wiped the kitchen table, put a bowl of water on it, and applied herself to cleaning the children of shame, who were too young to mind.

While she was thus engaged, Mr Miller, who had left the car at the corner because it was difficult to turn in front of the cottage, knocked at the open door and walked into the kitchen. Coming from the brilliant sunshine outside he was at first unable to see who was in the dark little kitchen, but a sense more intimate, more nostalgic than sight, suddenly seized upon his heart, making it stand still. For a moment he was a young man again on a hot summer morning, and Ella Morris in her check apron was scrubbing out the vicarage dustbin with Jeyes' Fluid before it was used for rubbish at the Church Lads' Brigade tea. Then, as his eyes became accustomed to the gloom, he saw Miss Morris, in an overall, seated at Mrs Thatcher's kitchen table, washing the faces and hands of Purse (Percy) and Glad (Gladys) Thatcher; so he said good afternoon.

'How do you do,' said Miss Morris. She finished drying Glad's face, emptied the bowl, and shook hands with Mr Miller. Mrs Thatcher began to cry again.

'That's enough,' said Miss Morris with kind authority. 'One of you get your mother's hat. We mustn't keep Mr Miller waiting.'

Doris took Mrs Thatcher's hat from a peg behind the door, rammed it on to her mother's unresisting head, and jerked her on to her feet, telling her not to keep Mr Miller waiting.

'Here's your purse, mother,' said Edna. 'You don't want to keep Mr Miller waiting.'

Mrs Thatcher, sobbing loudly, was propelled by her family towards the Vicar's car.

'Could I give you a lift, Miss Morris?' said the Vicar.

Miss Morris, who was folding her overall and putting it in her bag, thanked Mr Miller and said she would enjoy the walk back to Stories.

'Of course,' said Mr Miller doubtfully, 'I would not wish in any way to interfere, but if you could possibly see your way, without undue fatigue, to coming at least as far as the Vicarage, where I have to pick up the afternoon's post, I should be so very grateful. Mrs Thatcher is certain to cry all the way to Barchester and probably all the way back, and as I have to drive the car I am really very much at a loss.'

'If I can be of any real help I will come with pleasure,' said Miss Morris, and got into the back seat with Mrs Thatcher. Amid shrill cries from the Thatcher family the car moved off.

'I hope you made a good profit on the Fête, Mr Miller,' said Miss Morris. 'Now, Mrs Thatcher, you've had a nice cry and it's done you good and we all know you are very brave. Now you must be brave just once more for Jimmy. If he sees mother come into the ward crying, it will quite upset him.'

'Jimmy was always easy upset, just like me,' said Mrs Thatcher with some pride.

'Yes, we did very well, Miss Morris,' said the Vicar, speaking backwards, 'but a most unfortunate thing has occurred. Try as I will, I cannot get the accounts to balance, and the dreadful thing is that I seem to be seventeen and sixpence in pocket, quite apart from the profit.'

'Then the accounts must be wrong,' said Miss Morris with calm finality. 'There, Mrs Thatcher, that's better. Now you mustn't cry any more, or we'll have to ask Mr Miller to lend you a clean handkerchief.'

'Oh, Miss!' said Mrs Thatcher, agreeably shocked and horrified, but much calmer.

By this time they had arrived at the Vicarage, where Mr Miller and Miss Morris got out.

'Thank you very much for coming so far,' said the Vicar. 'I will just see if there are any letters for me and then I will take Mrs Thatcher on to Barchester.'

'I don't know,' said Miss Morris, with what was for her unusual diffidence on her own subject, 'if I could help you with the accounts at all. I am pretty good at them, and there is no hurry for me to get back.'

'Would you really,' said Mr Miller. 'Indeed, indeed I should be so grateful for your assistance. Everything is on my desk. If you would just allow me to show you my difficulties. And Hettie would bring you some tea.'

He led the way to his study, where a heap of bills, scrawled memoranda, receipts and odd documents lay in disorder on the writing-table. Miss Morris's eyes lighted at the sight and she took off her hat.

'Let me just get my spectacles,' she said, opening her bag. The overall in which she had been cleaning Mrs Thatcher's kitchen was hiding everything else, so she took it out and laid it on the table. A strong smell of disinfectant filled the air.

'That is Jeyes' Fluid,' said Mr Miller, his words spoken in a dead, level tone, forced almost with pain from him.

'You noticed it?' asked Miss Morris, feeling as if her own voice were coming from an immense distance.

'From the moment I came into Mrs Thatcher's kitchen and saw you ministering to that poor family,' said Mr Miller. 'Did you think I had ever forgotten?'

'I know that I hadn't,' said Miss Morris. 'It was the last day of happiness that I remember.'

'You were cleaning the Vicarage dustbin in your apron,' said Mr Miller, 'and your hair was blown across your face.'

'Do you remember that?' said Miss Morris. 'You put it back for me, because my hands were dirty. I suppose when things are far away there is nothing wrong in remembering them.'

She began to get her spectacles out, but found it difficult.

'Miss Morris,' said Mr Miller, speaking with what was clearly almost agony, 'I had a deep respect for your father and I have never ceased to regret the pain that I gave him, the disappointment of which I was the cause. For that I offer you my humble apology. But I cannot change my convictions, even if I lose everything on earth that I hold most dear; even if I have to suffer the almost unbearable pain of wounding what on earth I most reverence.'

Miss Morris's spectacle case fell from her hands on to the table. She wondered vaguely why it was so dark and why Mr Miller's voice came to her across infinite space. There was silence.

'I fear I have been discourteous,' said Mr Miller. 'You will, I trust, forgive me. I must take that poor woman to Barchester.'

He turned to go, but Miss Morris's voice made him turn to her again, though he did not look at her.

'I loved and respected my dear father more than anything in the world,' said Miss Morris, in her usual clear, controlled voice, 'but I cannot help seeing that he was sometimes wrong. He was unjust to you. So was I. Forgive his daughter.'

Mr Miller took a step towards Miss Morris. Her hair, as a rule so neat, was a little disordered by her work at Grumper's End and the drive back to the Vicarage.

'Your hair has blown across your face,' he said, touching it very gently. 'May I put it back?'

275

Then, because he and Miss Morris were so unused to outward forms of tenderness, they made no further sign.

'It has been a very long time,' said Miss Morris.

'Is that your only reproach?' said Mr Miller. 'I don't know how to bear that.'

'I have never reproached you. I only loved you,' said Miss Morris. 'I will soon get these papers tidy. Mrs Thatcher will be getting anxious.'

'How selfish happiness makes one,' said the Vicar. 'I will go at once. It doesn't take long.'

'Then I may still be here when you come back,' said Miss Morris.

'God bless you, very dear,' said Mr Miller and went out. In a moment Miss Morris heard the car start. She put on her spectacles, sat down, and was at once absorbed in the papers on the desk.

*

The hot, golden afternoon passed agreeably for Mrs Brandon. Having got Miss Morris safely away she lay down on the sofa in her room and went comfortably to sleep. At five o'clock she had tea with Delia, with a subcurrent of mild excitement at the thought of Noel Merton's visit. Hardly had they finished tea when a car drove up to the door and to their annoyance Mrs Grant got out, followed by her son.

'What on earth does Mrs Grant want to come in a car for?' said Delia, looking out of the window. 'It's Wheeler's big car from the garage and a lot of luggage. I hope she isn't taking Hilary away; it would be too sickening.'

But before she could indulge in any more theories, Mrs Grant was upon them, wearing in addition to her usual homespun suit and necklaces a kind of brigand's cape of coarse blue cloth.

'Addio!' she exclaimed, halting so suddenly and dramatically that her son banged into her from behind.

'But why?' said Mrs Brandon. 'You aren't going, are you?'

'I will sit down for five minutes,' said Mrs Grant. 'I am a gypsy. I come and go as fate wills. I am very glad to have seen my Boy in surroundings which he finds congenial, but for me this life is not possible. I bear no grudge against Amelia Brandon, and there is now nothing to keep me in England. Mrs Spindler, in spite of what Victoria Norton may say, does not wish to learn how to cook macaroni, and I refuse to eat her chops and puddings. I am going up to London at once and shall spend a day at my club, the Hypatia in Gower Street, and probably go to Italy on the following day. I believe there is a pilgrimage going to Rome and by joining it I could go more cheaply. It is quite a mistake to believe that Calabria is hot at this time of year. I am like the lizards, those graceful little creatures. I can spend all day with my brother the sun and feel refreshed. My Boy will join me there.'

'Oh, I say, mother,' said Mr Grant, 'I really can't. I've got heaps of work to do and I've got to read seriously all this autumn.'

'We will forget the fogs of London,' said Mrs Grant, waving them joyously away. 'Hilary needs the sun.'

'I'm awfully sorry, mother, but I simply won't,' said Mr Grant with such determination that Delia stared at him in surprise. Much as she liked her cousin, it had never occurred to her that he could assert himself against his mother, and she was at no pains to conceal her admiration.

'Then that is settled,' said Mrs Grant, rising with a majestic sweep of her cloak and a jingling of all her necklaces. 'I never fight against destiny. Woman must yield to man. Good-bye, Mrs Brandon. Good-bye, little Delia.'

Mrs Brandon, guiltily conscious of not having done much for Mrs Grant during her stay at Pomfret Madrigal, threw a passionate regret into her voice, to which Mrs Grant responded with equal fervour, pressing Mrs Brandon to visit her in Calabria at any time.

'I'd simply adore to,' said Mrs Brandon, 'but somehow I never seem to get abroad. I did go to Cannes once with my husband, but he died there, so I came back.'

'Cannes – Frinton,' said Mrs Grant musingly. 'The interweavings of destiny are strange. I shall miss my train. No, Hilary, don't come with me. Your gypsy mother needs no speeding on her way.'

With great agility she swept herself and her cloak into Wheeler's car, crying 'Avanti,' which Bert from the garage, who was driving, rightly conjectured to mean Barchester Central Station, for such was the destination that Mr Wheeler his employer had mentioned to him when giving him his instructions. The car disappeared down the drive.

'Come in the kitchen garden ·for a bit,' said Delia to her cousin. 'We might get some plums if Turpin isn't looking. I say, Hilary, you were marvellous with your mother.'

'I felt rather a beast,' said Mr Grant, 'but after all I've got to work. I mean I'm not going to starve, even without that beastly Abbey which thank goodness I haven't got, but one feels a frightful rotter doing nothing at my age, and mother doesn't understand that.'

'Besides, there's your novel,' said Delia.

'If ever my novel comes to anything, it will be all your doing,' said Mr Grant, finely ignoring the patient listening of Mrs Brandon, Mrs Morland and Mr Miller. 'If it weren't for you, I couldn't do it.'

'But it was Mrs Morland's idea,' said Delia, anxious to be quite fair before she could accept this praise.

'Yes, she did suggest it,' said Mr Grant, 'but you have been splendid about the whole thing from the beginning. I really feel there is no one I can talk to about myself and my work as well as I can to you. I awfully want to do something, Delia, and I wonder if you'd mind.'

'I'm sure I wouldn't,' said Delia. 'Hullo, Turpin wants to talk to me. What is it, Turpin?'

'I say, he looks dangerous,' said Mr Grant, for Turpin was advancing towards them from the far end of the grass walk which, with its herbaceous borders, divided the kitchen garden in two, looking like a paralytic old countryman on the stage, shouting angrily and brandishing a fork.

'Come and look, Miss Delia,' said Turpin, trembling with rage, 'come and look!'

He led the way towards the rich bed of manure where sprawled his beloved vegetable marrows. With a threatening gesture he jabbed his fork into the ground, stooped, and with infinite reverence turned the fattest marrow gently on one side. On its under surface, in misshapen letters, was too plainly visible the word HILARY

'That's my name!' said Mr Grant.

'Maybe it is, maybe it isn't,' said Turpin. 'What I want to know is who done it. I've laid awake thinking of that marrow, and now Sir Edmund's man'll have the laugh over me at the Flower Show. I'd have the laugh over the one that done it if I knowed who it was.'

'Well, I'm awfully sorry, Turpin, but I did it,' said Delia.

'You cut this young gentleman's name on my marrow, miss?' said Turpin. 'Of all the – '

But instead of finishing whatever dire thing it was he was going to say, Turpin began to chuckle in such a coughing and rumbling way that Delia and her cousin were alarmed.

'Do you think he'll burst?' Mr Grant whispered nervously to Delia.

But Turpin, his good temper miraculously recovered, was already moving away towards the tool-shed with his fork, chuckling to himself as he went, 'cut a young gentleman's name on my marrow, cut a young gentleman's name on my marrow,' until he was out of sight.

'That was the day we picked the gooseberries,' said Delia, not so much giving an explanation as a statement. 'I always frightfully wanted to carve something on that marrow, and I thought it would be nice for you to have your name on a prize marrow.'

Mr Grant was silent.

'Would you rather not?' said Delia.

'No, I like it immensely,' said Mr Grant. 'I was never allowed to carve my name on anything at home, not even on a pumpkin that we had in a little glasshouse, so I know exactly how you felt. I was wondering if what I wanted to tell you would be a good sort of thanking you.'

'What was it?' said Delia. 'I'm sure it would.'

'I thought I might dedicate Jehan le Capet to you,' said Mr Grant, trying to sound like a person who is in the habit of dedicating novels every day.

'Oh!' said Delia. 'But I thought you were going to dedicate him to mother.'

'That was when he was just a critical study,' said Mr Grant. 'But a novel is different, and I don't think your mother would

279

understand about le Capet's sex life, not really. So I thought I'd dedicate him to you.'

'What would you say?' asked Delia eagerly.

'I might just say, "To Delia".'

'How marvellous,' said Delia.

'Or, "To Delia Who Helped". Or I did think of "For Delia", but I think "For" is a little affected.'

'It would be rather nice to have something about the marrow,' said Delia wistfully. 'I mean, the book and the marrow do make a good sort of exchange, don't they?'

' "By just exchange one for the other given",' said Mr Grant musingly. 'You do hold mine dear, and yours, considering its size, I simply cannot miss; but that's affected too. I'll tell you what. I'll put simply, "To Delia Who Understood".'

'Oh!' Delia said again. 'Oh, Hilary, do you think you could possibly make it "Understands"?'

In her earnestness she stopped short and laid her hand on her cousin's arm.

'Of course I could,' he said, looking down with some pride at the intellect which, so he felt, he was calling into being. 'And what's more, I will.'

For gratitude Delia rubbed her head violently against his shoulder. Then they pursued their way towards the house and were soon laughing about nothing again in the sunshine.

*

In the drawing-room all was a cool, delicious, scented repose. Mrs Brandon, reclining elegantly on the sofa, flowers massed on a table behind her, flowers on a table by her side, was pensively doing nothing at all. On her face was an expression of amused and slightly guilty anticipation which her son Francis would have recognized at once.

Shortly after six o'clock she heard a car come up the drive, and a moment later Rose announced Mr Merton. Mrs Brandon, who was discovered working at her tapestry, looked up with a face of pleased surprise.

'How nice of you to come on this hot day,' she said to Mr Merton, holding out her hand with appealing lassitude.

Mr Merton held it for a second longer than was necessary and restored it to her with great care.

'Nothing would have kept me from coming,' he said, in his deep agreeable voice. 'The only thing that might have detained me was Lydia, who is so unacquainted with man that her tameness is occasionally quite shocking to me, but luckily she had got Tony Morland for the day and they have gone up the river.'

'She is such a nice girl,' said Mrs Brandon.

'I do love the entire lack of interest with which you made that remark,' said Mr Merton.

Mrs Brandon made no reply, but raised her eyes slowly from her work and looked at her guest with an air of complete candour.

'I can't tell you,' said Mr Merton, who was already enjoying himself immensely, 'how much I hoped I might find you alone.'

'I thought we could talk so much more comfortably,' said Mrs Brandon, again darting at her guest a soft glance, to which he delightedly attached its exact value.

After a little more desultory fencing, conducted with great skill on both sides, Mrs Brandon asked after Miss Brandon's maid.

'She has gone to a married sister at Swanage, so my father's clerk tells me,' said Mr Merton. 'She had fifty pounds a year left her by Miss Brandon, and all the contents of the sitting-room including the photographs. Also the gorillas.'

Mrs Brandon was silent for a moment, thinking of Sparks in a room at Swanage, furnished from the Abbey, full of the Brandon family photographs, guarded by the gorillas, and hardly knew whether to laugh or cry.

'You feel things more deeply than other people,' said Mr Merton.

'I know I do,' sighed Mrs Brandon. 'It's so stupid.'

'Not stupid at all. You can't help being sensitive,' said Mr Merton. 'Tell me – and then we will forget all these painful subjects – how is Miss Morris?'

'I don't exactly know,' said Mrs Brandon, suddenly becoming quite natural, 'but I hope very much she is engaged by now. Our Vicar, a delightful person, is a very old friend of hers, and I think used to admire her. He is very unworldly and when he heard of her legacy he wanted to withdraw, but it would be so foolish of him to spoil her chance of happiness because she has a little money, so I arranged for them to meet this afternoon, and as that was at half-past three and it is half-past six now, I really feel that something may have happened.'

'How like you,' said Mr Merton.

'One is so very grateful for any chance of making people happy,' said Mrs Brandon. 'One hasn't always been very happy oneself, so one does want it desperately for others.'

'I don't like to think that you have been unhappy,' said Mr Merton, throwing exactly the right shade of chivalrous admiration into his tone and look. So much indeed did he throw that his guardian angel, who was on the roof talking to Mrs Brandon's guardian angel, came hurriedly down through the ceiling to see if he was safe.

'I wouldn't trouble if I were you,' said Mrs Brandon's angel, following him. 'Mine can look after herself perfectly and I should say yours could too.'

'I daresay he can, but it's my duty to listen to everything,' said Mr Merton's angel firmly. 'Go back again, there's an angel, and I'll join you in a minute.'

'You'll find me somewhere upstairs,' said Mrs Brandon's angel and sped on strong wings into the cloudless blue sky.

Mrs Brandon laid down her work and looked at her hands.

'I was married very young,' she said simply, 'and knew very little. It's a stupid story; but there are things one doesn't forget.'

'I wish,' said Mr Merton, 'I could help you to forget them.'

'You do,' murmured Mrs Brandon, but couldn't help giving Mr Merton a conspirator's glance as she spoke.

'How charming of you to say so,' said Mr Merton. 'And how I hope that you will look on me as a real friend, as one who would do a great deal to make things easier for you.'

At this point Mr Merton's guardian angel nearly fell down off the ceiling in his anxiety to miss nothing.

'A friend,' said Mrs Brandon in a low thrilling voice. 'A friend. I feel about that word as Shelley felt about love. "One word is too often profaned – " '

'I know, I know,' said Mr Merton, in tones that matched her

own. 'But you must also remember that one feeling is too falsely disclaimed for me, if I may be allowed to alter the poet's choice of pronoun, to disclaim it.'

He looked deeply into Mrs Brandon's eyes and she looked deeply into his. What they saw there amused them so much that they began to laugh.

Mr Merton's guardian angel, puzzled but on the whole satisfied, spread his wings and soon his path was vague in distant spheres.